Twisted Revelations

August Knights MC

Book #5

The Twisted Series

By:
Keta Kendric

Cover: Steamy Designs
Editing: A. L. Barron

ISBN: 978-1-956650-16-7/Twisted Revelations

Contents

PART #1   9
INTRODUCTION   9
CHAPTER ONE   15
CHAPTER TWO   23
CHAPTER THREE   29
CHAPTER FOUR   35
CHAPTER FIVE   39
CHAPTER SIX   47
CHAPTER SEVEN   53
CHAPTER EIGHT   63
CHAPTER NINE   71
CHAPTER TEN   83
CHAPTER ELEVEN   91
CHAPTER TWELVE   95
CHAPTER THIRTEEN   107
CHAPTER FOURTEEN   113
CHAPTER FIFTEEN   121
CHAPTER SIXTEEN   127
CHAPTER SEVENTEEN   137
CHAPTER EIGHTEEN   145
CHAPTER NINETEEN   157
CHAPTER TWENTY   163
CHAPTER TWENTY-ONE   173
CHAPTER TWENTY-TWO   187
CHAPTER TWENTY-THREE   197
CHAPTER TWENTY-FOUR   203
CHAPTER TWENTY-FIVE   215
CHAPTER TWENTY-SIX   221
CHAPTER TWENTY-SEVEN   229
CHAPTER TWENTY-EIGHT   237
CHAPTER TWENTY-NINE   247
CHAPTER THIRTY   253
CHAPTER THIRTY-ONE   259
CHAPTER THIRTY-TWO   267
PART II   273
CHAPTER THIRTY-THREE   273
CHAPTER THIRTY-FOUR   281
CHAPTER THIRTY-FIVE   287

CHAPTER THIRTY-SIX   295
CHAPTER THIRTY-SEVEN   305
CHAPTER THIRTY-EIGHT   311
CHAPTER THIRTY-NINE   317
CHAPTER FORTY   323
CHAPTER FORTY-ONE   333
CHAPTER FORTY-TWO   339
CHAPTER FORTY-THREE   345
CHAPTER FORTY-FOUR   355
CHAPTER FORTY-FIVE   361
CHAPTER FORTY-SIX   371
CHAPTER FORTY-SEVEN   377
CHAPTER FORTY-EIGHT   383
CHAPTER FORTY-NINE   389
CHAPTER FIFTY   397
CHAPTER FIFTY-ONE   403
CHAPTER FIFTY-TWO   413
CHAPTER FIFTY-THREE   423
CHAPTER FIFTY-FOUR   431
CHAPTER FIFTY-FIVE   435
CHAPTER FIFTY-SIX   443
CHAPTER FIFTY-SEVEN   449
CHAPTER FIFTY-EIGHT   453
EPILOGUE   457
OTHER TITLES BY KETA KENDRIC   465

Synopsis

Beverly: For years, Laura and I sat helplessly on the sidelines while our best friend Megan ran from a deadly cartel. When Megan went radio silent, and strange men came creeping out of the darkness, we believed we were in the cartel's crosshairs. Unable to depend on the law when Laura is taken, desperation leads me to reach out to an unconventional source for help.

Laura: Taken. They took the wrong one. Either they were going to let me go, or I'd make them kill me. Beverly's call for help summoned two mercenaries so adept at killing I wasn't sure if we should run from them or the cartel chasing us.
How were we supposed to know the men coming to protect us knew how to stoke the fires of hell and use the flames to burn it to oblivion?

Warning: This book is a multicultural romance that contains explicit sexual content and is intended for adults. If you are easily triggered by morally grey characters, explicit language and graphic violence, this is not the book for you. Please be advised.

Note: This book follows the timelines of Twisted Secrets Book #3 and Twisted Obsession Book #4. Although I believe this book can be read as a standalone, it is highly suggested you read the series in order for surprising plot twists and for historical context of the main characters.

Part #1

Introduction

It was the telling way my Nike's tapped a wild beat across the dusty pavement that revealed our urgent dilemma. Beverly's bare feet slapped the ground after she ran clean out of her flats. I dragged her along, my fingers digging into her forearm.

A lone pole leaned against the darkness, its haggard stance as draining as the inadequate lighting it provided. Our heaving breaths ignited the dark and urged us to move faster even as our bodies screamed in protest.

The hard slap and unsteady slide of hard-bottomed dress shoes revealed a key characteristic about the men chasing us. They hadn't prepared for a foot chase. The insinuation that their plan would be an easy task gave us a slight advantage as we put more distance between us and the men chasing us.

The Crestwood Recreation Center at Dorchester and The Crestwood Recreation Center at MacArthur were the centers that employed us. They were help facilities for youth and young kids during the daylight hours, but at night, freaks lurked in every dark crack, awaiting the chance to act out their sinister intentions.

This evening the freaks had emerged and were chasing Beverly and me for reasons we weren't waiting around to find out. We, Laura Parker and Beverly Hudson, were known in the area for the assistance we provided young people.

With Bev's car in the shop, I'd insisted she remain at the center until I picked her up rather than her attempting to catch the city bus. We shared an apartment, but we rarely arrived or departed at the same time.

"As soon as we get around that building, I'm popping my trunk. You hop in." My words shot out in Beverly's direction over my labored breaths and thumping feet.

"No. They're chasing us with guns. Are you crazy?" Beverly tossed her choppy words back at me.

The answer to Beverly's question about my state of mind was *yes*. I was indeed crazy. However, I wasn't crazy enough to allow whoever was chasing us to take us both. They hadn't fired their weapons, so I *assumed* their intent was to take us alive.

Before this chase began, my hackles had rose while waiting for Beverly to lock the thick, barred doors to the center. However my internal sensors hadn't reacted soon enough. The darkness opened and spit out two dark figures approaching us from the edge of the building to our right. I noticed the lone car in the lot but ignored it since vehicles often loitered there.

One of the figures shouted in a demanding tone, but my brain refused to unscramble the words. My keen eyes immediately caught the gleam of a gun, the white of their skin, and the dark suits they wore. I snatched Beverly's arm and took off to the left, shouting for her to run like fire-eyed demons were chasing us.

My beat-up blue Toyota Camry was parked in the alley between the center and the old pawn shop next door as usual. If I could get to the gun under my driver's seat, I planned to make someone eat hot lead.

Our sporadic movements and chaotic mental state in the midst of being chased landed my face against Beverly's shoulder when I attempted to glance back. Our legs got tangled, but we adjusted and prevented a fall. I aimed my key fob at my trunk and prayed the raggedy mother-fucker would pop open.

"I'm not leaving you. We..." Bev attempted to say.

My flattened palms connected with her back, causing her to suck in a harsh breath before she stumbled into the trunk from my hard shove. She was forced to pick up her long legs and tuck them inside before I tossed the keys in with her and slammed it shut.

I dashed to the driver's side door, lifting and jerking the door handle. A cold voice called at my back, but didn't stop my attempt to get the door open. The trunk had decided to work, but my tricky driver's side door picked this specific time to let me down.

"Stop or I'll shoot you in the back." The sound vibrated across my neck, and the truth of his warning rang out in his harsh tone. I was shot before and didn't want another hell-lit bullet racing through my tender brown meat.

"Where's your friend?" The cold voice questioned, as I caught a glimpse of him pointing past me into the darkness with his gun. On the other side of the lopsided wooden fence was a residential neighborhood. Barking dogs, the unmistakable sound of gunshots, and the angry shouts of people arguing in the distance sounded. I wanted to see him take his ass over that fence and face the drama on the other side.

"She's gone," I finally answered. "But, I decided to stay behind so I can take out the fucking trash."

"You have a real smart mouth for someone with a gun aimed at the back of her head," his gruff voice sounded, growing louder as he closed the distance between us. His accent suggested he was Hispanic.

"Mr. Gun-wielding Bad-guy, do you have any idea where you're at?" I questioned, chancing a glance back at him. "Having a gun aimed at me in this neighborhood doesn't mean shit."

My lips twitched with the need to keep mouthing off, but the hard steps of his friend's approach grew closer, and my brave words stalled on my tongue. I was willing to go one on one, but tangling with two men would be a dumb decision.

"The friend got away," the winded voice of the second man sounded behind me. They assumed Beverly had gotten away. *Good.* The only way to keep her safe at this point was to lead them away from my car and go with them willingly.

When the one at my back spun me, I expected to stare into the barrel of his gun. Instead, he slapped cuffs against my wrists. He swiped them on so fast I was sure he had cop in his DNA. I lifted my knee, making it travel up at a fast rate, but my intent to deflate his balls was blocked.

He caught my game before I had time to play. He snatched me by my cuffed hands and spun me before shoving me in the direction he wanted me to go.

"Who the fuck are you and where the fuck are you taking me?" I spat my question at them through clenched teeth. The vow I made to stop cursing had just flown out the fucking window, thanks to these assholes. The buddy of the cuff slinger took up an easy stride next to us.

"We have a few questions for you before we take you to see our boss. Those redneck bikers in Florida are protecting your slippery little friend, but let's see if anyone comes for you."

Who the hell was he talking about?

My brain fought to make the connections. *Megan?* Did these assholes know where she was?

"Megan? Do you know where she is?" I heaved out, needing to know. A hard shove was the man's reply.

"The lies have started already," he chuckled, shaking his head.

Megan had been missing for months, but Beverly and I refused to accept that she was dead. Her disappearance had us one dial away from calling the FBI.

"I can't wait to meet this boss of yours," I taunted. "I'm shaking in my tennis shoes," I mouthed off sarcastically while glancing back at my car, praying that Beverly wouldn't open the trunk too soon.

"Shut the fuck up and keep moving. We'll find your friends."

I was clueless as to where they were taking me, but I'd already made the vow. I was either going to escape or die trying.

Chapter One

Laura

After trading the cuffs for zip-ties, those musty mother-fuckers tossed me into their trunk like I was a bag of month-old trash. With my hands clipped together behind me and my feet zip-tied, I couldn't kick or break myself free.

At five-foot-two and a hundred and five pounds, I didn't look like a threat to anyone, and I prayed my size fooled the two who took me. If they gave me an inch, I'd take a mile and make their lives a living hell.

The rough, scratchy sack they tossed over my head made breathing difficult, but I managed, sucking in dust and recycled air. On a sigh, I rested my head against a spare tire as a large chunk of metal poked into my side and joined the potholes in making my ride a miserable one.

When the crush of pebbles sounded, and the engine idled down, I lifted my head, straining to listen for clues to my whereabouts. My ears perked when the vehicle came to a complete stop. Aside from car exhaust, there weren't any other noticeable scents present.

I'd accepted they were taking me to face my impending rape, torture, or murder. Possibly all three. *Why? Who were they?* It had to have something to do with the people who were chasing Megan. We hadn't heard from her since the tattooed, pretend detective came searching for her months ago.

The trunk release disengaged before it popped open and the barrel of a gun was shoved into my face. My lips pursed like the two men shining a bright light in my face were bothering me. One produced a pocket knife and cut both sets of my zip-ties.

He gripped my upper arm and yanked me from the cramped confines. When my feet connected with the ground, I faked a trip before I stomped my foot into his Achilles tendon, causing the man to stumble. He fought to stay upright, his weakened leg wobbling, but he managed to keep me in his bruising grip.

Since he was kind enough to keep me in an upright position, it gave me the opportunity to introduce my knee to his dick. All the air in his lungs burst from his open mouth on impact, forcing him to release the hold he had on me.

Fortunately, his friend walked ahead of us, confident I was under control. While Mr. Hurt Dick struggled through his pain, I took off and managed a full sprint. My feet ate up the concrete as I ran in a zigzag pattern, hoping to dodge a bullet.

"Fuck!" I screamed into the night as a big hand grasped the back of my shirt and twisted. I was lifted from the ground with ease and tossed across a sturdy shoulder like a sack of potatoes. Limp Dick's long-legged friend had chased me down.

"Put me down, you dick-faced bastard. I'm not telling you shit. I'm going to make you kill me first," I barked, meaning every word.

"As you wish, little cunt. I'm going to enjoy shutting that smart mouth of yours up," he chuckled.

"Why don't you eat a smelly dick and chase it down with a glass of rat poison?"

Although my view was upside down, it didn't stop me from scanning my surroundings. We were in an industrial area surrounded by warehouses.

The man carrying me laughed at my comments, his back level with my inverted view. If my arms were long enough, I'd kidney punch his ass just to see how far I could make his back arch.

The limping man walking next to us leaned closer. He had the nerve to stare down at me with a teasing smirk on his face.

"What the fuck are you looking at? Walking around scaring people, looking like a popped pimple." My comments caused the one carrying me to rumble with laughter again.

The partner I lobbed the insult at snickered while holding the door open to allow us in as I squirmed, kicked, and bucked like a raging bull. My attempts were useless against the man's strength, but I wasn't going down without a fight.

My foot became caught in the man's shirt, and I attempted to rip it from his body.

Smack!

A loud whack came across the back of my thighs. The heavy-handed lick infuriated me further, and a burst of strength allowed me the inch I needed to sink my teeth into his back.

Immediately, I was whipped through the air, and my back struck the hard floor, knocking the oxygen from my lungs. I heaved, fighting to catch my next breath as my inflamed tailbone throbbed with unrelenting pain.

When a big fist came flying at my head, I dodged it in the nick of time. The impact of the jerk's fist when it struck the concrete floor sent a small vibration through me. His cursing shouts of pain followed the fleshy whack. I prayed every bone in his hand was shattered into pieces.

The one thing that stopped me from introducing his nuts to the bottom of my Nike's was the sound of the metallic *click*. Douche number two aimed his pistol at my forehead, and his serious expression revealed his readi-ness to kill me.

"Calm down before I blow a hole through your fore-head," his strained voice warned. Since I was content with my forehead being intact, I stalled my attempts to kick their asses—for now.

The one I bit gripped my shoulder, attempting to rip it from the socket as he lifted me from the floor and shoved me into a standing position. I didn't help, making him work.

He shoved me deeper into the warehouse. The scent of oil mixed with armpit musk hit me in the face before curling my nose hairs. Wooden crates stood against the dimly-lit interior, stacked nearly to the ceiling.

My gaze brushed past a small forklift and a yellow pallet jack. White packing peanuts littered the floor and floated against the shift in the air our movement created.

We'd taken three turns through a maze of wall-high crates before reaching a black door that stood out against the plain, concrete gray walls. The one with the firm grip on my arm used my body to bump the cracked door the rest of the way open.

A two-way mirror on the wall to my left indicated I was being led into their interrogation room. I was marched across the short expanse of the brightly-lit room before he slung me into a worn, wooden chair. I lurched back as the chair grunted, struggling on its ancient legs to stay put un-der the abrupt intrusion of my weight.

I didn't resist when the man caught my left wrist in his tight grip. He cuffed me to a round metal bolt drilled into the center of the wooden tabletop. I scanned my sur-roundings as the sound of the cuffs locking into place signified the finality of my capture.

The room was standard size. Large enough not to be constricting with the big men hovering above me. Aside from another wooden chair that sat near the door, the table

I was forced to sit behind and the chair I sat in were the only furnishings. A checkered black and white pattern made up the dirty floor tiles. Uncovered fluorescent lights hummed above me.

The scent of urine and cleaning products dominated the air. Whoever they tortured before me had pissed themselves, and the strong power of bleach hadn't gotten rid of the smell .

How the hell was I going to get myself out of this one? Growing up poor, motherless, and running the deadly streets of the Crestwood neighborhood, I had no choice but to be tough, but I was worried this situation might be insurmountable.

I claimed to be motherless, but the truth was known by a select few. My mother had been a zombie my entire childhood. Crack, heroin, meth — she didn't care what drug she shoved into her body. Monique Parker hadn't had a desire to live in the reality of her existence, so drugs became the magic she used to make herself disappear.

My current situation yanked me from the memories of my childhood despair. With my forearms pressed into the table, I grabbed ahold of the bolt I was anchored to and held myself steady. I started to shake against the table while my deadly gaze volleyed between the men. I was sure they assumed they were intimidating me, but I'd been stared down by bigger and better.

"Stop shaking the fucking table, you hard-headed little bitch," the one with my teeth prints decorating a portion of his back edged out through bared teeth. I could see it all over his face. He wanted to beat the shit out of me.

"Cover your ass. Oh shit, my bad, that's your face resembling a fat hairy ass," I tossed at him, adding tension to his already infuriating expression.

What the hell did they want from me? Earlier, they mentioned a friend, who I believed was Megan. It brought forth the memory of the visit Beverly and I had gotten from the fake detective who came sniffing around after her. Their comments made me believe they knew Megan's whereabouts.

As soon as the one I bit shuffled to the door and took the seat there, I sent my foot repeatedly into the table leg to my right. The one left to interrogate me barked a few questions at me, yelling above the noise I made.

"Stop kicking the fucking table, you crazy bitch!"

Irritation was etched in the deep frowns on the man's face. He drew his gun again, threatening me with the same tired line about blowing my brains out. High on adrenaline, I was ready this time, my body set abuzz by the natural drug.

He may as well have pulled the fucking trigger because the only two options I had were to die or escape.

When the *crack* of the wobbly table leg sounded, I stopped kicking it. I eased back in the chair, the old wood creaking beneath me as I stared my capturer down as solidly as he stared at me.

He hadn't caught on to the notion yet that his intimidation tactics weren't working on me. While he holstered his gun, I tilted my head, glaring around him to find the other one.

His shoulder rolled, no doubt feeling the sting of my bite. A smirk twisted my lips before I clicked my teeth together in a biting gesture, taunting him. He pointed a stiff finger, shaking it at me. "You're going to pay for that, bitch. Let's see how smug you are when I make you drink your own piss."

My eyes rolled with ease, dismissing him and his words before I shot my gaze at the one standing over me.

"What the fuck do you want? I don't know shit, so you might as well let me go or put a fucking bullet in my head."

"Megan Jones. Lacey Daniels. Pick a name. I don't care. Where the fuck is she? And before you tell me you don't know, we know you've been in contact with her."

My gaze remained locked on his, unblinking. My nonverbal response put a deeper crease in his forehead. His fist clenched at his sides as his heavy breaths blew spit from his chapped lips. When his hand came down on the lopsided table, it shook as the unsteady legs danced under it. The leg I broke began to lean inward, barely holding in place.

The man's fists remained planted on the table as his strained glare stayed on me. His tanned skin had turned a glossy pink and was glistening with a fresh layer of perspiration. I took pleasure in working his last nerve and stretching his patience like hot gum.

I released a deep sigh before I tossed my chin up in defiance and awaited his next move.

Chapter Two

Beverly

Lying still and calming my breaths allowed me to feel the chill in the air. March had rolled in and the cool temperature that usually hung out in February lingered. The tremble in my lips spread to other parts of me as I fumbled with objects in the dark trunk, searching for the lever that would open it.

After pulling the cord, the trunk popped open, and I eased out. Tears streamed down my face at the notion that Laura had allowed those men to take her to save me. They would kill her if I didn't figure out a way to find her first.

My initial instinct was to call the men we grew up with from the streets. They weren't afraid of anyone or anything. Laura was also close friends with a drug kingpin named Kadeem St. James who took immense pride in bodying people.

Driving Laura's old, faded blue Toyota she refused to get rid of, I headed to Kadeem's place instead of calling him. He would take seeing me in person more seriously than a call. Kadeem was Laura's self-proclaimed brother, so I was certain he'd be willing to help me find her.

I hated the police, and although my friend needed help as soon as possible, I believed in the streets more than I believed in the law. The cops in our neck of the woods didn't waste their energy to help people who looked like me. If I needed to, I'd kiss their asses later—if kissing cop ass was what it took to find Laura.

***

Upon arrival at the Ashwood Projects, I went through the hood inspection process before I was allowed to drive up and park in front of Kadeem's building. The guys knew my face because of Laura. She'd taken me to Kadeem's spot several times when we needed assistance getting a few of the kids at the centers out of sticky situations with gangs.

I exited the car and winced as one of Kadeem's soldiers frisked me and felt me up in the process. A low growl in his throat slipped out as his hand glided across my ass. Stressed about Laura, I ignored his intrusion, and fought back tears, praying she was okay.

The man went about his business, checking the inside of the car while making kissing sounds and licking his weed-darkened lips at me. When he was convinced I wasn't a threat to any of the armed men standing about who could kill me with the flick of their finger, he released me to enter the front door.

I ambled up the two flights of stairs that led to Kadeem's apartment, knocked, and waited. The metal door I stood in front of had to be the most expensive upgrade in the building. The small metal lookout revealed a set of pearly whites smiling at me.

The door creaked open before male eyes scanned me with intentional ease.

"Reggie called up and said you needed to see Kadeem about something urgent. If you wasn't so damn fine, I'd give you a hard time, but since you made my night, come in," he expressed, winking at me.

In dark jeans, a long-sleeved checkered top, and fake brown leather flats, I wasn't dressed to impress anyone. The man acted like he'd done me a favor. He hadn't done a damn thing special because as soon as I let Kadeem know what happened to Laura, he would uproot hell to find her.

I stepped into Kadeem's nicely decorated apartment and was met with the fresh scent of jasmine and the low, relaxing melody of smooth jazz. The space was something from a magazine while the outside was drenched in a fresh coat of hell on earth.

Kadeem sat at his dining table eating gourmet food from Randell's, a high-end restaurant nowhere near this hood. He and Laura claimed they were sister and brother since she was fourteen and he was sixteen. In the streets we grew up in, you made your own family.

His hand gestured to the chair in front of him. I eased into it and fought to keep tears from dropping from my puffy, red eyes. An incessant ache squeezed my heart as my legs kept jumping and my mind was overwhelmed with negative ideas.

"What's going on with Laura?" Concern sparked in his gaze.

"My car is in the shop, so Laura swung by the center to pick me up. When we walked outside, two men dressed in dark suits were waiting for us. When they went for their guns, we ran. Laura stuck me in the trunk of her car and let the men take her to save me. I don't know where they took her. I don't know what they're going to do to her," I pushed the words out through my constricting throat. My shoulders slumped as I fought to keep myself together long enough to tell him everything I knew.

Kadeem grilled me for details, ignoring my sobs and tears. In addition to the dark figures chasing us, I recalled seeing a dark-colored, possibly gray Audi in the dimly-lit lot.

I was left at the table for a while as Kadeem paced multiple calls in which he yelled incessantly at people on the other end of the line. Once he ended his third call, he approached the table like a stalking wild animal, his phone gripped knuckle-tight in his hand. He would never say it, but he was as worried as I was about Laura.

"What can you tell me about the tattooed white boy who questioned you and Laura about six months back?" The menacing darkness that fell over his face had me afraid to answer.

How in the world had he found out someone had come to see us? He was talking about the man who attempted to pass himself off as a detective searching for Megan. When I took too long to answer, he snapped his fingers, three loud flicks in front of my face. I jumped, blinking as I fought to gather myself.

"Word on the streets is there was a group of Mexicans snooping around after the white boy showed up. Last time I talked to Laura, she told me that she was feeling strange vibes like she was being watched. I told her to come to me if she believed some shit was about to pop off."

Laura hadn't revealed a thing to me, probably unwilling to worry me with her concerns.

"You remember the girl me and Laura used to hang out with when we were younger? Megan?"

He nodded, remembering Megan.

"The man who came was searching for her, but I don't know if he had anything to do with Laura being taken tonight. The guys who took Laura had Spanish accents," I informed him.

Our brief interaction with the would-be detective hadn't been hostile. Did he know where Megan was? Had he found her?

Now that Kadeem had me thinking, I remembered one of the men who chased us tonight mentioned to Laura that our friend was possibly being protected by rednecks. Had he been talking about Megan?

Months ago, Laura and I were interviewed by Detective Mark Griffin. We were convinced the man wasn't a real detective. We called Megan about him showing up and questioning us about her.

She was usually stressed about who was chasing her. However, with this detective, I distinctly remember her laughing at Laura's reaction when I described him as tattooed and sexy. Her nonchalant reaction had Laura and me thinking she knew the man. There was one way to find out. I was going to call Detective Griffin. The real cops weren't going to help us, but maybe the fake one would.

I didn't bother sharing my ideas with Kadeem since I was grasping at straws, desperate enough to make a deal with the devil. I didn't care who they were associated with, as long as they agreed to help find Laura and possibly lead us to Megan. I jumped at Kadeem's loud clap.

"No, I don't want to stay here," I answered his question when it registered. "I'll get a cheap room for a few nights."

"We are going to find her," Kadeem reassured, and I believed him.

"You're welcome to stay here if you change your mind. It's not safe for you out there on your own."

"I'll be fine," I lied.

Chapter Three

Beverly

The drive back to my apartment had me wired like hot sparks were flying off the edges of my ripped apart nerves. Inching the car through the darkness, I crept into the alley behind my building, my head on a constant swivel like an addict. Pebbles crunched under Laura's slick tires as I squinted, driving without headlights.

My attempt to exit the car undetected was ruined by the elongated squeak of the driver's side door. I tiptoed through the night with nothing but the alley stink edging me closer to the back entrance.

I tripped over my own feet, searching for someone to pop out at any moment. I'd been careful when driving, checking for tails, but I was a novice at dodging woman-snatching bad guys. Therefore, I was about as jumpy as a cat avoiding a puddle.

The sturdy back door to our building appeared locked, but I knew as well as the other residents that the heavy door was for show. The dim interior lighting peeked out when I snatched the door open.

I dashed toward the stairs and ran up, struggling to keep my hasty steps quiet until I reached the third floor. I poked my head past the stairwell, peeking down my hall and thankful to find it empty. With my keys ready in one hand and one of my trusty switchblades in the other, I ran to our apartment with purpose.

As soon as I keyed the door open, I slammed it shut, and allowed relief to sweep through me. To stay on the safe side, I dragged one of the creaky wooden chairs from our small dining room and propped it under the front door knob. The only other way out was through one of the bedroom windows without the aid of a fire escape.

My feet stomped heavily across the floor as I entered my kitchen, yanking drawers open and tossing items out of my way. I rifled through the two rows of drawers until I found the business card the fake detective had given me.

"Detective Mark Griffin," I read his name on the card. "Did he know who took my friends?"

Although I was eager to dial the number on the card, I needed to assure my safety first.

I packed a quick bag and left my building the same way I entered it. Once I drove myself safely from my neighborhood, I sighed, blowing out a long relieving breath.

"Laura," her name seeped out into the interior of her car as I swiped at my teary eyes. My drive to the outer edge of Houston allowed me to let my mind race with ideas on how to find her.

I drove past two motels and decided on the third I came upon. I chose the area at random, a pinpoint on the map, so I believed I was safe until I figured out my next move.

The scruffy-haired desk clerk insisted there were only doubles left although the parking lot was nearly empty. I didn't argue, but my lips connected with the back of my credit card, thankful it had gone through. My bank account was on life support, and most of the money I made at work usually went back into the center for one reason or another.

After parking Laura's car on the opposite side of the building my room was located on, I locked myself inside the room. My busy mind kept me from being bothered by the stale scent that greeted when I entered the room.

I slung my purse and backpack on the bed and plopped down in the burgundy velvet-covered chair that sat next to the scratched varnished finish of the table. The stench of smoke permeated the room, although I requested nonsmoking.

Without further hesitation, I dialed the number on the card with shaky fingers, hoping I wasn't about to make the situation worse. A male voice answered the call and sounded like the man who questioned me months ago.

"Detective Griffin," my shaky voice called out. "We spoke several months ago about a friend of mine: Megan. I'm calling because we lost contact with her after you came searching for her. Now, another of my friends has been taken, and…"

My tight tongue refused to push out the rest of my sentence, and a throaty cry escaped instead.

"Beverly?" the man questioned.

"Yes," I whispered into the phone, my voice hardly working.

"Is Laura the friend that has been taken?"

"Yes. You remember us?" A pinch of hope cushioned my nerves at the notion that his brief encounter with us was intact.

"Actually, I've never met you. It was my cousin, Aaron, you spoke to. Unfortunately, he was killed about five months ago."

The news took my last bit of breath. I couldn't piece myself together long enough to ask the questions stacked up on my tongue. Had his cousin been killed by the same men who took Laura? Was Megan dead too? Who were they?

The man's voice jarred me back to reality. "Megan is with me. She's fine, but for a while she wasn't talking."

I breathed a long sigh of relief at the news that Megan was okay before a round of throaty cries burst free.

If he were helping Megan, would he be willing to help Laura and me too?

An urgent flow of rambling ideas stopped me in my tracks, prompting me to recall all aspects of the situation. Was this guy telling me what I wanted to hear? He could have been a part of the team responsible for taking Laura. How could I be sure that Megan was okay?

"Can I speak to Megan?" I tested, cutting into the litany of questions he was asking.

"Beverly?" Her shaky voice was like the first spark of sunshine breaking through dark thunderclouds.

I gasped at the familiar sound. "Megan." Her name dragged across my tongue, vibrating through my constricting throat.

"I'm okay. I'm so sorry I haven't called before now. I lost my phone, and I-I wasn't doing well." Her voice was cracking as badly as mine. The weeping sadness in her tone hinted that she was still struggling.

When I began asking questions, needing to know what happened to her, the man returned. This time, he grilled me as hard as Kadeem did.

I revealed everything that happened to Laura and me while the man, Ansel, as he'd identified himself, listened. He questioned me periodically for specific details.

Ansel revealed a few details about how Megan ended up with him in California and let me know it had all started right here in Texas.

"I'm going to send a few friends to your location to help find Laura. They're some of the best...." he paused. "They're some of the best trackers I know."

I wasn't as quick a study as some, but I knew he was about to say something other than his friends were trackers. If these men were helping Megan from the kind of trouble I knew she was running from, they were more than just *trackers*.

After I revealed to Ansel where I was staying and that I had enough good sense to hide, he informed me that his friends would link up with me before daybreak. He handed the phone back to Megan, and we cried and talked until my phone died.

I flipped the dead phone in my hand, thankful I hadn't been too disoriented to forget my charger. The knowledge that help was on the way sent relief sweeping through me. As fast as I was filled with relief, it was snuffed out when Laura crossed my mind. Fresh tears started, and nothing but seeing Laura again would stop them.

Would the help that I enlisted to find Laura be enough or were they already too late?

Chapter Four

Derrick

At ninety percent into cracking through layers of firewalls that had taken me a half day to dig a digital tunnel through, Ansel's number popped up on my phone and drew my attention from my task. I'd been working off and on with him on a project I personally labeled Operation Avenge Aaron while Ansel called it Operation Take Six.

Ansel reminded me of Aaron so much that we became fast friends after Aaron's death. As a matter of fact, Dax and I had only recently left California after a few weeks with Ansel at his house in the hills.

"What's up?" I greeted after I swiped to answer and tapped the speaker button.

"D, I have a big fucking problem," he announced, which was classic Ansel. He didn't hesitate to get straight to the point. Whatever the news was, he was always straight, no chasers, just like his cousin.

"One of Megan's friends has been abducted, and I think it has something to do with DG6. Are you still in Texas?"

"No, but I can book myself a flight and be there in a few hours. Do you have any details?" I asked, my interest piqued. Ansel relayed the details he'd gathered, which convinced me that DG6 was all over the situation.

DG6, also known as the Dominquez Cartel, was one of the deadliest in the country. We'd faced off with them in Texas in a failed rescue mission that had ended with Aaron's death.

Laura and Beverly. I'd never met them, but recalled leading Aaron to them when he was searching for Megan. Now that Megan was safely hidden with Ansel, DG6 was targeting her friends.

Megan had gone silent after Aaron's death, walking around like a ghost, partially existing. I could sympathize with her because I missed Aaron too. He was one of those people who would go to war for anyone he cared about, and you didn't just become his friend, you became his *family*. Ansel was the same way. Drawing me from my musings, his voice returned.

"You remember what we discussed about chopping off the heads of this DG6 snake?"

"I'm already tracking. You can call this Operation WTF for Watch the Friends. If we get an opportunity to take out an original member of this cartel, you can count his ass as good as gone," I expressed with confidence.

I sensed Ansel's smile through the phone. "Thanks, D. I appreciate it, man."

"No problem," I replied. With my senses hyped up, I was ready to get this mission started. I didn't care that I was in the middle of another mission. It wouldn't be the first time I worked double duty.

After dialing the number Ansel gave me for Beverly, we talked briefly. Her sullen tone was laced with the broken syllables that made her repeat herself. She'd requested that I send her a snapshot of my face so she could ID me when I met her. She may have been in distress over her friend, but she was smart. I didn't keep her on the line long but made sure we exchanged basic information.

I dialed Dax and relayed the story to him, but Ansel had already beaten me to it. Dax's enthusiasm about the impending danger had me laughing. He was one of the best dressed killers I knew. He relished the excitement of a mission and rarely turned down a chance to be engrossed in danger.

With a family as rich as the Rockefellers, he had access to the best resources money could buy. The men in our group jumped at the chance to work with Dax because he lavished you with the best of everything, no matter what the mission called for.

Dax had crawled through the same gutters as we had in the military and in life, but he was not going to forgo being pampered unless it was necessary.

When we first met in the military, my initial assumption was that he was a spoiled rich kid rebelling against his family. It only took our first mission together for me to understand that I had misjudged him. Dax may have come from money, but something much deeper and darker drove him, something he would never discuss in full detail, no matter how many times we pried.

Several hours later, the engine of my rental idled down as I slowed to check out the location surrounding the address Beverly provided. Eyes peeled, I searched the dark perimeter of the seedy motel before turning into the parking lot.

Dim lights anchored to the outer walls provided sparse lighting around the white-brick building with red doors standing out on each room. I parked a safe distance from the intended room. My neck constantly swiveled as I strolled to the door and knocked twice like I said I would when I chatted briefly with Beverly on the phone.

Her shadow didn't break the thin line of light below the door or darkened the peephole, but her words found my ears.

"Place your face to the crack in the door when I open it so I can see you. If you try anything funny, I'll slice your neck open like a ripe watermelon," she warned.

Dayum!

I did as she instructed and placed my face next to the crack. She eased the door open, but the chain kept it secured. When she'd stared long enough, she closed the door and the jingle of her undoing the chain sounded.

The door was sprung open before she stepped aside to allow me to enter. I walked past her, turning my head from her with tightly shut eyes before biting into my bottom lip. The glimpse I saw through the crack was a tease.

It was petty of me to think it, but I was praying Beverly was a homely woman who'd let herself go. However, she unknowingly introduced me to a new sub-operation because Operation Distract Derrick was underway. Beverly Hudson was sexy as hell.

My first full visual of her had widened my eyes. She had silky, dark brown skin, greenish-brown eyes that could be classified as hazel, and a body perfectly proportioned for her height of at least five-eight. She wore her hair in a straight, well-kept bob and it was *her hair* and not a wig or extensions. She wasn't the kind of thick that verged on being fat. She was fit-thick with noticeable curves.

Why did she have to be my type? Why did she have to look so damn good? She wasn't too much, but enough to entice and evoke pure lust.

After locking the door, she turned to face me, and the tears standing in her beautiful, distressed eyes ripped my lustful thinking to shreds.

Chapter Five

Dax

As I drove up to the Spangler Motel, my gaze lingered on the sign that hung lopsided in the parking lot marquee, lit with slanted red letters. The metal pole it once stood on had been struck by something, and the owners hadn't bothered to fix it.

I was forced to switch off the car's ventilation as the foul odor of road kill crept in and thickened the air inside the cab. The place was a fleapit, and my skin had already started to itch.

After parking my black BMW 750i, I studied my surroundings, and then crept to door 110. My car stuck out like a sore thumb, but the situation sounded dire and I didn't have time to switch vehicles. A missing woman who was possibly taken by one of the worst cartels in the country needed me. It sounded like trouble—my kind of trouble.

Before my knuckles struck the dusty red door, D sprang it open and stepped back to allow me in. How the hell had he beaten me here, when he was in New Orleans, and I was in Dallas? Once he closed us into the musty room, we gave each other a brotherly hug, at which point my eyes landed on the woman sitting at the desk.

"Hello," I turned to introduce myself. I reached out my hand, but my eyes were glued on the most beautiful set of eyes I'd seen on a woman in a long time. "I'm Dax."

She took my hand. "Beverly." I didn't miss the hopeless gloom that sat in her gaze. She fought to project strength although her eyes were glistening with tears by the time I let go of her hand.

She was certainly easy on the eyes, and I didn't miss that D's eyes were on constant watch. He stepped around me and took a seat at the foot of the lumpy bed before revealing the details we had so far. He already had two laptops sitting on the desk and at some point would attempt to track down her friend with the digital magic only he could create.

Beverly continued filling me in on what had taken place with her and her friend, Laura. Aaron had briefly mentioned talking to the women before he was killed by DG6 in one of the worst missions of my life.

As a group, we'd soldiered through the trenches of hell in foreign countries but had never suffered a loss so devastating as the one that befell Aaron. I for one hadn't fully come to terms with the notion of losing Aaron. Knowing the group who took his life continued to taunt us with their presence was all the motivation I needed to join the fight.

Although I was labeled a playboy who indulged in many casual relationships, I took offense to men who picked on women. It wasn't that I didn't believe women couldn't fight their own battles, but groups like DG6 were bullies, bruiting forces that picked on *defenseless* targets.

"There's no need for a lot of clues to know that this is DG6," I posed the obvious, eyeing D. "They probably took Laura because they are going to torture her for information on Megan."

D attempted to stop me with rapid eye movements in Beverly's direction, but it was too late. My insensitive words had frozen her in terror. I wasn't used to tempering my words. I'd not worked with many people I couldn't speak frankly in front of.

"My apologies, Beverly," I offered with my hand pressed above my heart. "But if we don't find Laura within the next forty-eight hours...." I let my words trail off. I didn't need to complete the sentence. She nodded her understanding with her lips pinched in determination.

Beverly and D switched places as I continued to question her, attempting to squeeze every bit of information out of her. She was in a mild state of shock and unable to recall anything substantial except a quick snapshot of the vehicle she'd spotted in the center's parking lot. It was the same information she gave D. She was surprisingly mindful enough to reach out to Aaron, even though he'd used an alias. It was smart and impressive.

"I've got something. Sometimes, this shit is too easy," D stated as he continued working the keyboard.

"CCTV gave me enough snapshots to piece together a plate of the vehicle spotted in the center's lot." He glanced back, directing his statement at us before turning back around and pointing at the screen.

He made the task sound easy, but he'd probably found a way to sharpen the license plate after it had been bounced off a glass and reflected off a puddle of water. Upon further inspection, I noticed it was much more difficult than I assumed. He'd taken hundreds of snapshots of the back of the car, capturing them from an unknown number of angles until he'd pieced together a license plate number like one would a jigsaw puzzle.

"Dark Gray Audi A8," he continued. "The plate popped up at several locations, but it was last spotted before disappearing on Industrial Parkway. The place is a warehouse estate with only two roads that lead back to the city. Based on footage from the last four hours, the vehicle hasn't left the area."

The expression of hope on Beverly's face softened the lines of her distress. "You think we can save her before they hurt her?"

Her question tiptoed around what was truly on her mind. The way her knee bounced, she feared her friend was already dead.

D placed a hand atop hers. "We'll find her," he reassured.

Truth was, we didn't know where she was in that sea of warehouses or if she were living or dead. Either way, we would still hunt them down.

I retrieved my phone from my suit jacket before dialing and lifting it to my ear. I needed to put a few plans in place to make things a little easier on us. With distance between us, I stood near the bathroom to carry on my conversation. Once I was done, I returned to the group.

"My assistant will book us an upgrade. We're going to need more space and someplace more secure," I stated.

I gave the room a once over, fighting to keep a frown off my face. The massive dip in the center of the second bed made it appear that someone we couldn't see was sitting in the space. The cheap golden frame of the picture above the bed Beverly sat on was falling apart.

My brow hitched at the sight I spotted. Was that a cinder block holding the bed up?

The place was a dump. Gum, spilled food, dirt, and unknown stains littered the green checkered carpet they hadn't upgraded since the seventies. A black and green mold stain in the shape of a man's face sat in the ceiling near the wall unit.

Relocating was a must and it wasn't because I believed I was too good for the room. I'd had to live in worse places. However, if we were going to do our job and do it as effectively as we were able to, we needed a space with a lot more to offer. My phone vibrated, calling my attention.

"Our suite is ready. D, I'll text you the address."

"Good." He knew me well enough to know I was not going to stay here unless it was necessary.

"I've found out where that Audi stopped," D updated.

Beverly jumped from the bed at D's words. "You did? Is Laura there?" The prospect of hope in her tone wasn't lost. She'd found one friend and lost another in the same night and was managing the emotional war taking place inside her well.

"I can't pull any visible images, but thermal images confirm that all inside the warehouse the Audi stopped at are alive," he updated, causing her to send a relieved breath through her weak smile.

We stood at D's shoulder as he explained where the warehouse was in relation to our location. We studied the blueprints and the considerably weak security measures the group had in place. We tossed around ideas about how we would search for and extract Laura, provided she was one of the heat signatures inside the warehouse.

"Wait. Only the two of you are going to go in there?" Beverly pointed at the screen, shaking her head. "All of those moving red dots are bad guys, right?" She was skeptical of our proposal for helping her friend.

D turned to face her. "Beverly, only *one* of us is going in there," he corrected. "It's best not to send an army. It's what they will be expecting. If one of us goes in, our chances of finding Laura and getting her out will be better."

"One." She laughed before she pointed between us. "*One* of you is going in there to get Laura? Oh God," she murmured before plopping down on the edge of the bed.

D took her hand. I envied his knack for keeping people calm.

"Beverly, I can assure you. We've done this type of operation before. If one of us goes in there, we aren't going to leave that building until we have Laura, even if it means destroying everyone inside."

Those words lifted her brows. She glanced back and forth between us, questioning who she'd truly gotten involved with. She stared, face strained, taking us in fully before nodding.

"I'll meet you two later at our new location," I announced. I'd assigned myself the job of going after Laura. D jerked his neck back at my words, his expression unreadable, but I knew better.

"I know you like to live up to your 'silent assassin' image," D stated, revealing my nickname from the military. "But that warehouse is surrounded by other buildings in an area where help won't come quickly or easily," he pointed out. "Are you sure you want to do this? I can't pinpoint where Laura might be inside the building, so you'd be going in blind," he warned.

"Yes. I figured as much," I confirmed, allowing a bit of the necessary arrogance needed for this type of mission to shine through.

Beverly's eyes volleyed between us as tension rode her body. She clearly had doubts about our ability to pull off the mission, and she should. Facts were, we couldn't guarantee it would be a success. We'd worked this type of mission before, yes, but like all assignments, you never knew when it would be your last.

D's penetrating gaze locked on mine. His stare said what he didn't in words out of respect for Beverly. I could picture a litany of words hovering above his tongue, telling me I was being arrogant when he was sitting there willing to trade places. I commented on his hard stare.

"I'll be silent. I'll be … *vigilant*," I confirmed before flashing a smile that revealed that the darkness of hell was following me into that building.

He nodded his understanding. "You're the only motherfucker I know who can dress your darkness up as well as you dress your body. Be careful," he warned, chuckling and handing me an earpiece. "It's long range, so you should be able to hear me from the new location. If not, use your phone, but only if you must," he instructed as a hint of concern reflected in his eyes but dissolved when a mischievous smile crept across my lips.

He eyed me for a while, not willing to say out loud the things we'd normally say to each other amid a deadly mission in front of Beverly. If we had to die, it would be as a result of attempting to do something good, to help the good guys, or to dispel an evil threat to the world. Did we live righteous lives? No, we didn't. However, we'd encountered real-world devils that made us look like the saints.

D turned to Beverly when we were done with our stare down. "Pardon my earlier language. I've been meaning to quit cursing, but it has a way of adding flavor to my limited vocabulary."

A smile crept across her lips. "No need to apologize. I fucking understand better than you think."

We laughed, but he kept his eyes on her, locking her in place with a serious expression. "We are going to find Laura," he reassured.

"If she's in that building, I'll find her," I added, knowing she needed the positive boost.

Uncertainty remained in her gaze and stress kept her body coiled tight. However, she had no idea she'd just received a promise from two men who knew how to stoke the fires of Hell and use the flames to burn it to oblivion.

Chapter Six

Laura

When their interrogation tactics failed to work on me, the men went for a break. Two hours of them yelling and knocking things around was a waste of time.

They were gone so long I started to nod off. It was their waiting game tactic, I supposed.

My head jerked up when they reentered the room, filling the suffocating space with their smug ugliness. They placed, what I assumed was their torture kit, a shiny wooden box, on the edge of the other side of the table.

As one of the freaks drew closer, bending across the table, I leaned in to meet him, positioning my chest against the table's edge. My free hand tightened around the table leg that I'd loosened.

Maintaining my position, I glanced through my lashes at the asshole standing above me, attempting to assert his worthless authority. It was obvious they didn't know what to do with me.

"Lady, save yourself a fucking beating and answer our questions," he urged, staring me down. If they had orders from whoever was running this show to put hands on me, they would have done it already. I gave up nothing, only my cold, deadly glare.

His menacing expression deepened as he leaned closer. His hot breath washed over my face as he barked threatening words that fueled my anger.

"I'm going to fuck up that pretty little face of yours. Knock a few of those nice straight teeth out. Break a few bones...." he continued, taunting me with what I assumed was his scary voice. His intimidation tactics weren't doing anything but making my body coil to maintain the angry outburst teetering at the edge of my restraint. His buddy stood near the door, snickering.

When the man leaned closer, closing more space between us, hovering less than a foot above me, a smile teased my lips. He was close enough that his dark pupils stood out in his whiskey-brown eyes. "I'm going to..."

Bam!

The loud *whack* sounded before blood and spittle flew across the room. I'd yanked the table leg free and busted him upside the head with it, attempting to knock his damn jawbone clean off its hinges.

The table shook from our unsteady movements, him wobbling in an attempt to figure out where he was, and me leaning against it for leverage. I remained in place as he staggered back, with enough good sense remaining to get the hell away from me.

His buddy checked him out as I stood from the splintery chair and pointed the table leg at them. Blood poured from the man's busted mouth, and I prayed that I'd at least knocked out a few teeth or had broken his jaw.

His gurgling voice found its way through the trauma, blood sliding down his chin. "I'm going to kill you, bitch!" He shrieked, holding his mouth with one hand and pointing at me with the other like he was mimicking Celie from *The Color Purple*.

His body jetted up and down, releasing pure, untamed hatred under his friend's tight hold. If I weren't cuffed to the damn table, I'd be fucking them both up. My lips pinched into a tight knot, eager to get at the man as badly as he aimed to get at me.

"We can't kill her because Sorio wants that privilege, especially after the Florida incident," the one who still had all his teeth spat. "We have to find out where that other bitch is located. Sorio is obsessed with finding her, and you know how he gets whenever he doesn't get what he wants," he reminded the one with the busted mouth.

Rage consumed the man, chomping at his nerves as he fumed and kept a firm grip on his busted mouth. His free arm flapped about uselessly under his friend's hold as he continued his attempts to lunge at me.

"I don't care! I don't care!" His words were muffled by flowing blood and his swelling jaw. Blood and spit dripped from his mouth and smacked the floor as his flaming words and angling body seethed to exact his revenge.

"I think that crazy bitch broke my fucking jaw," he revealed, touching his fingertips to his face before glancing at his bloody fingers. If I were stronger, I'd have knocked his neck off his shoulders and stepped over his cold dead body before I did the same to his friend.

His body continued to jerk erratically, but his friend kept a firm hold of him. I would break more than his jaw if he came near me again.

"Wait by the door. I'll handle the questioning," his friend proposed as he eyed the guy's smashed-up face. There was pity in his expression before his lips drew into a tight line, probably his attempt to keep from laughing.

The one who aimed to question me stepped closer, hesitant. Cautious. I maintained my composure, hoping he'd be stupid enough to step into my striking range. When he stood across the wobbly table from me, I sent the table leg swinging in his direction. He dodged my attempt by a hair, and the *click* of his gun sounded, aimed at the spot between my eyes.

"Drop the fucking stick or I'm going to split your head in two," he threatened, his words laced with his intent. He mistakenly assumed his words were a threat to me, but my adrenaline was revved so high I shook with rage. His threat was idle chitchat. I was banking on a quick kill shot from one of them since I was beginning to believe death was my only way out of this mess.

Common sense eluded me when my crazy kicked in, and instead of dropping the table leg like a sane person would have, I swung it at the man's gun, connecting and knocking it from his hand.

His wounded expression exhibited pain as he fanned his injured hand through the air, revealing blood.

"Fuck this shit. Kill that wild bitch!" His busted-mouth partner attempted to shout as he stood at the door holding his face together. There was fire shining in his gaze when he aimed his gun at me, the same kind of fire that blazed through my veins.

In a matter of seconds, the one nearest me picked up his gun and aimed too. Their fingers itched to press their triggers. In my last seconds of life, I accepted that I wasn't ready to die, but what other option did I have? Play victim so they could torture me and prolong my death?

I hated to leave Beverly like this, knowing she'd do everything in her power to find me. The hard pounding of my heart quaked through me as fear and regret battled it to take the number one spot in my head. But, even as I faced death, I was determined to die with a little dignity. I wasn't going to beg and I sure as hell wasn't going to cry. My eyelids fell at the sight of their weapons and fuming faces trained on me.

As soon as my lids closed, I was drenched in darkness, and the sound of my last breaths was the tune I'd die to.

Pop! Pop!

Two pops signified my end. It happened so fast, I didn't feel the bullet's impact and the pops were low like the sound had been turned down. After a few seconds of me continuing to draw breaths, I allowed one eye to lift.

What the...? Who the...?

Chapter Seven

Dax

The two men yelling out threats had their backs to the door. I snuck into what I believed was a failed interrogation attempt. The men's annoyance with Laura had distracted them, and left them vulnerable. Neither guilt nor remorse surfaced when I let off two quick rounds, one landing in the back of each of their heads.

They never knew what hit them as the sound of their limp bodies tumbled to the floor. The mess of their blown-out brains left splashes of thick blood and chunks on the floor and ceiling and continued to ooze onto the dirty, checkered floor. I'd done them a favor. A quick death was what you prayed for whenever you subjected yourself to this kind of life.

I bent to retrieve the cuff key from one of the stiffs, being careful not to let his exposed parts dirty my new suit. The strong odor of blood and open wounds filled my nostrils and dropped down to my stomach. When I turned his body, a guttural breath blew past his busted lips.

"Who the fuck are you?" Came the heated question lobbed at me by the feisty little lady named Laura. She couldn't have been but an inch over five feet. Her hair was in braids gathered to the right side of her head and hung past her chest.

Her eyes were big brown ovals that sat perfectly in her face. They were the kind of big eyes revered as beautiful. However, hers retained a depth of danger I'd seen reflected in my own.

She wore a fitted, burgundy T-shirt and snug-fitting, ripped jeans that hugged her small curves. She looked like jailbait, and if I didn't already know her age, I'd assume she was a teen.

According to D, she was a lesbian, so I expected a buff dude-woman, not this petite beauty with a good grasp on her femininity. Her appearance had trashed my stereotype of what I assumed a lesbian should look like.

"You come near this table, and I'm going to fuck you up too!" she shouted, meaning every word. She may not have had the appearance of a man, but she had the attitude of one.

Although I used a silencer, my actions had likely alerted the stiff's friends. The interrogation was being viewed through a two-way mirror and via the small camera in the corner above Laura's head.

I'd left two more dead on the other side of that mirror. The men had been thoroughly entertained by the way she handled their friends until I shut them up. However, there was still the matter of the person, or persons monitoring the camera feed. D would eventually, if he already hadn't, find a way to make whatever they recorded disappear.

Laura glared at me with flaring opposition when I aimed and took out the camera.

She was one tough woman. Cuffed to a table, odds stacked against her, and threatened with torture and death, she'd stood tall and fought. Even when she was assuredly about to die, it almost seemed she'd welcomed it. Her eyes had fallen closed before she lifted her head and sent them one last *"Fuck you."*

Only someone who'd been through hell could embrace death in that manner. I couldn't help respecting such bravery even as I wondered how I would convince her that I was there to help.

"I have no doubt you'll attempt to do what you say," I commented. "But, I'm here to help. You're Laura, right?"

She didn't have to confirm what I already knew. My statement was meant to break the ice, but Laura was all fire. I edged closer to the table with caution, holding out the cuff key with her pointing that bloody table leg at me.

"I don't know you, so your words mean nothing. Toss the key, Mr. Here-to-help," she spat.

I sat the key atop the table and slid it across before backing off and keeping an eye on the door behind me. Approaching footsteps were faint but growing closer.

The clicking of the cuffs being undone registered as I crept closer to the two-way mirror. With my back against the wall facing Laura, I kept one eye on her and the other on the door.

I hunkered low to hide from anyone coming to check things out. Once they spotted their men laid out and dead, they would kill anything that moved.

Laura's earlier reaction to the men had paused me too. When I discovered her true intentions—that she was baiting them to kill her—I sprang into action.

She eased from behind the table, uncertainty flashing in her gaze that alternated between the dead men and me. A deep crease lined my forehead when she bent across the dead man I took the cuff key from. She peeled back his fingers before she jerked his gun free of his death-clenched hand.

"What are you doing? You don't need a gun. I'm here to get you out," I hissed in her direction.

She, of all people, didn't need a gun in her deadly hands. She didn't trust me and was crazy enough to shoot me since she hadn't yet concluded my purpose.

"What the fuck does it look like I'm doing?" She answered my question with a colorful one of her own as the metal sounded from her cocking the weapon.

"If you're here to help, you shouldn't mind me having a gun," she added, staying in a hunched position before she started to move toward the opposite side of the mirror from me. She pinned her back to the wall and waited.

We couldn't see through the two-way mirror, but the faint sound of someone's approach on the other side registered. The door popped open in front of us, and neither of us wasted time pulling our triggers.

The first man caught two to the chest and one to the head, his body jerking violently as the bullets ripped him apart. My shots were silent, and Laura's rang out loud and sure. The second man at the door took a clean headshot from my deadly partner. She was an excellent shot. From my position, I couldn't see the others, but was aware they lingered outside the door.

When the window shattered between us, I stood, took aim and took out another one. I'd disconnected the hallway lights, so only scant lighting illuminated the area outside the window. I ducked behind the wall to avoid approaching bullets before I chanced a quick peek down the long, dim hall.

Laura's gun sounded loud and demanding as I concentrated and steadied my aim at another approaching from a distance in the hall. My gun kicked, sending fast-moving death into the darkness and my target. He stumbled around like a drunk before he dropped to the floor.

"This way!" I shouted, pointing out the cleared path in the direction of the doorway that would lead us to freedom. I wasn't sure Laura trusted me enough not to shoot me, but we had to move before we became sitting ducks.

I hopped through the busted-out window with ease as I scanned the area. Laura, with her short stature, faced a bit of difficulty in her attempt to hop across the wall. I gripped her forearm and yanked her across. As soon as her feet struck the ground, fire flashed from her pistol as she took down the man who turned the corner in our direction.

No one gave chase as we ran the expanse of the hall, exited a side door, and maneuvered the twists and turns between warehouses to get to my car. Laura didn't voice a complaint as she remained on guard. Our feet beat up the ground, and our harsh breaths added life to the darkness we traveled through.

The shadow of my black car stood against the darkness enough for me to make it out. I'd backed it into the alley for an easier getaway. A few clicks of the key fob in my hand caused the lights to flash once, announcing to anyone nearby I'd unlocked the car right as the engine roared to life.

Laura ran to the passenger's side, climbed in, and hunkered low without me having to tell her. I hopped in, keyed a secondary code, and sped along the tight alley without headlights. There were no other cars on the deserted street we turned onto, only the large structures of warehouses that all looked the same.

After minutes of the engine's roar and our accelerated breathing, it pleased me that no cars approached from either direction. The infrared D provided into the warehouse had revealed at least twenty bodies, so I expected them to give chase.

A long stretch of silence filled the interior of my car as we approached the flowing traffic of the city and turned into the hectic movements. Laura's neck continued to snap back in the direction we left and faced front before she eyeballed the side mirror.

The dash lighting revealed the gun gripped tight in her hand, waiting for a chance to be fired.

"So, what are you? Some rich wanna-be hit man?" Her eyes were glued to the side mirror, searching for a tail.

"I'm the man who just saved your life. Besides, I wasn't the one inciting my own death." I scanned the rearview mirror.

"I wasn't about to let those assholes torture me or do something worse. I'd rather die the quick ending *I* incite than suffer a torturous one for no reason. If you're truly the help, where the hell is Beverly? Is she okay? Or better yet, where the hell is Megan?"

"How could you possibly connect me to Megan when you don't know who the hell I am?"

"I actually didn't connect anything. First off, there was a fake detective who came searching for Megan months back. The assholes who just took me repeatedly questioned me about Megan's whereabouts and insisted that there were white guys protecting her. I assumed if you're here to help me, it meant Beverly found you somehow."

"Beverly is fine. She's with my friend, D, which is where we're headed as soon as I know for certain that we don't have a tail. Megan is fine also. She's in California with our friend, Ansel. He's keeping her safe from the same crew that's apparently hunting you."

My words satisfied her, but she remained quiet. I kept a keen eye on the rearview.

"Trust me," she said, lifting the gun, "If we had a tail, I'd have spotted them by now, and they would have caught some of this heat."

I didn't doubt that. I didn't know what to make of this woman. If I hadn't shown up, she'd be dead or everyone in that warehouse would be.

"So, Suit-and-tie. What's your story? Do you always go around killing people and attempting rescue missions dressed like you're about to receive an Academy Award? Montblanc watch, a tailor-cut suit, Ferragamo oxfords," she rambled off accurately, identifying my attire, proving she paid more attention than I assumed. It was impressive.

"First, my name's Dax, and I'd appreciate you addressing me that way. Second, I didn't attempt a rescue mission. I *completed* one, saving you before you ended up getting yourself killed."

"Whatever," she grumbled as she bent and fished around in her back pocket. A small object, obscured by the darkness, was in her hand. I sensed her assessing gaze on me as the low click of my cigarette lighter sounded.

When the lighter popped up, she removed it. A few seconds later, the burning glow of orange floated through the dim interior. When the flames caught the tobacco of her cigarette, she cracked her window as a pathetic show of respect for my property.

"Would you put that cigarette out and respect my car? I don't smoke, and you should have asked before lighting up," I disciplined her, irritated.

"Sorry. Not a cigarette," she choked out before taking another long drag, the hot orange tip flaring to life.

When the scent drifted up my nose, my foot stomped on the brake, causing her to fight the force of the interior momentum. She managed to avoid slamming into the dash as her lips kept the lit *not* cigarette in her mouth.

From my control panel, I rolled her window the rest of the way down before snatching what was a half of a blunt from her lips and tossed it through her window. My finger pointed in her direction like a father disciplining his child.

"You're next if you don't respect me and my property."

"Are you crazy? That was certified moon rock," she yelled like I was the one in the wrong. This woman was certifiably nuts.

"I don't care if it was the earth's crust. You need to keep a level head. You were abducted by a cartel. They are going to keep coming after you until they get what they want. Getting high is not the solution in this situation," I persisted , certain my words weren't making an impact on her half-dead brain cells.

A teasing laugh sounded. "I don't know how you relieve your stress, but you just tossed the one thing that's going to keep me calm and easy going."

I left the windows down and eased back onto the highway. Fifteen minutes, and I already wanted to throttle this woman.

Since we'd left bodies in that warehouse, we needed to find DG6's back-up locations, safe houses, or places they frequented so we could find the target we truly needed to eliminate.

"Thank God," I mouthed under my breath when I drove into the Grand Majestic Hotel's parking garage. Laura had talked non-stop about all she needed to do at the center that she managed. She acted like she hadn't been at the business end of several weapons. It was hard to forget she'd also killed at least two men.

"Yep, you're most definitely Richie Rich if this is where you're staying," came her condescending words. She had yet to thank me for saving her because in her convoluted mind, she'd saved herself.

There was no use replying to her statement. All I wanted was to find out how to put an end to the threat, call up three or four one-night stands, and take my family's yacht out for a week-long cruise. I sensed that, with Laura in this mix, this would be a mission from hell.

After parking, I rounded the car to open her door, but she met me at the back. We rode the elevator in silence, her continuing to size me up.

I sneaked a glance now that she stood under the strong lights of the elevator. She would be a beautiful woman if you could brush aside her prickly attitude, the furrow that sat like a permanent fixture on her forehead, and the unforgiving sting of anger set in her big brown eyes.

She was a perfectly baked brown, darker than caramel, but lighter than mahogany. Her skin was flawless and makeup free, projecting a misty glow. My tongue slipped across my bottom lip when my gaze traced the outline of her body. Sexy-slim was the best way to describe her petite frame that revealed curves where they were meant to be on a woman's body.

The deadly gaze she shot me for staring too long was a cold glass of ice water to my senses. How could I be attracted to a woman who had the temperament of a dragon, the attitude of a grumpy cat, and the personality of an alpha male?

It was a misjudgment on my part. Exhaustion had set in and hindered my sound decision making because I'd forgone my usual post-assignment break.

We exited the elevator on the top floor, our suite the only one on the floor. As soon as I keyed open the door and allowed the little ball of trouble to enter the room, her gaze found Beverly. They ran to each other, clinging to each other for dear life as they swayed back and forth.

I closed the door and shot a glance in D's direction. He popped his head up as a gesture of greeting and thankfulness I was okay. His gaze left mine and his smile deepened at the sight of the ladies.

"D, that's Laura, the rude one who didn't allow me the chance to properly introduce her," I grumbled, not hiding the irritation in my tone.

His smile revealed he wasn't bothered, nor did he care about introductions. He was all about the mission now. He'd been engrossed in enough intrigue to whet his appetite. If I was honest with myself, I was all in when Ansel called me.

"I'll go and prep the back bedroom so we can figure out our next move," I informed him. The ladies hadn't moved. They were leaning in a huddle, likely planning more problems for us to solve. My hand twisted the knob as my shoulder bumped open the door that led to the second bedroom at the back of the suite.

Chapter Eight

Laura

After my reunion with Beverly, I introduced myself to D. For reasons unknown, I liked him, and there weren't many men I liked right away. He was outgoing and friendly and understood my personality enough not to get offended by the off-handed shit that flew from my mouth.

"So, where did Richie Rich go? We're not the kind of company he likes to keep or something?" I asked D.

"No, he's making preparations. We have some business to attend to that may help us figure out how to stop this group. They will keep after you ladies now that you're on their radar," D advised, choosing his words carefully.

Before I requested he elaborate, Dax exited the thick, dark-wood door that led to another part of the large suite. My excitement over reuniting with Beverly had prevented me from checking out the place that clearly cost more per night than I made in a year.

Victorian-style furnishings, two crystal chandeliers over the oversized couch, a loveseat, and chairs, a shiny grand piano in one corner, human-sized porcelain statues sat prominently in their spaces.

The floor was so glossy and clean you could check your makeup in it, the ceiling so high your voice called back to you. The shine sparkling off the blue waters from the infinity pool on the balcony was bright enough to blind me.

The apartment Beverly and I shared could sit inside the open living-dining area three times. This wasn't a suite. It was a *house*. This was one of those places if I broke something inside it, they may as well send me to jail because they would never be able to collect. White, dark brown, and gray made up the color scheme and although the colors together should have been dull, in this place they popped with life.

Dax drew the door closed behind him, his stance almost protective. My gaze swiveled past him and landed on the door he exited, letting him know I wanted to know what he was hiding.

"What's up, Richie Rich?" I questioned as I stepped into his path, knowing he didn't like the nickname I chose for him. Beverly and D went silent in the background.

"My name's *Dax*. And what I'm up to is nothing you need to be concerned about," he grumbled, his stiff tone matching his rigid posture.

My forehead wrinkled, and I folded my arms across my chest, staring him down like I wasn't the one whose height didn't go past his shoulder.

The amount of arrogance he projected was off the charts. It drifted off him like an oversaturation of testosterone, making me burp in my throat to keep from gagging. He wasn't a bad-looking man as far as men went. Once a year, I was kind enough to give one of them credit, and this was my annual nicety.

Dax owned the whole tall, dark, and gray-eyed swagger market. His eyes weren't a dull gray. They were steely like he had liquid silver running through them. Manscaped to perfection, his dark hair was cut low and streaked with natural light-brown highlights. His chin was dusted with a day or two of scruff, but the rest of his face was baby-bottom smooth, likely from a facial. His straight teeth were so bright he could walk right into a toothpaste commercial.

We remained in place, staring each other down as I took my time drafting a reply that I knew he didn't want to hear.

"Like hell, I don't need to be concerned. I'm one of the hunted. More than that, I don't want to sit around with my fingers up my ass while strangers risk their lives to protect mine. No offense D," I tossed over my shoulder. "I can be useful. I can help. I'm not some weak broad who intends to let someone else fight my battles."

Beverly closed her eyes and lifted her head to the ceiling. Without hearing a word, I knew she was praying I wouldn't mess up the help we'd been given. She also knew I would test these men, aiming to prove the truthfulness of their willingness to help us. I didn't know them and therefore, I wasn't quick to relinquish my trust.

In the corner of my eye, I spotted a wide grin on D's face. The deep frown that creased Dax's face displayed every trace of his irritation with me. What was his problem? If he had a problem with strong women, he needed to get over it or send me on my way now. If he knew Megan, he should have already known we weren't the meek type.

His facial expression was unreadable, but the coiled tension emanating from his body cut like a harsh icy wind.

"I'll be back, D," he announced, ignoring me and my comments altogether before he stepped around me, brushing my shoulder. When he eased the front door closed behind him, I glanced at D.

"What's his deal?"

"He's probably never had a woman confront or talk to him that way. As you can tell by this suite, he comes from privilege and the women in his circle are very demure, prim, pampered, and submissive," he informed as he attempted to stifle a grin.

"Humph," I grunted and squinted when I picked up a hint of warning in D's expression.

"What? You want to tell me something, but you're not sure you should?" I flashed him a hopeful expression.

"Come on, D, spill it," I urged with more pleading in my tone, hoping my Puss-In-Boots eyes would work in my favor like they sometimes did.

"If you haven't noticed, Bev and I are in the thick of this shit. We can handle more truth than you think we can," I said, hoping I was persuading him to talk.

His playful, emerald eyes went up as he contemplated revealing more.

"He's one of the highest paid assassins in the country. He only takes high-profile targets. Much higher than these DG6 pricks hunting you."

I'm sure his words were meant to scare me into leaving Dax alone, but all he'd just done was piqued my interest.

"I like you, D, and that's saying a lot because I don't like your species. You're a straight shooter, and I respect that about you," I complimented, pointing, and smiling in his direction.

At those words, I picked up what must have been his keycard and faced the front door.

"Laura, where are you going? Leave that man alone. You shouldn't be wandering off by yourself anyway," Beverly warned, concerned.

"I'll be right back," I announced. I patted Beverly's hand after giving her a quick hug.

"I have heat. Besides, D's got eyes on me," I assured her as I approached the front door.

I'd been eyeing the computer like a hawk. D had found a way to hack into the hotel's cameras. While they assumed I was being an irritating bitch, I was ear and eye hustling my ass off, refusing to be left in the dark about what concerned our lives.

D attempted to call after me, but Beverly, knowing me the way she did, murmured, "Just let her go, D. You do know that telling her he kills people for a living made her more interested, right?"

I grinned at Beverly's comment before I pulled the door closed behind me. After I entered the code I'd seen Dax punch into the elevator on our way up, I rode it to level five. I took the stairs the rest of the way down to garage level three, parking space 335. I eased up to Dax's car as he was wheeling one of the hotel's large food carts toward the back of it. I assumed I was sneaking up on him, but his voice caught me off guard.

"What are you doing here? You need to keep a low profile and stop putting yourself in harm's way. It's my duty to keep you safe, and I can't do that if you're eager to die anyway," his voice was low but firm, and precise enough for me to understand every word.

"I'm not eager to die. I would like to help," I replied honestly. "My soul is restless. A lot in my life is messed up: bad decisions, stupid mistakes, but there is one thing I've always done, which is fight for myself and those I care about."

Dax paused to consider my words before he shrugged and popped the trunk of his BMW. Who in the hell went around rescuing people in a hundred-thousand-dollar car?

The value of Dax's car went up in smoke, and my lips fell apart at the sight of the man stuffed inside his trunk.

"While you were tempting your fate, I was making sure we at least had our next lead," he uttered, his voice monotone.

"Well, damn, Richie Rich!" I exclaimed, shaking my head as I stared at the unconscious man. I glanced around, searching for cameras.

"Don't worry, I've already visited the surveillance room, and D has this level on blackout for now," he updated.

Dax was not your average killer. He'd taken this man from a guarded warehouse, secured him in the trunk, and weaved his way through an army of killers to find me. I owed him more respect than I was giving, but I was too arrogant and hard-headed to say it.

"So, what's the plan, Richie Rich? Are we about to find out about this DG6 original or what?" I questioned, loving how he fought not to cringe each time I called him that nickname. "You plan on beating the information we need out of him?" I continued, pointing at the man who was sleeping like a fat, well-fed baby.

"*We*?" His brow arched high while eyeing me pensively.

"That's what I said. Are you hard of hearing?"

Based on his unbothered expression, my abrasive tone didn't bother him as much as I assumed. It irritated him, but for the most part, when I was being flippant, he brushed it off and moved on to his next thought.

"How do you know about the original? Did D tell you?" His expression didn't reveal a thing.

"I've been picking up the information you and D have been keeping from us. I can read between the lines better than you think. I know you intend to take out an original member of this cartel. Someone they call No Face. Your logic is to take out a leader, hoping the hit they have on us *might* disappear."

He maintained a poker face, but I saw a hint of something I couldn't identify flash before he turned his attention to the man in the trunk. He leaned in, shuffling the man's body around until his forearms were under his shoulders.

"Instead of watching, why don't you make yourself useful and grab his feet," he ordered, trying to be the boss of me. His face was darkened by the shadows cast by the raised trunk, but I heard the smugness in his tone.

My arms folded across my chest, and I stiffened my stance, mainly to get on his nerves further. A deep scowl etched his forehead before a weak, "Please," squeezed past his lips. He was learning my personality far faster than I expected.

I get on his nerves, but he's letting me help. A wily smirk accompanied my devious thought.

I gripped the man's feet and grunted as I lifted my portion of his weight. With the food cart turned sideways, we made quick work of stuffing the man into it. When shoving with my hands didn't work, I kicked his leg into the cart.

Dax stood shaking his head at me with a grimace on his face. If he didn't know it before, he knew it now: my ass was plum crazy. We were dealing with a cartel, so it was safe to say a certain amount of crazy was necessary.

After securing the car, Dax turned the cart upright, causing the man's body to thump as it shifted. What kind of drugs had the man been given? He didn't exhibit any signs of waking up.

I recalled my blunt Dax had thrown out his window. He probably assumed I was a pothead but smoking a *Black and Mild* or a blunt every once in a while helped me think, especially when the world was closing in on me.

The wheels of the cart squeaked an annoying elongated yell as Dax pushed it. I walked along the side of the area that opened to our cargo with my lips poked out, whistling.

Dax's abrupt halt caused me to stop and the body inside the cart shifted once more.

"The Whistle Song at a time like this? Nice," he mumbled under his breath, shaking his head at me before he restarted the cart.

The fact he knew what song I was whistling had revealed more about him. Maybe that stick wasn't as far up his ass as I originally assumed. He was rich, dangerous, and apparently, hiding a personality.

Chapter Nine

Dax

With our prisoner secured, I glanced at my accomplice, Laura. Was she truly going to watch me torture this guy?

When we wheeled the cart through the common area of the suite, Beverly and D stared at us. D knew what was about to happen, but Beverly was clueless and even more so when we continued to roll the cart through the door that led to the back bedroom. Neither Laura nor I uttered a word as their eyes followed us.

I sent Laura from the room to allow me time to finish setting up the scene. She left without protest when I promised to come and get her when I was ready.

When I stepped into the living area fifteen minutes later, I found Laura and Beverly standing at D's shoulder and him explaining something to them. Unlike mine, his patience was something to be revered. He could charm the pants off the devil's wife. I, on the other hand, was usually filled with biting anger that caused me to become irritated too easily.

D had their full attention. "Take out Santino Dominquez. It's the easiest way to make the death note on your heads disappear."

"What if taking out Mr. No Face Santino doesn't work and the group chasing us keeps coming? Why do they call him No Face anyway? Is he disfigured or something?" Laura questioned.

"They call him No Face, because no one that's tried to identify him has seen his face. Although our main goal will be Santino, we will also put a concerted effort into identifying the specific group targeting you. However, taking out the group before taking out a big fish like Santino could spook him, so we have to be careful how we execute. We also have to consider the link between the DG6 targets our friends in California are gearing up to take down. We have to plan and execute with all these moving parts in mind, which could very well mean us laying low and waiting for the right time to strike."

D was being more open with the ladies than I'd expected. However, my gaze landed on Laura and narrowed. She'd nagged him for details I'm sure. My eyes met hers before I tilted my head toward the door.

How far was she willing to go? I was interested in finding out. She was clueless as to who she was about to be locked in a room with. The suits I wore, my put-together persona, and even my family's wealth had long ago become the cover that hid the depths of my darkness.

I opened the door like the gentleman I was taught to be and allowed Laura to enter the room first. The man was hanging from chains that were clamped to the sturdy hooks I'd anchored to the ceiling. He was stripped of every thread of clothing except his underwear.

His body swayed like a light breeze was blowing him, the chains belting out a squeaky melody. Laura's gaze was locked on the man as she stepped closer, observing the room's setup. Thick plastic covered the floors, furniture, and ceiling. I eased the door closed, and the sound of the lock sliding into place drew Laura's eyes in my direction.

"You don't have to stay for this part. It can get quite..." I paused for effect. "*Bloody.*"

"I'm from Crestwood. Bloody is a norm I've had to live with all my life."

"Suit yourself, but I recommend you suit up," I suggested before pointing at the slicker suit I usually wore when I put in this kind of wet work.

Without question, she started pulling on the thick clear plastic over her clothes. The suit swallowed her, but she was more interested in getting this session started than being swallowed by plastic.

"Aren't people going to hear him if he screams?" She questioned while pacing and observing the man at different angles. She was inquisitive, and I noticed there wasn't much she missed.

"This suite's the only living space on this floor, and this room is soundproof. That's one of the main reasons why I chose this hotel," I informed her before pointing at the man. "He can scream until the fat lady joins him and no one will hear it."

A smile tickled her lips and her expression filled with a devilish glow. I wasn't used to having an audience when I worked, but I was intrigued by my little follower. The idea that she was into women still hadn't settled into my head. I didn't see or sense it in her, not that you could sense something as complex as a personal trait.

Her gaze followed my movement when I lifted the smelling salts from my worktable. With the salts under the man's nose, his head jerked and his body stiffened and released as he came awake with a start and fought against the restraints gripping his wrist.

A set of bloodshot eyes snapped open and met ours. Confusion wrinkled the man's face. His mouth dropped open at the sight of me and remained open at the sight of Laura. A glimpse at his naked body heightened his despair as he attempted to yank free of the thick restraints.

"What? Who?" His neck turned rapidly as his useless kicks whipped through the air.

"I'm going to ask you a few questions. I'll ask them *once*," I started, my tone severe. "I'm going to start cutting you, and I won't stop until I hear the answers I seek." My words were delivered with crisp precision so there would be no confusion about what would happen if I didn't get what I wanted.

The man attempted to speak, but the clouds of death that filled my gaze and a finger in front of my lips silenced him. Laura stood in place, her gaze roaming from me to the man. She was a talker, loved to hear the sound of her own voice, but she knew when to keep her mouth closed.

"Are there any more groups prepared to chase these women? Who ordered their capture and why? Where is Santino Dominguez? Where is his home? What place or places does he frequent?"

The man's arms grew tight as he attempted to pull free of the unbreakable restraints. He tensed, and his gaze clouded with fear.

"There are no other groups. We were told to capture the women, but I don't know who made the order. I don't know where Santino is either," he alleged in a low, squeaky tone. I could see Laura from the side shake her head, likely knowing far better than this man that he hadn't given me the answers I wanted to hear.

I turned to face the table allowing an exhausted sigh to escape. The shiny scalpel gleamed in my eager hand before I added a drop of liquid to the edge of the blade. Laura's shadow met me before her warmth settled near me, her stealthy steps not making a sound.

A question emerged in her expression but disappeared when she glanced at the bottle, labeled NaCl. "Sodium Chloride," she translated in a low tone. She glanced up at me, her face creased with curiosity.

"You're going to put salt in his wounds?" she questioned before a smile flashed across her face.

The surprise that flashed in my expression was brief, but I failed to extinguish it fast enough before she saw it.

"Oh!" She pointed at the bottle with a raised brow. "Because I'm from the hood, I'm not supposed to know my periodic symbols?"

Guilty. This was the second, maybe even third time I misjudged her, attempting to place her into my preconceived views.

"You're right, but it's not just salt. I've added an extra ingredient that will give his pain sensors more bang for their buck," I informed, causing her curious brows to lift and the man to squirm.

"Microscopic sea lice," I revealed. "When...."

She lifted her hand, cutting me off. "Did you say *sea lice*? As in, tiny insects that are going to get under his skin with that salt and bite the fuck out of him?"

The man started screaming "No!" repeatedly at this point. Whether it was her intention or not, her statement had the man about ready to piss himself and me biting the back of my lip to conceal the laugh that threatened to escape.

The man's gaze was locked on me as I pointed at the bottle of liquid, loving that he appeared ready to talk now.

"When I cut him, this will burn like the devil's holding a flame thrower set on Hell against his skin. The salty liquid and lice will eat into the opening and attack the pain sensors. It aches like a construction worker is jack-hammering his way out of your body."

Laura's eyes lifted from the blade in my hand and met mine. Her low tone sounded, "You've had this done to you."

It was more a statement than a question, her putting together pieces I didn't know she'd discovered. She was clever, listened well enough to pick out clues, and pieced together minute details like an expert puzzle solver.

I nodded before turning to the man and sending the blade across his abdomen, leaving his mouth wide with surprise, and his body frozen in shock. The cut wasn't deep, but blood seeped to the surface and painted his pale skin. It highlighted the two-inch gashed I gifted him.

The man began to wiggle like a hooked fish out of water, making the chains grumble with solid thumps. His gut-wrenching yells followed and filled the room when the burn lit up his pain sensors.

"I don't know. I don't know. Oh! God! Please don't do this," he begged.

I had lurked around the warehouse for twenty minutes before I found Laura. In that time, I observed who was in charge, who gave the orders, and who was most likely to know the whereabouts of the big fish we were determined to catch. This man was the lucky winner.

Another drop of liquid fell and skated across the blade, pink from the blood left behind. I delivered two more quick slashes to the man's body. One landed across his thigh and the other opened his forearm. His yells vibrated off the plastic-covered walls as his body bucked hard enough to make the chains *clink* and rip the skin from his bound wrists.

Blood flowed from his wrist down his arms like long rips were being torn into his skin. His pleas and yells went on for a full minute before they ceased into throaty whimpers.

I'd done this enough times to know the average person broke around number fifty, at which point their pain would lead them to believe they'd been set ablaze. It was also when the pain began to eat at your mentality and blur your thinking.

This was my preferred method of torture because, like Laura concluded, it had been done to me. I knew every stage of the pain like I knew my own name. And so far, they've always talked.

At cut number twenty-nine, the man pissed himself. The putrid liquid mixed with his blood and spilled to the floor, causing Laura to take a step back to keep from getting splashed. The man yelled loud enough to rattle the walls. I assumed his shrieking would find her compassion and weaken her resolve, but I was wrong.

The strong scent of blood mixed with urine tightened my throat. Laura wasn't at all affected by the sight of the bloody man or the scent that tunneled through our nasal passages like a bulldozer.

I spun the blade in my hand and handed it to her, handle first. She'd been quiet, assessing, and I believed, enjoying the scene. The man's mental abilities were breaking down faster than I expected. The idea of lice crawling under his ripped open skin and eating into him had his mind in knots. His eyes were wide enough to pop from their sockets.

The plastic-covered floor, ceiling, and Laura's coveralls were painted in splashes of blood. She wasn't disturbed, which was perplexing, but given what I'd seen of her so far, it made sense.

A quick study, she approached the table, not forgetting to add a drop of liquid to the blade. She turned to the man, glaring into his eyes before lifting and holding the blade in midair. The man screamed his throat raw at the sight of the blade waiting to eat through his flesh.

Eyes bulged with terror, he begged, but his words were wasted on me. The blade sliced across his lower abdominals. His cries were filled with pleas for mercy, but the cut hadn't delivered the desired effect. Laura's cut was too deep.

She stiffened at my touch but didn't protest when I stood behind her and took her hand in mine, even as my warm breath coated her neck.

"Your cut was too deep," I whispered. Laura had the devil in her, and she wasn't shy about letting him out to play. She was only allowing me this privilege because I had invited her into my sick playroom.

My lips flirted with her ear this time, taking advantage of the situation. At close proximity, her scent cut through the rusted odor of blood and the ammonia stench of piss. Despite all she went through tonight, the scent of warm cotton candy drifted off her.

Concentrating on teaching her, I kept a firm grip on her blade hand.

"Keep the cuts near the surface, that way the liquid seeps into his pain sensors slowly. Go too deep, it'll hurt, but not enough to make him talk," I pointed out.

"Okay," she replied, her gaze fixed on the begging man. She added another drop to the blade, and like before, she moved leisurely. When she sliced him this time, the blade raced across his chest. It ripped straight through his right nipple, slicing it in half. Even after she pulled the blade back, his skin continued to rip, the bottom half of his nipple falling away from the top.

I placed my mouth over her ear to speak over the piercing sound of the man's yells. "Do you see the distress rolling through his body?" She nodded. "He's breaking. A few more like that and he's going to give us an answer to at least one of my questions."

When she sent the blade up his jaw, slicing from the corner of his open lips, it exposed the inside of his mouth and flashed us a snapshot of his molars. The man's screams turned into a high pitched squeal, his open mouth stretching the ripped apart skin.

The gruesome cut caused my brow to lift as I eyed Laura unblinkingly. She stared into the man's eyes, blade steady in her hand as she waited for answers.

After Laura had delivered two of the most brutal slashes the man had received, the words, "Greenbrier Hotel," fumbled across his trembling lips and hissed from the opening in the side of his jaw.

His terrified gaze was locked on Laura, no doubt seeing the devil. When she made a slight movement, he flinched before his hoarse voice broke free. "No-no...no others after the women. Sa-Sa-Santino frequents The Greenbrier Hotel. He's a-a silent p-partner. It's where he gathers for meetings and sometimes stays."

"Answer the other questions," I urged, my tone severe enough to stop his sniveling cries. His sluggish gaze remained on my deadly one. He wanted to skirt the other questions because he gave up the hotel.

"Make the cuts more frequent. If I don't hear what I need to, cut deeper so he can bleed to death," I instructed.

"Okay," Laura responded, not concerned that she was about to kill this man.

Hanging on to the edge of life and death, the man's body was a map of the cuts we'd dispensed. Blood rained onto the plastic below him and formed a pool at his feet. My suit had been destroyed, but it was worth it.

With his blood damn near running on empty and his body shivering with cold, the man began whispering something that sounded different from his shrill yelling.

He fought to spit his words past his trembling lips, unaware that he was sitting at death's doorstep. Without a blood transfusion in the next few minutes, his survival was a pipe dream. However, we had to leave him with hope to keep him talking. Laura's understanding of my intention, however warped they were, impressed me even more.

"1236 Halo Heights," he repeated, his brain stuck on the words and numbers. After a full minute of him repeating the same address, his body started to convulse, fighting to keep his last bit of life's energy. "Lu-lu-lu, Sa-sa-San," he attempted before his tense body jerked against the chains, his tortured flesh oozing the last of his fresh blood that would stop when his heart gave up the fight.

Too far gone to answer my remaining questions, Laura and I stood in place until the man went silent and still. The light in his eyes dimmed as his mouth went slack. His eyebrows fluttered and dropped but they didn't shut all the way. I took the bloody scalpel from Laura's hand and placed it on the table before I returned to a position beside her.

"Perfect," I complimented before I brushed my lips across her smooth brown cheek.

She lurched back like she'd been scalded, slapping at her cheek to knock my peck from her satiny skin. My lips twitched as I attempted to restrain a laugh. Her palm remained against her cheek when she spun to face me, aiming her head so I'd noticed the seriousness in her stern glint.

"The next time you put your lips anywhere near me, you will be picking them up from the floor," she threatened. "If your twisted mind thinks there's perfection in death, you're half past crazy."

I took her threat and her comment about my state of mind with a smile. She stood glaring at me, holding her cheek for a long moment before she relaxed and allowed silence to fill the space once more.

"Now what?" She glanced at me expectantly before returning her attention to the dead man before us.

"You helped me kill him," I pointed out. "Now, you get to help me dispose of him."

Again, I expected resistance, disgust perhaps, anything that revealed her compassion, but Laura gave none. She was as broken as me, and I doubted compassion surfaced in her often, if at all.

"Were there really sea lice in that salt water?"

Glancing at her, I couldn't help a smile. Her acute sense of awareness and inquisitive nature served her well.

"No. There was only salt. It would burn badly enough for him to think something was biting him."

She was not at all what I had expected, proving my first impression of her wasn't an accurate one. She caught me staring again.

"I know what that look means, Richie Rich," she said, side-eying me. "Don't make this situation any weirder than it already is. I'm in love with the sweet taste of pussy and will never cross over to your side of the fence."

My ego refused to let her have the last word. "First, I don't believe in never and neither should you. And for the record, Laura, you couldn't handle me if I texted you instructions."

My lips twitched with a satisfied smile as I turned to face the body, loving the dumbstruck look my words put on her sassy face.

Chapter Ten

Dax

From one eye, I observed D work his tech magic. Using the clues we gathered to locate the hotel Santino frequented, D was also able to confirm he owned it. The drug kingpin was likely using the legit business to wash his dirty drug money.

What I presumed was a substantial clue, 1236 Halo Heights, the address the man kept sputtering, hadn't turned up anything of significance. It wasn't an address registered in the state of Texas.

From my other eye, I watched the ladies. They were glued together on the couch speaking in hushed tones. Why would DG6 spend so much time and energy tracking them down?

Their pretty faces revealed nothing, but their reactions to the danger hovering over their lives was being met with unusual calm and unbreakable resistance. I spotted a bruise on the back of Laura's arm, but I knew not to press her about it unless her needs were serious. I'd never met a woman who wanted a front-row seat as well as becoming an active participant in torture.

After blood and body fluids started to flow, most people couldn't take the scent, let alone the yelling and screaming. What had these women been through that would allow them to endure such graphic violence?

I was intrigued by Laura. If she wasn't a devout lesbian, she would have definitely been on my radar.

"Are you sure she's twenty-five?" I asked D because everything about her was confusing to me.

"Yep, she's as grown as you and me," he replied as his grin grew wide at my question.

Laura's look was fresh and young and she carried an innocence about her that didn't match her personality. She could easily pass for a teen, and did that make me a pervert for being attracted to her? I preferred a leggy woman with an ample chest and a nice round bottom, but Laura's personality made up for what she lacked in height and the rest of her was perfectly placed.

"You can forget about it. If her stomach is strong enough to watch you torture someone to death, her mentality is strong enough to resist your charms. She's all about the great cat chase anyway," D reminded me, knowing what I was thinking and teasing me for going there.

I returned my attention to him, shaking my head but knowing I was already latched on to my next target.

"I'm trying to wrap my head around her," I admitted. "She didn't just watch me torture the guy I snatched, she *participated*. She was even quiet long enough to let me give her pointers."

D lifted an eyebrow. "I'm starting to believe those two..." He tilted his head in the direction of the ladies. "They're cut from the same cloth as Megan."

"Do you get the feeling that DG6 wants them for more than Megan's whereabouts?" I questioned because something about the situation didn't add up.

"Yes. I think they're holding secrets. The same kind Megan was holding that has us at war with this cartel in the first place." His statement came out matter of fact, like being at war with a cartel wasn't a deadly endeavor.

"They aren't going to tell us a thing if we ask outright. So, we are going to have to think strategically when it comes to handling them," I commented, fascinated and irritated at the same time.

"If they can be handled at all," D quipped.

Laura's gaze met mine when I glanced back. "They can be handled," I mumbled, talking to him, but keeping my gaze on her. "They just need a special kind of handling."

***

Laura

My gaze caught flecks of light peeking in through the window that sneaked a warm brush against my arm. Its eager brightness had just begun to crack the darkness at 04:45 a.m.

Releasing a lazy yawn, my gaze found the set of gray eyes that kept staring in my direction. We'd shared a sick bonding experience over a dead man, but it didn't mean we were friends.

I appreciated him agreeing to help us, but if he expected me to show my appreciation on my back, he needed to hit pause and delete on his mental control panel.

"Are you okay, Laura? What's with the mean looks you've been giving the guys, particularly Dax? Don't go treating them like dirt because they're the wrong sex. I need you to remember that they're risking their lives to protect us from an enemy that had you chained to a table and about to kill you hours ago."

"I know, Bev. I just don't like the way he keeps looking at me. I already schooled him on what I like, and it was like he didn't even acknowledge my words." I rolled my eyes at Dax. Was that a smirk I just saw on his face before he returned his attention to D?

Bev's hand rested atop mine, tearing my pointed gaze from Dax's back. A pair of relaxed fit designer jeans and a black long-sleeve fitted shirt highlighted his build. He was fit in a way that you immediately knew he frequented the gym, his medium frame molded to precision.

What I truly wanted to know was how someone like him, who obviously had money, ended up at the business end of a blade and in a torture session I only wished on my worst enemy? He burned a suit and accessories worth more than everything I owned, including my car. He was rolling around in a hundred-thousand-dollar vehicle, transporting bodies, and subjecting it to gunfire. Who did that?

"Do you think those DG6 guys are going to come after us again? It's only now that I fully understood why Megan kept running," Beverly said, regaining my attention.

"If GI Joe and The Tech King stick around and don't get us all killed, I think we'll be fine."

I stood, dragging Beverly up with me. "What I won't do is sit by with my tail tucked between my legs."

Bev yanked me back when I started to walk toward the men who hovered over the laptop.

"Laura, they hunt bad guys for a living, I think," Beverly said with uncertainty. "Let them work. If they need us they will let us know," she continued, her pleading gaze speaking after her words stopped.

"Bev, how long have you known me? The only reason I wasn't out there helping Megan was because she was smart enough not to tell me where she was going. The shit killed me. I couldn't even help my own damn friend."

I threw my hand around Beverly's waist and dragged her along with me, causing her shoes to scrape against the shiny floor. She could say what she wanted, but I noticed the eye-heat she shared with the tech geek. She was attracted to him and likely fighting every instinct to avoid giving in to temptation while he did nothing to hide his attraction.

"What are you guys talking about? What are *we* about to do next?"

Dax stared upside my head, straightening his stance. "We're all going to chill for a day or two until we have a solid plan. Think you can stay calm that long?" Sarcasm dripped from his voice. His smirk and tone hadn't been missed. Surprisingly, instead of my nose turning up at him, my lips decided to bend into a smile. Why the hell was I smiling? Quickly, I decided I needed to ignore Dax and concentrate on D.

"So, what have you found out so far? Do we have any more actionable intel?"

The men cast each other a quick glance before they turned their gazes on me. After a moment of us staring each other down, they decided it was better to let me in on what they were planning or risk me running off at the mouth. It was day one, and they had already latched on to my personality.

Ten minutes after my question, my damn mind was in shambles listening to D talk in his tech language to Dax who apparently understood every word. He talked about digital mapping and using encryption manipulation data to corrupt firewalls like I had a damn clue as to what any of it was. Bev had long ago left the conversation, not caring about deciphering any of it.

They talked in their cyber code to throw me off, but I caught enough to get the gist of what they were saying. I'd also latched on to them planning to use digital technology to find out how our target moved if they could find an accurate snapshot of his face. They believed the group chasing us was tied to Santino.

In my opinion, this wasn't necessarily good. It meant we had to take out Santino before we zeroed in on the specific men coming for us.

Something I'd forgotten hit me, causing me to tap D on the shoulder in the middle of a sentence about grayware and a series of numbers I think was code for certain words. I placed the object I withdrew from my jean's pocket on the table next to the keyboard, nudging Dax in the side as I squeezed between the two men. I could have stepped to the other side of D, but vexing Dax made me feel better. I sensed his gaze boring into me until it fell on the brown wallet I placed on the desk in front of D.

"I took it off one of the stiffs we killed at the warehouse. That should get you more clues, right?"

D's smile came first. Dax stared between the wallet and me, likely sorry he hadn't come up with the idea.

I stared up at him. "You took a body. I took a wallet. Brains versus brawn, Dax," I teased, enjoying another chance to pluck at his nerve strings.

He shook his head before a smile crept across his lips, his head tilting sideways. "You've had that the whole time and waited until after we tortured, killed, and disposed of a body before giving it up?"

My shoulders lifted before I turned away from Dax's eyes that were squinted in curiosity.

"This is huge. Smart!" D exclaimed. "I could kiss you for this," he expressed before cracking the wallet open and immediately pulling out the contents. He was giddy like a kid at Christmas, a smile wide with excitement animated his every move.

"Please, keep your lips to yourself if you want to keep them," I warned D. He smiled at my retort rather than take offense, letting me know we would get along fine.

D lifted a hand. "I know. I know. I'm the wrong gender. But, this is great and...." His words stopped when he extracted a keycard from The Greenbrier Hotel. It was the same hotel we'd tortured a man to find out was owned by Santino Dominquez.

A quick glance at Beverly showed her playing a game on her phone. She couldn't care less about chasing down bad guys. She was a girly girl who didn't mind a man fighting for her. She was the kind of woman who allowed a man to carry her heavy shopping bags or open a pickle jar. I didn't hold it against her because the world needed women like her to tone down the testosterone buildup that would suffocate and kill us all if it weren't controlled.

I, on the other hand, had a chip the size of Texas on each of my shoulders and couldn't care less about stroking a man's ego. I had my own ego.

D placed the credit cards down but kept one pinched between his fingers. When he began peeling off the skin of the card, I noticed it wasn't a credit card at all. It was a digital storage device.

I was prepared to ask how to read a device like that, but he produced a small black box, the size of a deck of cards, which he attached to the computer. He stuck the card into the reader, but all that popped up were numbers and letters, scrambled and roving across the screen like tiny fast moving insects.

"This is amazing," he said. He'd converted the large fancy desk into a mini computer lab, two laptops attached to three larger monitors along with equipment I couldn't name.

"I'm glad you think it's amazing. It's a jumble of letters and numbers," I pointed out, not understanding the amazing part of it. Dax's wide smile suggested he knew what we were looking at?

"It's going to take time, but I can crack this. Hopefully, it's DG6 secrets we can use against them."

Okay, so the depth of these men went deeper than testosterone-driven killers and egos. They were intelligent, leading me to believe that me and Bev might make our next birthdays.

"Hey, guys," I called to them in a low tone, awaiting their attention. "Thank you for stepping up and helping us. Not everyone is willing or crazy enough to help strangers like this." It wasn't as gracious a thank you as I aimed to give, but I was trying.

"You're welcome," D smiled up at me. Dax nodded once in my direction and turned away, but I sensed him side-eyeing me.

Chapter Eleven

Laura

The next time my eyes snapped open, I found my feet resting across Beverly's warm lap. Her face was crinkled into a deep frown as she stared at her phone. I withdrew my earbuds, reluctant to let go of H.E.R whispering in my ears.

Rapid keystrokes led my eyes to D facing his laptop and working like he was getting paid.

"Was he there all night?" I asked Beverly. "Where is the other one? Did you sleep any?"

Beverly was a night owl and worried like she was the world's mother. I could sleep through a train wreck and wake up wondering where I'd lost my missing limbs.

"The guys switched out. D went to take a nap and just returned. They are going at it hard, cracking some codes. So far, they are sure it has something to do with the group's money laundering activities. Also, they said they won't leave us until they are sure of our safety," she stated as a smile spread across her face.

"What are you smiling about?" I questioned before glancing at my cheap plastic watch. It was after eight, so I'd gotten a few hours of sleep.

"Don't you think it's sweet? They won't leave us to fight this group alone. They are taking their jobs seriously, too."

"Yes, they're very sweet," I muttered, my tone so sarcastic it turned Beverly's joyful smile into a frown.

"I'm pretty sure they kill people for a living, Bev, therefore I do believe we might be doing them a favor," I pointed out, being my usual grumpy self.

"Laura," Beverly called in a whisper as she eyed D's back, hoping he hadn't overheard my comment. I fell back on the couch, stretching my fatigued body.

"Laura," Beverly sang my name again, low and syrupy. It was the sugary voice she used when she wanted to butter me up for a favor or tell me something she knew I didn't want to hear. I popped back up, eyeing her with suspicion.

"I went to Kadeem for help when I didn't know how to find you. As soon as I knew you were safe, I let him know," she updated, shifting her gaze away from mine. My hand cupped my forehead as I squeezed my throbbing temples. I stared at her, not blinking.

"Even though I let him know you were okay," she continued. "He still wants to see you, and you know he has a way of finding out about everything. He knew that someone was helping us without me telling him. He wants you to bring one of the guys with you today."

"Fuck," I muttered under my breath. The last thing we needed was Kadeem tangled up with this cartel. He no doubt had Mexicans lined up in front of his blood-thirsty men in a hood version of a firing squad.

"I'm sorry, Laura, but I didn't know who else to turn to because the cops aren't going to help us."

I cupped her warm hand, folding it between mine. "You did good, Bev. You used the resources you had and did what it took to find me. I appreciate you for that. I'll go and see Kadeem later and take Dax with me. My feelings would be less hurt if Kadeem killed him over D."

Beverly's hand came down on my thigh with a hard slap. "You should be ashamed of yourself for saying something like that."

My laugh sounded and she failed to hide hers, knowing it was normal for me to be a sarcastic asshole.

Another hour of D going at that computer was about all I could take. Bev had finally fallen asleep, her head lying across my lap. I eased her head away to satisfy my urge to be nosey.

I tiptoed to the back of the suite and peeked in on Dax asleep in the torture room. We'd managed to get it back to normal after all the bloody hell we caused.

My constant hovering at D's shoulder a few minutes later caused him to pull me up a chair next to his. I sat and allowed him to blow my mind and when I could take no more, I shuffled back to the couch.

"Beverly," I woke her so we could shower and get something to eat at the restaurant downstairs. D was certain we'd be fine as long as we didn't leave the security of the hotel.

Beverly rose, glancing at her surroundings before she sat up. Next thing I knew she was hugging me and planting a kiss on my cheek. That was Beverly all day, the loving one. After returning her hug, I patted her arm before suggesting again that we get cleaned up. My gaze shot to the door that led down the hall to the second bedroom before I approached D.

"We're going to get cleaned up and go downstairs for something to eat. Do you want anything?" I asked him, attempting to exhibit gratitude since he was partially the reason I continued to draw breath.

"No. I'll go later or call in room service, but thanks," he replied with a gracious smile. He turned back to the computer screen before his fingers went back to work.

***

Beverly

While Laura showered, I was stuck in the room with D. He didn't hide his interest in me, and it was hard for me to hide mine in him. However, I was afraid of what a man like him could do to me.

He was impressively good-looking and scary smart on that computer. He was the kind of man you fell all over yourself for knowing he would eventually rip your heart out and hand you what was left of it. I didn't need it confirmed, to know he'd left a trail of hearts in his wake, and I was determined not to be one of them.

"I hope I'm not wrong in assuming that you're interested in me," I blurted, making his grin appear.

"That's correct," he offered, his lips twitching into a wide smile.

"Would I be wrong in assuming that you're not looking for anything long-term?" I questioned, hoping he'd be honest. He pursed his lips, clearly considering my question.

"You're right. Currently, my life doesn't allow me to pursue anything long-term."

"I'm honestly flattered you are interested in me. It's a huge compliment. However, I've been through the wringer with men and promised myself I wasn't going to be anyone else's one-night stand or temporary fulfillment. I would like something more meaningful with at least the chance of being long-term," I told him, watching his face drop a bit.

"I understand better than you think. As much as I'd love to give you what you'd like, I can't promise it. What do you say? Let's take things day by day and concentrate on securing your safety? And, allow whatever will or will not happen between us unfold as it should or shouldn't."

His gracious attitude on what I assumed would be a difficult subject had me grinning and more at ease.

Chapter Twelve

Dax

"Are you sure this is a good idea?" I asked, needing to know where Laura was taking me. She insisted it would be better if we took her car. I'm sure to aid in avoiding the extra attention my skin color would draw.

"Say what you mean, Dax. You usually have more to say," she stated, her teasing tone irking my nerves.

"You're taking me into your hood where I'll likely be the only white man, an outsider. Don't you think that's a good enough reason for me to be concerned?" I questioned, glancing around when the businesses and buildings started to look more haggard, some boarded and some abandoned as we approached the heart of Crestwood.

Crumbling red-brown, dirty-white, and ash-gray bricks made up the buildings, some several stories high, some single-storied duplexes, and houses, all mingled together. Cracked door frames, weathered wood, useless bars on windows and doors passed my view as neighbors and friends hung out on their porches and balconies.

The streets weren't littered with trash, but they were bustling with people standing around, talking, smoking, and drinking, block-party style. Dingy clothing hung from balconies and open windows that didn't have screens. People peeked at us as onlookers on the streets gawked and pointed.

"I ain't a killer but don't push me…." Tupac's lyrics spilled from Laura's radio. The sound was set low, so the lyrics seeped into the car's interior like subliminal messages hinting at what we might face.

"You're with me, Dax. I'm not going to let anything happen to you," she promised, flashing a calming gaze in my direction. Although I knew firsthand how tough she was, she couldn't guarantee my life if things went bad. I believed she misunderstood my apprehension. It wasn't because I was afraid of what would happen to *me*.

"I figured you for the biggest advocate for my demise," I finally replied to her statement, noticing more fingers pointing and eyes scanning as they spotted me. Although different types of music warred with each other, it became background to the eyes that followed Laura's car as we rolled down the block.

She chose to ignore my quip. I coiled tighter when two men stood in the path of her car, making her come to a screeching stop. Their weapons were visible, but thankfully, they remained tucked into their waists.

My hand sat on my holstered pistol, concealed by my dark suit jacket. My spare rested against my ankle. Laura hadn't suggested I leave my weapons, a clue that we were entering the lion's den. It wasn't visible, but I knew she had hidden the pistol she'd taken from the warehouse.

The man standing to Laura's side of the car side-stepped around the hood and approached as she rolled her noisy window down, the loud squeak calling out like a woman screaming.

"What the fuck do you want, Jay?" Her gaze remained aimed straight ahead, and her tone wasn't the least bit humble, even with the gun in the man's waist staring at the side of her face. The man bent and peered inside the car, causing her to yank away from his intrusion.

"We can't allow you to pass. Who is that you have with you? We don't know him." His hostile expression remained pinned on me.

"He's with me. That's all the fuck you need to know. Now, tell Buck to get his ass out of my way before I run him over," she expressed as she revved the car engine, making the overused pistons growl under the hood. The man stood his ground and refused to relay Laura's warning to his friend.

Clink! Clink!

The loud sound of the gun she drew and slapped on the dash of the car, made the big man at her window stumble back in surprise. She glared at the ceiling of her car, her head moving from side to side in irritation. "Jesus, please build a fence around my trigger finger, so I won't pop a cap in this nigga's ass."

The black nine-millimeter she threw on the dash wasn't the same as the silver Beretta she'd left the warehouse with, which meant she was in possession of at least two guns. Her deadly glare panned to the man at her left.

"Are we going to have a fucking problem? You're getting on my goddamn nerves, Jay. Now, step the fuck back and let me pass before I have to explain to Kadeem why I killed your ass!"

The man lifted his hands and took another step back. "Hey, Buck," he called to the man standing in front of the car who had never taken his gaze off me. "Let her pass. You know how she gets when she hasn't had pussy in a while."

"What about *him*?" Buck questioned, pointing at me.

"Kadeem will take care of him if there's a problem," the man confirmed like I wasn't sitting here.

I reeled at the harsh manner in which Laura was handling this serious situation. She took off, her small foot slamming on the gas, almost taking Buck's right hip with us before he cleared the front of the car.

"It's okay. You're good," she assured me, staring straight ahead. "The only language they know is curse words and guns," she continued like her actions were the answers to my mounting concerns.

I didn't know Kadeem's motives for requesting to meet me. All Laura would say was that Beverly had enlisted him to help find her last night and he was like a brother who wanted to meet the man who helped them.

When we drove up to the building located a few blocks down the road from where the men stopped us, I was reluctant to exit the vehicle. My trust was placed in a woman I wasn't a hundred percent sure didn't continue to cling to the urge to kill me simply because I was a man. I overheard one of her conversations with Beverly, and she talked about men like we were all rabid dogs who needed to be put down.

After exiting the car, I followed her up a set of dusty gray cement steps, sensing eyes on me from every direction. This was the first time I'd experienced what it must be like to be a minority. It was unsettling and humbling in a way that opened me up to appreciate some of the freedoms I took for granted.

Once we entered the building, a little of my tension evaporated until we cleared the stairs and approached an intimidating metal door. When a small metal window slid open, smiling eyes met Laura, but turned wide when they landed on me. A tiny black camera, no bigger than the tip of my finger, sat camouflaged by the black rim of the door. I'd have missed it if I didn't have a trained eye.

"Kadeem asked me to come. He wanted me to bring the man who helped me. So, here he is. Now, open the fucking door, Barry!" she yelled at the eyes.

"My name's Chopper now and..."

Clink! Clink!

She produced the gun so fast I was clueless as to where she drew it from. The barrel sat inches from the forehead of the wide-eyed man at the door.

"You better open this damn door before you end up with another new name, like Dead Dick Bastard," she said, spitting her words at the man's face.

She wore skinny jeans, a fitted acid washed, navy T-shirt, and a black pair of those wedge-heeled sneakers. The attire clung to her small, curvy frame and highlighted her nicest features. It wasn't the kind of outfit I expected to see on a lesbian, but what the hell did I know? I was just now discovering a new breed of women after meeting Megan months ago and again after a short time of being around Laura and Beverly.

"Fucking chill, Laura, damn!" Barry whined before she dropped the gun and shoved it down the back of her pants. She left it visible, but I was sure it wasn't the same place she'd had it tucked previously because my eyes had been glued to her ass on our way up the stairs.

The metal slid closed, and the locks being disengaged on the other side of the door sounded. When the door squeaked open, I followed Laura inside. She scooted aside a man who was taller than my six-two frame and about as wide as the door. Next to him, she was a little person, but the big man flinched out of her way.

The interior of the apartment was nothing like outside. White and gold made up the color scheme as chic, French-designed furnishings decorated the living room and visible dining area. Was that an authentic Van Gogh hanging on the wall above the couch?

The loud clap of the door being shut sounded behind me.

"Laura, only you would upset the balance of nature by bringing a white boy into this hood. How the hell did you even get this far?" A voice questioned before the man it belonged to came into view.

The man, who I assumed was Kadeem, walked around the door frame of what must have been his kitchen and waved his hand in her direction. About my height, he was bulkier, and like Laura, he wasn't what I expected.

Dressed in a midnight black button up with silky designer slacks, he moved with an air of confidence. His skin was a pale caramel, his hair short and wavy.

"Never mind. Shots weren't fired, so you obviously bullied your way in," he continued, answering his own question.

After he gave her a once over, which wasn't the kind of look you gave a sister figure, he turned his gaze in my direction.

"So, you're the one who helped this little trouble-maker get out of the shit she's gotten into with a *fucking cartel*?" he shouted the last few words in Laura's direction, highlighting that he was aware of the danger she was in and that he'd been dragged into now.

His penetrating gaze trapped mine. "How the fuck did she end up in the hands of one of the most dangerous cartels in this country? How the fuck did she end up with a white boy for a protector?"

Laura eyed Kadeem, slicing him to pieces with her sharp gaze, but like me, he didn't take her attitude to heart.

"First, I can handle my own shit," she spat. "I was well on my way to taking care of the situation before he showed up." She tossed a thumb in my direction, but her sharp eyes remained on Kadeem.

I jumped in, my gaze pinned on the side of Laura's head. "First, the situation was out of control." I turned to Kadeem. "Second, I'd appreciate it if you'd show me some respect or at least acknowledge that I risked my life to save hers."

Laura's mouth dropped. Kadeem hid his reaction behind a stone face, but his tensed body revealed he was as shocked as Laura. She did a splendid job on the drive over explaining how dangerous Kadeem was, but she couldn't know I didn't care who he was or where we were. I'd stand my ground no matter what.

Besides, I still had both my weapons, and if something was supposed to go down, it would have already happened. Kadeem assessed me, his gaze scanning me from head to toe. I tilted my head in Laura's direction, but my sharp-eyed gaze remained locked with Kadeem's.

"I'm compelled to babysit her until this is over because if left to her own devices, she's going to end up dead," I added, firm in my conviction.

"Now, wait a damn minute!" Laura shouted, pointing an angry finger in my direction. "I know you didn't say you're babysitting me?" Her face was as fixed as her stiff stance, set to rip me to shreds. "I didn't ask for your damn help, and if I recall correctly, I was keeping bullets out of your ass, too."

My hand met my forehead and squeezed, knowing she wasn't going to stop her ranting until she was ready. It was the smile on Kadeem's face that allowed me to tune out the slew of curse words Laura slung at us both.

"Okay, you're right. Dax, is it?" Kadeem asked, ignoring Laura's rant as I'd quickly learned to do.

"Yes," I answered as she continued to huff and puff in the background. Kadeem reached out his hand to shake mine, finally breaking the tension between us. I took his hand with a firm grip.

"Kadeem," he finally relented. "I respect anyone who will take on a group like DG6. Dealing with them is toxic to your health. I gather it would be a mistake to misjudge you as well?" he asked, giving me a once over.

"Yes." We finally let each other's hands go, but our gazes remained locked. "Judging me wrong would be a *grave* mistake." I let my arrogance speak.

"What the fuck?" Laura stated, her head toggling back and forth between us. "So, you two are starting a bromance now. You want me to grab you some beers and tampons?"

"Yes. Beers would be nice, Laura. Thanks for asking," Kadeem tossed sarcastically in her direction.

Laura glared at him with murder in her gaze before she aimed it at me.

"The beers, Laura," I added, causing her anger to shoot through Kadeem's roof.

"Such unrestrained anger.... Where does it all come from?" Kadeem questioned as he eyed Laura with intrigue.

"When anger rises, think of the consequences," he quoted with a finger aimed at her like a teacher coaching a student.

"Okay, Confucius, like you don't have anger issues," she shot back at him. Her knowing who he quoted revealed yet another layer to a woman with more depth than any I'd ever met in my circle.

"Are you going to get those beers or what?" Kadeem questioned before she stomped off toward his kitchen. He continued aiming his words at her back, "If Beverly hadn't called me back to let me know you'd been found, I would've executed three men connected to that cartel, and shot up a damn warehouse looking for you."

At those words, I knew I'd misread Kadeem as much as he'd misread me.

"You can have a seat. You saved my sister, so you're pretty much family now," he said. His smile met his eyes for the first time. "Only white family we've ever had around here, but we got you if you ever need anything from us," he continued.

He wasn't being deceptive. His care for Laura ran deep.

"I appreciate that," I replied as I sat on the plush leather couch. His place hinted that Kadeem was a lot more cultured than he let on. Laura had jokingly mentioned that he was one book short of being insane. I never met a highly-intelligent, drug-dealing criminal before, especially not one who liked to read. It didn't make sense that he was a drug dealer when he seemed smart enough to do anything else.

"I know what you're thinking," Kadeem said before taking the Corona Laura handed him. She handed me the other and sat a few slices of lime atop a white saucer on the table in front of us. For her, a bottle of water was pinched between her fingers. The big man she threatened to re-nickname stood at the door, quiet and observing.

"What am I thinking?" I asked Kadeem in response to his statement. Laura sat on the other end of the couch I sat on, observing us. Kadeem sat in a nice sturdy beige chair.

"Why waste my time being a drug dealer?" he replied, knowingly. I took a sip of beer, enjoying the cold refreshment although I wasn't a beer drinker.

"I was supposed to finish college to get out of the hood and help my family get out. Although my father was one of the biggest dealers in the city, he never forced this life on us. He gave us a choice. This life eventually killed him and my two brothers. My mother became a slave to the drugs until they killed her. After my brothers were gone, I got into this for revenge and got it," he confessed without a hint of guilt in his tone.

"I found that once you get sucked into this, it's as addictive as the drugs you sell. See enough death, deal in enough death, be the cause of enough death, and pretty soon it becomes a part of who you are. After my father, the hood needed a leader or they would've faced a hostile takeover. I became that leader by default, and they allowed me the time I needed to let my balls drop, so to speak. And trust me, they are better off with me than they would have been with the alternatives."

In a way, I understood. I didn't doubt what he was saying was true. He'd been forced to become a monster to save himself and the people he cared about. In Kadeem's case, he became a drug lord and based on what I witnessed so far, he was a well-respected one.

We discussed strategy for staying under the radar from DG6 and keeping Laura and Beverly safe. After thirty minutes of more questions from Kadeem and eye rolls from Laura, we were released with Kadeem's blessing. I'd also gained a direct line to him and an ally against DG6.

The first ten minutes of our drive back to the hotel was in silence, but I sensed Laura's slick eyes on me.

"What?" I asked without glancing in her direction.

"I know it's not safe to return to my apartment, so I'm going to swing by a shopping center so I can get some extra clothes," she announced.

"Okay," I answered as a smile crossed my lips, knowing she was itching to say more.

"How did you get the outfit you have on," I questioned. It wasn't what she was wearing at the warehouse.

"Bev packed me a change of clothes when she snuck back into our apartment last night."

They lived together, a factor I hadn't considered. Come to think of it, I didn't know much of anything about these women. As soon as she turned the car in the direction she needed to go, silence fell between us again.

"So, you and Kadeem," I started, aware I was about to disturb a hornet's nest by insinuating what I suspected. "You two ever dated before you declared yourselves sister and brother?"

Her neck swung in my direction so fast she jerked the steering wheel, making her slick tires screech.

"What the hell kind of crazy-ass question is that? Hell no, we never dated. What part of me being a lesbian don't you understand?" she questioned, glaring at me for so long I feared she'd run us off the road.

"I asked because he wasn't looking at you like you were his little sister or a lesbian. His eyes were filled with lust. Desire. Want. Almost a burning need," I pointed out.

A deep retching sound from her throat filled the inside of her noisy car. "I think I just threw up in my mouth," she expressed before rolling down her squeaky window and faking a spitting gesture.

"I'm telling you what I saw. The military trained me to notice things, and I'm pretty sure Kadeem wants to be more than your brother."

I laughed at how disturbed her facial expression was in reaction to my statements. She assumed her lesbian status was the key to making her off-limits to men, but she couldn't have been more wrong.

"Enough, please. I don't need to hear this. You're going to mess up the way I see him," she said, sounding genuinely distressed about my revelations. I left it alone. Instead, I was about to make another suggestion I knew she wasn't going to like.

"I think we should share a bedroom and D and Beverly should. That way..."

"Hell no! I noticed the way the geek squad was eyeballing Beverly. I can aim and shoot as well as you can," she boasted before releasing a deep sigh.

Night had started to settle, but even in the hazy interior of the car, the V in the center of her forehead highlighted her irritation. I didn't know what it was, but I found that I enjoyed irritating her.

"Before I was so rudely interrupted by your unnecessary outburst," I continued. "I was suggesting we make the split for safety reasons. That way each team will have an ex-member of Special Forces with them. I know you can shoot, Laura, that's not the point. I know you will not hesitate to put a bullet in someone if they touch Beverly and that includes me and D, but I'm thinking strategy."

She didn't say anything for a long while as she considered my suggestion.

"Special Forces, huh? That explains a lot," she stated, side-eying me. "I wondered why a single man came into a warehouse of armed men to find a woman he didn't know."

"You sound like you're impressed," I replied teasingly.

"It's hard not to be," she admitted, keeping her face straight ahead. "I know I've got a big mouth, but I give credit where credit is due. You guys know your shit, so I guess I'll be sharing a room."

She stared pointedly at me, taking her eyes dangerously off the road again. "Don't make shit weird, Dax. We are barely all right, damn sure not friends."

My hands lifted in mock surrender. "Strategy for safety, that's all," I declared, hiding my insidious smirk by glancing out my window.

Once back at the hotel, we ordered room service, and D and I took turns decoding the chip. I'd taken selected coursework in information technology but being around D, I'd picked up enough to hack my way into a few useful sources. I wasn't on his level, but he was willing over the years to teach me the most useful tricks of his trade.

Chapter Thirteen

Laura

At one in the morning, my body's call for rest was about to be answered as I prepared for bed. The notion of sharing a room with Dax bothered me at first, but my worry was eased with Beverly's acceptance of the arrangement.

She liked the idea of having a personal protector. *"There are double beds. It's not like we have to sleep in the same bed as them,"* she'd pointed out.

Fresh from a shower, I washed away a day that never wanted to end. Gray eyes were on me as soon as I strolled out of the bathroom and made my way across the room to my bed. The irritating frown etched on Dax's face caused me to return a scowl in his direction.

If he knew me, he'd keep his mouth shut and not say one word because I was a grumpy asshole when I was tired. "You're being weird as fuck right now," I muttered in his direction. He didn't bother with a reply, but his eyes were aimed at me until I reached my bed.

Once I climbed in, I adjusted my pillows, threw my arms behind my head and prepared to relax for a minute before I passed out. Khalid's song "Better," spilled low from the earbuds I was about to plug in. Music before I fell asleep always eased my mind.

"Do you plan on covering yourself?" Dax questioned, his voice traveling across the room with enough volume to strike me upside my head.

I popped open one eye and aimed it at him. Shorts and a tank, how much more covered was I supposed to get? Did I need to invest in a burqa? With a deep sigh, my eyes fell closed again, ignoring him and his damn question. If he believed he was controlling me and my every action, he had the wrong damn idea.

I relaxed into the mattress, allowing more of today's tension to ease from my muscles. This was a gorgeous suite, so it would be wise to enjoy it before I returned to my lumpy mattress at home which was older than me.

Finally. Silence fell over me, and a satisfied smile danced across my lips.

A few seconds later, a shadow disturbed the space around me, causing my eyes to snap open to the sight of Dax standing above me. His bed hadn't squeaked, the mattress hadn't creaked, nor had the sound of footsteps registered moving across the floor. Nothing had alerted me to his approach until he was in my face like a fucking homicidal lunatic.

"You're not wearing a bra, and that's disrespectful to me as your roommate," he scolded, standing above me like he was the damn brassiere police.

"What does it matter? I'm wearing a shirt. Besides, they didn't have my bra size at the store, so I was forced to hand wash mine in the sink," I told him as I tucked my arms back behind my head.

"Are you planning on sleeping like that?" He was hovering like a deranged stalker.

"How the fuck else am I supposed to sleep? What's your damn problem? I'm laying here minding my own business, and you're hounding me about a damn bra?" The crease of irritation in my forehead was about to crack my skin. I gave him one of my signature eye rolls to portray my irritation, praying it had the power to get him away from me.

"The problem is you're a woman, and I'm a man. You shouldn't be walking around me like that," his eyes were on my tits.

My elbows dipped into the firm mattress as I eased up higher and glanced down, turning my head from one tit to the next before I lifted my gaze to him. My face was pinched in annoyance and an ache that wasn't there before pinged inside my head. He was giving me a damn headache.

"You're making this shit harder than it has to be. I'm sure you've seen your fair share of tits, so why the hell would my little tit-tots bother you?"

"You're an attractive woman, Laura. I'm a man. I don't need you distracting me," he stated matter-of-factly. His straightforward statement caught me off guard.

When I found my voice, it spilled out all at once. "Need I remind you that I'm a *lesbian*? And it's not like I'm well-endowed enough in the chest to distract you anyway. What…"

The rest of my sentence was stalled because his long arms reached across me, gripped the sheets and slung them across me. The whole time he was maneuvering the covers, I was attempting to shove him, but his body was so solid and strong it was like pushing a brick wall.

He fussed as he wrapped me to his satisfaction. "It doesn't matter about your size," he mumbled as he tucked the covers he folded me into. He continued to manhandle me like I wasn't slinging every curse word I knew at him. "On your frame, they are a distraction, so cover yourself around me, lesbian or not."

By the time he was done, I was swathed and baby-wrapped to perfection. Instead of being upset at his behavior, I fought to keep from laughing out loud. I enjoyed pissing him off, and it was becoming apparent a lot of my actions irked him even when I didn't mean for them to.

My eyes remained on his retreating back as he stomped off to the bathroom for his shower.

***

Beverly

The chemistry between Derrick and me was off the charts. Even after our talk, he stared without hiding that he was checking me out. Although the attraction tugged at the strings holding my resolve together, I couldn't help thinking there was something missing.

It was flattering that a man that good-looking was keeping an eye on me, but I'd been through it all before. The charmers. The ones who issued false promises. The ones who wanted a quick hit and run. The ones who looked good enough to make you forget about principles.

When a pattern of drive-by sex and drive-by relationships started to emerge, I decided to take a step back from men. My cookie and emotions were on lockdown until I felt otherwise. It would take a genie to make me take the chains off, and I was hoping like hell D didn't have the magical combination that would lead me to remove them.

He was tall, well built, with smiling eyes, and a fun personality. His brown hair had length on the top but was cut low on the sides and back. He was well put together, not a thing out of place. There was no denying how sexy he was. But, however tempting he was, I was choosing to face the cold, hard truths of our situation and stick to the rules I set for myself where it concerned men. I wanted a deeper connection other than just sex.

So far, we've managed five days without a major incident. Dax and Laura bickered like an old-school husband-and-wife team. Every time Dax made a suggestion, Laura would oppose it. When Laura would suggest something, Dax would take issue with it. At times, D or I would chance stepping between them to get them to calm down.

Although it was a trying transition, I think D and I were falling into friendship with each other. He didn't sleep much at night, so for the most part, the bedroom was mine. He spent a lot of his time on that computer.

A few days ago, my gaze trailed his movement while he planted three guns in different locations throughout the huge suite. There was no telling what Dax had hidden as well. If someone were daring enough to enter, they would end up getting lit up like a Christmas tree.

Laura and I ganged up on the men and convinced them to allow us to check in at the centers. City grants, donations, and sponsors kept the doors open, but it took hard work and constant networking to stay afloat.

We had assistants, volunteers, and a system set in place if we couldn't be there, but I missed the kids. I think it was Laura's threat that she'd take me and speed off in her old Toyota that eventually convinced the men to concede to our request.

Chapter Fourteen

Dax

We escorted the ladies to Beverly's center yesterday. While D kept a close watch on the ladies inside the facility, I'd chosen to spend most of my time outside as a lookout. Today, we were heading to Laura's facility. We were reluctant to split up the team and risk DG6 snagging one of the women so we maintained a close knit team mentality.

I was on constant guard while pulling into the parking lot of Laura's center less than five miles from the one Beverly managed. It wasn't in the best part of the city, and although it needed renovations, the building stood strong and provided a retreat for kids and teens who didn't have anywhere else to go.

Like meeting Kadeem for the first time, coming to these centers struck me with another round of humbling realizations that forced me to think about how privileged I truly was. The front interior of the center was a large open bay type room with a few worn folding tables and cheap plastic chairs neatly arranged about the space.

The fluorescent lights in the ceiling had clear coverings over them in certain areas and exposed in others. Aside from the front door, the expansive front wall I believed was once glass was bricked. At a distance, I spotted a wide hallway that led to an indoor gym area and a few rooms labeled with the activities available inside.

No sooner had we cleared the front doors and stepped fully into the building, than three children, five to seven years in age, came barreling toward Laura.

Three sets of tiny brown arms fought for space around her small waist, and she lavished each of them with strong hugs before they let her go. The sight forced me to fight to keep my eyes from going wide. I assumed she didn't have a maternal bone in her body and ate small children for snacks. It was yet another assumption I prematurely made about her that didn't hold an ounce of truth.

"I missed you, Ms. Parker!" The little boy exclaimed as his words pushed through the area where he was missing a front tooth.

"Me too," one of the two little girls announced, eyeing her with the kind of admiration a child aims at a mother.

"I missed you too," the other one chimed in, not wanting to be left out.

While she was attached to the children, others passed her, speaking, smiling, and tapping her shoulder to get her attention. It was clear she was well liked around this center.

"I missed you guys too. Have you all been keeping up with your lessons?"

"My favorite doctor," she said, cradling the little boy's head. "My favorite teacher," she continued, touching the next. "My favorite interior designer," she expressed, pulling the last little girl's long ponytail and making her giggle.

"Where's my favorite engineer?" she scanned the area for another one of the children.

"He wasn't feeling well. He's in the bathroom," the little boy replied.

Laura turned toward me, and for the first time the children's attention left her and landed on me too.

"Kids, this is my friend, Mr. Marshand, she offered as an explanation for his presence. He's helping me solve a problem so I can come back to work," she reassured them, concern etched on her face. "I'm going to go and check on Kenneth. I'll be right back," she announced before taking off toward what must have been the bathrooms.

Three little hands reached out, attached to the biggest smiles, and jovial giggling voices. I shook each of their hands. "Thank you for helping Ms. Parker," the little boy stated.

"She's always nice to us," the little girl with the long ponytail added. The way the little girl expressed her statement implied she didn't encounter many nice people.

Laura was gone for a while, but I had to admit, I was enjoying getting my ear talked off. The children were painting me a picture of a side of Laura she never would have voluntarily revealed. However, my worry increased after she was gone for about ten minutes and hadn't returned.

"Will you guys show me to the bathroom," I questioned, getting firm agreements from the children. Each girl took one of my hands and led me down one of two halls and pointed me to the male restroom at the end.

When I walked in, I found Laura with a mop in her hand, cleaning up a puddle of vomit. She glanced up at me with a weak smile before her gaze landed on the child curled atop a thick fluffy towel.

"What happened," I questioned. "Is he okay? How can I help?"

"He'll be fine. He's my favorite engineer," she said, aiming her voice at the child. Her melancholy tone wasn't missed. Something more was happening, and I was at a loss as to what to do. She finished a final sweep of the floor, leaving the broken and cracked tiles glistening clean as the light scent of bleach and pine permeated the area.

She dumped the water down the toilet before shoving the mop and bucket into a stall that was converted into a closet. I stood in place, waiting for her to say something, *anything* to clue me in on what was wrong. Her haunting expression, her downturned lips, and sluggish movements concerned me. I'd never seen Laura like this. She looked beaten down, helpless, heartbroken. She washed her hands and glanced at me before going to the obviously sick child.

She bent, checking the child's forehead before she shoved her small arms under his neck and legs and lifted him. I hurried over to help.

"No, I've got him. If you weren't here, it would just be us. Open the door, please," she requested, her tone low and solemn. I didn't argue. The child was too heavy for her to carry, but her steps never wavered as she turned onto the hall.

"The last door on the left. Open it, please," she called across her shoulder. I ran a few paces ahead and opened the door for them. The fact that she'd said please twice *to me*, was a clear indication that this situation was serious.

She stepped through the door and didn't stop until she laid the little boy atop a small loveseat that sat across from what must have been her desk.

I eased inside, silently observing as she plucked a pillow and blanket from a closet that had a thick black sheet hanging in the front of it as a door. She approached the little boy, covering him with the blanket and making him comfortable.

This was a side of Laura I'd never expected, a layer of her personality she shielded with a toughness she rarely put down . You'd never see this side of her unless she allowed it. Talking about judging a book incorrectly by its cover. Never saw this coming. These kids worshipped the ground she walked on, and she adored them with a nurturing passion I didn't know she possessed.

"I know it hurts, baby. Was your granny able to pick up your medicine this week?" she questioned the little boy.

A weak, "Yes ma'am," fell across his lips as she rubbed his curly head of hair. She placed a kiss on his cheek. "Try to get some rest. I'll come back and check on you, okay?" He shook his head this time, a frown of pain etching his face.

She cast a glance in my direction before she headed for the door, pain and defeat prominent in her expression. Her watery eyes were filled with a depth of sorrow that reached into me, and I was forced to stop myself from gripping and pulling her into my arms to make it disappear.

Once we were outside the office, she left the door cracked and started back toward the main common area of the center. I gripped her shoulder, stopping her.

"What's wrong with that little boy?" I asked, my face pinched in concern for the child and her.

"Cancer," she whispered. "He takes treatments every other week, but…" She shook her head, warding off the grief of the situation. "His grandmother says the treatments aren't working. The cancer's too aggressive. They're too poor to opt for better care, so he has to take what the government pays for, which is usually test drugs, some that haven't even been approved by the FDA."

Her hopeless gaze flashed back toward her office. "He loves to come here and interact with the other kids. He and his grandmother live in the Maplewood Projects, so this is one of a few places he can come and play and not get caught in the mess the streets are always stirring up."

My hand closed around hers, hating to see her so discouraged. She was a different person here, not the feisty alpha female in which I was initially introduced.

"I'm sorry, Laura. I wish there was something I could do."

She jerked her hand away from mine, the crease in her forehead deepening into anger. "What are you sorry for? None of this is your fault. This is life. Many of us have to face more of the harsher sides of it. We live through what gets dumped on us and make the best of it in the process."

She pushed her finger into her chest. "I take what I have or what I'm given and do my best to make what is needed, especially here," she said, forcing a smile onto her face.

The emotional aches I saw played out on her face. The pure defeat pressed down her small shoulders. She made it all disappear, swallowed it for the kid's sake before leaving me to stand in the middle of the hall with my mouth hanging open. Staring at her back, I realized that I'd never been so proud of someone.

Spending the day with Laura and the kids at the center was an eye-opening experience. There were teen boys and girls, gymslip mothers with their babies, preteens, and a woman who came seeking sanctuary away from an abusive man.

Laura refused to allow the woman to stay around the children but provided her help by calling someone who came and picked her up. The woman was so grateful that she'd cried and kissed Laura's hands. I was getting a lesson in life I didn't know I needed.

Laura introduced me to several of the center's volunteer workers. I listened in on enough of her and Beverly's conversations over the past week to understand money was always tight, and they, along with a few others, received meager paychecks.

I overheard her speaking briefly about a new sponsor the center had picked up, and the conversation had piqued my interest. My family donated money to multiple charities each year, but we never delved into what our donations did for people. We never took an active interest in what the money was being used for, or more specifically, who it would help.

My mother always said everything happens for a reason, and I was certain that this was one of those times. I was supposed to meet Laura and I most certainly needed to experience what went on at the centers she and Beverly ran. I needed to encounter the kinds of problems people faced that people like me had the ability to help solve but were ignorant about. This was a situation I'd never have understood if I hadn't encountered it first-hand.

I faced hard times, but I never knew how bad others had it because I always had an endless supply of money at my disposal. Laura and Beverly's centers would be receiving a boost from an anonymous donor. They just didn't know it yet.

Chapter Fifteen

Laura

The next night.

The firm hand placed over my mouth stopped my sharp intake of breath. In the dead of night, I took a moment to process the urgent actions unfolding as I went into fight mode.

The blinking digital numbers on the bedside clock flashed 01:52. Was I ever going to get more than two hours of sleep?

"Get up. Put your clothes on as fast as you can," Dax ordered, his words demanding. "We have unwanted company on the way." The unmistakable sound of a bullet being primed highlighted his words.

The lamp on the table between our beds spilled the only light into the room. Dax stood at the window covered by the blackout curtains and peeked out. We had the rear view of the building that showed us nothing but the top of the parking garage and a tight alley below that separated us from the backs of more high-rise buildings.

The first thing I grabbed was the gun I'd tucked under the edge of the mattress for situations like this and just in case Dax decided to get out of hand. I paused when I noticed a silencer had been attached. My lips twitched into a smile until I remembered that we were about to face a possible attack.

There was no time for modesty. I tugged off the T-shirt I was sleeping in and rummaged through my backpack for a top. My shorts went zipping down my legs, and I went for the fresh pair of jeans I took out with the shirt. When I sensed eyes on me, I glanced over my shoulder into the stunned face of Dax.

Gun in hand, mouth agape; he made no attempt to hide his gawking. His gaze raked over my ass wrapped in silky blue panties and trailed down my legs and back up. I didn't have time to start an argument, so I ignored him and continued my task.

"How do you know we have company?" I asked as I shoved my first leg into my pants.

His gaze remained on my ass as I hurriedly dressed. "D caught them on camera. They found a way through hotel security and obtained a key and code to the elevator. We obviously underestimated their abilities."

The finger below his earlobe revealed that he and D were communicating. I was the only thing that got him to drop his gaze from me.

"Three minutes," Dax relayed. D carried enough tech gear to have his own convention, so I shouldn't have been surprised. However, I was impressed with the level of sophistication these men were revealing. Gun in hand and at the ready, I followed Dax out of the door.

Bev and D were already at the front door. Seeing a gun in Bev's hand stalled my uneasy movements, but given that we were on a cartel hit list, it was necessary. D directed her to the dining room area and had her lie, prone behind the thick wooden table.

"If it's not me, D, or Beverly, shoot them. Aim for the head or heart," Dax whispered to me in the same commanding tone as D had to Beverly. The rules of engagement were simple: shoot to kill.

"Got it," I answered as I glanced back at Bev's location.

"We're not going to let anything happen to either of you," Dax assured us, his words sounding like a promise.

He led me in the opposite direction, standing me between the two walls that formed a nook that led to the large common area bathroom. With his gaze on mine, he lowered his hand in a gesture for me to stay low.

Once he positioned me with the walls as my protection, I peeked out at his retreating back. His movement was as silent as the night as he took up the post closest to the front door. Nothing but the door when it opened would keep him from being spotted, and it bothered me that I couldn't see Beverly or D from my area.

When the room went black from Dax flipping off the lights, I tucked myself into place and raised my gun. The open blinds illuminated the area and showcased the dark view, letting in the moonlight and the busy sparkle of the city outside.

"Twenty seconds," a faint whisper sounded, and I couldn't tell if it was D or Dax. *How many were there and how had they found us?* It was two of the many questions I hadn't had time to ask Dax.

The whine of the keycard reader was followed by a click and a double beep. They must have assumed we were sleeping. The silence that filled the interior of the large space pressed down on me—the quiet before the storm.

My heart pounded, sensing the presence of danger before the door squeaked open at a leisurely pace, followed by a loud thump. Was that a body hitting the floor or my heart beating away at my chest cavity?

I peeked. The door continued to widen, and the light from the hall crept across the floor. Two shadowy figures entered the living room, their identities protected by the darkness they faced.

Their guns were aimed in opposite directions as they stepped further inside with caution. They wore full head-to-toe tactical gear like law enforcement, proving that we weren't dealing with run-of-the-mill amateurs.

Where the hell was Dax? He was no longer at the door. My anxiety kicked up a notch when one of the intruders approached the area near Beverly's location, and the other proceeded in my direction. Two more entered through the front door and were trailed by another.

The fifth man sprang into alert mode, scanning every direction. When four more came charging in, my anxiety imploded and my nerves caught fire. Four would have evened the odds, but nine was a complication. The last man closed and locked the door behind him, drenching the room in moonlit darkness.

Were D and Dax as good as the résumé I was building on them suggested? We were locked inside a penthouse with nine well-armed and determined killers. Men who had enough resources to track us down and find their way into a secured top-floor penthouse in a building I assumed was impenetrable.

At the first sound of gunfire, my finger automatically hovered over my trigger. The silenced gun taps weren't that silent inside the suite. At least four shots were fired, the sounds coming from every direction. No sooner than I peeked around the wall than all hell broke loose. Muzzle flashes from weapons, tracer rounds traveling across the space like fireworks, and the unmistakable sound of a fight in progress drew me from my hole.

I ducked, dodging a fist that came flying toward my head. Dax was engaged in hand-to-hand combat with one of the killers. He was doing martial arts, more skills he possessed that I was discovering in the heat of battle.

When the bad guy's gun went skidding across the floor, I picked it up and dashed in Beverly's direction. My right foot was snagged by a lifeless body in my haste, making me stumble to the floor. The large couch shielded me from the kitchen and dining area.

A guttural moan drew my attention. The man Dax was fighting was on the floor, but he wasn't dead as he crawled toward a fallen bottle of wine from the bar to use as a weapon.

The idea was driven clean out of his head when I lifted my gun, aimed, and watched half of his face explode in the mirror in front of him. I turned on my back, using the dead man I stumbled over to prop myself up.

Furniture moving noises came from the bedroom Bev and D shared. A man's loud roar sounded, followed by the subdued double tap of a weapon going off.

I crawled across the body I used as my prop. My knee sank into the stomach and caused the body to move underneath me. The hair-raising growl escaping the body raised goosebumps on my arms.

When the lights snapped on, Dax's gun was aimed in my direction. I caught the sight of a muzzle flash and glanced back in time to see a body falling into the nook I just abandoned. By the time I glanced back in Dax's direction, he'd vanished again.

On my hands and knees, I crawled to the edge of the large sofa to see if I could spot Beverly. The sight that filled my view was a large splattering of head contents on the table Beverly was no longer hiding behind. Instead, a limp body lying stomach down appeared not to have a head attached.

Two bodies lay slumped at the front door, blood running like spilled water around them. They were likely attempting to make an escape once they discovered they had ambushed the wrong people.

The sound of another fight had my head turning in every direction. We had transformed this expensive luxury suite into a murder house, and I prayed all our crew was still breathing. The rusted scent of blood mixing with the unmistakable odor of gun smoke dominated the air inside the suite now. The suffocating mixture clogged my nasal passages, traveled down my throat, and rested in the pit of my stomach.

Where the hell is Beverly?

No sooner than I thought it, the hairs on the back of my neck stood, and a chill consumed my entire body.

Chapter Sixteen

Laura

Dax and D emerged like I had summoned them, their gazes locked behind me. With the large sofa blocking most of my view, I was unable to see what captured their attention. I rose onto my knees, and my gaze followed the direction in which they now aimed their weapons.

"Let her go," D's voice whispered across the room like a deadly lullaby. He and Dax took easy steps, closing in on the fidgety man who had a gun aimed at Beverly. With her back to the wall, he was forced to stand beside her with one hand gripping her arm as the other kept his gun pressed firmly against her head. Her gun sat on the floor, out of her reach.

"Stay back! Stay back or I'll shoot her!" He shouted, his thick Spanish accent slurring his words. His attention was aimed at D and Dax, his gun wobbling with each yell.

The man's concern with D and Dax's approach distracted him from a more imminent danger. He should have been worried about the person next to him. I'd never known Beverly to not be carrying a blade.

My eyes widened when the switchblade danced to a flashy opening in her hand. It was one of a set of three, custom-made, that her father had given her.

I feared she'd get herself shot, although I knew how quick she was. The man glanced briefly in my direction, shock freezing him in place before dramatic spurts of blood burst free like his neck was being ripped open from the inside out. He didn't even know he was dying yet.

When the blade went in a second time, it remained there, stuck in his neck as blood gushed around the artery Beverly opened. The man's gun was forgotten, thudding against the floor as his hands automatically went to his neck to keep blood inside his body.

Beverly kicked his gun from his reach and ran to put distance between them. I met her halfway, my body colliding into hers.

I hadn't a clue as to what was next in this fucked up situation. Didn't care. Beverly and I were together and alive to see another day.

"We have to go, ladies," Dax announced.

"I didn't spot anymore, but it doesn't mean there aren't any," D stated as he turned and aimed in the direction of a groan behind him and let off two rounds. The man's body danced from the dark opening before his knees gave out and he stumbled to the floor, his head burst open as one of his eyes hung from the socket.

"They managed to sneak men past the cameras, so we don't know if they have any more waiting. We also need to find out how the hell they found us," D continued, his tone filled with irritation.

D took pride in what he did, and it didn't sit well with him that these men infiltrated our hideaway and he hadn't seen it coming until it was happening. Bev and I moved with swift purpose, grabbing our shit and preparing to leave this active crime scene.

The man Bev stabbed had slumped to the floor, choking and gurgling blood, clawing at his neck. D and Dax weren't worried about him, so I wasn't either. His wide eyes were snow white as he glared at us for help. There wasn't shit we could do for him. Death was standing above him, smiling, waiting to snatch his soul.

Bev made sure she retrieved her knife from the man's neck, jerking it free like she was upset she'd had to get it dirty. We all met near the front door. Dax had his phone to his ear while glancing back at the horrific scene that would likely draw every law enforcement agency in the country.

"The penthouse suite. Nine. I'll call the manager to put this floor on lockdown," Dax continued to speak into his phone, his face creased in irritation. I didn't understand what was happening and I didn't get a chance to question it as we hopped across the two bloody bodies on our way out the front door.

D was leading, and we followed, with Dax as our eyes in the back. We left the penthouse with nine dead bodies and neither D nor Dax appeared the least bit worried.

When we arrived on the first and not the third floor of the parking structure, the lights of a dark gray Jaguar XJ flashed. The car started with a crawling roar, and I glanced at Dax.

"My assistant," was all he said. This was smart. The people hunting us would be expecting a BMW or my Camry which were still on the third floor. We tossed in our bags and a medium-sized suitcase of D's equipment into the trunk.

Bev and I climbed inside when the men opened the back doors for us. Dax drove leisurely as we eased from the garage in one of the smoothest rides I'd been in. His eyes found mine as he glanced in the mirror.

"Was that your family's hotel back there?" I questioned. D glanced back with a smile. He was sitting in the front seat working on a tablet device.

"You'd make an excellent detective. How did you reach the conclusion of that being my family's hotel?" Dax asked, the curiosity in his tone edging out.

"The call you made. Some unlucky person is going to clean up the massacre we left in that penthouse, aren't they? And the way you call up your assistant and order up cars and ten-thousand-dollar a night penthouse suites has me thinking your assistant is a super-computer. Also, you don't get a suite with soundproofing unless it's your own personal touch," I pointed out.

Dax was interesting enough that I Googled him as soon as I convinced D to tell me his last name. The man was Texas royalty. Why he ran around putting his life in jeopardy was a mystery. His people had enough money to run the government. When I searched for information on the hotel and the nightly rate of the suite we were staying in, I nearly choked on my tongue.

His smiling eyes lingered on me in the mirror until we broke contact. I relaxed into the seat before sliding closer and resting my head on Bev's shoulder. Her shaking hand had been clinging to mine since we slid into the back of the car.

Unlike me, Beverly wasn't willing to kill anyone unless she was forced to do it. She would beat herself up over the man she stabbed until she forced herself to accept that she didn't have any other choice.

My head lifted from her shoulder when Dax pulled the car into a rest stop that resembled the set of a horror film. Three semi-trucks were lined up on the dusty, dirt-covered parking lot decorated with potholes the size of small ditches. Woodlands surrounded the place, and a solitary country road was the lone pathway cut through them.

How far out of the city limits had we traveled? Far enough that the gas pumps didn't have card readers. A toothless old man sat on the outside of the station's entrance on a wooden bench spitting his tobacco juice into an old Crisco can in the middle of the night. This was likely what he did for fun on a Saturday night.

The old man's curious gaze hadn't left us since we drove up to the pump. We weren't there for gas because a quick peek showed the gage pointed at full. Dax turned, peering across the seat at me. His words were aimed at D, but his gaze was locked on me.

"I think they may have put a bug on her," Dax stated. His words sent a quick stream of panic through me. D's eyes turned on me, joining Dax's. There was no way I had a bug on me. *How? When?*

"That's the quickest way they could have found us. You wouldn't happen to have packed a bug detector?" Dax asked D, finally turning his eyes away and releasing the hold he had on me.

"Yep," D replied nonchalantly, like packing a device that detects bugs was as normal as packing an extra set of underwear. Their words and scanning eyes had me patting myself down although I was sure I hadn't been bugged.

"Are you saying they put a bug on me from when I was abducted? It's been five, no, six days ago. Why didn't they come sooner? Where could they have possibly put it?" I questioned. My words were choppy because Bev had started to help me with the pat down.

"Besides, when they took me, I didn't give them a chance to put anything on me. They were too busy keeping me from kicking their asses."

"As I witnessed," came Dax's confirmation. "It likely took them days to figure out a way into the penthouse once they located the tracker. We need to see if there is one, so we can eliminate the possibility and prevent them from finding us again."

"I've changed clothes every day since the night I was taken, and the clothes I wore that night were washed by the hotel's laundry service," I added while continuing to pat myself down.

"Where do you think the idea for waterproof phones came from?" D asked, his words had my eyes creeping up to his face.

"You were in contact with them too. How do you know it's not *you* who was bugged?" I questioned Dax.

"I burned everything I wore that night with the body. I need to check you," Dax insisted, and it wasn't a request.

"D, will you get the detector please?"

Dax hopped out, opened my door and waited. My gaze followed D as he exited the car and walked back to the trunk before he met Dax at my door. They stared at me like I was a specimen under a microscope before Dax was handed a piece of equipment that appeared to be borrowed from the *Ghostbusters*.

"Grab your backpack and let's go," Dax urged as he headed toward the rest stop bathroom. At minimum this was a place where ten unsolved homicides had occurred. Dirt fought the spray-painted walls for dominance and cigarette butts littered the path. Reluctantly, I yanked my backpack from the trunk D had left open and followed Dax.

My nose wrinkled as soon as I crossed the threshold into the smelly den of shit and sin. The light above the single sink buzzed as it glimmered between dim and light, making our dreadful surroundings pulse like a packed club. The single leaky toilet had a stream of water flowing toward the dirty, clogged drain in the middle of the floor.

Dax locked us inside as he strolled past me and stood with his back to the sink. Not a stranger to the criminal world, I dropped my bag, lifted my hands at my side, and spread my legs shoulder width apart.

His brow lifted at my action before he flicked a button on the device. It emitted a low squall that competed with the hum of the flickering light.

Dax took his time passing the device along my body, eyeing me as he did. He liked this. I believed he sensed his closeness made me nervous. I didn't like it, yet it was strangely comforting. I hated what I didn't understand, and this was one of the reasons I didn't like Dax.

My eyes rolled when he slapped the back of his hand to the inside of my calf to widen my stance. My tight jeans stretched taut against my body. I'd been trying for years and had finally started to gain weight, so most of my clothes were tight as hell. My bank account needed a money transfusion, so I'd not been able to catch my wardrobe up with my body.

The instrument's squeak elongated when he passed it above my shoe. The sound drew our attention and caused me to go still.

When Dax stood fully upright, my gaze lifted with him as his eyes held mine hostage. I struggled to keep my face impassive, but the strange connection we shared had the hairs on the back of my neck standing and my muscles tensing tighter. The intensity of the energy between us increased and my brows twitched and gave him a glimpse of what his presence had the ability to do to me.

He broke our trance when he flipped the machine off before turning and placing it on the nasty cement floor. His fingers clamped around my wrist before he directed me to the sink.

"What is it? Is there something on me?" I questioned, my anticipation of what he may have found hardened my already sharp tone. I was so busy staring down at my shoes, where the instrument beeped the loudest, I was thrown off guard when Dax placed his hands under my shoulders and lifted me.

He sat me on the sink and took my left foot in his hand, leaving me no choice but to swallow my surprise and grip his sturdy shoulders for support.

"You could have asked me to hop up here." Venom dripped from my hissing voice. "You couldn't help showing off your ego by manhandling me, huh?" I gave him an evil side-eye he ignored.

"Yes," he answered with no shame as he searched my lower leg and shoe. How could he already be so adept at handling my attitude? Warmth radiated from his strong hand wrapped around my leg as he thumbed and fingered my calf before he lowered his movements. He bent for a closer look at the area, which caused my grip on his shoulders to tighten.

My fingers dug into the hard cords of his muscles, pulling my attention from his inspection. My examining gaze was aimed at my hand clawing into his shoulders. Why the hell did I enjoy the way his hard muscles felt under my fingertips? *Strange.* I ignored my odd behavior and eyed him closer.

Dax was one of those men who was used to getting his way with women. I knew as much the moment I met him. His dark brown hair was cut low on the side with a few inches on top that he styled with a gel that probably cost more than everything I wore. It had a pricy scent, like something I couldn't afford to sniff. He looked expensive. Everything about him was always neat, and he never dressed in anything less than the best.

He wasn't pale, nor was he darkly tanned either. His light complexion was fresh and natural versus the artificial look from a tanning bed.

Although I'd never kissed a man's lips, his were enticing, not too plump or thin, but revealing a noticeable succulence like he'd just been thoroughly kissed. They were pale pink, wet, and seductive in a way that enticed me to want to test their suppleness with my own.

What the fuck am I thinking?

He fingered my shoe, and his brows knitted with curiosity and drew my attention from my up-close assessment of him.

He picked at something that made the sound of a button being tapped. He continued to pick and tug until he detached a clear white disk the size of a dime from my shoe. The bug had a thin strip of metal in the center, the part that must have kept it clamped to my shoe.

Dax lifted the device, allowing me to examine it.

"This is a pretty high-tech bug," he confirmed, studying it. "It's probably why they didn't give chase when we left the warehouse. I'll check you again to make sure this is the only one."

He proceeded with a more thorough check than the first time. When he traced the outlines of my breast and kept his gaze pinned on mine, it took a great degree of mental fortitude to remain calm and not squirm or pretend it didn't affect me.

When he allowed his hands to fall over my ass, I took the unnerving intrusion, swallowing a ball of lust that attempted to tell on me.

A deep sigh of relief and even deeper eye rolls were cast on him when he decided he was done. His deceitful ass knew what he was doing. He was taking full advantage of my current situation, knowing I wouldn't have allowed him to go that far otherwise.

Dax locked Beverly in the running car and brought D in to study the tracker before they decided to flush it down the toilet. I couldn't recall a time when the men had time to place a tracker on me. It had to have been when they'd shoved a sack over my head and put me in the trunk of their car. The assholes had tagged me like I was livestock.

It didn't matter now. Their link to us was severed. Instead of us being the hunted, we at least leveled the playing field now. Dax put in a call to his infamous assistant, and we had a new place to stay within minutes.

By the time I lifted my head and rubbed sleep from my eyes, we'd weaved a trail across several interstate highways, doubled back to the city, and lost ourselves in downtown Houston. Dax drove us into the garage of an M. Exclusive Hotel.

I'd read about the hotels, the M standing for Millionaire. This kind of place was too expensive for even my dreams. Now, I was about to stay at one, compliments of Mr. Long Money.

Chapter Seventeen

Dax

It didn't take us long to settle into the new suite, despite what we went through at the last one. At my strong insistence, I shared the upstairs bedroom with Laura but found myself spending the majority of my time on the downstairs couch to avoid the woman who was beginning to give me fits.

The waiting during a mission was always the worst part. Add Laura to the mix and my days were turning into endless rounds of torture. I'd survived ten days so far and didn't know how much longer I would last.

Despite my personal demons, D and I had managed to build a résumé on our No Face target, Santino Dominquez. I'd have liked to have tackled DG6 sooner. However, we had to stick to the plan of aligning our mission to take out Santino with the missions ramping up in California and Mexico.

If we took out Santino Dominquez before our friends in California and Mexico executed their plan, we could inadvertently jeopardize their mission, spooking their multiple targets. Also, our thinking was to take out the whole hive of DG6 leaders on a close timeline. The team in California was larger and prepared to take out Tomas, an original, and his sons Alonso and Fernando.

We decoded the storage device that D took from the wallet Laura had lifted. It was information that listed hundreds of businesses that laundered money for DG6. If this type of information ended up with an organization like the FBI, it could result in the kind of damage to DG6 they wouldn't be able to recover from. DG6 was a sinking ship as far as I was concerned and accomplishing our missions in Texas, California, and Mexico would solidify their downfall.

"Where are you going?" Laura questioned as she approached and scanned my outfit. In her presence, my nerves tightened like a fist had gripped them. After connecting with the softer side of Laura at the center and spending time around her, she was growing on me like a lovely wild vine.

However, after that day at the center, her attitude toward me worsened, and she sought to pluck at my nerves even more so than usual.

I was using the hotel gym nightly. Laura insisted on walking around with those shorts on and although she respected my wishes, and wore a bra to bed, it was too late. I'd already seen too much. My urge to bury my dick in her balls deep was becoming unbearable.

I didn't know if it was because I knew I couldn't have her or because she wasn't the least bit attracted to me, but whatever the reason, it had the opposite effect on me. I hid a wicked attraction to her, even though she plucked my last dying nerve.

"I'm sitting here in this chair minding my own business," I said sarcastically, finally answering her question.

"I mean where are you going dressed like that? You look like you're about to go on a fashion shoot or something," she expressed, eyeing me up and down. She knew that I dressed well, even when I spent the full day inside the suite. Her aim was to get something started.

D and Beverly had gotten used to our banter and didn't get involved when we started up.

"I don't have to be going anywhere to look nice, but thank you for the compliment." I smiled. "The fact that you think I look like a model is the first of many of your secret compliments that you've expressed out loud," I informed, noticing when my lack of irritation and leading words had dampened her urge to annoy me further.

I'd survived weeks with this woman who did everything in her power to rattle me to pieces. Sometimes, she wasn't aiming to irritate, but she did just the same.

Like now, we were preparing to stake out The Greenbrier Hotel where we'd identified multiple DG6 lower-level targets. Thanks to D keeping a constant spying eye out, we were gathering valuable insight on the hotel.

Ansel and crew in California had set their go-live date for the same night The Greenbrier would have their annual charity event. D had confirmed that Santino Dominquez would be in attendance since he'd sponsored the ball for the last five years.

However good the digital intel was, it was always better to investigate the location in which we would be working, in person. Kind of like casing a bank before you robbed it.

I closed my eyes and prayed for mercy from the double dose of havoc this little loudmouth woman was causing me. However, "Why can't I come?" zipped into my ears.

Laura buzzed at my ear like a busy-body bee, and I had the perfect thing to calm her down. If I didn't think she'd shoot me dead, I'd have just fucked her already.

"How old are you?" Her question came from left field.

"Twenty-eight. What does my age have to do with anything?"

"In *all those years*, you haven't learned when someone is not going to take no for an answer?"

"I suppose twenty-five years isn't nearly enough time for you to have figured out that when I tell you *no*, it's final," I expressed, eyeing her, and waiting for more of her words to come crashing against my eardrum.

"You're a damn egomaniac who wants a woman to stay in her place. Pompous ass." Her jibs didn't affect me in the way she assumed as I was beginning to enjoy the back-and-forth spats we shared.

D placed a delicate hand on one of her set shoulders, interrupting the hard glare she set on me. He drew her attention before our argument could spiral out of control. She loved to challenge me, testing to see how far she had to push to get me to lose my cool.

D took his time explaining why she couldn't go on our recon mission. By the time he was done, she flashed him an appreciative smile and thanked him. She treated him differently than she treated me. *Why?*

Maybe she treated him better, but I believed I knew her well enough to know that she hadn't given up her quest to go on a mission with one of us. She stepped away from D and shot me a sharp glare before joining Beverly on the couch.

Laura was all fire and would burn you down to your socks without a second glance. The sight of her now was enough to unravel the gentlemanly ways that had been drilled into me during my upbringing. She was not my type at all, but I'd be damned if she didn't have my dick trying to climb out of my pants.

The logic of my attraction to her wasn't adding up. What was it about her that drove me crazy? She knew how to rip my peace to shreds, and I liked it. She made life more interesting. I believed she knew I enjoyed her fiery personality enough that I'd put up with her, sassy mouth and all.

The women in my circle were eager to please. It didn't mean some of them couldn't be exciting. Some were certified freaks behind closed doors. However, none posed a challenge. They didn't care to know me, the *real* me. As long as they knew my last name, I could have been a walking brick.

My authority, which I knew wasn't always right, was never challenged. I was never told my ideas were horrible or that my decisions didn't make sense. I didn't have to fight for a woman's attention. I was never interested in peeking into their minds because I never saw anything interesting enough on the surface to go that deep.

Laura wasn't afraid to let me have it. She certainly spoke her mind and expressed when she didn't like my ideas. At first, it was irritating because it was something I wasn't used to, but it was quickly becoming something I appreciated about her.

She made me think twice, think deeper, and harder. She didn't care about my last name or that my family had money. She was more impressed with the dangerous aspects of me, the side of me I hid. I believed she was attracted to my darkness and so was I to hers.

If only I could get her to drop that persona of lesbianism for one night and let me play with her flames.

***

Derrick

Dax was playing with a massive fire, and he was going to get burned alive. These women weren't weak or clueless. They'd lived life: the good, the bad, and the ugly. They knew what hell was like on all five senses.

However, Dax was one of the most determined men I knew. He wanted Laura, and from the way he'd been watching her since night one, his *want* was growing stronger. He was hardheaded as hell, and no matter how many pep talks or warnings I gave, I knew he would only try harder.

Laura was a challenge he was fixated on, but she wasn't just any woman. She was fearless, and even if he found a way, she wasn't going to be easy on him because she was as hardheaded as him.

He was in gym clothes now. I cast a quick glance at Laura before my gaze traveled to Dax's back as he exited the front door, heading for the gym again. Did she have any idea he was frequenting the gym more than usual because of her?

My buzzing phone drew my attention from a situation that wasn't going to end pretty. It was Aaron's number that popped up. Each time his number flashed, I knew it was Ansel, but it also flooded me with memories. Aaron was the closest thing I had to a brother, and after nearly six months, I continued to feel the sting of his death. I answered the call.

"Hey, man, what's up? Y'all good in Cali?" I called into the phone, waiting for Ansel to answer.

"Derrick Wesley Michaels?" a voice that wasn't Ansel's called into the phone with a smooth tone. There was only one person who knew my middle name, and he was dead.

"Who the fuck is this? Knox? Look, I don't have time for no motherfucking jokes. Who is this?" I questioned, instantly irritated that someone would be that cruel. They were making my fucking hood come out playing these games. I was usually the cool and collected one, but when people wanted to act stupid, I'd give it right back.

"It's me D, *Aaron*," the voice that sounded like Aaron proclaimed.

What kind of tech were they using to pull this off? I decided to test them.

"Prove it, motherfucker," I replied. "Yemen, operation, how many, and why?"

"Black Death, five, nerve gas. We were stuck in that fucking place for four months," came a quick reply, causing my loud gasp to escape. Beverly and Laura sat staring.

"Knox! What the fuck, man? How the fuck are you talking to me right now?"

"It's a long-ass story, D. Death had me by the fucking balls, but that dark evil bastard wasn't ready for me yet."

"No fucking shit!" I exclaimed, slapping my hand against the desk.

"D, Ansel's been filling me in on the plan y'all have been working on to take out the leaders of DG6. I'm not at full strength, but I'll be damned if I sit around while you all deal with these poisonous serpents."

"Man, I can't believe this shit. Wait until I tell Dax that your nine-lives-having ass is still alive. Motherfucker got more lives than a *Mortal Kombat* character."

Only Aaron could make me speak complete sentences in curse words. A few chuckles sounded in the background on his end before a shadow approached and stopped right next to me. Laura. Her pinched expression represented the question she wanted answered.

"After we assumed you died, we fully intended to go ape-shit and kill as many DG6 members as we could, but Ansel stopped us. He got us to calm the fuck down and think about how you would go at this. So, we slowed our roll, and now, we're in line to put DG6 out of commission. With the top gone, the rest of those fucking leeches are going to feed off and devour each other until there's nothing but pieces left."

I filled him in on what we were working on form our end before ending the call.

Nothing could take the smile off my face after I hung up with Aaron. For six long months we believed we'd lost him. We mourned him. We traveled back into enemy territory to search for his body.

"So, your friend, the one who spoke with me and Beverly about Megan, he's alive?"

"I don't know how, but he's alive, and ready to take these guys out as much as we are," I replied.

My smile deepened as I stood, squeezed Laura's small shoulder, and marched toward the door. I had to get to the gym and deliver the amazing news to Dax.

Chapter Eighteen

Dax

I was smiling for no reason for the past few days. Knowing Aaron was alive was the best news I received in a long time. I requested to see him for myself, so D set us up on a secure link that allowed us to talk and see him.

When we found out Aaron had escaped the farm with a member of the Dominquez family, we made several attempts to see if Regina could identify Santino for us. Unfortunately, she'd not had any real exposure to the Dominquez side of her family until they took her and held her captive.

We were also successful in getting the ladies back to the centers for another visit without incident. Visiting the centers was the highlight of Beverly and Laura's time. Other than her sneaking onto the balcony to smoke a Black-n-Mild every once in a while, it wasn't hard to discern that being at the center was Laura's therapy.

Her need to help people, particularly teens and children, was the one thing she coveted as much as her friendship with Beverly and Megan. They were her life, and she would unquestionably sacrifice everything to protect them. She was rarely on her phone, but whenever she was, it was with Megan or someone from the center.

She presented the Laura people needed, but she became Laura, the beast, behind the scenes to protect them from threats, some they would never know existed.

The more time and effort we poured into the mission, the more useful information we gained on DG6. The one thing we hadn't found was an easier way to take down Santino. The man was better protected than the president. We were tracking his movements for a month and had only spotted him twice with his face obscured from view each time.

Whether it was wearing dark shades, a low cap, or a group of people's heads blocking him, Santino always had a way to protect his face and never remained outside any building past a few minutes. Hence, his nickname: No Face.

D wanted a shot of his face so he could use it on facial recognition software that would allow us to track his movements. Santino was more than likely aware of the many ways he could be tracked, so he protected his face like an invaluable treasure.

Mentally, I refused to relinquish the internal battle I was fighting. It kept calling up the woman who was in my head too frequently. She was clueless to the fact that I was intensely attracted to her, although she was unavailable in every way possible.

I wasn't sure why I said yes, but she argued her way into my recon mission at The Greenbrier today. The one I'd turned her down from attending a thousand times. The same mission D assumed he'd talked her out of going on. My gaze landed on D who shook his head at me, his teasing smile on blast.

Laura stood at my shoulder, breathing down my neck as I packed the last few items. I shoved the binoculars and listening devices into my bag along with one of D's laptops.

She surprised the heck out of me with her disguise. The long-sleeve button-up shirt, the loose-fitting jeans, and tennis shoes had transformed her into a teen boy.

Unless you knew her, she hadn't left a trace of her womanhood exposed.

The mission was simple: go in, snoop, and gather intel to see if we could get eyes on Santino.

***

Laura

I finally wore Dax down with my bickering, and he allowed me to tag along with him to track our target. He stood at my back, his body so close the heat made me appreciate the winding breeze that swept past my face.

On the fourth-floor balcony of a random empty room of the hotel facing The Greenbrier, we spied on a group of men who Dax and D identified as DG6. They were the closest associates of Santino Dominquez. We'd been observing his men's activities and the outside view of the penthouse D was certain Santino lived in, for nearly an hour.

We had no luck getting a glimpse inside the penthouse, not even when Dax dragged me to the dusty, bird-shit-splattered top of the hotel for a better view across the distance. The drapes remained shut tight, and not even a glimmer of movement stirred inside.

I did get a glimpse of the helipad landing area on the far side of the penthouse roof. It provided an excellent escape route if forces stormed Santino's guards and entered his protected living space.

Peering through binoculars, Dax spoke into my ear, pointing out specific members of Santino's crew. He knew their names through intel gathered by D. It surprised me to find out the men were a mixture of races, unexpected for a Mexican cartel leader.

"Any of these men we're spying on could be Santino? How do you know he's not in plain sight and using a shadow to keep his cover," I glanced back at Dax.

"D has run all of their faces and more. They've also identified Santino by name, confirming for us who our target is. But we like to have a back-up plan," he stated, his warm fresh breath coating my face. His closeness had set my body abuzz, but there was no way in hell I was admitting it to him.

Dax and I came down from our perch atop the building. We had to get close enough to the men so the listening devices could pick up their conversations clearly. Before we started, I requested a restroom break.

After I returned, I tugged my baseball cap low over my eyes before blending into the crowd at the hotel restaurant. I chose the table next to the group. I typed useless words into one of D's laptops. My irrational mind typed words like, *"Fuck DG6. Fuck your cartel. Die all you sons-of-bitches,"* as I listened for keywords in the group's conversation about Santino.

No one paid attention to me because half of the guests scattered around the restaurant had laptops and digital devices too.

The listening device Dax had clipped to the sleeve of my shirt picked up every sound down to one of the men breathing. The smaller listening device in my ear allowed me to hear what Dax heard.

Dax sat inside the lobby of the hotel around the corner from the restaurant. For the first twenty minutes, nothing important was mentioned. The men bragged about their latest high-dollar purchases and the women they were screwing.

"How long do you think he's going to stay at the ball this year?" One of the men's questions caught my attention. He was likely unaware, but with the listening device, it was easy to discern his tone had leveled out and softened, indicating he didn't want anyone outside his table hearing his question.

"Probably only a few minutes as usual, but he expressed that he wanted to shake hands with Stockton. They have a big deal going on between their companies."

"You know how Santino is. He's protective of his reputation," another pointed out.

This was the kind of information we needed. We had audio confirmation that Santino would be at the ball, possibly shaking hands with a business partner. We suspected this since he was the sponsor, but hearing verbal confirmation solidified our plan and put us closer to taking him out.

We listened for another half-hour until the men dispersed. Dax kept eyes on them from his location. Two went up the elevators, likely going up to the penthouse. The other two headed outside.

Instead of moving along, I took a seat on a plush couch near the large spinning glass doors when I noticed the men waiting for the valet to drive up with their vehicles.

Dax swept past me and strolled toward the front door before he tossed a head gesture in my direction for me to follow. I adjusted my cap and shoved my pants lower. Since I had an ass now, I had to go up four sizes to hide it.

My eyes met those of the one I assumed was the leader of the group I was just spying on, based on their conversation. He'd talked the least, but the others often looked to him for answers. When his eyes locked with mine and an angry glare was directed at me, I lowered my head and hissed at Dax who was a few paces in front of me, making his way to the street we needed to cross to get to his car.

"I think I've been made," I squeezed out while maintaining an air of nonchalance as the cold gaze I met remained on me.

"How were you made? You make a better man than me," Dax replied, failing to hide the smile in his voice while I was being serious.

I dodged a group of three businessmen in suits who acted like they owned the damn sidewalk. Cars zipped past us and other pedestrians as they maneuvered their bodies in every direction, dodging cars and each other. Revved engines, squealing brakes, laughter, and shouting all mingled into one chaotic melody.

"I think he remembers me sitting next to them at the table," I continued, glancing back as we marched across the street. I widened my shorter steps to keep up with Dax's long-legged strides. Another quick glance back revealed the man staring at me with a deep frown on his face. Instinctively, I tugged my cap down lower like that would help.

"Laura," Dax called, getting my attention. "I'm going to need you to drive."

My steps hitched, the large tennis shoes I wore scraped the warm asphalt. "I can't drive a stick. I've done it once, and it wasn't a smooth ride," I informed.

"Good," he replied. "There's no better time than now for you to learn," he announced matter-of-factly.

With hesitance in my stride, I walked around the car and approached the driver's side. Dax had already climbed into the passenger's seat and slammed the door shut. Today, he drove a dark blue 1969 Mustang with white racing stripes, so there was no switching from standard to automatic like I noticed in his other cars.

As soon as I climbed into the car, Dax shoved the key into the ignition. "Start it and get ready. He's climbing into his car and staring in our direction."

The seat grunted as I inched it to the closest setting to the steering wheel and bent the mirrors to my sights as quickly as possible. Dax snapped on his seatbelt and sat low in the seat as he stared from his tinted window.

"He hasn't alerted his friend, but that frown on his face is saying that he's interested in us," Dax confirmed.

After snapping on my seatbelt, I flipped the keys, shoved my feet down on the clutch and brake, and prayed I would recall the one lesson Kadeem had given me in stick-shift driving seven years ago.

"You remember how to take off?"

"Hell no!" I replied.

"Good," he mouthed as he continued to stare out the window. "Left foot, hold clutch, right foot, hold brake, stick in first gear, ease off the clutch as you ease down on the gas. When the engine sounds like it's yelling at you, reverse foot order and shift to the second gear. Go now, Laura!"

"What? Wait! What?" I muttered, staring at my feet and the stick that vibrated in tune with the running engine. I stopped thinking when the cold gleam of metal flashed across my view. Dax drew his weapon from its holster.

Our bodies jerked on my shaky start, and my head ached, scrambling to recall what to do next. Was this Dax's way of getting me back for insisting I go with him?

The engine screamed for release as buildings and people in my peripheral area began to roll by, "Second, Laura. Now. He's coming after us," Dax yelled as he cocked his pistol, the metal playing a tune for the screaming engine.

"Shit," I cursed before I threw my foot down on the clutch and yanked the stick down and into second. The clutch stuck with a metal scraping roar as the car hiccupped loudly. I lurched so hard I white-knuckled the steering wheel to keep from slamming into it.

"Faster, Laura! Faster!" Dax yelled as his grip tightened on his pistol. "Take the next right," he ordered as my gaze caught the man chasing us, zooming past cars to catch up with us.

"Clutch and third," Dax yelled as he started to lower his window. How in the hell was he so calm while I was driving a car I didn't know how to drive with the cartel on our trail?

I threw the car into third, and it questioned my skills by bucking forward and lurching back before it decided it wanted to go. The car swerved around the corner and after all I'd been through we were only up to forty-five. After nearly clipping a parked blue Chevy Tahoe, I straightened out the protesting car and gave it more gas, preparing to take it up to the next gear.

There was a huge intersection up ahead, and although our lane was moving through the light, they were crawling across the intersection.

"Dax!" I called, not knowing where to put my feet or the car for that matter. The approaching intersection and line of cars was racing toward us instead of the other way around.

"Go around them! Don't stop," he yelled. That was easy for him to say—he wasn't the one driving. If we could make it past that intersection alive, it would lead to the onramp that flowed into the openness of the less congested interstate.

"Faster! Faster!" Dax yelled as the sight of the slower-moving cars up ahead grew larger in my view. I couldn't remember what gear I was in and didn't have time to figure it out. The way the car was growling, I needed to change something fast.

The light silver Acura chasing us grew larger, streaking closer to us like a silver bullet. I stomped my foot on the clutch and yanked the stick down to the fourth gear. There was no fifth gear like I'd seen in other manual transmission cars, due to this car being a limited edition Boss 429 Mustang. The car stopped yelling, but its roar continued—loud and demanding.

Dax's left hand gripped the dash as he steadied his gun in the other hand. He hadn't complained once about my shitty driving or the strong odor of burned rubber, brakes, and clutch.

As soon as the white car ahead of us eased into the intersection, I nearly ran up its ass before zooming around the right side to prevent the lips of Dax's car from kissing its white ass.

The Acura giving chase barely missed it as his squealing tires screamed and a truck he swerved in front of missed his side by an inch. The chase was on now, and I was up to sixty in a forty-five zone.

Now, I could breathe and concentrate on not hitting anyone, but the sharp curve that turned us onto the interstate arrived too quickly. I took it with the tires squealing and the car leaning hard on the driver's side shocks and axel.

As soon as the coast was clear, the silver Acura was at our side, the driver staring me in the face with his gun aimed at my head. Dax was aiming right back, ready to trade bullets with him.

"Brake!" Dax ordered. I stomped the shit out of the brakes, letting the Acura speed past us, and causing a cloud of white smoke to swallow us. By the grace of God, nothing was behind us. I hadn't even checked. I assumed Dax had since he ordered me to hit the brakes.

In my haste to get rid of our stalker, the slow-moving car coughed and burped, letting me know it needed something.

"Second," Dax called in my direction since I couldn't get the car to go faster or stop jerking. The loud scratching of gears sounded as I yanked the stick from fourth and shoved it into second to get us moving again.

"D, we are at Wayside Drive merging onto the 610 loop headed eastbound. We picked up a tail and are about to be engaged in a gunfight. We need a blackout on CCTV. Local police will be involved."

I didn't spot the Acura as I shifted gears with minor jerks this time. Where had he gone? Us swishing past cars sounded through Dax's cracked window. "Roll your window down," Dax commanded. I did as he said but stared in his direction for an explanation.

"Lean back," Dax ordered, his tone was loud enough to break the swishing wind but ominous enough to raise goosebumps on my arm. That's when I noticed the Acura, creeping up the passage meant for law enforcement. He turned onto the road, so he wasn't aiming to ram us but to keep up with us. Cars behind me and to my right prevented me from stopping, and I had no place to go but forward.

When Dax aimed his gun in my direction, I eyeballed him like he'd lost his natural mind. The gun sat less than a foot from the front of my face. He closed one eye, held a steady aim and inched it closer to my open window. I was too stunned to move or say anything.

The car was driving itself because my focus was on Dax. This crazy ass man was not about to….

The single shot left Dax's gun. I swear, time and space slowed and allowed me to see every action. The gun bucked, the silencer saving my eardrums. A sliver of fire sparked from the barrel as the bullet exited. The glass in the Acura's passenger side window splintered before the force of the bullet tossed the driver's head sideways.

The Acura veered off the highway before it collided into the thick cement Jersey barrier. The car crumpled into a tight wad of mangled metal, the hood and engine forced into the back, crushing the driver immediately. An explosion erupted over my right shoulder, flashing a blue and orange mixture that painted the sky a lively portrait of smoke and fire.

Thankfully, no other vehicles were involved in the crash. I was unaware of how fast we were going until my stressed gaze found the needle pointing at eighty.

I rolled my window back up, drenching the cab of the car in silence. My adrenaline flowed steadily; my breaths chasing throaty heaves before wheezing back in. This kind of tension was worse than having a gun aimed at my head.

My heavy foot eased off the gas as I glanced in the side-view mirror at the wreckage we were leaving behind. A thick cloud of black smoke polluted the air, and only a tiny piece of the car's silver finish was visible.

"You did well," Dax complimented as he swiped a number on his phone and placed it to his ear.

"I'm going to need a clean-up on 610 eastbound near Mykawa Road, single car accident. If it's attached to his body, the driver has a bullet in his head. Local authorities will be involved. Let them do their jobs, but get that bullet."

The fuck? I stared in Dax's direction, my eyes wide, my questions no doubt expressed on my face.

"You shot a DG6 member dead," I pointed out. "He's crashed in a fatal accident that the world is gawking at and turning into a live broadcast with phones. But that's not the kicker. Did you just call your famous assistant to retrieve a bullet from a man that probably looks like a bowl of chili?"

My thumb was aimed across my shoulder, although the sight of the scene was no longer in my view.

The car's roaring engine was the last of my worries at this point. "Your assistant can make this kind of heat a non-issue?" I questioned, not caring he was on the phone.

"Yes," Dax answered simply, aiming his words in my direction before continuing his conversation on the phone.

My face crinkled before I glanced back in the mirror. Why would he need the bullet anyway? I stared in his direction once again. He sat his phone against his chest, and I could hear the person's voice as he stared at me.

"Think, little assassin. You know why I want that bullet," he quizzed, knowing my question before I asked it.

I pointed at the area where he placed the gun under his jacket. "No bullet, no assassination, no spooking the rest of DG6. Just a fatal car crash," I offered, my brain latching on to this crazy shit way too fast.

His answer was the sneaky smile he flashed in my direction before he went back to his conversation on the phone. Now, I had an idea of what happened to the nine we left in that suite.

After all this time, D's initial warning about Dax was just hitting home. Who the hell were Beverly and I cozied up with? These men had the ability to get away with as much, if not more, than the cartel that we were running from.

On second thought, maybe the cartel was running from *them*.

Chapter Nineteen

Dax

Laura continued to impress me. She thought like a killer, so there wasn't much she missed in a world I assumed she'd get lost within. She would rip me a new one if I revealed to her that I was responsible for luring that Acura-driving DG6 member after us.

When I bumped into him in the lobby, I pointed her out to the man, telling him that she'd lifted his wallet. I had the man's wallet. My plan was not to kill him, but to test Laura's reaction under a different type of pressure.

Like a fool, the man had taken the bait and followed. His wallet hadn't produced any substantial findings, but he was one less cartel hound we had to worry about.

My devious ideas went up in flames when Laura and Beverly came into view. Tonight, we had reservations at Charlie's, one of the best restaurants in the city that happened to be located inside the massive hotel in which we currently resided.

Of course, D had hacked his way into their surveillance system, which was an added bonus that would give us a leg up if DG6 lurked. He also added us to the top of the reservation list. We hadn't encountered any other threats and believed keeping surveillance and staying on guard was enough to risk treating the ladies to dinner.

When I suggested sending them shopping earlier today, it was the first time I didn't hear a complaint from Laura's mouth. The hotel housed at least seven high-end boutiques that they visited. I'd have liked to offer them more, considering the dangers they faced, but their safety was our priority.

I didn't bother asking D what he was wearing. Like Aaron, D would put on a pair of jeans and a T-shirt and call it an outfit.

The dresses Laura and Beverly had chosen for dinner provided me another glimpse into their personalities. They had a superb sense of style and knew how to play up their best features in a classy way that I appreciated.

Beverly had chosen a teal-green one-shoulder dress, and although her chest was fully covered, the exposed shoulder led your eyes to that well-developed area. The lower half of the dress fanned out, kissing her figure, but not hugging.

Laura had chosen a sleek little black dress that dipped low in the chest and stopped above her knees. The dress was simple in cut, but on Laura it became unique. The dark eye-play with her makeup had me mesmerized. The daringly high heels she wore stretched out her petite frame. She was gorgeous in a way that gripped my attention and made her linger in my head even when I wasn't looking directly at her.

I was proud to accompany them tonight. A pleasant smile greeted me when I approached the booth after seating the ladies in the waiting area of the restaurant. D hung back, to do a last scan of the inside and outside of the hotel.

"Reservation for four, under Dax," I relayed.

"Yes. Mr. Dax, your table will be ready shortly," the Maître d' replied.

"Thanks," I called back to the man before I turned and approached the ladies to let them know we would be seated shortly. The smiles on their faces revealed their happiness to partake in something besides car chases and hanging out in the suite.

After D's arrival, we waited and lost ourselves in small talk that drew our attention away from how much time had passed. I returned to the booth, but instead of a gracious smile this time, a glare of disdain was lobbed at me.

"No need to come up. I'll call you when the table's ready," the man expressed in a clipped tone before his gaze panned to the ladies and D. Why did it feel like an iceberg had dropped on us? I nodded in his direction once before I stepped away to retake my seat, determined not to mess up everyone's night because I was so easily irritated.

One of Laura's famous eye rolls was gifted to the man as I sat waiting patiently. Two other couples were seated ahead of us, and I forced myself to believe that it was because we had a party of four and they were parties of two. I didn't have a habit of wining-and-dining the women I dated, so I was never met with any hostile reactions concerning who I chose to dine with or date.

After a few more hateful gazes were cast in our direction, I was ready to go off. My patience had evaporated. D was into something on his cell, and Beverly was his student, shaking her head at whatever he explained to her.

Laura eyeballed the host, and if the crease in her forehead got any deeper, I feared it might crack and start bleeding. I placed my hand atop her forearm. "Are you okay?"

"No, I'm not okay. We have reservations, we shouldn't be waiting like this. Host Asshole is making us wait because he doesn't like the company you and D are keeping," she stated what I was thinking but didn't want to believe. "He's probably a fucking republican," she continued, boiling.

"Laura, *I'm* a republican. You shouldn't assume the worst about a group by what you've decided to believe as truth."

Her sharp eyes met mine.

"Would you stop preaching what I already know and let me indulge in my misguided ways?"

My brow lifted before I shrugged. Laura may have been right about the reason for the host's cold shoulder but admitting it to her would only heighten her irritation.

"Dax, would you please use your white privilege and get this fool to release our table." she commented loud enough for the host to hear and to pull D and Beverly's attention. When the comment widened the eyes of the couple waiting, Beverly dropped her forehead into her palm to hide her face. D glared at me for answers.

I didn't offer a reply nor was I embarrassed because I was used to Laura's prickly attitude and unapologetic speech. My fingers brushed her smooth forearm before I stood and approached the host. I leaned across the podium where he sat high and mighty. My words edged out above a whisper.

"My name is Dax Marshand, from the Dallas Marshand's," I informed him, making his eyes go wide. "Yes, *those* Marshand's. If you don't show us to our table right fucking now, I'll not only buy this restaurant so I can fire your ass, I'll make sure you're blackballed in the entire state."

Although we got the royal treatment after the chat I had with the host, dinner was less than enjoyable. Every time a woman came along flirting with Laura, I couldn't keep frowns from darkening my facial expression. The fake smiles I presented were no better at hiding my displeasure.

D and Beverly had come to terms with their friendship and were having the time of their lives, laughing up a storm.

Laura was in her element, attracting beautiful women's attention. D would shake his head at me every time he noticed my pinched brow or the irritation I attempted but failed to hide.

However, when the lady pouring the wine decided to flirt with me instead of Laura, I noticed her tight expression and stiff posture right away. I entertained the woman, aiming to sharpen the sting in Laura's stalking gaze.

"Is that enough? I can give you more if you want it," the blonde pouring my red wine questioned playfully before giggling. The name tag that sat pinned on her over-inflated chest displayed her name was Karen.

I tilted my head, taking the time to allow my gaze to travel along her long legs and lean body. She was young, mid-twenties, and used to men flirting with her.

"If he wanted more, he would have asked for it," came Laura's voice when Karen leaned in closer to me with a ready smile. Laura tossed her linen across the floor, her gaze locked on the woman. "Now, be a good bitch and go fetch you a bone someplace else." Her tone was sharp enough to nick an artery and deadly enough to commit mass murder.

Karen's face turned beet red before she dropped the bottle and dashed away. Beverly and D had paused their conversation, their heads volleying between Laura and me.

"Were you born that rude?" My easy tone drew Laura's gaze from Karen's retreating back. "She was only doing her job." The woman was an afterthought. I was more intrigued by Laura's behavior. She rocked a finger back and forth between us.

"She didn't know if you were with me or not, yet she was willing to risk disrespecting me to openly flirt with you."

"She has a point," Beverly stated as D stared at me, but kept his mouth shut.

"You do have a point, Laura. But, you've flirted with the bread lady, and the salad lady slipped you her number," I pointed out. I kept to myself that I noticed her eyeing every pair of tits and ass in the place as well.

"He has a point," Beverly teased, her hand covering a smile. Laura turned her lip up at her friend before aiming her gaze back at me.

"That's beside the point. It was disrespectful," she proclaimed, her sharp words flung in my direction. I nodded before taking a sip of my wine to conceal my smile. Was she jealous? I hoped like hell that she *was* experiencing the emotion.

Minutes later, two men approached, carrying our orders on large trays balanced on their shoulders. I was grateful for the distraction. D and Beverly jumpstarted their conversation and Laura eventually ditched her attitude. However, I noticed she didn't flirt when the bread girl returned with a bright expectant smile in her direction.

Chapter Twenty

Laura

What the hell had I been thinking, acting like a jealous girlfriend at dinner? How could I be attracted to a man? Of all the men I could have been attracted to, why did it have to be Dax?

At the tender age of ten, I discovered my love for women after kissing the first girl who I claimed as my girlfriend. Our relationship lasted only a week, but I knew who I was and had never wavered in my preference.

Now, here I was fifteen years later, questioning who I was because of my attraction to the opposite sex. Not the opposite sex as a whole. I still despised men. But *him. Why?* The torturous realization caused an involuntary shiver to run through me.

The way he smelled: posh, smooth, and spicy all rolled into one unique scent was as unnerving as it was appealing. He looked interesting, important, and it hurt my mouth to say it, but handsome.

I even appreciated the way he invested in his appearance, always making sure he looked his best even when he was planning to deliver death. Maybe it was what sparked the attraction. He had no qualms with dispensing violence to anyone who stepped to him wrong.

He was the first man I witnessed stand up to Kadeem and still breathed. Not only that, Kadeem liked him well enough to open a direct line of communication. Each time he was on the phone with Kadeem, his teasing gaze would find me, reminding me of what he revealed to me about Kadeem's motivations where I was concerned.

Was I cheating on who I was because I couldn't control this stupid-ass attraction? Kendrick Lamar's voice filled my ears, but my inner-thoughts screamed louder than his captivating lyrics.

A familiar tone broke through the music and caught my attention, and it wasn't until the third chime I noticed it was my phone ringing. Reluctantly, I swiped my music off and answered, not bothering to ID the caller.

"Hello?"

"Laura, it's me, Ms. Noreen." Ms. Noreen Jackson was the grandmother of little Kenneth from the center.

"Is everything okay with Kenneth?" I questioned, my leg already jumping to contain the nervousness that had quickly filled me. Bev's eye caught my jittery leg and my phone at my ear.

She approached cautiously, taking the seat beside me on the couch. D had finally broken away from his laptop to hit the gym. Dax was on the balcony, taking a swim in the perfect water I'd dipped my legs into a few times.

"He's more than all right. We will be heading to Saint Anthony's Cancer Treatment Center in San Antonio in a few days. The hospital called and said that they have a spot for Kenny. They want to treat his cancer," she whispered, losing her voice as it started to crack.

Bev glanced into my face and gripped my hand, misreading my expression. We'd had so many joyless moments in our lives that it was easy to assume that things would go wrong. I placed the phone on speaker so she could hear the rest of Ms. Noreen's words.

"They want to admit him to the hospital so they can give him the best care. They even have a place for me to stay." She paused, and a sniff sounded. She was crying, but happy. "Laura, baby, I know you did this for us … I … I…."

Again, her voice faltered, and Beverly must have caught on to what she was saying because she placed her hand over her surprised expression and stared at me with a smiling gaze.

"I can't thank you enough for helping us. My grand-baby is going to get a chance to beat this cancer because of you," she expressed. The sheer joy in her tone filled me up and burst my heart wide open.

The peppery ache started behind my eyes as my rusted tear ducts produced a lazy flow of water. I gazed through the floor to ceiling windows that faced the balcony and found Dax, moving in the water. He did this. He was giving a woman and child a dream and most importantly, he gave them hope. He hadn't once mentioned or bragged about it, and I believed he never would.

"You're welcome, Ms. Noreen. I'm happy for you," I finally answered her. "However, I can't take credit because I didn't do anything. I want you to call me anytime with updates please."

"I will, baby. And I knew you'd be modest, but thank you just the same. You'll always be blessed for the things you do for all of us. I love you," she declared, full-on crying now.

"I love you too, Ms. Noreen. Kiss Kenneth for me," I requested before clicking off since my tears were on the verge of breaking free and spilling down my cheeks.

Bev and I talked briefly about the unexpected blessing. Once our excitement settled, and I sat quietly reflecting on all that had happened in only four weeks, I shoved Bev's knee to draw her attention from one of the Housewives' reality shows she was addicted to watching.

"I'm going to bed," I announced before standing.

It was a little after eight, early for my bedtime, but I wanted some alone time to think. My gaze landed on Dax once more, the moonlight revealing only the shadow of his back before I walked up the steps that led to our room.

I scratched my head and decided to distract myself by taking out my braids. They were good for another week, but there was only so much gel I could put on my edges before they started fighting back. I fished out my combs and brush and lined the bathroom sink with my shampoo and conditioner.

After changing back into my jeans and T-shirt I wore before our outing, I hung up the cute little black dress I'd worn to dinner. I flipped on the large television mounted to the wall, allowing it to act as my usual distraction to get myself through being stuck in this confined space with *him*.

I plopped down on the edge of the bed, tucked one of my legs underneath me, and began my task. I'd gotten only five of the twenty braids taken down when he strolled into the room. His quiet approach drew my attention when he stepped between the beds and sat on the side closest to mine.

He must have showered on the balcony because he was fully changed in a plain white T-shirt and black basketball shorts. A warm, fresh scent danced off of him and found its way to me.

He picked up one of the tracks of weave I'd taken down and stared at it before lifting his gaze to mine. I wanted him to say something crazy to give me an excuse to go off on him.

"Do you need any help?"

My curious gaze lifted to meet his before a deep crease folded across my forehead. "Have you had too much to drink? What the heck do you know about black hair?" I squinted at him as I continued to pull the next braid apart.

He stood, stepped over and sat beside me so close I reared back, staring, my rapid gaze scanning him up and down.

"I know more than you think I do," he stated, his gaze locked on mine. We sat staring at each other.

Something had changed. A weight had shifted. Shit couldn't get any weirder between us.

"Seriously, are you drunk?" I sniffed in his direction like I could scent the level of his drunkenness.

"No. I'm not drunk."

Curious to see what he'd do, I handed him the extra comb from the bedside table we shared. He took the comb, picked up one of my braids and went about his business of picking it apart.

What the....

My gaze went from his working hands to his face. What had gotten into him? He wasn't acting like his usual bossy self.

"You're being weird," I stated, attempting to cover up the strange vibes swarming within me. A veiled look washed over his features, so fleeting I was thinking maybe I imagined it.

"Seriously, you call me weird when you're the one who restricts herself to an all-female diet when you have fresh male at your disposal," he said, his expression remaining unreadable.

My lips twitched at his comment, but I forced myself to stifle my laugh. I assumed he knew my use of the word weird meant he was making me uncomfortable.

"You date a lot of black women?" I questioned him. I was sure he understood by now that my bluntness was simply a part of my personality.

The smirk on his face was laced with an arrogant edge. "I don't *date*," he stated before a blaze ignited in his gaze.

"You fuck and flee because you lose interest afterwards," I added for him without indifference. "I understand it better than you think. You're attracted, you hit, it's either good or bad, you move on. There isn't a real investment," I stated, revealing my relationship history because I believe it mirrored his.

"Can I ask you something?" He separated the weave from my real hair and reached across me to sit it atop the rows stacked there. I froze when his body brushed mine, uncertain about being close to him.

"Yeah," I finally answered, ignoring how my heartrate had sped up. I could feel it pulse in my neck.

"Please don't take this the wrong way. I'm simply ignorant on this matter," he admitted and paused to await my acknowledgment.

I nodded, interested in what he was about to say.

"Tonight was the first time I've seen you interact with women, so I have no doubt that you're gay. But, you don't act or dress like any of the more dominant lesbians I've encountered. I don't understand the way you are in comparison to what I think I know," he disclosed, his confusion apparent.

My tension eased, grateful he was only trying to understand me.

"I date women. Therefore, I'm going to have some fashion sense. When I was younger, I used to dress like a boy. I had a short haircut and everything. It wasn't until I did a favor for a friend of mine, when I was sixteen, that my view of myself was altered. I'll always fight for the underdog. It's the one area where I don't care if you're a man or woman, boy or girl. I hate bullies. I hate seeing people get picked on that can't or don't know how to fight for themselves."

After a deep sigh, I continued. "There was this boy, Michael Davison. The kids always picked on him because he was poor and he didn't have nice clothes. Like mine, his mother was a well-known crack addict. He told me he wanted to go to his senior prom, but he knew he'd never work up the nerve to ask any of the girls. He was sure they'd be too ashamed to attend with him or laugh in his face if he asked. He desperately wanted this one good thing from his horrible experience in high school. He was a senior and I was a junior, and I agreed to go with him. When the time came, I picked a nice dress, let Beverly do my hair, and makeup, and damn near scared the shit out of myself after seeing the results. What surprised me most was I didn't dislike what I saw in the mirror."

Thinking about Michael's reaction to my reveal drew an instant smile. "When Michael saw me, he didn't even recognize me. I'd never seen anyone smile as much as he smiled that night. He understood that I didn't want him romantically, but he told me all night that he was the luckiest boy in high school because he was at his senior prom with the prettiest girl in the school. I assumed he was being nice because I agreed to go with him. But, a lot of the other students reacted the same way."

Was I really sharing one of my corny high school stories with this man? That fact alone was a telling sign that kept reminding me Dax and I shared a connection. I blinked the disturbing idea away so I could finish the story.

"Michael had more popularity in one night than he'd had in four years of high school, and I ended up discovering a different side of myself. I was hit on that night by girls and guys. It helped me understand that I didn't have to make myself into the image of a male to date girls. Since that night, I embraced being a woman. Crazy thing was I pulled way more women embracing my femininity."

Dax had taken down three of my braids while listening to my story and was working on the fourth.

"I love that story because you discovered a part of yourself that you'd chosen to hide or more so, believed you had to hide."

I nodded, recalling the night had meant as much to me as it had to Michael.

"You have beautiful hair," he complimented as he pulled at the shoulder-length frizzy mess emerging from the braids we were nearly finished taking out. My sandy hair was undecided, a texture I could wear natural, but was stuck between wanting to be curly and wanting to be an afro.

"Thank you," I finally replied to his compliment, not meeting his gaze. "How do you know about weaves and taking it out?" I questioned, eager for his answer.

"I date a lot of women, but there was this one. Pretty, long auburn hair, gorgeous body. We went at it hot and heavy, to the point where I gripped her hair. She was into the sex as much as I was so she must have forgotten to warn me about her hair. I gripped a hand full and yanked."

My mouth dropped open as his wide smile met mine. "No," I replied to his smiling expression, shaking my head.

"Yes," he replied. "I yanked her wig off. It wasn't a full wig, but a half. Back then I was in my early twenties and I didn't know anything about partial wigs, extensions, or weaves. At first, having that much of her hair in my hand had me thinking I'd scalped her. Finding that she wasn't concerned was a relief."

My laughter sounded as I imagined him snatching the woman's wig in the middle of fucking her.

"So, did you stop when you snatched out her partial?"

"Hell, no. It messed up my stroke a little bit, but I was on a mission, and she didn't stop me. She actually jerked the wig from my hand and tossed it when I didn't know what to do with it. After that night, I learned all I needed to know about lace fronts, partials, sew-ins, and braids."

I was hooting and howling with laughter with the knowledge that Dax was actually funny and proving bit by bit how much I misjudged him.

"That's a good one, Dax. Funny," I stated, noticing I called him by his name and not by one of the nicknames I usually called him. For the first time, we shared parts of ourselves with each other and genuine laughter.

Chapter Twenty-one

Laura

After some coaxing on my part, Dax promised to get with D and make plans, so we would get another chance to check up on activities at the centers. He hadn't put up as big a fight as I expected. I assume it was the hair-bonding experience that softened him up.

Once I was done with my shower and hair, I was ready for a good night's rest. I'd managed to coax my hair into a sleek ponytail and my scalp felt like it had been re-born. A silly smile kept popping up at the notion of reuniting with the kids soon.

I sensed Dax's eyes on me as soon as I walked across the room. I was dressed in a new, silk pajama short set, compliments of Dax's black card. When he gave Beverly and me his credit card and set us loose inside the hotel shopping plaza, we were not modest in our spending, especially when he insisted we not be.

I didn't make enough to afford real silk, so I enjoyed the soft slide of it against my skin. I was, to a certain extent, allowing myself to be spoiled for the first time in my life. The lingering threat of imminent death made me think twice about squandering certain opportunities.

At the side of my bed near the wall, I placed my shampoo and conditioner back into my toiletry bag before sliding it back under the bed. When I stood, I jumped because Dax was standing right behind me.

"Dax, what the fuck? Are you trying to give me a damn heart attack?" I stared, my brow tightly clenched. I was beginning to understand why they called him the silent assassin. The man could sneak up on his own damn shadow.

"My apologies. I didn't mean to scare you. I have one more question for you," he stated, but his stormy gaze revealed more than just a question.

"You couldn't ask from your side of the room?" I squinted, trying to figure out his reason for venturing into my territory. Again.

"One question and an honest answer, and I'll leave you alone," he assured.

"Okay. Get on with this question." I urged, ready for him to leave my personal space.

He took a step closer, boxing me in with the bed to my right and walls to my back and left sides. His shining gray eyes were glued to mine as he inched closer still, causing the air around me to stiffen. I'd never been a wimp, so I stood my ground, waiting to see what this crazy man wanted.

We were damn near face to face at this point, with me glancing up, and him peering down at me. The heavy silence that filled the room was broken by our heavy breathing and flickering gazes.

I didn't know how much more of his weirdness I could take. I'd never wanted a man, but there was something about Dax that stirred cravings I never expected to feel. Like now, my heat level wasn't just hot. Lava flares were flaming around me.

His words broke into my inflamed mind. "Are you attracted to me, Laura?" His gray eyes narrowed and focused on me with firm intensity, turning my heart into a fist that pounded against my chest cavity.

"No," breezed past my lips way too fast.

He shook his head, not accepting my answer before taking another step. This time I did back up, but the wall stopped me.

"I don't believe you," he whispered, his words sweeping warmly across my face. "The military trained me to notice things," he reminded me. "I've respected your choices, but I'm afraid I've run out of the will to keep pretending."

He tapped a finger against his temple. "I can't get you out of my head, and I can no longer suppress my need to know what your mouth tastes like, to know what your body feels like against mine, to know what it feels like to be inside you."

I gasped, struggling for each breath as the chaotic pulse within me started to vibrate across my skin. Every stitch of clothes on me had gone up in flames. Next thing I knew, his warm lips were on mine, and mine yielded before gliding against his.

The combination of his soft lips and firm body pressed against mine sent an ache of passion thundering through me. There was nothing rushed about the kiss. It was slow and deliberate, impacting and meaningful in a way that it would be remembered.

I breathed him in, taking in his heady scent, one I'd already admitted to liking. My heart pounded, the thumping beat igniting the pulse in my neck and the one between my legs. He was kissing my lips, but the thrilling impact traveled all over my body. When his eager wet tongue slid across my lips, enticing me to open my mouth, I snapped out of the spell and came to my senses.

My fingers crawled over rippling abs and taut skin. His body heat poured through his shirt and into my shaking hand. I splayed my fingers over his strong chest and found the strength to shove him off me.

"Are you crazy? Get away from me!" I yelled, breathless.

My mind was set ablaze with the memory of what we were just doing. My brief moment of insanity was replaced by a burning anger that raced through me and came alive in my head. My palm opened and I reached my right hand way back into another dimension and sent it across his cheek so hard that his head jerked forcefully to the side. He kept his head turned, his eyes closed, as he allowed the sting of my slap to dissolve.

I couldn't believe I smacked him, but he deserved it, and I was ready to face whatever would follow. He turned and stared at me, moving his jaw left and right, to regain sensation in it. The hand I used to smack him stung as tingly sparks of pain flared inside my palm.

Back against the wall, my chest heaved up and down from his attack as I waited to meet his fury. However, it wasn't anger or fury that greeted me. A smile spread slowly across his lips, even as my handprint started to take shape on his face.

His fingers traced the edge of my jaw, making me shiver. "You enjoyed my kiss. I can tell by the look in your eyes that I've made your pussy wet." His tone was blunt and arrogant, him speaking the facts as he believed them.

He pressed his hand against the wall on either side of my head, boxing me in, before he lowered his head and placed his lips against my ear. "Your body is begging me to fuck you," he whispered. His hot words sent a sharp pang of lust through me, and I choked down a moan. I believe this was the first time he'd cursed out loud—one of those men who saved his misbehaving for the bedroom.

He nipped my earlobe before he drew back enough to glance into my eyes. His gaze dropped to my nipples, which were hard enough that my bra didn't hide the print of them pressing against my top. I didn't give a damn what my body expressed, I wasn't conceding to whatever plans he was hatching in his delusional brain.

"Don't flatter yourself, Richie Rich. Before I fuck you, I'd go to hell with my pussy dripping gas." At this point, I didn't know if I was turned on or angry. The line kept blurring, and his closeness was driving me nuts.

He struck again, with smooth aggression. His lips were on mine so fast I swallowed my gasp. His tongue slipped into my mouth, and I didn't fight it. I couldn't or maybe I didn't want to. He thrust his body against mine, pinning me to the wall as his hardness sank into my stomach.

His hands were everywhere, caressing, squeezing, and rubbing. When he filled his palms with my ass and lifted, my legs went around his waist. The strong pulsing beat between my legs was being stroked by the big bulge he nudged me with. The force of the urges roaming inside of me overrode my good sense as I leaned into him, deepening our kiss.

Never had I allowed a man this type of control. I never wanted one this close to me. My top was being slipped off as his lips plied mine, and his tongue explored the inside of my mouth. Our faces parted long enough for my top to be slipped over my head.

His lips didn't return to my mouth, but to my neck as he rained kisses down the side and kept dipping lower until he pinched my hard bra-covered nipple between his lips. A loud gasp escaped when a strong shot of pleasure hit me in the chest and shot down to my pussy, making me moan.

My legs were anchored around him so tightly, there was a chance I may leave him bruised. Keeping me pinned to the wall, he eased the top half of his body back, pinning my lust heavy gaze before he gripped the neck of his T-shirt and yanked it up. I helped, catching the bottom front and lifting it, working it over his head and off his left arm once he freed it from the right.

My gaze landed on a large tattoo, a partial sleeve that covered most of his right shoulder and bicep. It had something to do with the military. I wasn't fully functional at this point to really decipher the design.

Was I about to do this? I'd never had the curious urges I was experiencing. The idea of being with a man was usually enough to make me nauseous.

What was so different about Dax? I'd never thirsted for anyone before, man or woman. The cloud of lust that surrounded me was thick enough for me to lose myself within the smoky plums.

I couldn't do this. *Could I?* I needed to stop this before we went too far. *Shouldn't I?*

Dax's eyes found mine and remained on them like he sensed what I was thinking.

"It's just me and you, Laura. No one has to know if you don't want them to," he assured before landing a soft wet kiss on my lips that emitted enough of a spark to burn away most of my doubt. His lips traced across my jaw until they were at my left ear.

"Do you feel that?" His warm breath eased across my skin like a roaming kiss. Right now, there were many sensations surfacing. I didn't know to which he was referring. He had my panties so wet, they were sticking to me.

"It's passion. Chemistry. Lust. Desire," he whispered before pulling my lobe between his hot lips. When he caught it between his teeth, a throaty moan bubbled in my throat. "We are lucky to have this, Laura. Many never experience anything close," he continued.

His lips took mine again, except this time the kiss was tender, sparking with a passion that invaded my full body and caused me to whimper. He was using whatever magic he had to keep me from talking myself out of this.

Lust and desire were brought on by an arousing kiss. *His* kiss. When we sensed something extra stirring between us, we stopped the kiss and our gazes locked. The way he regarded me with knowing intensity caused me to drop my gaze.

Me backing down from something was not like me at all. There was this deep tugging of emotions and an unfamiliar need that lingered after we drew our faces apart.

Like now, the tingle in my lips continued, and the tightening in my chest wasn't loosening. The pulse in my neck thumped before it dropped and fluttered in my belly, keeping a steady rhythm. I didn't like this connection with him, yet I couldn't help feeding on it. I hated Dax for making me feel this way, yet I liked him for it at the same time.

"Let's enjoy this. Say you want to enjoy this. Please, Laura," he urged against my lips in a desperate whisper.

I drew my head back so I could stare into his eyes again, finally summoning enough strength to lift my gaze.

"I want to enjoy it. This *one* time," I stated firmly.

"This one time," he repeated my words with a hot whisper before he turned and moved us to the bed. He placed me on top of the mattress, unwrapping my legs from his waist. He didn't waste a moment as his lips went to my collarbone and trailed down my body until he was at my shorts.

I lifted without question for him to ease my silky shorts down. His lips connected with my inner thigh for a second before he dragged the material over my hyper-sensitive skin as his eyes feasted on me, observing every reaction.

He tossed my shorts aside as soon as he freed me of them. His hands returned to me in seconds, worshiping my body, making my hips sway for more of the kind of attention I never before allowed myself to experience.

He kissed the area above my panties and let his wet tongue glide up until it dipped into my belly button, eliciting another lazy moan from me.

"Don't move a muscle," he commanded before easing from the bed and walking to the bedside table.

How could I move? The world as I knew it had been shaken up and was spinning backwards on its damaged axis. It wasn't until the black and gold square filled my view that I noticed the condom. I'd never been this reckless and out of control. My head fell back into the mattress as doubt filled me once more.

"You're thinking way too much. It's too late to turn back now," he uttered. His voice was so heavy with lust it fluttered across my body like a caress as his hand dropped to his shorts. My gaze fell to the bulge there, eager to see if it was as big as it felt against me earlier.

When he dropped his shorts and stood upright, his dick sprang up, ready, deep pink, and *big*. It was bigger than my damn strap-on. My lips parted, and I swallowed before my gaze met with his. "Shit. You need to put a leash on that thing," I commented, still gawking. His lips turned up into an arrogant smirk, but he didn't comment.

Moving quickly, he climbed back into bed with me and took a ready position between my legs. He'd taken over my brain power, and I'd done nothing but let him do it. Otherwise I would have been making better decisions by now.

An overwhelming heavy sensation flared back to life in the core of my sex and had my eyes falling back to his big pink dick. He hovered over me, making me squirm before he lowered, meshing his hot body against mine. My nipples were puckered so tight they ached, and he noticed.

Through my thin bra, he pinched one between his fingers and gently tugged the other between his teeth. I drew in a deep sip of air as my eyes slammed shut. I shuddered against the sparks of desire his mouth created.

I could never recall a time that these impulses had surged through me. When his dick nudged my hip, a snapshot of it so big and imposing invaded my mind.

"I thought white men were supposed to be small," was the insensitive remark that slipped from my lips as he swiftly took my bra and began to slide my panties down my legs.

"That's nothing but a stereotype. You've been looping me into a lot of those since we met. And, I'll admit, I've put you into a few as well. We're learning a lesson in assuming," he said while accomplishing his mission of ridding me of my soaked panties.

"You can say that again," I whispered over a deep sigh. Next thing I knew he was sliding over me with ease, making our bodies meld together. I spread my legs wider to allow him to fit more comfortably as he kissed me, sucking on my tongue like it was a flavorsome morsel of caramel.

I liked the pressure of his weight on top of me, the heaviness leveling me out physically. When he dipped his head and pulled my nipple between his wet lips and sucked, my mouth dropped open, and I no longer cared about stifling my moans. My pussy flooded and an urgent need crackled through my core and rumbled through my torso.

His hand slipped over my hip, and he used his middle finger to smear my wetness. "Shit, you're dripping wet," he hissed out, before his eyes slid closed on a deep inhale. He ripped the condom open and slipped it on with expert precision.

I was flowing so fluidly the scent of my arousal reached my nose.

"I've never been with a man before," I reminded him before I closed my eyes and waited for him to enter me.

"I know. I'll go slowly," he replied to my outburst as he cupped my chin in his palm and turned my head so that we were face to face. He hadn't understood what I was saying. I didn't fear much, but I was afraid of this.

With my gaze locked on his, I rephrased my statement. "I've never been penetrated, not even with a sex toy."

This time my statement registered. His dropped jaw and wide-eyed gape remained on me. "Shit. Laura. Fuck!" tore from him on a harsh whisper. His body went limp on top of mine before he buried his face in my neck.

When he lifted his head, he stared, allowing his gaze to travel across our entangled bodies. My revelation had heightened his arousal if his harsh breathing was an indication. His dick was three times harder than it was moments ago as well.

"I thought lesbians used strap-ons, dildos, vibrators, your hands, fingers, fist...."

"I was always the alpha. I get off on getting women off. I never had a desire to do anything else," I revealed.

He didn't comment. Fully realizing I was technically a virgin. He started kissing his way down my body and teasing my nipples to the point of almost making me come. His kisses trailed lower and lower until his warm breath teased my aching center.

"I want to know what your pussy tastes like. Can I find out?"

I nodded before I even grasped what I was doing. For once, I was glad I didn't like any hair down there, so keeping that area manicured was easy.

He took a firm grip of my knees and spread my legs wider. He kept glancing up at me, eager for me to witness what he was about to do as well as assessing my reaction.

It started with another kiss, him introducing his lips to my lower ones. He extended his tongue, widened it and licked from the star of my ass all the way up to my clit. I rose from the mattress, chasing his mouth as a long and loud moan started at my chest and eased past my throat.

He took his time introducing his tongue and lips to every part of my pussy, spreading my lips with his tongue, before he licked up and down every seam. The shit he was doing to me drove me insane. I couldn't catch a full breath. The charged pleasure traveling from his mouth into my crazed body couldn't have been natural.

He was making magic with his tongue, and I had no shame in accepting the pleasure he dished out. My pelvis muscle tightened with each thrust of my hips to receive every flick, every lick, and every suck.

"Fuck!" I cried out when his tongue delved in deep, so deep he hit multiple hot spots that made my inner thighs quake.

I found the strength to lift my head and glance down in time to see one of my slick brown lips between his pink ones, giving it a light tug before his tongue eased out and delved past the area he sucked. His eyes found mine, continuing to watch me watch him.

"Your pussy tastes like ice cream melting on my tongue," he whispered. His words set my pulse to an erratic beat and caused me to overflow with wetness.

The way he placed his hands under my ass, aiming my pelvis up. He was like a cat, not a house cat, but a wild one, like a lion or tiger drinking from my bowl of milk. He delved deeper, circling his tongue into my wet opening. I didn't know how to react.

"Shit, Dax. Fuck!" I cried before I sipped on huge bursts of air. My legs started to quiver first. A sensational shiver traveled across the rest of me, releasing a burning pleasure that caused me to lose control of myself.

Instinctively, I rotated my hips, attempting to ease the building ache in my core, but Dax would not allow my satisfaction to end as quickly as I was aiming for. I think he enjoyed teasing me as much as pleasuring me.

I gushed so fluidly, the covers under me were drenched and I didn't care. I was lost in the overwhelming impulses that kept building until they yanked at my core, enveloped my body, and ripped me to pieces.

The powerful orgasm froze me before I was forced into convulsions and shattered all over again. I was drenched so deep into the pleasure buildup I didn't notice my hands were gripping Dax's head and shoving face deeper into my soaking wet heat.

He showed me he didn't have a problem when he came up for air with a satisfied smile before his tongue slid across his lips, tasting the remnants of my orgasm.

This time when he fitted his weight against me, I was better prepared to accept him into my body. He placed the warm head at my opening and delivered an easy push that eased past my lips, spreading them until the head licked at the entrance of my walls and enticed them to quiver with anticipation.

He eased more in, the pressure present, but not painful. The next thrust nudged the barrier that had never been breached. He froze when I tensed and seemed as afraid as I was moments ago.

My lips caressed his ear. "I want to know what it feels like," I urged, convincing him to continue.

His eyes widened at my words and a fire ignited within him, the heat pouring off his warm, hard body and soaking into me. He thrust harder this time, and something inside of me snapped the instant he pushed passed the only valuable jewel I ever owned. It was the one precious gift I protected with an iron-clad will when I was a young girl. There was pain, but if there was one thing I understood well, it was the unapologetic burn of pain.

It didn't hurt, though. Not in the way I was led to believe it should. It brought with it a spark of passion I embraced.

An unexplainable compulsion I would never get to experience again, began to flow around us. The sensation sank further with each thrust until he was seated deep inside.

He pinned me with his intense gaze while continuing to slide in and out of me. "It's amazing how your little pretty pussy can take this much dick," he gritted out. His words were part compliment, part male arrogance. I was too overwhelmed, too stuffed, and too intoxicated with lust to do anything other than moan out my pleasure and chase my next breath.

The heel of one of my feet dug into the back of his hard calf, the other slipped up and down the back of his strong thigh with each movement. He was being careful with me, but I didn't want him to be. I witnessed enough sexual acts as a child and teen to know this wasn't the way it went down.

I had enough sex of my own to know there was not much room for tenderness in the act. The begging and pleading for me to go harder and faster always emerged, and now, I was finally experiencing the why behind the urgency.

Chapter Twenty-two

Dax

How could this beautiful woman be a virgin? I understood that to her she wasn't a virgin because she'd had sex many times. However, in my head and understanding, she was untouched, a person who'd never had sexual intercourse and therefore a virgin in every sense of the word.

The news of her sexual status had set my lust to an explosive level and caused my dick to grow harder. I had to fight like hell to keep myself calm for her sake.

Laura was sexy as sin. The warm glow of her brown skin, the flawlessness of it, the curves of her perky tits, the swell of her perfect ass, and the lushness of her body against mine. Every part played a role in seducing me and left me no choice but to explore her fully.

My lips hovered an inch from hers now, my gaze peering deep enough to reach into her mind.

"You can go harder." Her hot words winded into my ear. She was asking me to do the one thing I was struggling not to do. I was being a gentleman because of her delicate state.

I lifted my head enough to level my gaze with hers. "No. I won't go harder. You're searching...."

A deep groan escaped when my easy thrust met her eager upward movement. I paused to align my sight with hers, aiming to finish the thought she caused me to forget.

"I won't go harder until I need to. You're searching for an excuse to say that this was bad, but I'm not going to give you one," I insisted before I restarted my slow movements, pleasuring her body to hopefully appease her troubled mind.

She was already sorry about us being together and we'd only just begun. However, I had something she didn't. Experience in pleasing the opposite sex. My mission was to fill her body with an overwhelming desire that would build until it blazed into uninhibited ecstasy.

By the time I was done, I wanted her to think about how soon the next time would come, instead of going along with that ridiculous pact that this be our only time together.

"This is between you and me," I reminded her when I sensed her thinking too hard again, doubting what we were sharing. My words put a spark of encouragement in her that I intended to keep stroking.

When our bodies rode the rhythm of the desire stirring between us, I knew I was in trouble. Fire raced through my veins, chased by unrestricted pleasure. Laura's little body was an emotion inducing, pleasure packed powerhouse that already had me obsessed.

Once her doubt dissolved, her body came alive beneath me and accepted every inch I offered.

"My God, your pussy. So fucking good," I blurted, my inner-thoughts forcing their way out of my head. I glanced down at our connected bodies, not believing I'd been able to resist her for so long. There was no way we could do this once and not want more.

My dopamine levels had rocketed off the charts. Laura was an addiction that surpassed the others that I'd experienced. Ten times as addictive and twice as deadly.

A series of low moans mingled with her accelerated breathing and spilled into my ear. Her seductive cries were the only music I needed. Her fingers gripped my waist, tugging at my back, as her legs spread wider to allow me to go deeper and intensify the high we fed each other.

We cried and moaned together as the sweet desire I had fought, and she'd pretended didn't exist, overtook us. Our heavy breaths and sighs filled the room. We weren't hiding from each other anymore, and for the first time since knowing her, Laura Parker allowed me to see her fully.

The smooth skin of her shoulder was pulled taut between my lips before it met my tongue. I allowed my teeth to clench her skin before sucking, the action keeping me from falling apart too quickly.

I don't know where the idea came from, but I couldn't resist voicing it. "So, how does it feel going to hell with your pussy dripping gas?" I questioned, making her earlier words resurface.

She squeezed her already snug walls around my dick, and a deep gasp flew past my lips, making my heart leap into my throat.

"How does it feel having your dick taken by uncharted territory," she asked, unable to resist countering my question and putting me in my place. My eyes grew wide, and an antagonistic spark took a hold of me. However, when I turned my hips at the right angle…. "Oh, shit!" was forced from our mouths as we caught the same rhythm and rode it for all it was worth.

"This pussy," I breathed out, unable to hold back my lust induced words.

"That dick," she returned, over a languid moan.

"Dax," her sultry voice stretched out my name and tickled my eardrum as she began to flutter around me below. Her spasming around me, and the sound of my name spilling past her lips in passion was my undoing.

"So tight, so deep, so wet," I squeezed out. Her pussy was strangling my dick in the best possible way. My orgasm hit so hard I lost my breath and couldn't call on the mental strength I needed to take my next. She was killing me, the only woman to ever set me aflame and reduce me to a pile of ashes.

I gasped, choking on the most intoxicating pleasure I ever experienced. This was the hardest I'd ever cum in my life. Helpless, I could do nothing but take the fierce infusion of passion, lust, and an emotion I didn't want to give a name.

After a moment, our breathing synced and leveled out as we clung to each other until the fairy tale dissolved and reality floated back into our world.

***

Laura

"Are you okay?" Dax's eyes had darkened to a smoky gray as he stared down, asking me a question I wasn't sure I knew how to answer.

As if I would ever be okay again. I was a lesbian who had sex with a man for the first time. To top it all off, I acted like his little slut in the process. I enjoyed it instead of hating it like I was supposed to.

"Yes," I finally answered, attempting to catch my breath.

Why isn't he getting off me? Why the hell is he looking at me like that?

The chaos in his expression was reflected in the tight creases of his face, inches from mine. The warmth of his quick breaths caressed my hot skin as we breathed the same oxygen.

"I wanted to be a gentleman, Laura. I promise you I tried. But…." A long, pregnant pause followed his *but*. The realization that his dick remained stiff and inside me hit as hard as the twisted glint in his gaze. His expression clearly said, *"You know you done fucked up, right?"*

"Dax?" I questioned, searching for any hint of the man I just had sex with. He drew back and surged forward with no warning, taking my breath, and not giving me a chance to recover it.

"I took my time with you because you were a virgin," he clarified his earlier statement. The impact of his thrust hit harder this time. "You're no longer a virgin, Laura. Now that I know your little pussy can take my dick, it's time to fuck."

His harsh whisper kissed my face as he fucked me harder, driving me into the mattress. His arrogant words should have spiked my anger, but they were turning me on.

His lips were at my ear as his hand cupped my face in a tight grip. "Since you informed me we can only do this once...," he breathed out, leaving the sentence unfinished. I was certain he knew that this was not what I meant when I said that.

I yelled out when he jerked me up and twisted me around so fast I was unaware of which way I faced until my mind caught up with the movement. I found myself glancing down at him, his back pinned against the headboard, me straddling his lap, his length already buried inside me.

"Wh... what?"

He cut off my question, placing his fingertips over my lips. "I was taught to be a gentleman, so I'm going to give you a chance to fuck me before I fuck you," he expressed before sending his tongue, gliding deep into my mouth.

He didn't stop his mouth play until one of my nipples was being tugged between his teeth. There was no gentle pull or light tongue stroking this time. This time was all about the joining of pain and pleasure in an unholy ceremony of sin.

With my nipple pinched between his gleaming white teeth, he glared up at me, pure evil dancing in his gaze.

"What are you waiting for, Laura? I need you fucking me, proving you're every bit as bad-ass as I know you are."

Shocked, turned on, and uncertain, I stared. What happened to the suit-wearing, well-to-do, goody-two-shoes? The challenge of his words kickstarted my energy and gave me a boost.

I placed one hand on his sturdy shoulder for leverage. He sucked the thumb of my other hand into his mouth. The sensation of his tongue and teeth and the suctioning against my finger added to my already heightened lust level.

Slow, wavy movements started my ride, testing the waters to see if I could take him this way without having to go through vaginal reconstructive surgery.

The fact that I never did this before surfaced, but my body instinctively knew what to do. The first few waves produced a lusty vibe that enticed me to go faster as he sucked on my tits like they were sweet ripe strawberries.

When I started fucking him harder, faster, and took him in deeper, he dropped my tits and leaned his head against the headboard, eyes rolling in his head. "Laura, that feels *so* fucking good," his words were edged out on a long breath.

I was being selfish, grinding out my own pleasure, but the knowledge I could bring him as much as my own desire spiked my lust to the boiling point. His body tensed beneath mine as his fingers glided across my ass until he palmed my cheeks.

His actions started to mirror mine, riding along with the flow of my movements. The tight pull of his abs and thighs flexed against my rotating hips as I allowed myself to feed on the lust that the deep swirling penetration produced. I couldn't decide what I liked more, the spikes of pain or the booming pleasure that kept beating it back.

"That's it. Fuck me!" he yelled as I allowed myself to sink deeper into the pleasure-pain swirl that built a solid foundation of another orgasm. His face turned up to mine as I was riding him like a jockey on steroids.

I was doing fine until he gave me the expression that did me in. It was so nasty and dirty. His eyes penetrating, his nostrils flaring, his lips slightly turned up at the corner as he gripped my ass and punctuated each of my rotating thrusts. We worked his dick so far up my pussy that my stomach mistook it for something it needed to digest.

I'd just had first-time opposite sex one act ago, yet my body and mind were set to a ravenous state I believed Dax had reached in and dragged to the surface of me. My pussy had starved itself for twenty-five years and now that she was eating, she was being a greedy bitch.

One, two, three jerky turns, and I blew the hell up, "Dax! Fuck! You fucking... Shit!" I couldn't spit my curse words out in an orderly fashion as an over accumulation of pleasure, pain, and emotions consumed me whole.

Moments later, I found myself draped over Dax like a wet scarf, my bones rubbery. My face was buried in his neck, my arms limp across his shoulders, and the front of me glued to the front of him.

I was afraid to back off his dick because I feared it had gone deep enough to be stuck. However, I had a more pressing issues to be concerned about. His dick was still hard.

What the fuck?

"Why the hell is your dick still hard? Did you pop a Viagra or something?" I questioned, my face squinted in confusion. His hands ran up my spread thighs before he allowed them to skim up my arms and nudge me back, putting a little space between our heaving bodies.

The first thing I noticed was that smug smile on his face. "All I need is the proper motivation. The sight of you makes my dick hard," he replied as his heavy-lidded eyes,

as persuasive as his touch, traveled over my sex-damp-
ened body.

"Speaking of hard," he pointed out before his dick
moved inside me and caused me to whimper and squeeze
my thighs against his abs. The lust-crazed gaze and hint
of determination in his expression revealed that he wasn't
done. I shook my head to calm the buzzing energy that
started to flow off his body.

"I couldn't possibly go again," I stated, hoping he'd
take pity on me. My hope was washed away when his sinful lips went crashing into mine. He lifted and flipped me
over so fast, I was given no chance to get up and run to
save what was left of my pussy. The man was going to
fuck me to death. I was sure of it. Was he punishing me or
was he proving how much I didn't know?

He positioned me on all fours, with my stupid body
conforming to his demands. My knees and arms were
hardly strong enough to hold up my own weight. He used
his shirt that he'd tossed earlier to wipe away the juices I
was drenched in.

The ripping of another condom wrapper sounded. He
cleaned his dick before sliding the new one onto his
length. Instead of running, my hot ass stayed in position,
staring back at him.

"You do understand, I've never had any of this done
to me before tonight," I pointed out, in case he forgot.

Smack!

The loud lick he delivered across my ass was his reply. Next thing I knew, his mouth was on my pussy, and
my damn body responded when I started dripping all over
his tongue. What the hell was happening? Was my body
repaying me for depriving it for so long? Once I was
drenched, he aligned his dick and prepared to enter me
from behind.

I needed my hands to hold myself up, but they were
too weak and I was unable to defend myself or swat him

away. I asked for it and was getting more than I bargained for. He didn't force it in. He eased his length in, bit by bit, stuffing me so full I ceased all movement.

Like the deranged lunatic he was, once he was sure he had me slick and open, he started fucking me like I'd smacked the shit out of his mother after calling her a bitch. My loud screams, if heard, would have someone calling the police on us.

My arms shook with the force of his thrusts, and I used my last bit of strength to lock myself in place. If I fell, I feared he might split me in two. The slushy sound of my slick pussy, the sound of his dick beating up my walls, and his balls and hips slapping my ass added to the out-of-control lust levels in the room.

The heady scent of our sex perfumed the air, a drug that kept our lust level on high. My legs and thighs shook and shivered as another orgasm bowed my sweaty back and sent shivers of lightning through my stomach before I was broken.

My arms noodled, giving out. I buried my face in the mattress, allowing it to absorb my throat-tickling screams. The rest of my body absorbed the hard pounding Dax was putting on me. Somehow, I survived it all until he came, cursing, and gripping my hips like his life was ending.

I couldn't recall how I ended up on the bed in the fetal position, but it was how I was lying when my eyelids fluttered open to Dax standing above me sipping from a bottle of water. His dick stared at me as well: dark pink, semi-hard, and hanging between his muscled thighs with pride.

There was an expression on his face, like he was deciding if he was done with me or not. If I ever needed a fucking blunt it was now. This was some life-changing shit I'd just been through, my mind relieved in one way and traumatized in another. I eased up on a shaky forearm and attempted to force my body toward the pillows.

"Let me help you," he offered in a sweet tone as he took my elbow and assisted me into an upright position. My desire to punch him in the face for being sweet after what he did to me had risen. He sat on the bed facing me, his weight jostling my sore body.

"Take these," he instructed. A glance at his open palm in front of my mouth revealed him holding two white pills.

"What are those?" My voice dragged like I was highly intoxicated.

"Ibuprofen. You'll be sore. I'm drawing you a hot bath," he announced as my mouth met his hand to accept the capsules. He must have noticed that my energy level was at zero because he lifted the water to my lips so I could drink.

Dax ended up carrying me to the bathroom and sitting me in a tub of fragrant, bubbly, hot water. He took his time bathing me as I struggled to keep my head lifted. The man had fucked me into a semi-conscious state. I was still fading in and out of consciousness when he dried my limp body and dressed me in a fresh T-shirt and panties.

He laid me down on his bed because mine was drenched in our juices. When he flipped the light off and climbed in with me, I didn't have the sense of mind to string any words of protest together. Instead, I shook my head, which didn't do a thing to deter him. He snuggled in, pulling me against him. I didn't have the strength to pull away.

He tucked my tensed body tighter against his, spooning me until I started to relax. He kept me pinned in his relaxing warmth until my breaths grew deep and my muscles released the tension I tried to cling to.

His warm breath brushed my skin before he buried his face in the back of my neck. The steady flow of his breaths lulled me into a relaxing drift until sleep dragged me under.

Chapter Twenty-three

Laura

I enjoyed watching the dancing flames of a fire. Something about the colorful flickers always drew my attention. No matter how minute the spark, a certain contentment and warmth would fill me. It was the magic of a combustible reaction. Carbon dioxide, water vapor, oxygen, and nitrogen coming together to produce a flame, something that had always been an inexplicable impossibility in my head.

Dax and I were similar to the chemicals that generated a flame. I didn't understand us. I didn't get how we could co-exist and produce something great. Something beautiful. Something in nature I didn't believe we should have been able to create.

We fought, argued, and had our back-and-forth banter, but when we let go of whatever doubts and anger resided within us, we were magic together.

I'd slept with a lot of women, more than I could even remember.

Was it possible I was saving myself, that specific part of myself, for someone I deemed worthy enough? Just like the beautiful flickers of a flame, I didn't understand the logic and reason didn't factor into my situation with Dax.

Although I cared for a few of the women I slept with, I never experienced those sparks and flickers he and I created together. I never cared about what any of them thought of me. I never cared if any of them were proud of me. I was certain none would risk their lives to save mine. This thing with Dax was suffocating and confusing and left me out of sorts, unlike myself.

I allowed shit to get out of hand. I let things go too far. How could I give in like that? I was never that weak, especially not where it concerned a man. He ignited a desire within me I never had before and found a way to ease the tension by pleasuring it.

"Aww!" I yelled up at the ceiling, glad that no one could hear me, including Dax who had exited the room. "Make these thoughts disappear. Make these absurd feelings evaporate into nothingness. I don't want any of it," I continued, shaking my head to pull myself together.

My eyes rolled at the low tunes spilling from my phone, Dru Hill telling me that somebody was sleeping in my bed. "No shit," I mumbled.

I rolled from the bed and dressed in slow motion, noticing it was past ten o'clock, the latest I'd slept in years. I hobbled, dragging myself down the stairs and into the living room. Beverly stared at my sluggish stride and immediately knew something was wrong.

Everything hurts. My arms, legs, hips, and thighs had gone through twelve rounds with a championship boxer. My fingers and toes ached. My hair follicles were sore. My curiosity had killed my cat. I promise, my pussy needed to be soaked in a tub of Neosporin ointment. I had no doubt that my shit was ruined, wrecked, destroyed and would never meow or purr right again.

Dax had the nerve to present a pleasant smile and greet me with a friendly, "Good morning." D followed suit, but all I could squeeze out was a grunt.

Look at him, acting all subdued and dignified, smiling and being polite. I wrinkled my nose when I sensed his gaze following my careful stride. *Asshole*. He knew what he did to me was unholy, sinful, and disturbing. And I couldn't get the shit out of my head. How sensational the sparks of desire. The flames of soul licking lust. How deep I allowed him inside my body.

I eased past him and D huddled around a laptop and sat on the couch next to Beverly before I laid my head in her lap.

"You okay?" The concern in her tone was apparent. I could picture it on her face.

"I'm good," I lied as I adjusted to get comfortable. Beverly wasn't going to buy that shit. Sooner or later, she would get to the bottom of my situation.

"Did you and Dax get into another one of your little spats?" She leaned in close to my ear, her stomach against my back. "I think he likes you," she whispered.

If only you knew. I must have liked him back to let him do what he did to me last night.

Bev wasn't done as her hushed words continued to flow into my ear. "But, since he knows he can't have you, he likes to keep up this little duel you two have going. Don't think I haven't been paying attention."

Thank the heavenly angels Beverly assumed it was our spats that had me sleeping late into the day and seeking out a lap for comfort. She rubbed my sore scalp and back with a soft stroke as she stared daggers at Dax's back.

A deep sigh escaped as I focused enough to concentrate on what Bev was asking me next.

"Are you sure you're okay? You keep zoning out on something." The concern on her face when I glanced up made me smile. It was good to know that someone in the world worried after me and cared if I lived or died. Before Beverly and Megan, I didn't know what it was like to have someone care about me.

With a deep sigh, I lied to my best friend a second time. I lied because I couldn't tell her what had really gone down. I wasn't sure if I'd ever tell her. All I wanted to do was pretend it never happened and make sure it never happened again.

"Yes. I'm fine," I finally answered. "He gets on my damn nerves," I continued as my eyes drifted closed, and I prayed for sleep to take me back.

"I'm ready for this to be over. A few more days and this operation goes live. We get to kill an original and put this manhunt to bed," I voiced, but in the back of my mind, I knew things were never that simple.

"You say that like it's so easy. You heard what the guys have been saying. The man is protected. He guards his face and identity like it's a sacred fixture. D says that's why we have a plan B in case the original plan doesn't work."

I shrugged. "Beverly, don't let these men's good behavior fool you. You don't get picked for black-ops because you're good. You get picked because you're the best. These men know how to play it cool. They take their time and learn. They are smart. They know how to be poised and calm under pressure. They've even trained themselves to be gentlemen. But, they don't fool me. Under that calm, composed, and well-manicured exterior lays a straight-up fucking killer. You know what that means?" I didn't give her time to answer before I moved on with my rant.

"It means their kill lists are probably higher than we can count, and sometimes, I wonder if DG6 is really who we should be running from. These men respect who they care about, but cross them, and you have pretty much signed your own death warrant. For some crazy-ass reason, and thanks to Megan, they like us, and I'm glad for it."

Beverly huffed at my words, releasing a deep exhale.

"Laura, I love you. I'd kill for you. You know this. But I need you to face one fact," she stated.

"What fact is that?"

"You are as bloodthirsty as you're painting those men to be. My logic might be messed up because of how we grew up, but the way I see it, it's justified when you kill to protect someone you care about or love against monsters like DG6."

***

Beverly

Laura was acting off. Being on the run from DG6 and being caged up with these men was taking a toll on her. As soon as her body relaxed and a few light snores sounded, I eased her head off my thigh.

I approached one of the main sources for her problems: *Dax*. Laura was right. He was an expert at letting you see what he wanted you to see, but I spotted bits and pieces of the hell I knew he was capable of unleashing.

"Can I talk to you for a minute?" I called to his back. He and D turned and stared at me.

"Sure," he answered.

He followed until I stopped near the front door, out of earshot of D. I didn't miss that he kept glancing at Laura as she slept on the couch.

"What did you do to my friend?" My accusatory stare met his and stilled.

"Nothing. What did she tell you?" he returned, his face not revealing a thing.

"She didn't tell me anything. But I'm not blind. She looks like you shot her dog or something. You know just because you guys are helping us, it doesn't mean you get to treat us any kind of way. I know Laura has a mouth on her, but she always means well, even if you can't see it right away. You have to be a bigger man, find a way to excuse that mouth, and see the loyal and beautiful person behind it."

"I'll talk to her. But, trust me, I've excused that mouth more than you could possibly know," he said. The playful twinge in his tone and the hint of a smile in his gaze melted my irritation, and I allowed a smile to creep across my lips.

I knew Laura better than anybody. She probably lost the fight they had and wouldn't be right again until she got the last word. Dax's smile mirrored mine until it dropped. Seriousness reflected in his gaze and put a wrinkle in his facial features.

"I was a little hard on her last night," he confirmed. "But, I'm sure you already know that if anybody could take a licking and keep ticking, it's Laura."

"You're right," I agreed. "Whatever you said, I'm sure you'll get it back with more gusto than you issued to her."

Dax nodded and an unreadable expression sat on his face. He wasn't eager to face Laura, but if there was one thing I was learning about these men, they stuck to their word.

Chapter Twenty-four

Dax

Beverly was always so sincere and carefree. She carried a warmth with her that rubbed off on others. However, the version of her that stood in front of me and defended Laura's honor would have dragged my soul from my body and set it on fire if I did anything to hurt her friend.

It took some convincing, but I lured Laura to the sitting area on the balcony that provided as much privacy as the bedroom we shared.

"Laura," I breathed her name like it hurt my tongue. She didn't say a word in return, merely glanced at me as I took a seat next to her. She sat staring at the city view, eating what I learned was one of her favorites breakfast meals: French toast with a tomato, cheese, and spinach omelet.

My smile grew at the sight of her eating the breakfast meal for early dinner, as she would assuredly be ready to eat again in a few hours. I was drawn to her, me, a magnet, and her, a ferromagnetic material—something tough like steel.

My eyes roamed before they lingered. I was unwisely growing an attachment to her and could watch her all day. Her sensuous lips with their kissable lushness. Her hair, a glowing sandy brown with natural red hued highlights. The curly texture had a beautiful wildness about it that fit her untamed personality. Her personality had grown on me as quickly as her dominating presence.

A deep breath filled my lungs before I lifted my face to the sky. The sun hadn't set yet, the temperature perfect with just enough breeze in the air to make you appreciate being outside.

Done with my mini-meditation, I concentrated on Laura. It bothered me that I couldn't read anything in her expression. We sat on the same cushioned bench with a small table sitting in front of us. I picked up a fresh piece of pineapple as she polished off her omelet and then started on the plate of fresh, mixed fruit.

There was enough space left between us to park a car, the emptiness there as a result of my uncertainty about our situation. I didn't think either of us was ready to discuss what happened between us last night. I certainly wasn't. I continued to process the emotions that popped up and sparked reminders of our bond.

I eased close enough so we didn't have to yell our conversation, but far enough to preserve her comfort. Her fresh scent, merged with her personal fragrance of cotton candy and wrapped around me. The scent caused me to fight the urge to hold her; against her will, I was sure, and pull her into my body.

My connection with Laura was on a different wavelength. I'd never experienced anything so authentic and rich with a vibrancy of life I fought to understand. No one, not even my closest brothers, had the power to drive a strong sense of purpose into my life.

Once, I believed I was meant to be the death dealer of the wealthy evildoers of this world, the ones who got away with heinous crimes because they could afford to do so.

Now, I contemplated life and what more I wanted from it. How could I make other's lives better without the incorporation of death? How could I help others find a purpose and make their lives matter?

My connection with Laura was as awe-inspiring as it was terrifying. Sex with her was out of this world, but there was also an emotional connection building and creeping out and revealing itself when we were together. I closed my eyes and a deep breath caused me to take in another whiff of her smooth, intoxicating essence.

I wanted to regain control of our situation, but it was beginning to feel like I'd never had any. I wanted Laura, and it frightened me that I wanted her over sex. I wanted to know the intricacies and inner workings of her mind. I wanted to know what would make her the happiest. Would she lay aside her established life as a lesbian to embrace a heterosexual relationship with me?

My inner-voice said no. Actually, it screamed *hell no!* But, I wanted to try anyway. Our relationship was deeper than sex, and I wanted the opportunity to prove it. For the first time in my life, I couldn't breathe. My chest tightened, my breaths went shallow, and I was overflowing with nervous tension. I desperately wanted someone I wasn't sure I'd ever get.

Being with Laura was...

"Are you going to start this conversation you insisted we have or what?" She stopped the reel of ideas turning in my head.

"I wanted to apologize if I said or did anything you didn't like last night."

She lifted a hand to stop me. "I'm fine. I didn't stop anything that happened, so you have nothing to apologize for. Besides, I know that Beverly talked to you and used that calm, easy-going tone she lays on while ripping you a new one at the same time probably prompted this."

My smile widened. "You're right, but even if Beverly and I hadn't talked, it doesn't mean that we don't need to talk. I figured you weren't ready and I didn't want to push."

"Thank you," she replied, eyeing me with suspicion, but not continuing.

My gaze locked on hers. I was unsure how to proceed and unable to overcome the heady effect she cast over me. I believed I was truly falling for Laura. I reached out but stopped myself, placing my hands on the table in front of me.

"Would you be willing to tell me what happened to you? What made you so tough, brutal, and deadly?" I questioned, changing the subject to beat back the emotions that wouldn't subside. The energy around me was so charged I was ready to talk about anything to muddle through it.

Her focused gaze was aimed at my legs while she contemplated my question. I waited, reluctant about a few of the decisions I made last night that continued to quarrel in my brain.

"From my first memory, I was subjected to my mother's neglect," she started, her words easing me. "Her inability to force out an ounce of care was something I just accepted, even when I found myself hungry because there was never any food in the refrigerator or cold because she couldn't keep the power on in the house or teased because I went to school with holes in my clothes, my hair not combed, or smelly because there wasn't any detergent to wash our clothes."

Instincts and observing the way she responded to certain situations hinted that she was likely neglected as a child. However, she'd managed to not let it hinder her the way she lavished the children at the center with care and compassion.

"By the time I was seven, I was stealing to feed and clothe myself. I was no one in a world that didn't care. The overlooked, the left for dead, the empty space no one paid attention to. I was what people didn't want to see and pretended wasn't there. One day, I was so hungry I broke into the food truck of the man who drove around our neighborhood selling plates. I didn't understand at the time the truck was also his way of selling drugs. I wiggled my way in and ate all that I could stuff into my body before stuffing my pockets. I managed to squeeze back through the crack left open by the small swinging window. Unfortunately for me, I was spotted by one of the dope man's lookouts. Shouts came from several directions, yelling for me to stop. The attention naturally forced me to run faster. My feet pounding the pavement made the only sound before a single gun blast rang out."

I was horrified at the notion. My head shook at her words, not wanting them to be true.

"The bullet struck my back with enough force to hurl me through the air. I hit the ground so hard it knocked the air from my lungs. The pain was so intense I shivered in an attempted to shake it away. The burn, so demanding, I lost the ability to move as it ate me alive. Someone started groping me, their rough touch jostling my little injured body. At first, I assumed they were attempting to help me, but instead their ugly words hit me as hard as that bullet had. *'Stupid little bitch was stealing food. Let's go'.*"

Dumbfounded, my back stiffened, as my eyes, unblinking remained on Laura whose face was aimed at the bright view of the city, her mind lost within the horrific memory.

"They shot me and left me there to die. I couldn't see them because I was afraid to unclench my eyes or even move. However, I could hear a group gathering to stare at me. No one bothered to help me, the overlooked, the left for dead, and the empty space they pretended wasn't there. They eventually left, every last person, and I remained there, scared, cold, with only silence for company. I knew how our hood was, people peeked from doors and windows, but as far as they were concerned, they hadn't seen or heard anything. I was a nine-year-old kid, shot in the back and no one cared. I lay there , struggling to breathe, the minutes feeling like hours."

Filled with biting emotions, I shook my head, my teeth sunk into my bottom lip. This explained her small circle of friends and why she was reluctant to let anyone into her life. Why she needed to be hard and tough, not only for herself but for those she cared about.

"By the time the paramedics arrived, I must have blacked out. I woke up to them moving me and calling for more medical supplies and equipment. I spent three weeks in the hospital with a collapsed lung and broken ribs. The bullet traveled through me and stopped just below the surface of my skin, under my left arm. Other than damaging my lung, it hadn't hit anything else vital. My mother visited me once and it was only at the insistence of the police after they gathered enough information from me to track her down. Believe it or not, that hospital stay was the best care, food, and comfort I'd received in my short life. It was one of the best things to have happened to me at that point. The way the medical team took care of me, checked on me, combed my hair. One even sang to me. It made me want to be that kind of comfort for someone one day."

Her weeping eyes and gloomy face tore at my heart. "I'm sorry this happened to you." I swallowed hard. I didn't know what else to say.

"You think that was it? I'm not even close to telling you how I became so tough as you put it," she stated with a huff of a laugh. I inched a bit closer. Laura was not going to want my sympathy, but she was getting it anyway. I placed a hand on her knee. When she didn't remove it, I left it there.

"One day, months after being shot, I walked into our roach-infested, Section 8, second-floor apartment to find my mother being attacked by one of her Johns. She had two types of Johns, the ones she screwed for drugs and the ones she screwed for money to get drugs. This one was beating her with no mercy, fist after pounding fist. I attempted to help, using one of the rusty candlestick holders that sat on our burned-out wooden coffee table. I struck the man over the head, but I wasn't strong enough for my lick to matter. He shoved me across the living room floor, sending me into the wall before I crumbled into a ball of pain. I crawled to my mother's room, and with each glance back, his fist continued to wail on her while she screamed for him to stop."

The fact she was telling this story, undoubtedly, one of the most difficult parts of her life, told of how far we'd come in our short time of getting to know each other. Although saddened by what she endured, I was grateful for her strength and humbled by her suffering.

"It took me forever to find the right shoebox, but I found the one my mother kept her gun in. I'd seen her pull the gun on one of her Johns after he screwed her and refused to give her the drugs she was fucking him for. By the time I returned to the living room with the gun, the man was choking her to death, telling her he would kill her and rape me when he was done."

My grip on Laura's leg tightened as a strong crease of concern wrinkled my face. Laura kept her gaze straight ahead. Her face had grown indifferent, hard.

"I aimed for his back and pulled the trigger. However, I caught him in the head which had his brains leaping from his head and hitting the couch as his body slumped over my mother's, shaking and twitching. My mother shoved him off her, letting his limp body tumble to the floor. His lifeless eyes were aimed at me, scolding me for shooting him. That's when I noticed bits of his brains were splattered on my mother's shirt near her shoulder. Instead of making sure I was okay after I shot that man in the head, she started searching his body for her drugs. I stood in place, gun hanging in my limp hand, immobile. I didn't know it then, but I was in shock. My mother, with her bruised and beaten body, stepped across the dead man, still leaking blood and took a seat on the open space of the couch."

Laura closed her eyes tight before reopening them, no doubt, picturing the horrific scene. The lump in my throat refused to go down as I fought to keep myself in place.

"My mother wasn't thankful that I saved her, letting me know she'd let go of life long before I came along. She sat on the couch next to the globs of brains, loaded her crack pipe and started sucking. The love of her life had been away too long, and not my wellbeing or the dead man that I killed laying at her feet were of any concern. I stood there until I thawed. I stumbled into my room and prayed that it was all a nightmare."

"Laura, I'm so sorry," I offered, unsure of what to say to someone who'd been through such tragedies at such a young age.

She released a deep sigh before glancing in my direction when I moved close enough that my knee brushed hers. I slipped my hand around her waist, but I didn't pull her closer, allowing my hand to rest there.

Laura shattered who I assumed she was, but this part of her filled in the shadowy parts. This part of her is what allowed her to walk into the darkness without fear.

"I walked into the living room and found my mother passed out, the dead body stiff at her feet. I woke her and was met with her fist for doing so. Before her eyes were fully opened, she was yelling at me to clean up the blood as she ran toward her bedroom to finally change her clothes. I was a nervous, shaking mess, but if I didn't find the strength to clean up the mess I made, she would beat me until I did. I threw up three times. I gagged, choking on the scent of the man's exposed head contents. My eyes watered and I quivered in fear and disgust as I scooped up chunks of flesh and bones and blood with a dirty wet dishrag."

At this point, I dredged up images of her as a young girl forced to kill a man for her mother and later forced to clean the horrific crime scene.

"My mother called another of her Johns, promising sex and drugs if he helped her with what she called a problem. When the man arrived, he didn't even flinch at the body. He aided my mother with rolling the man into the cheap dirty rug that sat under our couch before helping her carry him out. They took the body two buildings down and tossed it into the dumpster, knowing that a dead body in our hood, even if found, wasn't going to lead to a police investigation. As a matter of fact, the rug was worth more than the man's life."

My head shook back and forth for a long moment. I could hardly digest the gravity of what she went through and couldn't imagine living through it.

"My childhood mentality was fucked up for good by then. My mother never hugged me or soothed me or anything, and although I wanted it, I knew I'd never get it, not from her. Imagine living with a woman who you knew as your mother, but you didn't *know her*. I didn't know anything about her. I was never told stories of her childhood. I never knew if I had aunts or uncles, or grandparents. I never knew a time when she wasn't high on drugs. Did she finish high school? Who was my father? My mother was a complete stranger. I found out some of what I wanted to know from the streets, and they knew about as much as I did. Monique Parker was a crack-head hoe."

The psychological impact this must have had on her; I couldn't imagine not knowing the woman who had given me life.

"After I killed that man, I didn't think things with my mother could get any worse, but they did. Her drug use became chronic. Instead of just crack, she used whatever was available—meth, heroin, coke—it didn't matter. She wanted it and was willing to do anything to get it. Since she'd used up *her* body, she started to offer me up as payment, but I was smart enough to keep that gun close. When my mother couldn't get drugs, the one thing that made her feel better was beating the shit out of me."

Laura paused, and the far off stare she cast at the city were a representation of more untold chapters of her life.

"I received a lot of practice on how to take and appreciate pain. It was the one thing that I could always rely on from my mother. It was the one thing I promised myself I'd protect others from. I grew combative enough to fight anyone, but I never lifted a hand to hit my mother back. She deserved it, but I clung to a small level of respect simply because she was my mother."

Another pause followed a deep sigh and her pensive gaze lingered on a spot on the balcony floor.

"I had no idea how old she was, thirty, thirty-four maybe, but when my mother discovered she couldn't control me with beatings or curse words anymore, and that I wasn't going to let her Johns use me for sex, she allowed her brother, Dennis, to come and live with us after he offered her a couple hundred dollars a month in rent. Other than her saying so, I didn't believe he was really her brother. She'd offered him my room, but I refused to allow him to enter it. He turned the couch into his bed even with the reeking stain on it. It didn't take but a couple of weeks before he started to eyeball me with lust. I knew the look well, had seen it many times in the hungry eyes of my mother's Johns."

She shook her head automatically, but it didn't stop her words.

"Dennis repeatedly attacked me, each time I found a way to fight him off. Once he attacked me with my mother sitting on the couch too high to do anything, not that she would have. Another time, he slammed my head into the wall so hard I ended up with a concussion and spent three days in the hospital. He must have thought he'd killed me after the blow to my head had knocked me out because he disappeared for two weeks until he found out I was still alive. I couldn't get a break. I couldn't even be a kid. I was in and out of juvenile detention so much, the staff knew me. Most times I'd get myself tossed into juvie just to get away from my situation at home. I'd inherited adult situations and considered myself grown from the moment I could think on my own."

"Laura," I whispered as I drew her into my side whether she wanted my affection or not. She'd never gotten it from her mother, and I wanted her to know that I cared. I would tell her how much if I didn't fear her pushing me away.

"You wondered how I got this way, Dax, it wasn't overnight. By the time I was fourteen, I was in situations that made death as acceptable as living."

"And your mother? What happened to your mother?" I questioned while squeezing her tensed body against my side. She was retreating, and I didn't want her to hold back anything.

"Overdosed," she finally answered. "I found her dead a few months before my twelfth birthday. While most kids were fighting to escape the juvenile group home they often stuck me in, it was a big step up from the life I lived. I had so much practice being on my own that I was one of the only kids who knew how to sneak in and out of a group home without getting caught. I met Beverly in the same group home. There were twelve of us there. Beverly and I later met Megan at school, and we've been friends since."

She stopped abruptly, her gaze aimed over the balcony again, but I knew she wasn't seeing anything but what was in her head.

"This is why you're so dedicated to your friends and the kids at the club," I pointed out.

"The little ones," she said as a sad smile teased her lips. "They look at me like I'm a superhero when all I do is offer them a few necessities their parents either can't afford or don't care enough to provide. Food, a few decent clothing items, shoes, coats when it's cold. I attempt to give them a bit of the attention their parents refuse to give or don't know how to give."

She freely gives what she never received. Where had she learned how to bestow the type of compassion she was never taught to give and had never received?

"You're a better person for what you do," I told her. "You told me that you take what you are given and make what you need, and that's exactly what you do. Even with the hand you were dealt as a child, you've done more for others than the people out there prancing around calling themselves philanthropists. You're more inspiring than I believe you know."

"Thank you," she replied before I drew her all the way in and closed her into my arms. She allowed her body to relax into mine as she laid her head against my chest. There was more, I sensed it.

"What about the rest?" I questioned. "You don't have to tell me the details, but is death a part of what links you to the two people you are closest to in your life?"

Her body had grown so rigid I expected her to retreat, but she didn't. The faint trace of one word found my ear.

"Yes."

Chapter Twenty-five

Dax

Laura and I sat together and breathed, our bodies falling in sync. "Are you okay?" I whispered against her ear.

"I'm fine," she whispered back, her warm breath flowing against my chest. I knew she would be fine. She was one of the strongest women I ever met.

"Let's go back in before Beverly thinks I've done something else to you and rips me a new one," I suggested.

Her head snapped, her side eye sharp enough to cut down to the bone. "Wait one damn minute. I've just told you shit that I've only shared with two other people in this whole world and all you're going to say in return is, 'Let's go back.' Nope. Hell no! And no again. It's not going down like that," she barked.

Her eyes sat wide and daring, holding me in place. "You are going to sit right here and tell me how someone from one of the richest families in this country ended up getting tortured."

I swallowed. I hated talking about my childhood. My family shoved me into the offices of the best shrinks in the city, and they couldn't make me talk. My gaze panned over the balcony as I released a sharp breath, hoping the splendid view would drag me away.

However, Laura's intense gaze remained aimed at me. She'd backed out of my arms and put too much distance between us. She bent to get a better look at me and stared, waiting.

"It's just you and me, Dax. It's best to get it off your chest no matter how much you want to cling to it."

A tiny smile surfaced. "Are you sure you didn't go to school for mental health therapy?"

She chuckled but kept me pinned in her stern gaze. "I couldn't afford to go to school, but Bev and I pooled our money together so that she could go. She worked part-time, took all the classes, and ended up with a degree in social work. She'd come home and teach me everything useful. One degree, one price, but two students. All a part of our motto of using what we're given to make what we need," she affirmed as she released a deep breath.

With every passing moment, Laura was growing before me, amazing and shining in a light that she was unaware she created.

She wanted my back story, one I never intended to repeat in its entirety. The men I was closest to knew only half of it, and I'd known them for years. I was contemplating telling her everything after having known her for a month.

"I'll tell you my story if you do something for me in return," I tossed out.

"It's like that?" she questioned, one eyebrow stuck in the air. "I need to give up something, just because I'm interested in knowing more about you? The shit makes no sense," she muttered, frustrated.

Her head shook as she tossed her arms across her chest. I was tugging on the one nerve she had remaining. Where it once irritated me, I found her short fuse cute as long as I avoided getting blown apart by it.

"Laura, I'm not asking you to give up a kidney. I've never told anyone the full story. I want to tell you, but I'd like for you to sit closer, so I don't have to yell it."

A tiny smile peeked in my direction before she stood to sit closer. When she bent to take the seat, I stopped her with a firm hand across her ass. The action caused her to snap her neck around and glare at me. A questioning glint followed when she noticed me patting my lap as the place I wanted her to sit.

With great resistance on her part, I drew the human-sized stick of dynamite onto my lap, placing her so that her hips sat across my thighs, the back of her feet dangling at my left ankle.

"This is damn awkward. Just unnecessary," she muttered under her breath as I adjusted her on my lap. With the prospect of me telling her my story, she stayed in place, fussing the whole time.

Truth was, I just wanted to be close to her. I'd already decided that I wasn't going to persuade her to have sex again. By some miracle, I hoped that she enjoyed it enough to ask for it again. She was alpha enough to take it if she wanted it. Either way, I was willing to give her whatever she wanted.

She stared straight ahead which put her cheek inches from my mouth. I planted my lips against her warm skin, expecting her to pull away, and was surprised when she didn't. My forehead sat against the side of hers as I sank into the euphoric sensations her closeness wrapped me in.

Her small hand gripped my forearm, the other stroking my nape. One of her lashes brushed lightly over my skin. The smallest details of our closeness elicited a contented smile from me.

"Laura," I whispered, my breath kissing her cheek and bouncing back against my lips. Our gazes met and stilled when she faced me. This was it, the feeling-it-and-knowing-it moment. I was kicked in the chest with a powerful blow that prevented me from taking my next breath.

I was struck by one impacting revelation. My heart pumped emotions instead of blood. I connected to her special energy, the sparks sending tingles all over my body. I believed it would happen when I was well pre- pared for it, but like most things in my life, Laura had blown in like a hurricane and swept me away.

My gaze delved into her big brown eyes that stared back into my soul. There was no doubt, no confusion, and no pretenses in our exchange. There was no denying I had genuine feelings, overwhelmingly deep ones that didn't allow me the chance to convince myself otherwise.

When did this happen? Has it been happening since we met? How could I have overlooked such raw emo- tions? When had the tide turned from me lusting after her to caring so deeply?

There was nothing she could tell me to convince me she didn't sense the penetrating connection we shared. Her heavy-lidded eyes, intense stare, and harsh breaths re- vealed that she experienced every pang, tug, and tingle as me. The light tremble in her body mirrored the tremble that coursed through mine.

I took advantage of our state of heightened awareness and leaned in, my lips inches from hers, waiting. "Please," I breathed, begging for her kiss. I never begged anyone for anything, but for another taste of Laura, I accepted that I was willing to do just about anything.

At her slight movement toward me, I pressed my lips against hers, the warm, soft brush yielding her response to my begging whisper. The connection was immediate, the intensity taking my heartbeat from a pulsating thump to a hammering beat.

The warmth of her breaths, mingling with mine, the smooth surface of her lush lips, and the fiery impulses that forced me to cling to her, caused sensations to explode in my chest and drop to the pit of my stomach.

My aching hand coursed up her back, driving her closer, while her invigorating warmth wrapped around me tighter. My intention was to be closer to her, but this was better. Her flavor was sweet, enticing me to drag my lips across hers before delving deeper. When her tongue met mine on impulse alone, a shot of lust snapped our sweet kiss into one laced with a demanding desire.

We had to stop. We needed to. Once I went past a certain point with her, all the rules we set would crumble apart and I would end up dragging her to the nearest bed.

Thankfully, she was strong enough to stop our demanding desires. Our harsh breaths battled in the tight space we shared, her chest pressing hard against the rapid movement of mine, her arms around me now as mine were wrapped around her.

"How could it be so different?" she questioned, turning her gaze from mine and allowing it to pan the open space around us that I forgot existed. The sound of the city returned. The traveling sound of voices, honking horns, revved up engines, a lonely bird chirp, and the whispers of lost wind. I didn't hear any of these sounds while wrapped in Laura's hypnotizing caress.

"How could *what* be so different?" I asked, still attempting to get my breathing under control.

"Kissing a man. I assumed it would be the same as what I was used to." Her eyes squinted and reflected her confusion when they met mine. When they fell to my lips, and the tension in her face intensified, it drew my understanding. She was fighting to understand our connection in relation to the connection she had shared with women.

My head tilted before I sought her eyes. "Am I the first man you've kissed?"

"You're the first man I've done anything with," she confirmed. It pleased me that she wasn't ashamed to admit it nor did she sound sorry about it. The fists squeezing my heart tightened, humbling me in a way that reminded me of the special privileges I was being granted where it concerned my relationship with Laura.

"There are no words to explain how thankful I am that you chose to share yourself with me. I was a tad ravenous in receiving you because you had me so worked up, but I don't take it for granted. No one has ever deemed me worthy enough to bestow a gift as precious. You gave me one of the most valued gifts a woman owns." She searched my eyes for the truth I knew she saw in them.

The bond between us had been building and was now being dragged into the opening. We may not know how to deal with it, but we couldn't deny it. Our conversation paused for a long moment, but it hadn't sobered the heightened impulses stirring between us.

"Are you done stalling? Are you ready to tell me what happened to you?" Laura's questions put a stop to the depth of intimacy we were creating.

My hands locked around her waist, pulling her tighter into me. One of her arms remained draped around my neck, the other sat atop my arm. Having her this close to me filled me with a level of contentment, I never knew existed.

Chapter Twenty-six

Laura

This thing with Dax was getting way too deep, so I did what I did best, and displayed indifference.

He was reluctant to share with me why he was so deadly. Dax had deep demons, the kind that sent him in pursuit of delivering death to the powerful and wealthy. The kind of demons that made him disappear from his bed in the middle of the night. On many occasions I spotted his shadow creeping out of the room and attempting not to wake me.

His hands tightened around my waist as he prepared to finally tell me his story.

"On the night after my sixteenth birthday, I woke up to cold and darkness. I spent that night celebrating my sixteenth like some celebrated their twenty-first, partying the day and night away until it spilled into the day after. I stumbled around the unfamiliar place, fumbling through the darkness until I discovered that I'd ended up in a stuffy room I couldn't find a way out of. I couldn't recall how I'd gotten there and didn't remember being taken. The last thing I remembered was being out with my friends, drinking, and getting high."

His Adam's apple bobbed in his attempt to find the right words, and his warm breath brushed my face as I glanced away to give him a moment.

"I sat in the dank, dark space with time dragging on like days, dismissing the idea that it was my friends playing a cruel joke on me. After searching the area, I found that it was a standard-sized basement room. Tiny elongated windows, no wider than my spread hand, were blacked out. Only when the sun was at its highest, could I see rays of light peeking in. Those narrow beams provided the only clock. The area was empty except for a mattress, no covers, and a bucket for a bathroom. Food and water came once a day, some form of meat and stale bread."

My brows pinched, but I sat, balancing patience with my eagerness to know more.

"Ten steep wooden steps led up to a metal door at the top of the staircase surrounded by the cement walls that kept me prisoner. The people who took me never allowed me to see their faces. They would step down into the darkness to taunt me by telling me they were still negotiating with my family for my release. After a few more days of waiting, I started to wonder why my family hadn't paid to get me released. Had my captors been lying? Did my family even know I was missing? The first time they dragged me out of the darkness they cuffed my hands, sacked my head and led me to a shed. It was the first time they introduced me to the cutting."

He closed his eyes to the memory, making me tighten my grip on his forearm when he shivered.

"They kept their faces hidden behind masks and promised they'd keep cutting until my family gave them what they wanted. They were deliberate in their actions, so I could observe what they were doing before they delivered every single slash. The first day I received ten while they asked questions about my family I didn't know the answers to. Questions I believe they knew I wouldn't know like my father's business practices and business partners. A week later, after the first cuts were starting to scab, they gave me twenty more. After a month, I believed my family didn't care and they had chosen money over

TWISTED REVELATIONS · 223

me. As if things couldn't get any worse, the people who had me upped the ante."

The arm I had over his shoulder tightened, increasing the strength of the hold I had on him. Telling his story was a great source of distress for him, so much so, his body involuntarily reacted to his memories. The tremors, the light jerks, and the way his eyes would clench tight enough to tremble. They were actions I wasn't sure he was aware was happening.

"Sarah Morganson lived less than a half mile from my house. At the time, her parents were richer than mine. I knew her because I went to school with her. She was bright, pretty, and popular. Sarah and I weren't the best of friends, but we would stop and talk whenever we ran into each other. My capturers snatched her and threw her into that dark basement with me. I prayed they wouldn't do to her what they were doing to me. My prayers weren't answered because they did worse. They allowed Sarah to sit for three days and bond with me before they yanked her out."

The sound of the city murmured in the background, but my focus was on Dax. He'd dragged me in and made me care about his feelings.

"When Sarah returned, the darkness did nothing to hide her pain. She skirted away from me, yelling when I tried to comfort her. It took two days for her to trust me enough to allow me anywhere near her. She cried off and on the entire time, her weeping the only thing breaking up the darkness. When they came for her again, she begged for my help. I tried to fight, but for all my effort I was led to the shed, strung from the ceiling, and sliced open until my mind started to walk out on me. The pain...." He paused. The shivers running through his body were making their way into mine, allowing me a taste of his despair.

"I still feel it. I still find myself yelling out, knowing that it was in vain, begging for mercy, knowing that none would be given, and telling secrets that most teen boys would never tell a soul. I still feel my skin ripping apart, the blade sliding over the surface and leaving a trail of fiery aches, icy pricks, and stabbing pain that left me without the mental capacity or physical ability to control my bodily functions. They...." He faltered, unable to finish his next sentence. My hand skimmed delicately across his back.

"They did this repeatedly, ripping apart pieces of my soul each time it happened. I remember each time, remember every spot the blade landed. I can remember the hate in their eyes when they delivered each cut. I can recall the satisfaction they took in seeing me suffer, humiliated, and torn apart. Many nights Sarah's cries and mine colored the darkness. I suspected it, but Sarah revealed that they were raping her. They fed her the same story they fed me. That they were negotiating with her family for her release. I sat and listened as Sarah would comb every square inch of the dark basement room, searching for something to slit her wrist with. It became an obsession to her, to find something to end her life, and I was selfishly grateful she never found anything. She, like me, gave up the notion that our families would pull us from the situation."

A long sigh left him, and I comforted him the best I could. I squeezed his forearm to let him know I was there simultaneously rubbing his back to hopefully ease the pain he still harbored.

"I stopped counting the days, so I couldn't recall if it were day or night when Sarah came stumbling down the steps after they finished with her. We were each other's warmth, so she squeezed her battered body into mine and cried the most haunting cries I ever heard. I felt it. I felt her pain as deeply as I felt my own. Since we were without sight, we gently brushed over each other's cuts and bruises, the only salve we had to ease the pain. She begged me to help her die, and her pleading cries reached me in a way that I wanted to give her what she wanted.

"Dax, I can't possibly live through it again. It's worse than death. It's ripping apart my soul. My innocence has been ravished, turned into this dirty horrid thing that I can't live with, that I don't want to live with. Please, Dax. You have to set me free of this. You're the only one who can save me."

"It took hours, days, possibly weeks, of me listening to her pleas before I rose to my knees. I placed my feet against the wall, my tears falling as hard as hers. She scooted up to a sitting position in front of me. Neither of us said a thing because we'd talked about this in great detail many times before. However, I never imagined I'd actually have the guts to do it. Sarah knew about my martial arts training because her older brother was in one of my classes. She allowed her head to fall against my chest. *"Thank you, Dax,"* were the words she whispered before I leaned down and kissed her on the cheek. Placing my hands on her shoulders. I took my position like I was trained, locking my fingers around her jaw with a firm grip at the top of her head. Although I couldn't see a thing, I closed my eyes to summon every bit of strength I could muster and snapped her neck. No crying, pleading, or begging, she fell to the mattress instantly."

"Dax, shit," I uttered, unable to hold my tongue. I'd killed for vengeance. He'd had to do something much harder. He'd had to kill for mercy.

"I lay beside her until her body grew cold and stiff and I no longer sensed her presence in the dark space. She'd been set free of the hell we were cast into, and all I could think about was finding a way to set myself free."

The soft stroke of my fingers brushed up and down his nape as I drew my body into his, pressing tightly into his warmth. Was I providing him any level of comfort?

I'd never offered emotional support to anyone but teens, women, and children.

"When they came down the next day to get Sarah and found her dead, they pulled me from the basement along with her. Instead of taking me to the shed for torture, as I expected, I was led to a vehicle. With a sack over my head, I assumed they were taking Sarah and me to bury us. I was later slung from the vehicle and thrown onto the pavement. I didn't lift the sack off my head although my hands were free. I was held captive for so long that I just sat there with my head covered, hidden in the darkness I'd grown used to. Neither Sarah nor I was given any clothing to wear, so I was in the street, stark naked. A screaming woman jarred me, awakening my awareness. It took me a moment to discern that the woman was calling my name and a few beats more to realize it was my mother's voice I was hearing."

Dax squeezed me to him, his forehead dropping against the side of mine as he clung tighter. The sensation of our closeness scared me, but I believed it was something he needed, *we* needed.

"When the sack was yanked from my head, I glanced into the terrified faces of my parents. *"What have they done to you?"* was the question my mother kept repeating. She was afraid to touch me, could hardly stand to look in my direction. I was this hideous creature that my own mother feared. A twisted ankle and a broken wrist were the results of the car toss, but over time I was introduced to so much pain that I was unaware of my new injuries until I was in the hospital. It was when I got the first peek at myself and saw for myself why my mother couldn't look at me. They turned me into a monster with so many cuts that my skin appeared burned instead of sliced. I didn't understand why, but they spared most of my face, only leaving a few large gashes. My parents revealed that they were never contacted for ransom during the three months I had gone missing. It was the same with Sarah's family."

Why the hell would they take him if they didn't want money? My brows pinched.

"It took a lot of money, time, and resources, but my father found the man behind Sarah's and my abductions. A former business associate of my father's, Douglas Gonzales. The man believed my father and Sarah's father had stolen his business plan and cut him out of the deal . Douglas had established his own wealth without my father, but his bitterness was endless enough to seek payback against our parents by using us kids.

"With his resources, Douglas believed he was untouchable, but my father was relentless in his pursuit of avenging me. We never found Sarah's body and Douglas never outed me as her killer. He wanted us broken and he accomplished his mission. No matter my parents' attempts, no matter how much money they poured into shrinks, I was never the same after that horrific experience. I fought. I got into trouble. I got addicted to drugs. Pills mostly. I was even dumb enough to snort coke."

I didn't know how to respond to any of this. It sounded like he was talking about a different person.

"Today, I won't touch any type of drugs, not even if I need it for surgery or stitches. It took eight plastic surgeries before my mother could look at me without cringing. Doctors did an exceptional job of piecing me back together physically, but nothing could reconnect the emotional pieces that were ripped away from me. My family's money is what landed me under that blade. One of the reasons I use money so fluidly today is because I believe I've earned the right to. I take care of my appearance because I know how it feels to be a monster, to look like a monster."

"Damn, Dax," I muttered before releasing a low whistle. "That explains a lot about you I didn't understand. My initial impression was that you were an arrogant prick who used your money to influence situations in your favor. I'm learning that the things I assumed about you were based on surface impressions when your motive for what you do and why goes deeper than anything I could have imagined."

The impact of his story allowed me to see him more clearly, the *real* him. "You know pain personally. You know what rock bottom looks like." My gaze locked with his, allowing him to see the newfound respect I had for him.

At this closer view I saw the faint traces of one of the scars on his face. It was so faint along his cheek I don't believe I would have spotted it without knowing his story. His doctors had done one helluva job. The same money that caused him to be ripped apart was used to put him back together. I reached up and traced my finger along the faded scar. He didn't pull away and I believe it was relief resting in his gaze.

"You've experienced your own version of hell. You've stood in it and been burned down to ashes in the fiery pits, shaken hands with the devil, kissed the back of his withered, long-clawed hand—"

"Okay, Laura," he said, laughing at me. "I believe our pasts are what led to our connection. If you would embrace the connection we share—"

My finger against his lips stopped him. I refused to entertain him advocating for us to have a relationship no matter how deep our connection went. He would end up giving me the one disease I never wanted to catch. He was spreading it like the plague. Dax was spreading feelings, and I feared I was already catching them.

Chapter Twenty-seven

Beverly

Yesterday an urgent call from Aaron alerted us that DG6 decided to arrive a day earlier to Ansel's house than they originally planned. A fourth and unexpected target had also arrived on the scene in California: Sorio, the one who was responsible for sending men chasing after Megan for years and the reason this war was started.

DG6's unplanned move not only put Operation Take Six at risk, but our mission in Texas was also in jeopardy since we aligned our assignment with the team in California. We waited in silence as D worked to provide support with Dax's assistance.

I knew D was a valuable asset to this group, but I was only beginning to understand his worth when I watched him in Houston, making impossible things happen in California. When he talked about taking control of satellites and temporarily scrambling the California team's digital devices, I understood that he was someone a value couldn't be placed on. We saw bits of live feeds from the operation that popped up on D's laptop, and it resembled those videos where top government missions were being carried out by one of the SEAL teams.

Laura and I supplied D and Dax with food and refreshments, making them comfortable while they worked. Dax, in my opinion, had been hiding his abilities. He worked with D in front of an intimidating workstation, the set up resembling something from a science fiction film, with large external monitors, three laptops, and other attached devices I couldn't name. When D would call out a task, Dax would execute it on one of the computers. I'd never seen anything like these men. I never knew any men who had so many all-around skills and possessed that much knowledge.

D didn't disconnect with the team in California until they confirmed eliminating their targets and that the incident was contained from the media. Without television or social media influence, we were free to proceed with our mission on schedule. Our hope was by the time anyone discovered that four of the top men in DG6 were missing, we would have taken out the fifth.

We also kept in consideration that we had a team down in Mexico dealing with a sixth DG6 target. This thing wasn't just about me and Laura being targeted by this cartel family. It spanned different states and countries, making it bigger than either of us could have imagined. Seeing all of the effort it took to fight DG6 heightened my fear of this crew as well as what we may face attempting to take down an original member here in Texas.

***

Today, Laura and I flashed fake ID's to match the false identities D obtained for us. We entered the charity event without a hitch, strutting through the checkpoint in our over-priced dresses like we belonged.

At ten grand a seat, we were thankful for D's inventiveness in stealing us the identities of two cancellations. Santino was using the guise of raising money for the homeless as a cover to meet with his notorious associates who dealt in the sales of illegal goods and other illegal services.

The inside of the auditorium resembled a wedding party. Large, covered tables and chairs lined the main body of the open space. The color scheme was blue, accented with hues of purple and white.

Wavy blue material made up the ceiling and baseball-sized disco balls dangled from it like expensive chandeliers. Blue, purple, and white flowers accented the tables, sitting atop blue sparkling cloths.

Hundreds of matching flowers lined the floors, creating the aisles between the tables. The stage was decorated with a similar theme with brighter lighting.

Laura assumed the identity of Margo Carrington, a young heiress to her family's pharmaceutical manufacturing fortune. She wore a navy Giorgio Armani dress that stopped above her knees. The four-inch gold stilettos she wore made her legs look miles long. She knew how to dress for her body type and had the ability to make her five-foot-two height look six feet. I straightened her hair that tickled her shoulders, sleek and shimmering with volume. I did a nude natural makeup on her to highlight that beautiful, deep caramel skin of hers.

I assumed the identity of Juliette McCoy, widow of the late Fredrick McCoy, millionaire diamond dealer. I chose a royal blue Gucci dress. Although the dress swept the floor, it had a slit that reached up and cupped the top of my brown thigh. The dress was cut to give a tease of cleavage, but most of the focus was on the embellished waist and daring back exposure. My four-inch beige and gold Valentino heels made me one of the tallest women at the party and put a lot of male eyes in my direction.

Dax went as himself, the son of billionaires. Since the Marshand family was well known in the state of Texas, Dax called up his assistant and the next thing we knew he was on the list.

Our goal was to rub noses with the men identified as being closest to Santino and use them to reinforce his identity when he came down from his protected penthouse and attended the ball. Once we identify Santino, one of us would get close enough to tag him with a special tracker D gave each of us.

D assured that he'd take care of the rest, although he never revealed to Laura or me what "the rest" entailed. Our part of the mission was cut, dry, and simple. Mingle, identify, and tag.

We mingled, and although their stick-up-the-butt attitudes didn't suggest it, the men in attendance had sneaky hands they didn't hesitate to place on various parts of my body. I forced a gracious smile onto my lips, but I boiled on the inside.

Laura didn't give a damn about being courteous. She'd already slapped a few hands, but her actions did nothing but turn up the heat in this den of slithering reptiles.

The sight of Dax mingling helped to increase my confidence. The first leg of the mission was complete. We all got in without a hitch. My next step was to approach Eduardo Dominquez, the man confirmed to be Santino's cousin. Unfortunately, a crowd of drooling women currently surrounded him.

My tits hadn't failed me yet and there was no time like the present to put them to use. I poked out my chest, cast my smoky eyes in his direction, and prayed like hell it was enough to call his attention. The three mop sticks circling him failed to hold his fleeting attention anyway. After swiping a glass of champagne from a roving tray carried by a member of the serving staff, I took a sizable gulp.

When a hand brushed along my shoulder a few seconds later, I stifled a groan before I turned to face him.

I reached out for the hand he offered that sat mere inches from my stomach. His inquisitive gaze scanned me instead of paying attention to where his hand was directed. After taking a half step back, I took his hand.

"Eduardo. It's so nice to meet you," he introduced himself, his tone dripping with interest.

"Juliette," I replied with a gracious smile.

"I'd like to take you out some time," he offered, getting straight to the point and nearly making me spit out the sip of champagne I took.

"Can I at least find out what you like about me before we start going out? Or was that your way of telling me you're only interested in getting me on my back?"

I intended to play the submissive flirty girl, but he was the type who was already under my skin with that one sentence. I chose to speak to him in his language and based on the expression on his face he wasn't used to a woman talking to him that way. He liked the meek and coy ones he could manipulate and control.

A smile crept onto his lips. He was handsome, I'd give him that, but the devilishness in his dark stormy eyes revealed a different story.

"I like you. But, you...." he stated, giving me a once over. "You deserve a whole lot more time than one night. I'd make you my number one."

Wow! I was supposed to be flattered that he was willing to make me his main piece of ass. It took effort, but I pretended. I allowed my lips to part and flash my teeth, hoping it took the sting from my eyes. I shifted on my feet before lifting my shoulder to my cheek to drive home how *flattered* I was as I gagged on my unspoken curse words.

His gaze followed mine to the group of women he walked away from who had adopted the color jealous-green as their mascot. "They are eyeing me like they want to punch me in the face," I confirmed. He placed his hand in the small of my back before lowering his lips to my ear.

"I'd never let that happen. You are worth ten of those bitches. How about I escort you to the balcony for a bit of fresh air," he whispered. He lifted his free hand, aiming it toward the balcony.

***

Laura

If this man put his hand on my waist one more time, I was using the stem of this champagne glass to floss his teeth with. Oliver Dominquez was arrogant, even more so than Dax, who was giving the asshole as many evil side eyes as me.

He didn't like Oliver's hands on me. Was he jealous? A giggle escaped, and the douche bag in front of me assumed I was laughing at his corny-ass joke.

"Margo, you look young. Are you at least eighteen?" he asked, as his tongue swiped his lips for the hundredth time. Even if I was underage, this asshole wouldn't care. I nodded in reply, not in the mood to explain my age or anything about myself to this birdbrained fool. Used to being told I looked young, I believed my short stature and small frame had a lot to do with it.

"I understand your family is in the pharmaceutical manufacturing business. Do you work for your family?"

"Yes, but I dabble in my own side business. I'm more of a freelance head-hunter," I stated, glancing at the area of his neck I wanted to shove a broken piece of glass into.

My statement lifted his eyebrow, but I left it up to his interpretation.

"Margo, would you care to join me in my suite for a drink?"

"No!" Dax's harsh whisper sounded. The tiny ear mics D fitted us with had Dax and Beverly's voices going off inside my head like they'd become a part of my brain.

"It's the penthouse suite," he added when I took too long to answer. My sly smile met his slick one. "I'd love to see the penthouse," I gushed, ignoring Dax and D hissing, "No!" in my ear. It was about time Dax went and checked on Beverly before she ended up gutting the

bastard she was with. The tone she'd taken with her ad-
mirer was not one to be ignored.

We were supposed to wait until the famous Santino
came down from the penthouse, but I was about to walk
right into his house. On our way to the elevator, Oliver
and I passed Dax as he marched toward the balcony at a
swift pace to check on Beverly.

Chapter Twenty-eight

Dax

"Are you always this touchy-feely?" Beverly asked Eduardo, one of the two targets we identified as our links to Santino.

Laura's conversation buzzed in my ear, stopping me in my tracks. She was being extended a golden ticket to the penthouse, and my heart sank because I knew that telling her no would be useless.

D briefed us that the penthouse was fitted with specialized shielding that blocked most signals. Not only was she going off-script by going up to that penthouse, she was putting her life in jeopardy, subjecting herself to a place that would render her earpiece useless.

I headed toward the balcony as Beverly's tone indicated she currently needed me more than Laura. D urged me to stop Laura, but he knew as well as I did the request was useless.

"You bitches are all the same. Tease men to the point of getting our dicks hard and once you accomplish your goal, you leave us high and dry," Eduardo's voice sounded.

Without weapons, I'd have to subdue the man by hand if my vocal request didn't work. He and Beverly stood in the tightest corner of the balcony where other guests wouldn't spot them. The man was cornering Beverly. With heels on, she was nearly his height, but he managed to loom over her in a dominating fashion.

"Hello," I called to Edwardo's back, making sure my tone remained calm. "Is everyone okay?" I questioned, maintaining a non-threatening posture.

He turned to face me, keeping Beverly at his back.

"This is none of your business, buddy. You can turn around and head back now," he demanded, his tone as harsh as the deadly gleam flashing in his gaze.

"It doesn't seem like the lady wants your company," I persisted as Beverly's bright eyes peered across his shoulder at me. This man wasn't going to make this easy. His coiled posture and scrunched face announced his intent.

He reached back, his hand at her stomach and shoved Beverly into the stone wall behind him. I charged ahead but was stopped cold by the pistol he drew.

No weapons allowed, my ass.

Apparently, the no-weapons rule didn't apply to the Dominquez family. I lifted my hand in surrender as he dragged Beverly to stand in front of him. His gun, equipped with a silencer, was discreetly aimed at her side.

"Can you terminate the situation?" D's voice sounded in my ear. "Yes," I answered, calling attention to our volatile standoff.

The man tightened the grip he had around Beverly's waist as he spoke into his wristwatch, revealing he also had someone listening. His action confirmed what we already knew. The team who protected Santino was well equipped and prepared for attacks.

"First-floor balcony, now!" he snarled. My gaze remained on Beverly's, hoping she could read the words flowing through me, urging her to remain calm.

"You stuck your nose in the wrong business this time, buddy," the man confirmed, his crazed eyes meeting mine. His hand traveled up the side of Beverly's dress. He didn't stop his lewd movement until he groped her breast and caused her to cry out. I hated men who took what they didn't deserve without permission.

"And you, you temptress bitch, you teased the wrong man tonight," he growled into Beverly's ear while glaring at me.

Within seconds, approaching footsteps sounded before I was gripped roughly from behind, spun, and frisked. Beverly and I were led back inside the building. The hard press of a silenced gun remained poked into my back. The group of four surrounding us all possessed the main tools of my trade—guns.

They shoved, cursed, and threatened, but the entire time I studied them and their movements. They hadn't discovered yet that Beverly and I were impostors or that they were our doorway to Santino. It was possible that this mishap could work in our favor if it got my eyes on our pint-sized, trouble-making teammate and Santino.

59374 were the numbers keyed into the elevator to start it moving. When one of the men inserted the card attached to him by a plastic cord and hit 34, I stifled a smile. It wasn't smart to all be in the same space, but Beverly and I were about to join Laura in the penthouse.

Once I was shoved out of the elevator, my earpiece went silent. A minute later a short hallway led to the only thick wood door on the floor. Santino Dominquez's protection detail, the same ones me and Laura snooped earlier, confirmed that Santino sometimes resided in this building.

Two armed guards stood on either side of the elevator when we exited, and two stood outside the thick penthouse entrance door. D was right; Santino wasn't skimping on his guard detail. The door to the penthouse was opened in the same manner as the elevator: a code and a keycard.

Once the door popped open, I was shoved into the room, and the first thing to fill my view was Laura sitting on the large brown living room couch with Oliver, sipping champagne and laughing like she wasn't in the most dangerous place in the building.

She stared at the sight of Beverly and me, being escorted into the room. Panic flared in her gaze before she recaptured her fake smile. There was no sign of our main target, Santino. He could have been anywhere. The place was over five thousand square feet. We could be murdered in one area while our target escaped in another.

With the thick drapes drawn that would let the city view inside, Santino's penthouse was plunged into silent darkness. Even with the lights on, darkness pressed in with a suffocating force. The furnishings were all black and brown, and most of the tables and fixtures were glass. The place probably looked wonderful in the light of day, but at night, it revealed the characteristics of its owner.

Laura stood from the couch when she noticed guns aimed at Beverly and me, her gaze dancing back and forth between us before they landed on Beverly. "What are you doing to my girlfriend?" she shouted, staring at Eduardo who had his gun jammed into Beverly's side.

"Girlfriend?" Laura's new boyfriend, Oliver queried, his tone projecting hurt feelings.

"She teased me, so I intend to show her what I like to do to a tease," Eduardo spat, answering Laura's question before he pointed his gun at me. "Him, he wanted to be her hero, so we intend to show him what we do to heroes," Eduardo voiced his intentions, shaking his gun in my direction.

"You can't let him hurt my girl, Oliver," Laura pleaded, and the man contemplated her words, proving her potent charm.

"Let me have the girl, Eddie. You can do what you want with him," Oliver proposed, dismissing me like I was trash.

"Hell, no!" Eduardo replied, pointing at Beverly.

"If you think I'm going to give this up, you're loco." His gaze fanned down Beverly's body. If we didn't do something quickly, things would go from bad to worse.

Laura left Oliver and stepped within Beverly's personal space, stirring the tension in the room. The only reason she was getting away with that mouth and moving around in a room full of killers was because she was a sexy woman in a dress that had the ability to mess with a man's head.

However sexy Laura was, hands still managed to make their way to hips to finger their weapons. Eduardo watched Laura's approach with curiosity, not perceiving her as a real threat.

"Where the hell are you going?" He questioned her, his stern gaze blazing a trail down her petite frame.

She pointed a hand across her shoulder. "He may be afraid to stand up to you, but I'm not going to let you take my girlfriend and do ungodly things that only I'm supposed to do to her."

A few chuckles sounded and loosened the tightness of the suffocating tension in the room. The gun in my side wavered when the man laughed.

Standing behind Beverly, Eduardo smiled while eyeing Laura with more interest as his lust flared to life.

"How about I take you *both*?" he proposed to Laura. "Since you're so tough, I'll show you what I do to tough lesbian girls."

Before another word was uttered, Laura strutted up to Beverly, inched up on her toes, and placed her lips against hers. The gun-wielding men were as shocked as I was, watching them kiss.

The smile on the men's faces confirmed their interest, but none were as stunned as I was at Laura and Beverly's display. This was a twist I hadn't seen coming. Were they acting or were they more than friends? I was confused and oddly turned on.

"You're always pulling side-handed shit, Eddie. Fuck you!" Oliver yelled, upset because Laura had chosen Beverly and Eduardo over him. If Laura and Beverly were acting, they certainly achieved their goal because the men were distracted from their objective.

"I'm going back to the party," Oliver muttered as he flashed a fuck-you scowl to Eduardo.

Where the hell was Santino Dominquez while this was happening? Had he left the penthouse? Was he ever here?

The unmistakable whirl of rotors sounded, and the space around us grew quiet. It was so silent in fact, our erratic breaths produced the only sound.

"He's early," one of the men stated. "Get them the fuck out of here. He's going to flip the fuck out!" another yelled. They shoved us toward the front door, but I dragged my feet and faked a fall to stall them. Beverly and Laura caught on, staging their own little argument to stop the men's movement.

Eduardo was at the front door as the rest of us sounded like cattle being led out. Hushed urgent tones, barking orders, and shuffling feet all came to an abrupt stop when, a man I assumed was Santino, emerged from the back of the large penthouse.

His arrival sucked the air from the room. Everyone stilled, even the two who had taken a firm hold of me when I pretended I didn't know how to work my legs.

"Santino," someone whispered like the mere sight of him was a worship moment. He was in a button up, striped, blue and white shirt and dark slacks. His suit jacket was slung over his right shoulder.

Santino was not how I pictured him. Seeing him in person was an eye-popping revelation. His hair was dark, and although his skin was tanned, he didn't have conventional Mexican features.

Santino Dominquez was as white as me. Although I suspected one of his parents was a Dominquez, there was no Hispanic influence in his features. He was at least my height and either adopted or the non-Hispanic parent had a dominating influence on his genes.

D and I had seen that face before. D had run it through facial recognition and turned up a different name. Santino was getting away with being 'No Face' because he made his real face disappear behind a fake name and used a clever decoy when he went out in public.

His Caucasian features gave him the perfect cover and explained why he was so protective of his identity. He was also the youngest of the original six, a double cover, as many would have expected an older man. Santino was no older than thirty, although D confirmed that the young-est Dominquez should have been thirty-eight.

"What the fuck is going on here?" He pointed his pinky at the men. His deadly, roving gaze caused the men to hold their breaths. He inched closer, eyeing me from top to bottom. He stood so close his cologne cocooned me in an overpowering spicy fragrance that tickled my throat.

His visible shoulder holster, weapon, and clip of am-munition were on full display. He turned his furious gaze on Beverly and Laura who were being held at the front door before resting his attention on Eduardo.

"How many times have I told you about bringing hoes and strays in here? Get rid of them. Now!" He tossed his suit jacket across the back of the large couch and walked away, whistling like we were an irritating inter-ruption. He headed toward what must have been the kitchen.

How often did this happen? How many others had these men brought up to the penthouse and executed? They stood in place as silent as the night was dark and waited for their boss to disappear before shoving Beverly, Laura, and me across the room toward the balcony.

I knew from watching the place from an outside view that the balcony was a massive area that wrapped around the bend of the apartment, equipped with a full-sized pool, hot tub, and a few nooks and private sitting areas. Since they had the night for cover, killing us would be easy in this protected area thirty-four stories up.

An idea hit me. Did they do this to anyone not in their circle who could identify Santino? They would kill us with no qualms because we'd entered the penthouse and came face to face with a man who lived with no face.

Once outside, Eduardo held Beverly from behind like they were boyfriend and girlfriend, his arms draped around her waist. Two stood behind me as Laura continued arguing with the one aiming a gun at her. Oliver and another remained inside with Santino.

As soon as they shoved the balcony door shut, the wind suctioned it closed, giving us the sound-proofing we needed. The pool in the distance to our left provided light, unnaturally blue and waving across the area.

I didn't think. I acted. My elbow went flying into the underside of the chin of the man who stood at my right as the heel of my opposite foot stomped into the groin of the man on my left.

Holding his mouth, the man allowed me to seize his gun. Urgent yells rang out for me to stop and drop it, but their orders would be ignored unless they shot me. I didn't allow the men to step fully from the dark shadows of the building before I launched my attack. Therefore, their friends would risk shooting them to take me out. My knee was up in a flash, crushing the face of the one I relieved of his gun.

Within seconds, a bullet was in the top of the head of the one whose balls I rearranged, and two more bullets cracked open the chest of the one whose gun I took. On a spin, the barrel was aimed at Eduardo, who kept Beverly in a tight grip with a smirk on his face.

"Still trying for the fucking hero slot, I see. Nice moves, Daniel Wu, but you're not faster than a fucking bullet. You and these bitches are going to die." He wasn't too shaken up by his friend's deaths and hadn't even taken a second glance as I kept one in front of me as a shield and the other lay bloody at my feet. The shadows cast off the building provided an extra layer of protection.

Eduardo's steady aim nearly kissed Beverly's head. I pointed my weapon at his head in return, and the guy who had a tight hold on Laura targeted me. The dancing water of the pool made the dim view wave, so aiming and hitting your target with precision wasn't going to be easy.

If it were only my life on the line, Eduardo and his friend would already be dead, but I couldn't take the chance of them harming Beverly and Laura. The big, burly one who had Laura in his grips revealed his fear. It floated off him like steam. The intense triangle standoff would end in blood and death, hopefully theirs.

"You're outnumbered," Eduardo pointed out as he removed his gun from Beverly's head to take aim at me. I enjoyed witnessing the moment when a man allowed his ego to override his good sense. When a flash of metal flickered, and the shiny blade emerged, I was grateful for Eduardo's fatal mistake.

Chapter Twenty-nine

Dax

Eduardo assumed I was his main threat because I had the gun. I kept my gaze pinned on the man who held Beverly, admiring her swift movements. Proud she waited. Now, I think I understood her and Laura's kiss.

Beverly used her right hand to pinch the blade between her fingers lifting it from the top of her tongue. She spun from the tight grip Eduardo held across her upper chest. As swiftly as a cobra striking its target, she sent the blade up, slicing through his neck before thrusting into the inside of his gun arm.

The practiced movements were so beautifully executed that even with a gun aimed at my head, I gave the scene my full attention. Eduardo didn't know he was bleeding until he coughed, his forehead wrinkling with deep confusion. His gun arm shook with effort before it went limp. The heavy metal dropped to the ceramic tile covering the balcony floor.

Beverly had gotten to his radial nerve, stopping most of the motor functions in his arm. Agents were taught to shoot at certain areas to disarm a threat, and Beverly found it with a blade. She either had exceptional knowledge of human anatomy or she was trained because this was the second time she'd gotten herself out of a deadly situation with just a blade. It was only now I gathered that she wasn't operating on luck.

I aimed my weapon at the man holding Laura as I kept my eye on the unfolding activity between Beverly and Eduardo.

"What the fuck is wrong with you, Eddie?" His friend asked, his tone as shaky as the hand he kept around Laura. From his angle a few feet behind them, he was blind to the horror riding Eduardo's face or the blood that gushed from the severed vein in his neck.

Shock had Eduardo unable to do anything but stand in place as his blood poured from his body, wetting his pale blue button up, turning it black in the blue lighting.

The friend attempted to peek, bending his body around Laura's as Eduardo stumbled in my direction. The friend kept his gun aimed at me as Eduardo managed to reach for his neck with his working hand.

When Beverly made a move to step further away from a deranged Eduardo, his friend didn't know where to point his gun anymore. He waved it back and forth between Beverly and me and his grip on Laura grew tighter, lifting her off her feet. Her fingers dug into his forearm, to fight for the leverage she needed to keep from being choked.

Eduardo fisted the back of Beverly's dress, ripping it as she struggled to break free of his hold. His face was filled with a devil's fury as he snatched her back to him. When his grip slipped, the momentum sent Beverly crashing into the wall. The side of her head collided with the bricked finish before her body slid to the floor unmoving. Her chest continued to move up and down, but she was knocked out.

The sight of Beverly going down caused Laura to fight with her captor. I aimed my weapon but didn't have a clear shot of the man, Unfortunately the waving shadows increased my chances of hitting Laura.

A large projectile of blood gushed from Eduardo's mouth and painted the stony gray balcony floor. His body folded and he stumbled sideways. His blood pumped out in sharp spurts, his shirt so saturated that dark red droplets dripped from the material.

A moment of reckoning hit him before his eyes grew wide and he fell face first. The hard surface of the floor welcomed him and delivered a sickening crack when his head struck it. Blood spread rapidly, forming a puddle and putting the final touches to his bloody end.

Laura's captor was the last man standing. Because of his trembling fear, he was also the most dangerous. He'd somehow managed to take back his control over Laura, and inched them closer to the balcony's ledge. His twitching eye, his trembling hand, and his shuffling feet behind Laura revealed his desperation. He had a massive body, but he lacked confidence. He continued to switch the aim of his gun from Laura's head back to mine.

"I'll kill her!" He yelled, the gun waving at her head. Like with Beverly, I was at a loss. I wasn't willing to shoot the man without a clear shot while he aimed his gun at Laura's head. I much preferred him pointing it at me, so I yelled, taunting him, keeping his focus on me as I searched for an opportunity to take him out.

My actions on the balcony revealed a disadvantage I'd never before encountered. This was the only time I had stalled at taking out a threat. My love for Laura was proving to be one of my greatest weaknesses.

The man's yells rang out so loudly, I couldn't understand his threat once he switched from English to ranting in Spanish. His gun remained pressed against the side of her head. Her face was tightened and angry, making me shake my head because I knew what the expression meant. She wanted me to shoot him.

My unwillingness to shoot in his direction gave the man the upper hand, and he took advantage when he removed the gun from her head and aimed it at me. I saw the decision in his gaze. He knew I wasn't going to shoot at him while Laura was his shield.

The first bullet struck the wall behind me, the second hit the man I was using as my shield, and I lost my grip on his limp body. The force of the third bullet struck me in the side. I was spun in a circle before colliding into the wall near Beverly. The impact sent my gun flying into the shadows.

Before the man could get another round off, Laura struck his gun hand. She'd saved my life and put her own in jeopardy.

The man and Laura tussled for control of the gun. At my angle, I had a view of their dancing legs and swinging arms as they yelled indiscernible words at each other. I stood, but I was struck with a force of pain so strong, it crumbled me, causing me to grip my aching side.

I fought the pain, picked up my gun, and staggered toward Laura and the man. The view before me stopped me cold, freezing my blood in my veins.

The man had lifted Laura and was aiming to toss her over the balcony's railing. The sight of him about to end her life struck me like a lightning bolt and I fired, taking out his legs, but I was too late.

The sight of Laura tumbling across the barrier as she struggled to grab a hold of something that would stop her fall stopped my heart from beating. I reached the edge of the railing with a speed I didn't know I possessed.

My right hand grasped a hold of her forearm before her hand slipped off the edge of the ledge she was hanging on to by the tips of her fingers.

The hard yank of her flailing weight and my unsteady attempt at preventing the fall had us stretched to the max. We were a disastrous combination, me hanging over the railing with a slug in my side, and her dangling into the windy night with nothing to hang on to.

My short nails dug into her arm, drawing blood as I squeezed tighter. There was nothing but darkness and wind to contend with, and she had no leverage. My dressy, no-grip-bottom shoes slipped, making our situation that much more intense as I struggled to pull her up.

Blood gushed from my side, warm and thick as I trembled from the bullet burning my insides and the energy I was exerting to keep Laura from falling.

"Laura, your other arm, lift it so you can grip my free hand. I can't pull you up like this," I grunted my words.

At our angle, my free hand was higher than the one I clung to her with.

"I can't. I think it's knocked out of place." The wind stirred her words, but I caught enough to know that the arm she needed to lift was possibly injured.

"Come on, Laura. Please. You're the toughest woman I know. Lift that arm right now!" I ordered.

The determined set of her face and the tremble in her body revealed her efforts. Eyes shut tight, body shaking with exertion; she managed to lift her arm as high as her waist before it fell limp at her side.

A sharp gasp escaped when my biting grip slipped and inched up her forearm, sending her farther into the night that attempted to suck her in.

"Let go!" she yelled. "You're going to bleed to death." She must have seen my wounded side through the glass portion of the balcony. We were going to have a long talk about how easily she was willing to give up her life. Because of her childhood, she didn't know her worth. She didn't know what she meant to people, more specifically, to *me*.

"Laura, lift that fucking arm right now!" I yelled at her again, my breath growing more shallow and my strength dimming by the second. "If you're giving up this easily, fuck it, I'm giving up to," I barked. "We are either leaving here together or we're dying right here and now!"

The words were the harshest I'd said to her, but also the clearest I'd expressed yet.

Her body shook hard as her strains and grunts sounded into the night. I feared saying anything, even afraid to breathe as she lifted the arm past her waist. My blood flowed, snaking its way down my leg as I strained and grunted in my attempt to lift Laura closer to my hand that she fought to grasp.

When her shaking hand caressed the palm of my free hand, I gripped it, and sheer determination gave me the strength I needed to haul her across the balcony, my shoes slipping and sliding with my effort. We literally tumbled to the floor once her legs spilled across the railing.

We sat, tangled in each other's exhausted bodies, as our harsh breaths mingled with the wind. I positioned her atop my legs with her back against my chest as we allowed our wounded bodies to relax.

The idea of me coming so close to losing her was a hit I wasn't ready to face. Nothing in my life was more important than her staying alive. Nothing in my life had been more important than her.

"Beverly?" She questioned as I followed her tear-filled gaze.

"She'll be fine. She was knocked out from a blow to her head." Her body relaxed after my quick response .

"What about you? How are you?" She turned to get a better look at me.

"I'll be fine," I lied. Truth was I wasn't sure. Right now, I had to find a way to get her and Beverly to safety.

"You're not alright," she protested. "It looks like you've been shanked in a prison riot."

Only Laura could make me smile through my pain. I was thankful to have her with me despite the unknown dangers we had yet to face in our unfinished mission.

Chapter Thirty

Laura

My body had run hot to the point that lifting my head was a chore. We'd taken out the ass-face killers and now, we had to find a way to go back in to take out the intended target who was a walking identity thief if I ever saw one.

I needed my ass whipped for allowing myself to come up to the penthouse in the first place. This disaster was my fault. We all could have died, still could, and I would punish myself harder than anyone else if we made it out of this alive.

D had laid out the plan numerous times: mark the target when he entered the party and exit the building. If need be, D or Dax would go to the backup plan I wasn't supposed to know about. It involved a more extensive plan of taking control of Santino's helicopter.

What none of us could have known was the Santino who showed up at that party was likely going to be a decoy. My mistake had us face to face with the real Santino, but it could also cost us our lives. It became clear if anyone entered that penthouse who wasn't a Dominquez or employed by Santino, wouldn't leave alive.

"Why didn't the rest of them come out when we started fighting and shooting?" I questioned, glancing at the door.

"The door seals shut, and the wind sweeps most of the sound away from the building," Dax answered.

When the rusted scent of blood crept into my nose, I spun to take a better look at Dax, whose skin had gone pale. Blood had soaked through his shirt and jacket. The hard floor drove pain into my knees when I climbed from his lap to check his wound.

My efforts to go any further were stopped when his firm hand grasped mine. His back remained propped against the glass portion of the balcony. He pulled before gently repositioning me before he placed his mouth against my ear.

I glanced back at him before my eyes followed his deadly gaze. The man who tossed me over the balcony was propped against the wall that faced us. He needed to get past us to get back into the penthouse, but with a bullet in each leg, he was stuck.

His hand clutched his wounded legs as he eyed us, the waving blue currents around the bend from where he sat acting as his dim spotlight.

Dax placed the gun in my working hand, leaving my injured arm alone. He used his free hand to support the underside of the gun for me, keeping it steady. With the gun aimed at the man who shot Dax and attempted to kill me, my anger flared.

"Eliminate the target," were the words that wound into my ear before Dax's lips brushed my cheek.

My finger flexed against the trigger with ease followed by the view of the monstrous dark red splatter that painted the wall behind the would be killer. Giving the appearance of being electrocuted, his body jolted about with stiff dancing movements. Neither of us moved until the last of his life escaped, being swept away by the same dark wind that had attempted to take me.

"We have to go in there and kill Santino," I reminded Dax.

"I tagged him," Dax confirmed. "When he stood eye-balling us like we were trash and ordered these men to get rid of us. I clipped the tracker to his gun holster."

The strain in Dax's voice indicated how badly he was wounded. We needed to wake Beverly and find a way out of this penthouse. In our physical condition, the task would be hard considering the protection detail posted outside the front door and at the elevators, not to mention the rest of the group inside the apartment.

The hard plastic of the cell phone poked me in the chest, calling my attention in that direction. I'd shoved it down the front of my dress after I swiped it from Oliver. He'd tossed it on the coffee table as soon as we entered the suite, confirming that it didn't work inside the pent-house.

"Think you can use this to contact D? Oliver spilled that it works out here on the balcony when he tried to get me into the hot tub," I informed.

Dax's smile was answer enough. He shook his head and released a weak laugh before taking it. We hadn't bothered to bring phones into the building because we knew they'd be collected at the entrance. Although I wasn't sure it would work, my earpiece was knocked out, and I hadn't seen Dax's either.

I stood with my injured arm limp and heavy. With my good arm and teeth, I ripped a portion of the nearest dead man's shirt to tie the gun I'd taken to the inside of my thigh. I continued ripping the shirt to make a tourniquet for Dax's wound. He was ignoring it because he was trained to do so, but the shot was more serious than he was letting on.

Dax stood, despite his pain. It looked like Jack the Ripper had gotten a hold of him and shredded his side. With the phone to his ear, he gave D the short version of what we'd just went through. I tied the ripped shirt together before I approached and tied it around Dax's waist like a cummerbund.

Hopefully, D was giving Dax a roadmap to a way out of the building. Dax ducked low, using the glass portion of the balcony to block the wind before he placed the phone on speaker.

"I can't explain right now, but we have extra help," came D's words. "Two rings will mean the pathway to the elevator outside the penthouse doors will be clear. An armed woman wearing a Yale-blue dress will meet you at the elevator. As I have no clear view inside the penthouse, once you enter the living room, be ready to shoot."

Dax and I locked gazes at D's words.

"Since he has the tag on him, I can track Santino inside one of the upstairs bedrooms. Confirmed intel says there is another of his guard crews on the way. I'm controlling the elevator. It will take you to the second floor. Once there, you will meet a second woman in a turquoise dress. The ladies will help you exit the building."

Bits and pieces of D's voice broke up, but I understood enough to know that he had enlisted two women to help us.

Leaving Dax to finish with D, I crept towards Beverly. I was missing a shoe, so I tossed the other over the balcony to find its mate. After I shook her from her stupor, Beverly groaned as she fought to lift her head. I brushed away dirt particles that were stuck to the side of her cheek.

A small blood stain coated her hair on the top left side of her head, but there weren't any signs of major damage. Her hand lifted to the hurt area of her head as she groaned against the pain that emanated there. Her neck swiveled left and right, her gaze searching. Her eyes widened when she grasped where she was, and her anger flared to life at the sight of Eduardo.

Dax assisted me in helping her to stand. She wobbled but remained upright. Our asses had been kicked, but we were alive. Unfortunately, we were about to face another round of trouble once we entered that penthouse.

"Thanks for getting the blade," Beverly stated, glancing at Eduardo. "Because of him, I didn't get a chance to go to the bathroom," she continued, causing a frown of confusion to form on Dax's face before he glanced at me.

Thankfully, my persistence had paid off, and I had convinced Dax to take me on the recon mission of this hotel. Bev and I agreed that I should sneak in a few blades. I'd hidden them in the bathroom behind the tampon dispenser as extra security if things went sideways.

There was no way of knowing if the blades would be there tonight, but they had been. Once I was invited up to the penthouse, I wasn't going up without some form of protection. My short bathroom break had gotten me one of the blades, and I left the other in the bathroom for Beverly. When I spotted trouble standing at her back, I distracted the men and passed the blade to her.

"That's why you were so determined to go on that recon mission with me," Dax stated, piecing together one of me and Beverly's little side plans before he lifted the phone to his ear.

"Santino. We have weapons. We could take him out." Dax explained to D over the phone.

"No time. More trouble's on the way. Don't worry about him right now. Besides, you know how he looks. Two rings, be ready," D stated before the phone clicked off.

The three of us could have been zombies in Michael Jackson's "Thriller" video. My dress and Beverly's were turned into dirty rags as scrapes and bruises sat prominently on different areas of our bodies. Dax resembled a reanimated corpse. The wound must have stopped bleeding, as it hadn't soaked through the makeshift tourniquet yet. However, we had no idea what kind of internal injuries he may be suffering.

For once in my life, I was worried about a man I didn't consider family. I didn't want him to die. He'd risked his life multiple times for Beverly and me, and my hardheadedness had gotten all of us dragged into a situation we weren't meant to survive.

Had Dax been serious about dying along with me when I was hanging over that balcony? It was a question that kept blazing to life in my head.

Chapter Thirty-one

Dax

Ring! Ring!

The chime of the phone jarred us, pulling us from the stillness of our quiet wait. We huddled together, walking toward the door, me in the middle. I entered first, the gun leading us into the large living room.

As soon as they peered across the back of the couch they sat on and noticed we weren't their friends, the silenced weapon in my hand introduced hot led to two men, one of them Oliver. Their bodies sat slumped against each other, their blood thankfully, hidden by the back of the large black couch.

My gaze scanned the room before heading toward the front door, flipping the lights off to conceal the dirty deed that had just gone down. Six bodies…Housekeeping would be pissed.

It took willpower, but I fought the urge to creep through the penthouse to find Santino. Being that close to a target and leaving him alive was not something I was used to doing. However, the sight of Beverly and Laura reminded me that my main goal was to keep them safe.

The last thing I wanted was for them to be tangled up in this assignment as active participants, but the power of female persuasion was an entity of enormous strength, and here they were, walking through the devil's belly with me.

Beverly was at my side and Laura was at my back. If there was anyone coming up at our rear, even with one arm, I was confident she wouldn't hesitate to give them a one-way ticket to see Lucifer.

As soon as I pulled the front door open , we stepped across two bodies, the second time in weeks we had stepped across bodies at a front door.

Two more sat near the elevator. They lay at the foot of the lady in a Yale-blue dress, the one D had identified. She'd managed not to get a drop of blood on her dress or shiny beige platform heels. Had she taken out all these men on her own? Where the hell were all these alpha women coming from all of a sudden?

"Dax, Beverly, Laura?" Miss Yale questioned with a pinched brow. I nodded. Her fingertips stroked the spot below her ear, her eyes aiming up as she listened.

"D says, OTS," she expressed, confirming the code D would send to let me know I could trust this woman. I nodded again.

The elevator door opened upon our approach, and we climbed in without hesitation. The woman scanned the area once more before backing into the elevator with us. She'd taken a keycard off one of the dead men left in the hall and keyed in the code I memorized earlier.

We were lowered in silence, the flashing red numbers counting down our descent with a lingering pace and a noisy buzz with each new level.

Miss Yale stood near the lighted panel as Laura, Beverly, and I held up the back wall of the elevator. The lady's gaze never met ours. She kept her face aimed at the door and her silenced gun aimed at the floor.

The pain exploding in my side had me feeling woozy and my vision was starting to go in and out of focus. I snapped out of my temporary trance when I felt Laura shift next to me.

When we stopped at the third floor instead of the second, Yale Dress, Laura, and I had our weapons raised and aimed. I trusted D with my life, but going into the unknown had my hackles up, and I wasn't willing to take any chances.

When the doors parted, we were met with the same greeting—a gun aimed at us by a woman in a turquoise dress. Yale Dress dropped her weapon, so Laura and I dropped ours. The women were familiar because they too had been inside the ball.

D was holding out on me. Who the heck were these women? I appreciated the assistance, considering we were injured. However, I didn't know these women and remained vigilant as I scanned the dim hall we stepped into.

"This way," Miss Turquoise and the taller of the two stated as she pointed into the darkness behind us. Her gun scanned the area as much as her eyes did.

"We'll take you to D," Miss Yale volunteered.

They hadn't requested we surrender our weapons, so there was no imminent threat as far as I was concerned. We approached a door with a posted warning stating an alarm would sound if we exited.

"The alarm has been silenced," Miss Turquoise informed us without glancing back.

Miss Yale shoved her shoulder into the door to get it open. We entered the darkness of the parking garage, and the silent call of night met us.

Four parking spots away from the door was a white van decorated with the logo of Brick's Catering, the company that prepared the food for the event. Turquoise Dress was our faithful guard while we climbed into the back of the van and sat on the hard metal floor.

As we exited the garage and merged into the bustling city traffic, Laura's small hand wrapped around mine, filling me with warm sparks of energy that made me smile. Her simple gesture helped to decrease the pain in my side and caused my eyes to fall closed to the buzzing sensations charging through me.

She would never say it out loud, but she was worried about me. Taking care of people when they were down and out, hurt, or wounded was something she was good at, and I wasn't altogether sure she understood it was a gift. Beverly was on the opposite side of me, her head against my shoulder. We'd been through hell together.

We circled several of the towering buildings, their shadows following us, lurking as we moved along the one-way streets and dodged anxious motorists for ten minutes. Our bodies swayed when we made a hard turn to enter the garage of a building no less than three buildings down and to the back of The Greenbrier Hotel we just left.

The door of the van was snatched open, and D's face came into view. A beautiful woman in a royal blue dress stood next to him. There were no handshakes or introductions, only a meeting of the eyes. D knew these women. Based on how well organized they were, I believed they were agents or mercenaries. They dropped bodies, so they were of a high-level of law enforcement or a part of a well-established criminal organization.

"This is where we part ways. Send me a copy of the video," the woman in the royal-blue dress requested, staring at D. He and the woman locked gazes for a brief moment before he nodded, and all three of the women climbed back into the van.

My sharp stare met his smiling gaze for an explanation and found him shaking his head at me in the negative. Beverly and Laura remained silent, but their expectant gazes were also leveled on D.

"How bad is it?" D asked, glancing at my hunched body with a hint of pity in his gaze. I shrugged, pretending I was okay when I was ready to pass out. Sweat had pooled at the top of my forehead and my stomach was attempting to climb up my esophagus.

"This way," he stated, taking us in the opposite direction of where we entered the garage. The mystery ladies leaving in the van sounded behind us. We piled into the open and waiting elevator. As soon as the door closed behind us, D entered a code, stuck in a keycard, and started talking.

"You look like shit," he expressed, but the concern in his gaze wasn't missed. "I called your assistant. Help is waiting upstairs. Since I didn't know how badly you were injured, I requested level four," D informed.

"Good," I mumbled as more of my strength slipped.

"And the ladies who are helping us," D continued, pulling our attention. "All I can say is, top-secret, agent types, overlapping missions," he finished, aiming his head straight ahead as his voice bounced back to us.

Beverly and Laura stared at the back of his head, unaware they weren't getting anything else out of him. On the rare occasion D was tightlipped, it meant he was on a mission or about to start one. It wasn't uncommon for him to help us and be on an active mission of his own at the same time.

Despite how well we believed we knew D, he knew just as many people in the criminal world as in the law enforcement community. He was the only man I knew who walked on both sides of the law, with each side knowing about the other.

He knew how to balance his crimes in a way that made him the quintessential Mr. Untouchable. If one of my illegal activities were discovered, they wouldn't toss me into prison and bury me under it.

My eyes flickered closed. Laura's grip on my arm leveled me out. It occurred that neither of the ladies suggested I be taken to a hospital. Based on the way they handled deadly situations so far, I'd say they knew the protocol for the injured in our type of illegal situation.

My unsteady legs shook when I stepped off the elevator, but Laura had a firm grip on one of my arms, and Beverly had the other. I didn't protest their assistance because I was one breath away from blacking out. The scent of my blood drifted up my nose, making my nostrils flare as a wave of nausea closed my eyes.

When I staggered into the room, my eyes locked with gray eyes that resembled my own. Rick, my older brother by four years and only sibling, stared back at me. Concern etched his face as his gaze fell to my bloody side.

"What are you doing here?" I whispered, not wanting my brother anywhere near the shit I did.

"Your assistant called. I was close," he replied, shrugging. "Do you honestly think I would stay put, knowing you were hurt?" he questioned before he pointed to the table he'd set up.

I didn't have the strength to argue with him. Rick knew too much as it was. He knew that my task of handling security for our family sometimes consisted of illegal activity. He also knew I was on a hunt whenever I disappeared.

He never questioned me about my activities nor had he ever passed judgment. He'd been away at college pursuing his dream of becoming a doctor when I was taken. When he found out what happened to me, he put school on hold and came home. He was the one who sat with me through all of my surgeries. He was the only one with the strength to look at me without flinching. This was not the first time he was called to patch me up either.

Laura and Beverly moved me along before assisting me onto the table. The worry etched in their faces wasn't lost on me. They'd grown to care about me.

"Rick, check the ladies first. Beverly has a head injury and Laura's shoulder may be dislocated," I called out, pointing at them. He was already cutting me out of my jacket and working on the shirt.

When he paused midway and glanced at the ladies, they shook their heads.

"I'm good," Laura offered quickly, waving off my suggestion.

"I'm fine," Beverly followed.

D turned and glanced over his shoulder at us, his laptop glowing in front of him.

"I'll take care of the ladies," he said.

"You will?" they asked him in unison like they'd practiced the question. They obviously didn't know that the military made sure we had thorough medical training.

"Yes. But first I need to take care of Santino," D informed, making us all forget about being injured. My brother had to place his hand on my shoulder to get me to relax.

D transferred what was on his laptop screen to the large television monitor mounted to the wall.

"Do you see the blinking red dot?" he questioned.

"Yes," the ladies replied, their heads nodding. The camera D controlled panned to allow us to see the red dot inside the penthouse. The dot was Santino.

D split the images to allow us a continued view of the red dot as well as a second angled view outside the building.

"No way," Laura stated first. Beverly's mouth dropped open before they stood from the couch, their gazes locked on the monitor. I didn't know if it was my weakened condition that gave me bad eyesight, but it took me a while to spot the other image on the split screen.

The crane's long arm was turning from the building adjacent to the structure that housed Santino's penthouse. Attached to the crane were lengths of wire ropes that were wrapped around at least a two-ton cement boulder the size of a smart car.

We waited with bated breath as D aligned the boulder to the top of Santino's building. It hovered above where that red dot blinked, swaying with anticipation. We'd risked our lives, planned, plotted, and killed, just to get close enough to Santino to produce that red dot.

My brother paused cleaning my wounded area as he allowed the sight on the television to pull his attention. When D lifted the crane to as high as it could go, he released the huge block of cement. It fell through the sky— causing a heavy, silent death—before it crashed through the top of the building.

The impact sent an explosive boom, followed by a swish through the sky, the sounds swirling in through our cracked balcony door. The red dot flashed three more quick times before it went black. Sound stood still.

After the long silence lifted, the sound of honking horns, revving engines, and sirens broke through the night. I could hardly wait to hear how this story would be reported on the news.

Chapter Thirty-two

Laura

My hand clung to Beverly's as D examined the small knot that had formed on the top of her head. Her hair hid it, but D found it and did a thorough check before cleaning it.

He shined a light into her eyes, checking her pupils before he conducted a follow-the-finger-test that I'd seen doctors do. To say that these men impressed me was an understatement.

Whether they knew it or not, they had unveiled a different class of men to me. I learned more about the opposite sex in my short encounter with them than I'd learned throughout my life. There was a lot I closed myself to, and just as much I'd not taken the time to understand.

"I'll keep my eyes on you like a hawk for the next twenty-four to forty-eight hours," D informed Beverly, causing her to giggle. He placed his hands to either side of her chin and examined her, turning her head left and right.

"If you feel nauseated or faint, I need you to let me know right away."

"I will."

He glanced in my direction and allowed his gaze to fall to my limp arm. "You're next."

"Okay, Doctor D," I replied playfully.

As soon as he gripped my arm, I winced and fought not to cry out in pain. When a steady flow of adrenaline was pumping through me, I'd not given into the pain. Now, I swore my arm had been ripped out of the socket by Cujo.

D poked and prodded my shoulder to the point I wanted to punch him in his face. He squinted and smiled at me like he knew what I was thinking. When his smile dropped and he took on a more serious expression, I tensed.

"What's wrong?"

"You can take a lot of pain," he pointed out, lifting his gaze from my arm to meet mine. "Your shoulder is dislocated," he confirmed as he kept poking at it. "What's going to hurt worse is when it goes back in," he muttered with a grimace, his gaze locking on mine.

"Just get it over with," I replied to his look.

He pointed me to the largest area of the empty wall at the foot of Dax's setup. I stood in place as a bout of nervousness hit me at the anticipation of the pain I was about to face.

D turned me, positioning me so my good shoulder was parallel to the wall. I squinted in confusion. *Shouldn't it be the other way around*, I wondered like I knew anything about popping a shoulder back in place?

Beverly was right there with me, standing against the wall a few feet in front of me, her face etched in concern like she sensed my pain. Dax tensed on the table, eyeballing D and me. His brother had gotten him prepped and ready for surgery, using what I assumed was an imaging device to pinpoint the bullet's location. Dax refused whatever pain-reducing drug he was offered, and I understood why.

D's tall frame loomed at my injured side. He set his hands in place at certain areas of my lower arm and elbow, making me flinch and writhe in pain. "You ready?" he questioned, glancing down at me.

"Hell, no!" I replied, making him smile. There wasn't a quick jerk and lift technique like I'd seen on television. He moved only my lower arm, lifting and twisting it in a way I believed he was about to break it. When he'd gotten my arm well over my head, a loud pop rattled my bones and I swore my entire skeletal frame shifted before my body vibrated.

I swallowed a scream when the pain struck, causing me to clamp my legs together to keep from pissing all over myself. Body shaking, my eyes remained closed until the pain subsided enough for me to move again.

Immediately, my fist on my good side tightened before I aimed it at D, who stepped back a few paces, laughing.

"Hold on , killer. I think I got it back in on the first try." The teasing smile on his face remained. "Can you move it?" he asked, moving closer. After a deep sigh, I shrugged, easing my shoulder up before I rotated it in super slow motion.

"Lift it," D ordered as he assisted, placing his hand under my elbow. My smile grew wide when I was able to lift it without shitting bricks. *These damn men...*

My lips pinched into a tight smile. *Where were they when I was growing up?*

"Thanks, D," I voiced with sincerity before my eyes landed on Bev. Her smile was as wide as mine. Automatically, my gaze brushed past my newly-connected shoulder and landed back on Dax. He was lying flat, but his stressed eyes were on me.

No one in the room had mentioned that all of our injuries were my fault, a testament of not only their care but their compassion for an asshole like me.

D positioned the scarf around my neck and secured my arm inside. My gaze found Dax's while D continued to stabilize my arm. We'd done a bang-up job of hiding our affair, but we were likely blowing our cover tonight.

"I'm going to put you in this sling for a little while to keep your arm sturdy and make sure it sets right," D informed. I nodded my confirmation.

Once D was done babying my arm, I inched across the floor and stood to the opposite side of the table as Rick who had a scalpel in his hand. All the tools needed to extract the bullet from Dax's side were aligned on a surgical table next to the larger table he was lying atop.

Rick glanced at me and back down at Dax who was reaching for my hand. I gave it without question, releasing more of the secret I'd vowed to take to my grave.

When the blade was placed to his skin, his gaze remained locked on mine as all the horrors of hell flashed on his face. He was doing this without pain meds, and it dawned on me when the blade sat at his skin he was remembering his torture, how he'd been sliced to pieces until he'd lost his mind.

My grip on his hand grew tighter, noticing every emotion playing out on his face when the blade made the first cut. Throaty groans and deep heaving breaths followed when a pair of oversized tweezers went into the hole after the bullet. Trickles of thick dark blood seeped from the opening as Dax squeezed my hand and spat out his harsh breaths through gritted teeth.

Rick was quick and strategic with his movements, pulling the slug out and letting it drop with a *clink* into a small metal pan.

Dax and I didn't say a word. None were needed. I stood through the rest of his surgery, observing, empathizing, and caring for someone in that special way I never knew I was capable of giving.

After Rick finished patching up Dax, he hovered, taking care of his brother for a few hours as they talked in soft tones. Beverly and I had gone to one of the large bedrooms to get cleaned up.

I pretended to watch television while the question, *"What now?"* kept recycling through my brain. Were we finished? Were Bev and I free to return to our lives?

When Dax waved me over, I didn't know what to expect. His brother's deep and intense gray eyes met mine across the bed Dax now lay on. Was it intrigue in Rick's gaze? What had Dax been telling him about me?

"Rick, this is Laura, a good friend of mine. I'm advocating for more than friends, but she doesn't want any part of that," he expressed. Rick eyed his brother like he didn't know him, and my mouth dropped open and refused to close right away.

Rick recovered, lifting his hand to meet mine above Dax's bandaged torso. Dax's revelation left me baffled, because I didn't know how to respond.

***

Once Rick left, we found out our mission wasn't over yet. The guys wanted to stick around for a few weeks to make sure that eliminating Santino had freed us from any other lingering DG6 threats.

Now, I was on the phone with Megan. The happiness in her tone rang free. It meant that her big biker man was doing something right.

"Wait, what?" I shouted into my phone as the gum I was chewing flew past my lips, and I caught it, stopping it from flopping onto the gleaming marble floor.

"Who opened up the gates of hell and let this kind of shit slither into your brains?" I questioned Megan. Beverly dropped the book in her hand and slid across the couch like her ass was on a conveyor belt.

"What? What?" she whispered breathlessly, eyeing the phone in my hand. I placed the phone on speaker so she could hear Megan's big reveal. I needed a witness to confirm that I heard Megan right the first time.

"Aaron asked me to marry him. I said yes and I want you here for the ceremony," she repeated. Beverly's mouth dropped open, and one of my eyebrows lifted and remained stuck in the air.

"Hello? Are you there?" Megan questioned, knowing good and well her news had stunned us into dead silence.

Part II

Chapter Thirty-three

Beverly

I buzzed with excitement at the anticipation of reuniting with Megan. When she called and informed us she was getting married, the news floored me, but I couldn't have been happier for her.

Given the horrors she faced in her youth, I would support whatever brought her happiness. After Megan's news, I pried the phone from Laura's frozen grip before snapping my fingers at her face to get her blinking again.

So far, D and Dax were a blessing during the storm that had blown into our lives, and they continued to protect us like family. I was keeping a closer eye on Laura with Dax. They weren't fighting like they used to, and I was becoming increasingly convinced there was more happening between them than they were revealing.

Maybe we'd all grown to care for each other since the guys saved us from the DG6 monsters chasing us. Santino, an original member of DG6 was dead, but we found out that Sorio was the source who ordered his men to catch and capture us as well as put the hit out on Megan.

Although it was wise to be cautious, with the top of the vicious organization gone, we were able to roam freely.

Compliments of Dax, Laura and I were being spoiled rotten. In preparation for our trip to California, he treated us to another shopping spree that landed us designer shades, clothes, and even a few pieces of expensive undies.

My silk Carolina Herrera blouse hugged like strong arms, and my ripped boyfriend jeans fit like they were measured and tailored. My new Louboutin platform heels made perfectly-pitched clicks against the pavement as we were escorted in the direction of Dax's private plane.

The April weather was perfect for what I called the cute-girl outfits. I lived in the moment, my head so high in the air you'd think I was a king's daughter. For the most part, I stylized my outfits mindful of dressing to compliment my size. Thankfully, I was evenly portioned, and thick and curvy in the areas that drew the most attention—ass, hips, and chest.

Laura was in a cream Max Mara jumpsuit paired with a four-inch red and gold Saint Laurent gladiator heel. She had an eye for style that blew me away sometimes. She attracted a lot of unwanted attention from men she'd learn to brush off as smoothly as she'd learn to pick up women.

She had confidence in herself, but I believed she was clueless as to how gorgeous she truly was. She could pass for a girl in her teens which undoubtedly garnered her even more attention.

I hardly flinched at the pressure of her nails digging into my forearm when the first view of the plane came into view. Our eyes bucked, and our steps faltered, messing up the rhythm of the expensive-sounding clicks under my feet.

Dax stopped at the edge of the steps to assist us up, always the gentleman. Although I didn't see D, I sensed him somewhere out there, watching, being our eyes and ensuring our safety before he boarded.

Stepping onto the plane, my steps hitched when I made a sudden stop to enjoy the first view and inhale the scent of newness. I aimed my phone and snapped a photo, adding to a collection I was building during this journey. My hands skimmed the wide, peanut butter colored leather seats that flowed smoothly under my freshly manicured fingers.

Dax stepped into the cabin behind us. "I'll give you ladies a quick tour before we take off."

A full-sized bedroom, a kitchen that came with a cook, two flight attendants, the pilot and co-pilot, and rows of large reclining seats lined each side.

The cabin could seat ten people comfortably. The bathrooms, including one attached to the bedroom, was full sized. They weren't converted closets designed to allow everything inside to reach out and touch you. If this was how the other half lived, I wanted to be signed up.

If Laura hadn't been a determined lesbian, I would be forcing her down Dax's throat for the perks of knowing someone with his kind of connections. I quieted my shameful ideas of pimping out my friend and glanced up to give thanks for what we already had, especially our lives and safety.

D eventually climbed aboard. No sooner than the plane lifted from the ground, Laura's head was heavy against my shoulder. Awed by my surroundings, I sniffed another whiff of the new leather scent before I slid lower in the plush seat.

My mind was buzzing with unrelenting thoughts. I imagined what California would be like since I'd never visited the state. A moment later, I recalled Dax and Laura, sensing I was missing something.

When he escorted us into that large bedroom, I got the sense he would have liked Laura locked and alone in there with him. I recognized their chemistry, but the likeliness of it emerging into something meaningful was highly doubtful.

As a matter of fact, Dax didn't hide it. The way his hand kept brushing her back while taking us around the plane. The fact Laura had allowed it caused my eyebrows to sit high on my forehead. Also, his eyes were saying things she either ignored or didn't notice.

Dax was supposed to sit where I was, but Laura chased him off before tugging me into the seat. He ended up choosing to sit two seats ahead of us, across the aisle from D.

As one of the most stubborn people I knew, I was beginning to believe Laura liked Dax. However, I didn't think she would act on her interest. Or would she?

She respected him now as much as she respected Kadeem. However, she didn't sneak peeks at Kadeem or allow her gaze to linger on his body the way she did with Dax. He, not Kadeem, piqued her interest whether she wanted to admit it or not. For now, I'd cast aside my speculations, but Laura and I were going to have a talk.

My head dipped, my brain attempting to shut down while my mind fought to stay alert. When I jerked my neck up, my best friend was drooling all over the shoulder of my new expensive blouse, and the pilot was announcing our descent into San Diego. The sun hadn't fully set, so the view from the sky was a breath-stealing eye-popper.

The plane dropped lower, making my belly flip as my neck stretched to glimpse the bright, vibrant lands of California. Thanks to Megan, Laura and I were lucky enough to go on a few trips together. We met up for a girls' week in Hawaii, in the Bahamas, and in Belize. It was the safest way to see Megan without risking exposing her to DG6. Other than those trips, we only ever drove to a few other states outside the great state of Texas.

Once on the ground, we gathered our bags for the few days we were planning to spend with Megan. We had to return to Texas for our annual Rec-Celebration at the center, where we celebrated the achievements of members and picked up much-needed donations and a few new sponsors.

The scheduled event would cut our time short with Megan. However, it was well worth the sacrifice for the sake of the children and teens who had nothing and no one else to depend on. Now that we were free to see Megan whenever we wanted, we didn't feel bad about our short visit.

Upon our arrival at the airport, I wasn't surprised that a BMW SUV awaited us. The drive to Ansel's house was a quiet one. Laura and I stared past our tinted windows and pointed out interesting features as we took in our surroundings.

San Diego was beautiful, but the landscape eventually started to turn into wide-open hills and plains. We passed residences scattered along the hilly, wide-open path until we drove up to the tall gates of a mansion.

"Where the hell are we?" Laura whispered in my ear as her gaze panned the area. "You're telling me this redneck-ass biker is living like this?" She didn't care that she was insulting the man responsible for sending us help and for keeping Megan safe.

My shoulders lifted in a deep shrug. After what we were exposed to and becoming accustomed to from D and Dax along with our adventurous escapes and near-death moments in Texas, I didn't know what to expect from the rest of the crew.

We eased from our seats when the men opened our doors and reached in to help us out. The crisp breeze in the air was surprisingly warm and refreshing across my face. Unlike in Texas, the April breeze wasn't stiff and dry. I scanned everything, unwilling to miss a thing as my eyes bounced in their sockets.

The large glass door sprang open, and her cute little face dressed in a huge smile was the first thing I noticed. I didn't walk. I forgot I had heels on and ran up the steps to get to Megan. I lost my breath when our bodies crashed into each other and her arms flew around my neck. I lost more breath when Laura's body crashed into ours.

We remained locked in a tight body-shaking hold, screaming out our delight at a reunion that had taken way too long. We rocked soothingly, forgetting everything and anyone around us, our hums of joy vibrating around the circle. The men marched past us, carrying our bags into the living room.

When we managed to let go and ambled into the house, the first person I recognized was Aaron. Scrapes and bruises covered exposed parts of his body, but he wasn't bothered by his injuries. His gaze studied us with Megan.

It didn't take but a second of witnessing him and Megan make eye contact to know that everything we heard about his willingness to protect her rang true. Megan shared with us the details about Aaron's time in Texas of him being shot in the head and left for dead. Him remaining at her side proved his dedication to her. I prayed that I would someday find a man who would love me that much.

The one standing next to Aaron must have been Ansel. His arm was in a sling and bruises painted the exposed parts of his body as well. I reached out for Aaron's waiting hand. A scar decorated his head that wasn't there when he was pretending to be Detective Mark Griffin. His beard was longer and magnified his intense presence.

"Nice to see you again, Beverly." His firm grip swallowed my hand as he observed me with an expression I couldn't read.

"You as well. Thank you for taking care of Megan."

A tight nod followed my words as his gaze zoomed in on Megan who was giggling with Laura. Ansel's hand gripped mine next. His charming smile widened into a grin on his handsome face.

The pretty woman who stood a few paces from the men must have been Regina. She eased toward us with her hand outstretched, and her pensive expression suggested that she expected us to be hostile.

She was one of those beautiful women who had an air of privilege about her. However, a glance into her eyes unveiled a different story. Megan also revealed to us how Regina was held captive by her own family.

D and Dax were forthcoming in giving us information about this crew who had banded together to take out not one, but four major players of DG6. Whatever D and Dax hadn't revealed, Megan would fill in the blanks. Ansel's beautifully decorated living room drew my attention, making its own introduction.

"Welcome, ladies. Come in and make yourselves at home," Ansel announced. His smile enticed me to grin. He knew how to lay on the charm, but I knew right away that he was a handful of straight-up trouble.

Megan remained in the middle of Laura and me as she kept a firm grip on each of our arms, interlocking hers with ours. Laura winced when Megan gripped her injured arm but didn't complain. She wore the sling D put on her arm for a few days but tossed it when it got on her nerves.

We strolled further into the living room, as a group, with the men studying our movements. Arms joined, we sat on the couch, unwilling to let go of each other.

Ansel stepped up to the edge of the coffee table staring at us while Aaron and Regina took their seats in nearby chairs.

Ansel's gaze panned up from our connected arms before moving between Laura and me. I heard he was a tough guy like Aaron, but he better beware with Laura. The way his face tensed as he studied us didn't bother me, but Laura was a whole different story. She would shoot her mouth off at anybody no matter their reputation. The stare she reflected back at Ansel wasn't a pleasant one.

Chapter Thirty-four

Beverly

"Ladies, would you like anything to drink?" Ansel's facial expression softened, and the tension in Laura's face disappeared. Water was all we requested.

Ansel stepped away as Aaron started up a conversation, asking about our mission in Texas like D and Dax hadn't already filled him in on the trouble we stirred up and managed to live through.

Ansel returned and handed us cold bottles of Evian in the midst of us telling about how we came up with and enacted the plan to take down, No-face, Santino. The news reporting was kept local, so D sent the guys a recording of not only Santino's death, but of how it was reported.

The news headline highlighted how a lifelong resident of Houston ended up crushed to death in his penthouse after a crane malfunctioned. News reports claimed the only body found inside the penthouse was the resident. They took care in not releasing Santino's name.

D was still tightlipped about the group of women who helped us, but I believed they were the ones who removed the rest of those bodies from that penthouse. I distinctly remember spotting a pretty black butterfly tattoo peeking from the wrist of one of the women.

Aaron and Regina filled in more blanks about their time in Texas at the farm, and how Aaron had ended up there in the first place. A more vivid picture of what went down at that farm and a bigger piece of Regina's story strengthened my respect for Aaron and my empathy for her.

"So, you're telling me your crazy ass cousin Luis, who has a license to practice medicine, is a meth mixer who uses human ashes as an ingredient? And they had you cremating their victims?" Laura questioned Regina. She'd asked Regina the question twice, phrasing it a different way each time because she, like me, had trouble believing it.

Regina nodded. "My family is pure evil. Empathy wasn't a part of their genetic sequencing," she uttered more to herself than us. Seeing her in person allowed me to look past her being a member of the cartel that had been hunting us. She was a survivor like we were.

"I've heard strange shit, but this…" Laura continued shaking her head.

Regina nodded again before allowing a sad smile to grace her face. Her family had put her through pure hell.

"You're one of us now, Regina," I stated. Megan and Laura agreed, each reaching to offer a touching caress against her arm. "If any of your psychotic family members come searching for you, they will be met with opposing forces. You've allied with the right group," I reassured.

"By the way, that one…." I pointed at Ansel, keeping my tone low. "Judging by the way he keeps watching you, I'd say you won't ever have to worry about anyone touching you again in life. However, you might have to worry about him. He seems very intense," I noted as he and I broke eye contact, and I returned my attention to Regina.

After our stories and updates died down, Megan stood. "I've cooked for you guys."

Her announcement had us as giddy as sugared up children. Although she would never reveal it to anyone, Laura knew how to cook too. She, like me, had gotten a lot of practice at the center, cooking for the kids. She and

I had also gained a wealth of useless knowledge from the classes we gave as well as helping the children with their homework.

Megan glanced at Ansel. "Will you call the rest of the guys?"

"No problem," he replied as he stepped off and headed in the direction of the front door. There hadn't been anyone outside when we drove up, but D did mention when he was helping this crew over the digital airways in their operation that Ansel's house had a lot of secret coves.

We stood and followed Megan into the kitchen with Aaron and Regina on our trail. Seeing Aaron poke Regina playfully in the side revealed the level of his care for her. Whether she believed me or not, she was a part of this crazy group we were forming.

The rest of the crew gradually joined us around Ansel's large hardwood dining table. The first of the group we met were Rob and Galvin. D and Dax had spoken freely about the men, so it was nice to put faces to the names. The men, like D and Dax, had no problems getting a woman's attention.

Observing them, my smile never dropped. My gaze panned the group, noticing their differences and picking out the one underlying characteristic they shared. They all had that bad-boy killer swagger that didn't put them in the same categories with normal men.

When *he* walked in, my gaze froze, and my smile dropped for the first time. Megan introduced him as Luke. The man was at least six-foot-seven, eight, or nine. I didn't know, but *Jesus H. Christ*, he was fine. I remembered a conversation between D and Dax mentioning Lucas Bradshaw. This must be him.

He was a sparkling pale like a seashell that received the lightest trace of sun. Ivory, that's it. His skin was the same glimmering color of invaluable ivory. He was built like the ancient gods, arms long and corded with bulging muscles that poked at the shirt covering him. His charcoal gray slacks covered legs formed like they could take down a tank.

I didn't have to view what was under his Olympic-blue, V-neck, long-sleeve Henley to know that the rest of him was as impressive. Tattoos peeked from the edge of his sleeves. When I assumed things couldn't get any better, he sat directly across the table from me, and I got my first glimpse of his eyes.

They were light blue, but not boring or plain. His were a mixture of an electric and a darker China blue that made crystals look like cracked glass in comparison. They formed flawless gemstones that enticed you to get lost in them.

My face pinched in concern when I noticed the beauty in those eyes was tinged with pain that probably didn't allow him to trust easily. My eyes fell closed, and I forced myself to stop analyzing him. I was used to being in therapy mode at the center and therefore found myself evaluating the people I encountered.

Luke was a good-looking man from top to bottom, with a chiseled jawline that held up a prominent strong face with round features versus angular. There was something boyish in his features although he was all the man a woman could ever want.

It wasn't easy, but I managed to pull in bits and pieces of the conversation while I seriously eye-stalked Luke. When I could focus, eating and laughing my way through Megan's delicious food, I enjoyed myself immensely.

The group of men could pass for a dangerous version of a high-end stripper team. They all possessed unique assets and flaring airs of danger emanated from their pores and made it impossibly hard not to stare.

However unique they all were, I was drawn to the titan that sat across the table from me. His eyes met mine a few times, heightening my awareness of his thrilling presence. I sensed he knew my watchful eyes were on him. Make that, staring a hole through him.

Sitting, he was a head taller than everyone else, so I sat musing over his height. By most people's standards, five-foot-eight was tall for a woman. Therefore, I enjoyed every opportunity to glance up to a man. With this group, I was in man-height heaven.

Now, back to my tempting distraction. His brown hair verged on being a dark blond and was tapered short on the sides and no longer than an inch on top. The several good glimpses I caught of his crystal blue eyes had them already imprinted on my brain.

Luke thankfully had lips, not two spaces that sat against his face and curved up or down when he smiled or talked. They were the color of frozen pink lemonade, yet succulent and generously defined enough to contend with the fullness of mine. My teeth sank into the corner of my bottom lip as I continued to observe him.

"Beverly!" Laura called out, slapping my arm and ripping my gaze from Luke.

"Yes. Why are you yelling?" I asked, a touch of annoyance dancing across my tone.

"Megan asked if you wanted another plate," she replied.

I'd fallen so far into my own zone I missed that Megan was standing right beside me.

"No, thanks, I'm stuffed," I answered and fought to keep my gaze from creeping back across the table. The man was a marvel to be studied. He wasn't fat by any means, but he had enough muscle and body mass to send a lesser man scurrying for cover.

My gaze landed on his solid pecs as he chewed his food, silent and in his own world, a world he unknowingly drew me into. Sensing my eyes on him, his gaze lifted and met mine, catching me staring once again. I snapped my head down to the empty space in front of me since Megan had taken my plate.

Mentally, I was getting a full workout. The next half hour was spent forcing myself not to stare at Luke.

He mouthed very few words during the entire dinner. I balanced participating in the lively conversation and nibbling on apple pie while devouring the man in front of me. It was time I stopped stirring my coffee that I'd not taken a sip of yet before the group assumed I was attempting the hypnotizing ritual from the movie, *Get Out*.

We talked well into the midnight hour, but the fatigue of the flight as well as our adventures in Texas was catching up with us. Laura and I were sharing a bedroom that Megan showed us to earlier. I heaved a deep breath, preparing to get up from the table when I was content to sit there and stare at the magical view all night.

Chapter Thirty-five

Luke

Usually, I would've eaten and excused myself once I was done, but not this time. The view was too magnificent, and I couldn't help but marvel at it. I was used to being the weird, big guy who everyone stared at or pretended to ignore as they snatched glances at me. However, there was something different about the way Beverly stared at me.

She was a rare, majestic dark feline, but not one you wanted to pet. She was one you admired and became engrossed in studying. You observed her from afar because the danger of touching such a beauty was forbidden.

My hard stare was penetrating enough to make out that the inner circles of her eyes were a sparkling light brown, the larger outer band a light green with a darker green ring. The beauty of those eyes was contained by a canvas of a deeply toasted brown, so deliciously hued it teased my senses and tempted my tongue.

Her hair was styled in a thick above-the-shoulder bob that presented her face to the world, her neck long enough to bring elegance to the style. I was entranced the moment I met her and fought with every breath I took to contain my need to soak her in, record the sound of her voice, and remember every line, detail, and curve.

She was life. Waves of her energy pinged against my senses and enticed me to breathe in her vivacity and allow it to live within me. Galvin's heavy hand struck my arm, snapping me from my trance.

"This is the first time I've seen you look at anyone like that," he whispered, leaning against my shoulder. He shook his head, a smile shining across his teasing lips. "I can't say I blame you. With a view like this, I don't plan on giving my eyes a rest," he expressed, laughing before his gaze swept past the pie on his plate and landed back on Laura.

My attention returned to the one thing I wanted it lost on. Beverly. I didn't feel like a sideshow freak under her sparkling gaze. Was I being presumptuous in thinking that she might have found interest in my presence?

Maybe I was fooling myself into thinking she was interested in me, but my brain latched on to the idea. Some women bolted at the sight of me, others gawked rudely, and the ones who may have been interested were afraid to approach me.

I never took offense to the funny looks and sly comments. They feared my size and automatically assumed I was a bully. Without speaking a single word, I possessed the ability to intimidate people. They didn't care to know and never took the time to find out I was more than my outside appearance.

At twenty-four, I'd engaged in a handful of relationships that fizzled out within a month. *Too quiet. Too awkward. No personality. No depth.* Their perceptions of me were right to a certain point. However, I had deeper and darker things done to me, so their shallow jabs didn't worry me as much as they might have the next guy.

Either way, I never knew what to say to women because I never had enough time to figure out what they wanted. The ones I dated couldn't summon enough patience or time to meet my personality, and I didn't have the energy to chase after them when they lost interest.

As a result of my passive nature with women, my balls were royal blue, and there wasn't a thing I could do about it. There was only so much jerking off you could do before it became just another function that got you by.

At times, the idea of putting in an order for a mail-order bride came to mind, but I wasn't desperate enough to proceed with that measure yet. I fought the crinkle at the corner of my eyes and the smile that threatened to bend my lips at the idea of me ordering a bride. The guys would never let me live that decision down, but they didn't face the same problem as me. Women fell all over themselves for them, fought each other for them, and did shameless things to get their attention.

My gaze danced around the table until I found Megan. "Thank you, Megan. The food was delicious."

"You're welcome," she replied, her smile always friendly. I liked Megan. She treated me like the guys did, accepting me right away, joking and chatting with me like she'd known me for years.

Talking to the guys was easy. Since I was the youngest in the crew, they treated me like their little brother. I was lucky in that aspect because they were a group who wouldn't let me fail, no matter what.

However, and even with them setting me up on blind dates from time to time, I repeatedly struggled with women and relationships. I wasn't afraid of them. I simply didn't know what they wanted and didn't know the first thing about finding out what they wanted.

Asking the guys for advice was out of the question. They didn't need to know every detail of my life, especially not my troubles with the opposite sex. They'd taught me so much throughout the years, but I couldn't let them know that something that came naturally for them was difficult for me.

After entering the living room, Ansel stopped me. We had discussed him using resources from mine and Galvin's security firm since he volunteered to keep an eye on one of the cartel's most prized possessions—Regina.

During our chat, my attention was taken by the sight of Beverly heading toward the stairs.

Once Ansel and I were done, I headed up the stairs after I bid the few lingering in the large living room a good night. Galvin and I were prepared to head back home to Georgia in the early morning hours. We considered sticking around California for another week, but Ansel assured us that he could handle DG6 if they decided to come after Regina. Either way, he had us on speed dial.

Work was my saving grace. Galvin and I owned and ran a small firm that specialized in security contracting jobs with a small research and development team. I lost myself in my work so the nagging loneliness that lingered would stop haunting me.

When I turned into the upstairs hallway, the soft thump of her body collided into mine. "Whoops," she whispered and left a breezy warmth on my face. The air in my lungs stilled, refusing to go any further as the rest of me joined, sending me into a frozen state.

"Beverly," her name finally floated past my lips and thawed my frozen state. She was tall enough that she wasn't dwarfed by my height, and our collision had placed her directly in my hold.

One of my hands sat delicately on the side of her shoulder, the other on her waist. A fissure of energy shot into my fingers before zipping up my arms and settling into me. Beverly was the perfect amount of woman; her body was shapely, a world of firm-softness and warmth.

She gripped the forearm of the hand I had on her waist. Up close, her complexion was an entrancing cinnamon-chestnut mix enriched with flowing melted chocolate. Her lips were so intricately lush they sent my imagination soaring through the roof.

She glanced up as I glanced down and we stood in place, suspended in a magnetizing power that prevented us from letting go of each other. Her scent, her beauty, her warm and pleasing body was like the inside of one of my best fantasies. Rose petals sprinkled with cinnamon was the magical scent that surrounded me.

"Pardon me, ma'am. I wasn't paying attention to where I was going."

"*Ma'am?*" she mouthed silently before looking at me with a pinched brow. "No, I'm sorry. I wasn't watching where I was going."

Being from the south, I had a habit of calling everyone I didn't know ma'am and sir. The guys warned me that there were people who didn't like it. Although I was silent on most occasions, I attempted to be careful with how I addressed people.

We hadn't let go of each other, which reassured she wasn't afraid. I didn't want to turn her loose. She was so warm and pretty she could make me lose my will to be the polite gentleman I was normally. My throat and tongue forgot how to work, and I couldn't form a word to save my life.

What was even better than her hand on me was this close-up view. Her beautiful eyes sparkled with a light I prayed would one day shine on me. Her dark, flawless skin glimmered against the hallway lighting and possessed a hypnotic quality. I was sure I'd already considered that about her skin, but I was currently limited in my capacity to think.

At this closer view, I noticed that she, in fact, looked at me with interest in her gaze. Was I seeing what I wanted to see or was I fooling myself? Wouldn't be the first time I believed I saw something that wasn't there in the first place.

A smile inched across her lovely lush lips and set fire to my doubts. The tips of her fingers skimmed my forearm, making the hair on my arm stand before she let go and backed away.

Reluctantly, I let go too, not having a choice since she stepped back. The depth of her warmth dissipated at our disconnect, but her pretty green eyes remained on mine.

"Have a good night, Beverly," I greeted, loving the way her name sounded vibrating over my tongue and rolling off my lips.

"You too, Lucas. Have a good night," she returned as her smile widened and grew brighter. She stepped around my tall, bulky body, leaving me to stand and ponder our interaction.

If I glanced back, she'd know how much our short encounter had affected me, so I forced my legs to carry me to the room I shared with Galvin. My head twisted sideways. How did she know my name was Lucas? It wasn't far off from Luke, but I rarely used it.

A deep sigh escaped. Galvin and I were leaving in the morning, so there was no need for me to fool myself into thinking too much about beautiful Beverly. Her lush, curvy body, embracing warmth, friendly smile, intriguing eyes, and caring caress. My eyes fell closed at the idea of all the wonders she possessed.

"Luke," D called right as my hand turned the knob to enter my room. He approached, his phone glued to his hand. The light shining from the screen lit up his face. The man should've been blind by now since he was rarely without an electronic device.

"Yes," I answered, awaiting his reply.

"I'm on another assignment that popped up on the radar a little while back. I've been pulling double duty, but it looks like I'll have to make a move that will pull me out of Texas and send me to Vegas. I may not be able to escort Laura and Beverly back to Texas. Dax and I have plans to stick around for at least a few more weeks to make sure DG6 doesn't have any stragglers lingering around their area. The ladies have their own protection squad that will look out for them, but you know we don't like to leave anything unfinished."

My brow lifted, awaiting his point.

"You think either you or Galvin can take my place in Texas for a few weeks? Keep eyes on the ladies until we're sure they're safe?"

My teeth sank deep into the back of my lip to keep a smile at bay before I forced myself to answer.

"I can do it," I volunteered too enthusiastically. "I don't have anything pressing going on right now." I was actually behind on my work from helping Ansel, but if there was one thing that being around my friends gave me, it was a spark of excitement I couldn't find anywhere else. They were also my only family. If watching two beautiful women was what was needed, work would have to wait.

"Good," D stated as a wide grin crept across his lips. He placed a stiff hand atop my shoulder and caught me with a warning gaze. "Don't let those beautiful faces fool you. Those women are as deadly as we are and twice as distracting. A few times, I believed I would have to go into the hospital and get a priapism treatment.

I burst into laughter, shaking my head at D.

"I'll sit with you tomorrow, brief you, and answer any questions you might have," he added, shaking his head with a twisted smirk on his face.

"Okay." I acknowledged him and continued to skirt my excitement.

"Are you going to Megan and Aaron's wedding to-morrow?" I shook my head in the negative. I was ecstatic for Aaron and Megan, but I was not at all interested in a wedding. However, I understood the women needed to be there for their friend and would give them all the time they needed.

"I'll have to stick around until after the nuptials. I'll let Dax know that you'll be replacing me. It's a first-class trip compliments of his private plane," he added. We didn't hesitate to take advantage of the luxuries that came along with working with Dax.

"Good night. Talk to you tomorrow." He still had that teasing smirk on his face as he stepped away. If the encounter I just faced fending off my immediate attraction to Beverly was any indication, I was already in trouble.

"Good night," I called back to him as I entered the room. The idea of me being in the presence of Beverly caused my smile to spread as my face filled with warmth. I stood in place, my fingers tracing my jaw as my mind lingered on none other than her.

Chapter Thirty-six

Beverly

The surprising update that Luke would be joining Dax in escorting us back to Texas had me grinning from ear to ear. If I didn't fear killing myself in the process, I would turn a few cartwheels.

The man had only uttered a handful of words to me, had barely touched me, yet here I was excited about seeing him again. In all honesty, I didn't even know if he was interested in me or even attracted, but it didn't stop me from hoping.

Although I was certain it would never be bestowed on me, I wanted what Megan had with Aaron. The way one gazed at the other, you could feel the chemistry stirring in the air. His willingness to jump into the flames of hell for her. It was the most amazing thing I believe I'd ever witnessed in a couple. Observing them together made me shelve some of the years of abusive, unloving, and adulterous relationships I grew up watching.

Later. I convinced myself I wasn't going to cry, but the waterworks started when I witnessed Megan marry the love of her life. We spent the rest of the day with them, talking and joking around, and enjoying each other's company.

It saddened me to the core that we had to leave the next day, but we promised to link back up. Besides, Megan mentioned that she and Aaron were going on a honeymoon. The notion that she was free to live her life warmed my heart and made me that much more grateful to this merry band of hot bad-guys protecting us.

***

After our tear-filled goodbyes, the next day, we loaded back into the SUV and prepared to head back to Texas. I took a leisurely glance at the bright California skyline before I clumped up the steps of the plane.

I loved Laura with all my heart, but I was elated Dax had taken the seat next to her despite her protests. It meant I was left with a chance to sit next to the object of my attention.

Luke stepped onto the plane, and a sigh of relief swept past my lips as my gaze latched onto him. He gave a polite nod in my direction before he turned and helped the flight attendant close the door. I rose, sitting higher in my seat, my eyes tracking his every move.

Luke's structure was broad with enough muscles to keep a girl staring. He was a stylish dresser for a big guy. His crisp green button-up was rolled up to his elbows and his dark slacks were draped impeccably on his tall, strong frame. At the right angle, his pants brushed the corded muscles of his thighs that enticed my tongue to reach out and swipe across my lips.

Every time he bent his arms, I yearned to wrap my fingers around his biceps. My gaze lingered on each of his steps as I swallowed the urge to run my fingers up his thigh muscles to learn how they would feel rippling and gliding under my fingers.

Those eyes, so light and mysterious, looked like they hid an ocean of secrets I wouldn't mind uncovering. I still found it difficult to believe that a group of men who barely knew us were willing to volunteer their own safety and put their lives in jeopardy to keep us safe.

In learning and piecing together facts about this group, I was discovering most of them like me, Megan, and Laura had suffered through their own personal hells. I believed our tortured pasts were the foundations that stood under us all.

An easy breath slid past my lips before I allowed my gaze to drop. Verging along the lines of creeper, I was eyeing Luke way too hard. Once the door was secured, the flight attendant gushed and smiled before her hand locked around one of the biceps I was drooling over.

Luke bent before taking a step forward, obviously used to ducking under low-hanging ceilings. After making a quick scan of his choices, he moved forward and my eyes followed him. He decided on a place in the front of the plane like me. Unfortunately, it was the window seat across the aisle from mine.

Damn it!

My curiosity about him was beginning to overwhelm me, so I allowed the boldness I used when running the center to take over. I unstrapped myself from my seat at the window and sauntered across the aisle. Luke was making me set fire to the vow I made with myself about men.

"Is someone sitting here?" I pointed at the plush aisle seat next to Luke's. His crystal blue gaze met mine before falling to the seat in question.

"No," he replied before a flash of a smile glided across his pale pink lips.

"May I?" I asked as I took the seat without giving him a chance to say yes or no. There was a spark between us I wanted to explore. If I were making a mistake, so be it. This wouldn't be the first time, but this would at least be one of those times I believed the mistake would be worth it.

I didn't know Luke, didn't know a thing about the man other than he was a friend of Megan's husband,

Aaron, and they'd been in the military together. However, there was something about him that called to me.

I adjusted myself in the seat, my elbow brushing his arm while I soaked up the relaxing warmth he emitted. Although he filled it out, the wide, plush seat was a perfect fit for his tall, well-built body. My stalking gaze traveled the expanse of his long legs stretched out before him and stopped at his crossed feet and freezing. *Jesus.*

"If you don't mind my asking, what size shoe do you wear?" My curiosity was uncontrolled as I latched onto the crazy notion Megan had convinced me and Laura was true about a man's foot size.

"Fifteen," he answered, his tone low as his gaze raked up my jean-covered legs and stopped where my hand sat in my lap. A knowing smile crept across my lips. I wasn't the only one curious. This wasn't the first time I caught his eyes roaming over me with a lingering interest that mirrored my own.

My gaze panned back up his body, my shameless eyes stopping in the area they didn't need to go. Thankfully, I couldn't tell anything by the way he sat. Despite Megan's proclamation, I'd met men who were given the height, but when it came to their lower member, it had been neglected.

Stop it, Beverly!

I was being way too fast and thirsty and needed to temper my behavior and act like a lady.

Damn, he smells good.

Fiery spice and lavender, one part strength and masculinity and one part calming ease, formed an irresistible mixture that caught me and wouldn't release. My gaze stopped at the ink on his right forearm, exposed due to the sleeve of his shirt being rolled back.

My head tilted, eyes squinting as I figured out what I was looking at. It was the earth, shaped like an open-mouthed Pac-man with teeth, eating a man. Half the man's bloody body was hanging out of the mouth. The canvas surrounding the area was intricate symbols and patterns. If this type of imagery was on his forearm, I couldn't imagine what else was on his body.

"Strap yourself in, Beverly," he suggested in a smooth-as-silk tone. I was so busy eyeing him, I hadn't noticed until he touched my arm that he was handing me half of my seatbelt.

After snapping the belt together, I distracted myself by forcing my gaze past him and sending it out of the plane's window. I enjoyed viewing the takeoff, giddy at the sight of the plush hills and plains being lowered as the wide, expansive sky turned it all into a painting.

When land disappeared, and fat clouds turned the view snow white, I returned my attention to a more fascinating vision.

"So, Lucas. What do you do, besides link up with your friends and kill cartel members?" This time, I didn't miss the smile that graced his lips before the low tone of his laugh deepened my grin. At close view, I admired his lips. The medium plushness of them enticed me to imagine how they might feel pressed against mine.

"One of those friends, Galvin, and I own a small security firm in Georgia," he replied to the question I almost forgot I'd asked. Luke didn't talk much. It was like pulling teeth, and I would be at his wisdom teeth before he realized I'd taken any, especially when my curiosity was doing the driving.

I was never getting anywhere with him if I gave up before I discovered the answer to all the questions in my head. Either I was about to embarrass myself or have my curiosity satisfied. I leaned closer for a better view into those lovely eyes.

"Are you attracted to me, Luke?" I blurted, unwilling to release him from the grips of my probing gaze. I needed to know or I would continue to be consumed by my relentless curiosity.

He stared, not saying a word as I held my breath. If he didn't answer soon, I would pass out from lack of oxygen and deepen the depth of my embarrassment.

"Yes," fell from his sexy lips, low but audible enough to allow me to begin breathing again. I released the breath I was holding and allowed a smile to dance across my lips. An invisible hand brushed across my forehead as I sat back in my seat. His single word warmed my entire body.

"Are you attracted to me?" he questioned. The apprehension in his tone wasn't missed. I placed my hand atop his strong forearm, unable to help myself. The warm flesh-to-flesh contact distracted me. My dark ebony against his pale ivory was a seductive contrast that drew my attention and forced me to gather myself long enough to answer his question.

"If I weren't attracted to you, I wouldn't be sitting here embarrassing myself," I replied, laughing at my impulsive behavior. My words caused the tension in his shoulders to deflate, and for the first time, I noticed he was as stressed as I was waiting for my answer.

"Why?"

His question caused my brow to furrow in confusion.

Because you're sexy as hell and one of the most distracting men I've ever encountered.

"What do you mean why?" I answered his question with a question but continued. "Luke, I hardly know you, but I feel connected to you. You seem likable. You don't talk much, but I can work with you on that."

I enjoyed the big smile that brightened his face and found I like putting it there. I didn't believe he smiled a lot, and I hoped like hell I could change it.

"Most women are intimidated by my size," he volunteered. "They think I'm weird—a bully, awkward, big and dumb, slow and incapable even," he stated, placing his pointer finger to the side of his temple.

My hand remained on his tattooed forearm, and I think he liked it. I certainly did. The sight of my chocolate spread over his cream elicited all types of freaky fantasies. His sturdy body, positioned atop mine, the contrast of our complexions swirling together in erotic delight caused me to squeeze my legs together as I forced myself to concentrate.

"I don't think that at all," I finally said. "You mentioned you own your own security firm. It takes a sharp person to be in business. Besides, I've met your friends, and it doesn't take a wizard to know that you all are impressively smart to execute the things that you do and to take the risks in your lives as you do."

"Thank you, Beverly," he stated. The sincerity in his tone rang loud and clear. "Thank you for not judging me before we even spoke complete sentences. I've gotten used to people doing that, so it's what I expect."

"You're welcome," I replied, quickly thinking of a way to keep our conversation going. "Now, tell me more about this security company you own."

Luke knew how to talk after all. He just needed me to coax the words from him. Every time he went quiet on me, I started another conversation. By the time we were level in the sky, and the fasten seat belt sign was switched off, I'd found out Luke had a depth that shattered who he was on the surface.

He liked classic rock, played video games, and read sci-fi books in his free time. He grew up with his single father who was deceased but had owned a funeral home.

The details were sketchy, but he'd been emancipated at sixteen and joined the military a year later. He went quiet on me after this bit of news. I knew from working at the center that death was never an easy subject to broach especially when it was a close family member. However,

I got the impression that Luke and his father weren't close since he revealed getting emancipated.

He was evasive about answering questions about his father and growing up living on the top floor of a funeral home. His reluctance heightened my interest in the rest of the story. Something awful happened to Luke, and I was curious to know what it was. I wasn't a nosey person, but in this case, I was willing to wear the banner with pride if it got me closer to Luke.

Simply talking about the most difficult subjects was often what you needed to purge sadness. Seeing Luke's smile was almost better than hearing him talk. His timbre was deep but low and pleasant-sounding like he practiced a mild tone.

I understood his low-expectancy standard where it involved public opinion. Like mine, his profile was predetermined by society, and he was either ignored or gawked at. In my case, I attracted stalking eyes and unwanted catcalls.

Despite the attention, I was often regarded as the side-chick or one-night stand, titles that were food for depression and self-consciousness. Therefore, when I met a man who claimed genuine interest, I automatically assumed he was hiding something.

There were women who hated me on sight because their men coveted parts of my body, never considering the man's motivation. What good was a man's attention when the rest of me would be neglected? What good was a man's attention when his mission was to get what he wanted and toss me to the side later? How could women be jealous of that?

I chose to believe Luke's interest in me was genuine. He hadn't blatantly gawked at my tits yet. Midway through our flight, I faked a few yawns after I stopped questioning him and allowed the conversation to grow quiet.

On a deep sigh, my eyes fell closed as I allowed my head to drift closer to his sturdy shoulder. Once my head landed on his shoulder, I eased myself closer, relaxing into his firm warmth. I was out of order, out of pocket, and out of character. I was just plain out of it and didn't care.

After a paused moment of our connection, he turned toward me, allowing me more room to lean on him. That one move expressed what words never could have. Before long I started to drift, surprisingly comfortable with this man I hardly knew.

Chapter Thirty-seven

Luke

Beverly. She was all I could think about as the pilot announced our descent into the small private airport near Houston. When she rested her head against my shoulder, it was the most pleasing connection I ever shared with anyone. She wasn't like any woman I met before now.

Beverly knew how to make me open up and talk. She knew how to make me comfortable enough to share pieces of my personal life with her. Surprisingly, she was easy to talk to and had a kind spirit that spread warmth through me. When she asked me if I were attracted to her, I'd stopped breathing, unsure if she would make me regret the truth.

She was the first woman I purposely set myself up to run into. I doubted she knew that our *accidental* bump into each other in Ansel's hallway was planned just so I could touch her. I needed to know if she was as magical as she appeared. It was a need I never sought to satisfy before meeting Beverly.

From the moment Megan introduced us across Ansel's table, my eyes refused to stray too far away from her. Her inviting energy lured me into her world, and I was forced to apply great effort to stifle my stares across the table. This connection was a first, one I wanted to explore even if it meant me returning home to Georgia broken-hearted.

When the plane landed with a hard thump, my arm instinctively shot out in front of her, already protective over her. We unstrapped ourselves as we coasted closer to the disembarking area.

The brightness of the sun was eclipsed by dark clouds as a warm, humid breeze kissed our skin. The clouds may have rolled in and hidden the sun, but I was walking next to a woman who had the power to cast permanent rays of light above me.

Beverly. Her name kept whispering through my head and kissing my senses as we traveled in the direction where our waiting SUV was parked.

Beverly was walking beside me until Laura sprang up and swiped her away, slowing her steps as I proceeded forward. The ladies trailed Dax and me as we led them closer to the vehicle.

Once we stepped past the tall, wide doorway into the hanger, a wicked tingle crawled up my spine, slowing my steps. A glance at Dax revealed his furrowed face. A wave of danger chased my chill, and Dax's expression tightened as his steps slowed to match mine.

My right hand landed on my pistol. Beverly approached, and I lifted my left arm to keep her behind me. Dax was next to Laura using his body to keep her in place. I hadn't drawn my gun, but I scanned the area.

"What's wrong?" Beverly whispered the question while staying in place behind me.

"It could be nothing, but I sense that something's off," I answered while scanning and steadily backing us closer to the metal wall behind us, same as Dax was doing with Laura.

"What the hell is going on?" Laura questioned. Where had she drawn a gun from? It was attached to her small hand like mine and Dax's were.

"Stay here." I ordered using myself as a shield to keep Beverly protected before tucking her into the nook of the thick metal support beam. Dax did the same for Laura although I sensed she would keep moving if he hadn't pinned her body behind his and against the other beam.

Being exposed to multiple combat zones had sharpened my instincts. Trouble lurked, but I didn't know what kind, why, or how many until a pair of black boots emerged a second before a bullet whizzed past my head.

Who the hell was waiting for us at a private airport? I made out at least two, one at our left, toward the back of the tall open building and one further inside. Three vehicles and a thick wooden podium stood between the shooters and us. One of the vehicles was our SUV.

Our steps echoed a choppy beat as we positioned the ladies behind the back of the nearest vehicle. Thankfully, it was a large utility van that would provide adequate cover.

Dax twirled a finger in the air before a few hand gestures indicated his attempt to flank our attackers as I kept them busy. He took off for the doorway we entered, his silent steps unheard and not matching his fast-moving body as Laura and I covered him.

The first bullets pinged off the truck's metal exterior. Its large body prevented them from having a clear shot. Unfortunately, it also meant neither Laura nor I had a clear shot on them. One of the shooters turned his focus from us and started firing behind him, announcing Dax's arrival at the man's back.

"Stay low." I glanced back at Beverly. "Keep firing," I told Laura although she didn't need my words. I ran ahead when the bullets paused. At a clear view, I ran once more and positioned myself behind the front passenger's side of the hood of our ride, a black Lexus SUV.

The bullets started to come at me more frequently, but I accomplished my goal of keeping the danger away from Beverly and Laura.

When one of Laura's shots caused the man to duck, I had an opportunity to take up a good aim. When he rose to fire at us once more, my clean shot slammed into his skull. The shot must have distracted the friend because he went down a few seconds later, Dax on the back end, wreaking havoc.

Dax came into view, aimed at the fallen man, but didn't shoot. We needed to confirm who they were and how they knew where and when to find us. When I rose from the protection of the vehicle to approach Dax's area a shot punched me in the chest, the sound reaching out after the impact.

I was slung back by the powerful force but refused to fall.

"Luke!"

The sound of Beverly yelling my name registered before I aimed and fired. Laura was behind me, firing as well.

The sight of the hidden third man's body falling into the open doorway ahead of me to my right was a pleasant one. He wasn't dead, so I aimed and shot him again, pissed that he'd shot me. Another shot sounded and drew my attention from the dead man at the door.

Dax had shot the man he was questioning after he noticed I was shot. He approached me grudgingly, his eyes on the area I'd taken the bullet. Beverly attempted to move in my direction, but Laura dragged her back.

"There was only those three," Dax confirmed as he glared at my chest, his eyes wide and searching. The worry on his face caused me to crack a smile although my situation wasn't funny. When you were used to being spit on all your life and found a group of people who gave a damn, it was hard not to revel in the moments when you could plainly see their care.

Thankfully, the bullet hadn't gotten through the bulletproof shirt I wore under my dress shirt. The six members of our small R & D department were getting a huge raise. I expected to take on fire during Operation Take Six in California, and it was by chance that I chose to wear the newly acquired protective shirt to Texas.

Thankfully, I had, because the danger in Texas apparently hadn't died when the guys took out Santino Dominquez. Dax yanked my top shirt down, popping off a button to gain access to my chest.

He pulled down the taut material of the vest shirt, revealing a large bruise which was a welcomed sight considering the alternative. It sat prominently atop my pale skin, hues of blues and purples already beginning to show. The bruise was above my heart, close to my right shoulder and would serve as a reminder of how close I came to death.

"You okay, man? What is this? Are you wearing a vest? You scared the shit out of me," Dax stated breathlessly. He didn't hide the concern in his gaze. The care and concern were the main reasons I was willing to jump into the fire if any of them needed me.

"Prototype. I guess it's safe to say that it works," I gave him a crooked smile.

Dax threw his arms around me in a strong hug. It hurt like hell, but I reciprocated the gesture. When I glanced up, Laura and Beverly were standing near, staring.

Laura must have noticed Dax yanking my shirt down because she did the same. The top of her head was mid-level to my chest, but she owned the presence of mind that made her my height.

"Either you have the toughest skin in the world or this undershirt is a high-tech vest." Her large eyes searched my face, expecting an answer.

"New vest," I replied to Laura before my gaze fell on Beverly. Her wide eyes were filled with unshed tears. Were they for *me*? Before I could utter a word, Dax started up again.

"We need to go," he announced as he started the SUV.

"Get the ladies to safety. I'll clean this up."

"Are you sure?" Dax asked. A heavy coat of concern was still draped over him.

"Yes, I'll sweep this place and have them ready by the time you get back," I insisted as my gaze found one of the dead men.

"I'll talk to the employees," Dax informed. "They can redirect flights or stall them until we clean this up and figure out how they found us."

I nodded as Laura and Beverly climbed into the back of the SUV. Beverly's gaze met mine once more before Dax closed them inside.

Chapter Thirty-eight

Beverly

Dax left Luke alone. I wanted to protest, although I knew the men knew what they were doing. What if something went wrong? What if they missed something and there were more gun-wielding bad guys waiting?

Dax assured us Luke was safe, but my tension wouldn't be released until I saw him. "He'll take care of the bodies," was all Dax would say when I questioned him a second time about Luke.

Dax checked us into another M. Exclusive location and got us settled before he left to go and help Luke. To say we were being spoiled was an understatement. Knowing someone like Dax could ruin us. Hell, it already had. When he said he was taking you somewhere, you could be rest assured it would be a place to blow your mind.

Although I was surrounded by breathtaking beauty and lavish luxury, I couldn't force myself to sleep. I was too spun up to eat the juicy steak I ordered from room service on Dax's endless tab. I bit into my lip, eyes glued to the door, praying they would just walk in already.

We were aware of DG6's capabilities, not to mention they had an endless supply of soldiers who were willing and ready to die for the cartel.

"You like him, don't you?" Laura inquired. She'd polished off a steak bigger than her leg and was now cutting into mine. When she glanced up at me, her gaze dared me to lie.

"The pale giant. You like him," she didn't intend it as a question.

"You like *him*, don't you?" I questioned her in return, aiming my head in the direction of Dax's room. The suite he got us had two bedrooms, but he changed up the sleeping strategy this time, informing us he and Luke would take turns alternating between the smaller bedroom and extra-large couch in the living room while Laura and I would share the larger of the two bedrooms. He wanted one of them to be on guard as the first line of defense, which was fine with me since we were attacked as soon as we arrived.

I was thankful the sleeping arrangements were different from those of the first leg of the mission. I wasn't altogether sure I could stop myself from jumping Luke if he was closed inside a room with me.

"He kept a bullet out of my ass and put his life in danger for both of us more than once," was the answer Laura gave to my question. I squinted, struggling to remember what I asked. Since when had she cared enough to use what someone did for her as a justifiable answer?

I turned, pinning her with a sharp gaze. I wanted the truth.

"There is nothing there," she offered, meeting my probing eyes. "He will be gone in a week or two anyway," she finished, rolling her eyes.

I knew by that crease in her forehead that I wasn't getting more from her about Dax. So, I prepared to give her my answer about Luke.

"Yes. I like Luke. There's a calmness about him that feeds into me and relaxes me. His size causes people to judge him before they know him. They assume he's intimidating, weird even, when he's everything except that. However, I do sense he has a dangerous edge to him, and considering who his friends are, there has to be," I said, more as justification for my own understanding. "He has characteristics that I rarely find in men."

Laura lifted a skeptical brow. "And you found all this out on a two and a half hour plane ride. You know his whole life history. Are you planning on hooking up with this guy?"

There she went, acting like my mother. I liked Laura being protective of me, but this was one of those times I didn't want her to be. For once, I wanted to get to know someone I found interesting no matter how long it lasted. I stuffed my feelings and answered her questions.

"No, I don't know everything about Lucas, but I like him and I'm not going to be too quick to pass judgment on him."

She screwed her lip up. "Lucas, huh?"

"Please don't start with me, Laura. Why don't you go and get some rest? I'll join in a little bit."

"Why?" she questioned, that crease in her forehead dented. "So, you can stay up all night waiting for a man you met a few hours ago? What happened to your vow to find a permanent man? One who wants more than a fly-by-night relationship? What do you think this is going to be with this man?"

She was making my damn scalp itch, throwing my damn words back in my face. I knew what I said, and it was *my* vow if I wanted to break it. The whole time she was hiding her crush on Dax, I didn't bother her. Now that I think about it, she and Dax were cozier with each other. I should have known something was off when their arguments died down.

"I never bothered you about Dax, even though you kept whatever is going on between you two from me. Knowing you, you're probably giving that poor man fits with the unbreakable chastity belt you've strapped on. I'm at least willing to admit that I like Luke."

Laura was keeping secrets and was probably torturing Dax in the process. The way her eyes shot up at my statements caused my lips to twitch. I'd struck a nerve by suggesting she and Dax had something going on.

Were my suspicions about the way she and Dax were acting toward each other correct? Had Dax cracked through her concrete brain and the wrought-iron gate she kept around her heart, mind, body, and soul? I was starting to believe he may have cracked her code.

After a deep sigh and her ignoring my question, she stood. "I'm going to bed. If you want to waste your time, go ahead. Good night," she called back, and her clipped tone was not missed. I was pissing her off asking about Dax. Whether she admitted it or not, Dax had found a way to get under her thick skin.

"Good night," I called after her. If I chose to stress over a man I just met, so what? I'd stressed over much less in my time.

***

My eyes fluttered open as I struggled to piece together my surroundings. The hotel, the lovely suite Dax had rented for us. My head whipped around when I noticed a fluffy white blanket covering me, one I hadn't placed there. It was pitch dark outside, but the television provided enough lighting to reveal Luke sitting in the chair at my head.

I focused, catching on to the fact he wasn't asleep. He was sitting in the dark, staring at me sleeping. I didn't know if I was frightened or flattered, but I was glad to see him.

"Did you have any trouble?" I asked while easing up from the couch—his bed—until he and Dax decided on whatever guard duty measures they'd worked out.

"No. None," was all he volunteered before he laid his head back, finally breaking the stare he was aiming at me for who knew how long.

Now that Luke was okay, I could focus my stress on the incident at the airport, since Dax suspected we may have been followed there before we departed for Cali. He even went as far as to check Laura for bugs again, although I was sure he just wanted to get his hands on her.

He told us our flight wasn't registered, so the guys waiting on us had no idea where we went and must have staked out the private airport to spot us returning. This encounter reiterated the notion that we weren't dealing with low-level thugs. They were using viable resources to find us just as we used ours to take out one of their leaders.

Dax and Luke didn't seem bothered that the DG6 threat remained a factor. It almost looked like they were glad for the continued danger. I, on the other hand, was scared out of my wits for them and myself.

My feet kissed the gleaming floor as I eased off the couch and inched closer to him. His head lifted at my approach. The light shimmering from the television gave me a glimpse of the weariness reflected in his gaze.

"You can have your bed. I kept it warm for you," I said, fighting the urge to reach out and touch him. What was wrong with me? I was never this forward with men.

The smile that filled his face warmed me to the core and validated my unusual level of forwardness.

"Thank you, Beverly. I appreciate it." He stood, towering over my five-foot-eight frame. I enjoyed the height difference—loved that I, who often looked a man eye-to-eye, had to crane my neck up to one.

Apparently, I could use only one body part at a time. Since my eyes were in use, my mind didn't know how to tell my legs to move me out of Luke's path. We stood in place, staring at each other. Was this our thing? Was this even a thing?

I was usually reserved when it came to relationships, protecting my feelings from the normal and expected rejection. Luke was more reserved than I was, so it made me the aggressor when I was anything but one.

"Thank you for protecting us, Luke, and for risking your life to save ours," I stated, needing to do something besides stare.

His hand rose, waiting in mid-air, but he held back. "You're welcome. It's my pleasure. I have a problem with a group of armed men hunting down women." His statement caused a wide smile to cross my lips.

We lingered there, sharing the warmth and buzzing energy. I swayed, gravitating toward him by a force I was powerless to fight. It was like the space around us was alive with this verve that forced us closer, and it wasn't something to be ignored.

I reached out to where he was shot earlier, knowing there was a huge bruise there. My fingers feathered over the area as our gazes remained locked.

"Good night, Luke," I whispered, desiring more, but fighting my urge. I didn't want to come on too strong and have him think I was throwing myself at him. However, I wanted Luke to want me, but I didn't know how to get to the next level.

"Good night, Beverly," he whispered before heading to the couch. My legs decided to move, but I stood at the door to the bedroom, fighting not to look back. Finally, I turned the knob and opened the door, meeting Laura's light snores on the way inside.

Chapter Thirty-nine

Luke

Food, music, and festive times flowed inside and outside the center. It was a packed house since Beverly and Laura consolidated the members of both centers to have their annual event at Beverly's location.

Streamers hung from the ceiling and balloons floated about the space. Those ones that lost the infusion of helium drifted to the floor and were being kicked playfully about by moving bodies.

Laura and Dax were engaged in a game of dominos on the opposite side of the building from Beverly and me. Three fully-stocked tables of food, punch, and soda lined the front wall and were manned by the center's volunteers. Laughter, dancing, and mingling bodies of the center's kids and teens and some of their parents filled the space with life.

Escorting Beverly to her function and observing the way she reacted with the children and teens revealed the reason why she enjoyed her work. She gave her attention to each person who needed it and sought ways to defuse the problems put before her.

For a crying pregnant teen, she became a counselor. When a kid's feet were hanging from his worn shoes, she made one call and produced a new pair of shoes for him. They were a size too big and cheap, but the boy cherished them like she'd given him a brick of gold.

I was currently losing my Monopoly money to a pair of nine-year-old snaggle-toothed twin boys and the eight-year-old girl who bossed them around. One of my eyes was always on Beverly and the entrance. She'd had to pull me out of the parking lot, although I spotted the additional protection she and Laura had enlisted.

Currently, she was speaking to a teen girl, no more than fifteen, and from what I could make out, the girl had an abusive boyfriend. Her right eye was black and swollen, and her bottom lip was split right down the middle.

"He gives my mom drugs, so she's going to let him in if he comes to the house." The girl's cracking voice found its way to my ear.

"Is this the first time he's done this?" Beverly held the girl's face between her palms, examining it.

"Yes. I think he was showing off in front of his friends."

"I know a place you can go for a few days. I don't know the next time I'm going to be here at the center, so I need you to text or call me if he puts his hands on you again. Don't let this become a habit," she urged, eyeing the girl with the sternness of a disciplining mother.

"Yes, ma'am." The girl nodded and tossed her arms around Beverly in a long hug before walking toward the back of the center.

I sharpened my focus so I could tune out the background noise and concentrate on the two phone calls Beverly made, filling in whatever blanks I couldn't hear by reading her lovely lips.

First, there was the one call where she smiled and talked to secure a place for the girl to stay. The second was the call that left her face tinted in darkness as she gripped the phone like she was choking someone. The second call was to the person who would pay the girl's abuser a visit. She'd asked the girl for the abuser's age to make sure he was old enough to catch the beatdown she was about to send him.

Being at the center opened my eyes. I faced my share of demons, but some of the kids here lived a hellish life the rest of the world ignored or didn't care to see. All they had to depend on was Beverly and the volunteers.

I approached as soon as she was alone because I knew it wouldn't last long.

"Beverly," I called. I loved saying her name.

"Luke," she replied, her smile embracing me in ways I didn't understand.

"I'm impressed with the work you do here. I believe it is severely under-appreciated and deserves more support. I'd like to become a sponsor?"

That lovely smile brightened her face, making her green eyes twinkle. "Thank you. Are you serious? You'd sponsor us?"

"Of course I would. You're doing amazing work here," I praised her. I meant every word, but I'd have said and done anything to make her smile like she was now.

When her gaze lifted and her smile dissolved, I spun to figure out what had stolen her happiness. A light-skinned African-American man was heading in our direction. He was tall, about six-two, and muscular. He reminded me of Dax in the expensive way he was dressed in a full suit. His possessive gaze was locked on Beverly, and I immediately took on a protective stance. A step placed me in front of her.

"It's okay," Beverly assured me, but I wasn't budging until *I* was sure. The man approached, but he would have to go through me to get to her. I gripped her waist and nudged her further behind me, her feet scraping the floor from my quick movement.

"It's okay, Luke. That's Kadeem," she offered as her fingers wrapped around the bicep of the arm I used to keep her in place.

"It's okay, big man," Kadeem stated, his cocky attitude on full display. Dax had informed me about Kadeem, and I understood his attachment to Laura, but would he also lay his life on the line for Beverly? I didn't know the answer to that question, so I stood my ground and waited for his reaction.

"I don't know where they keep finding you crazy ass white boys, but you're fucking serious, aren't you?" He squinted when I didn't answer, attempting to figure me out.

Silence was the answer I provided to his question as the tension between us started to spark to life. The music and the crush of voices that filled the space had faded into dull murmurs. My senses were focused on the man in front of me.

Beverly remained quiet, likely sensing I wasn't going to let Kadeem near her until I was ready. The tension between him and me filled the room and threatened to blow the roof off the building.

I lifted my gaze from his and put it on the two armed men he had standing at the entrance, awaiting his order to take me out if he believed it necessary. My gaze dropped from his men and zeroed in on Kadeem's strong glare, letting him know that I wasn't deterred by his men or his position of authority.

Our standoff drew gazes although we weren't speaking a word to each other. Beverly's fingers dug deeper into my arm, but she remained silent.

"I'm not a fucking threat," he pushed out through tightened lips and gritted teeth. "Beverly is family," he offered, his jaw ticking as he glared at me with unrestrained anger bounding from him. He wasn't used to being denied or disobeyed, and my unrelenting behavior was more of a threat to his ego than anything else.

If he couldn't sit his ego aside long enough to protect what he vowed to, it meant he wasn't truthful to his word.

If he couldn't control his anger, he didn't need to be around Beverly. I didn't budge. I didn't relax my stance or pull my gaze away from his until the veil of his anger dissolved.

As soon as I allowed my hand to drop from Beverly's waist, she let go of my arm and stepped around to my left shoulder. Dax and Laura were rushing in our direction at a rapid speed, but it wasn't necessary.

"Hey, Kadeem," Beverly's sweet voice sounded. "Hi Bev," he said without dropping his gaze from mine. His tone was back to its normal timbre. At the realization, I aimed a positive glance at Beverly before I stepped away from Kadeem to allow them time to talk.

"Where the fuck do you and Laura keep finding those suicidal-ass white-boys?" He asked Beverly behind me before I allowed a smirk to glide across my lips. He had no idea.

Chapter Forty

Beverly

Luke's standoff with Kadeem had scared the shit out of me. I knew Kadeem and how easily he snapped and killed people. But at that moment, Luke frightened me more. Although he scared me breathless, he also left me over-flowing with pride. He didn't speak a word to Kadeem, yet I got the sense that the men understood each other.

Laura and I picked up a few new sponsors, including Luke. Hearing the kids raving about the good time they were having made my heart swell. Luke and Dax were po-lite enough to help with the cleanup.

Although he tried, it was easy to tell Dax wasn't used to cleaning anything by the way he was sloshing dirty mop water across the floor. Luke put him out of his misery and took control.

Dax and Laura departed a half hour ahead of us be-cause I wanted to linger. There was still more cleaning to do by the time we prepared to leave, but I chastised myself when I realized I was babying the volunteers who assured me that they would take care of it.

Luke marched around the dark BMW M760i, com-pliments of Dax. He opened my door and assisted me inside. Chivalry was a nonexistent practice for most of the men in my world. However dangerous our protectors were, they harbored respect toward women in a way I wasn't used to but appreciated.

Luke was my very own big and sexy bodyguard. His strong presence provided a level of security that left me believing I was safe from everything. He agreed to take me back to my apartment so I could pack a few more of our things. I enjoyed being spoiled, but each time Dax purchased things for us, a twinge of guilt surfaced.

Luke took my apartment keys, opened the door, and entered first. He stood me near the inside of the front door after locking it so he could check the rest of the apartment before I proceeded to pack a bag.

I exited my bedroom with a large backpack stuffed with clothes and lots of undies. If this DG6 crew continued the chase, I was determined to at least have clean underwear while running. I took a few more moments to go into Laura's room that she rarely stayed in and packed her a few things.

We'd been sharing an apartment since high school and have never had one problem. For one, Laura was hardly here. If she wasn't spending the night at some woman's place, she passed out on the couch in her office at the center. I never understood how she slept at the center at night when the surrounding area turned into an active warzone.

"Ready?" I asked Luke as I headed toward the front door. In no time, Luke was at my back, pulling me from the door. "Stay behind me," he stated, his face and his serious gaze locked on the door.

I gladly stayed in place behind him. The small amount of contact with his strong hand wrapped around my arm already had my lust stirring. Why the heck was I lusting at a time like this? Lust should be the last thing to surface, but here it was, urging me to take in a deep whiff of his spicy-lavender scent.

Once Luke established our pathway back to his car was clear, he took my bag and slung it across his sturdy shoulder as I followed him down the stairs. I didn't miss that his free hand—his gun hand, was at his side. I couldn't spot the gun, and anyone passing probably wouldn't notice it either, but I knew he had it primed and ready.

Once he secured me in the car, I scanned my surroundings much like Luke did, refusing to allow myself to become too complacent. DG6 was a force to fear, and taking the threat lightly wasn't smart.

"Where are we headed?" I asked, peering out my window at the darkness. Dax called and informed us that we would be switching locations to be on the safe side. At this point, it didn't matter where he took us because it was always more extravagant than any place I'd stayed in.

"It's a secluded place about an hour away. He and Laura already have our belongings and are going to meet us there," he replied as he adjusted the seat. The seats must have been preset for Dax. Each time Luke entered he had to move it back as far as it would go to accommodate his size.

I inhaled deeply, allowing myself to relax into my seat. Between the new car scent and Luke's invigorating aroma, a mood candle may as well have been burning.

My head automatically turned in his direction as he shifted the car, heading toward our new destination. We coasted in silence for a few minutes until we reached the busy intersection we needed to take.

"Do you think—"

Bam!

My neck snapped, and I lurched. Luke maneuvered the steering wheel as we spun out of control. Less than five minutes into the drive and we were being hit by a vehicle neither of us saw coming.

They must have had their lights flipped off. Thankfully, they clipped the front fender, so Luke was able to shift the car into gear and speed away. The tires screeched out a protest as we made our getaway.

The vehicle gave chase, aiming to ram us again and proving it wasn't a random hit and run. However, their SUV was no match for the BMW's V12 engine. I didn't know much about cars, but hearing Laura's discussions with Dax about cars hadn't been lost on me. I couldn't remember how much horsepower they said the car had, but Luke was giving it a workout as the SUV struggled to keep up with us.

The car swerved, squealed, and grunted against the highway to avoid our relentless pursuers, but Luke kept us going. Due to the congestion of the busy intersection, we were forced into a residential neighborhood. We avoided a few near misses of people's empty trash cans that were flipped onto the road's edge and forgotten by the owners after trash pick-up.

The rearview mirror revealed a black SUV, fast moving and relentless in its quest to keep up with us. The windows were tinted so dark, it blended with the night and caused the vehicle to be invisible in certain areas.

Luke made the BMW's engine roar, but the SUV continued to close the distance, preparing to ram us. I gripped the, *"oh shit bar"* above my head, preparing for the impact. Their high beams flipped on, blinding us while revealing they were close enough to kiss our rear end.

My eyes were glued shut in preparation for the impact, but Luke forced a sharp turn to the left and sped down another street doing sixty in a twenty-five mile per hour zone. The houses and porch lights flashed past my vision. Thankfully, it was too late at 11:34 p.m. for kids or people to be outside.

"I know you don't like guns," Luke stated before handing me one. I couldn't have named what kind of gun it was if my life depended on it, but I took it.

"I don't, but I know how trigger happy these DG6 people are."

Luke drove like a mad man; his last sharp turn caused my stomach to flip-flop as we cut the corner onto a dark, lifeless street that housed the back of a shopping plaza.

A loud, demanding punch struck my window, and I instinctively ducked, straining against the seatbelt to take cover.

"Don't be afraid, the car is bulletproof," Luke informed. Was the knowledge of the bulletproofing supposed to ease the stress of us being shot at? Bullets continued to punch at the windows with maddening force as we raced down the dark street being chased by black death.

When Luke slowed the BMW, I prepared to ask if he was crazy until he spun the vehicle around so fast I was slung across the center console, my head nearly brushing his shoulder. The shock of our sudden turn had my arms and hands flailing about, attempting to find something to steady myself.

The bottom portion of the seatbelt gripped my lower half, warning of our erratic movements. Luke turned the vehicle so we faced the bad guys. The lights of their vehicle grew closer, lighting the way around us. They weren't stopping, and Luke wasn't moving. He flipped our headlights off so we'd die an even darker death.

"Please tell me you're not about to do what I think you're about to do," I challenged, knowing the inevitable truth. After that standoff with Kadeem, I was convinced nothing frightened this man. However, this type of shit terrified me. I wasn't on his level. I was afraid to die. I was afraid to get shot. I was deathly afraid to die in a head-on collision.

"Luke." My tone was low and shaking with fear.

The tires screamed, shaking under the car, attempting to convince Luke to shake off this crazy idea. We took off with the BMW lurching onwards like it was on a suicide mission. With no headlights on, my vision was playing tricks with my eyes, and I couldn't tell how far we were away from the vehicle speeding toward us. I slammed my eyes shut. I didn't need, nor did I want to see the moment before the impact.

"Lord, please forgive me for all my sins. I tried to do right by Your glorious name and pray that I've done enough good to win Your favor. All I ask is that You take me fast." I prayed with my eyes glued shut.

My heart was in competition with the revved-up engine. I could feel it beating in my throat, the speeding thumps spilling from my mouth as I continued to pray.

"Jesus, please take that wheel because the driver has gone mad." My eyes were trembling, my voice throaty and filled with begging intensity.

As we sped ahead to meet our assured death, my brain chose to acknowledge time on a whole new level. We had to have been speeding toward death for an hour. With my eyes still clenched tight, I recognized the squeal of tires and the unmistakable sound of a car crashing.

I pried my eyes apart and whipped my neck around at the cloud of dust behind us. It wasn't us. We'd survived. We weren't dead. They were the ones who chickened out. Our headlights were on now.

My lips fell apart as I eyeballed Luke in the dim cab of the car. Without warning, I started slapping at his right arm like a child throwing a tantrum. My hands bounced off his hard arm, my licks not affecting him one bit.

"I can't believe you almost killed me," I whispered as I hit his arm once more for effect. The solid smack sounded off inside the cab of the car, and he had the nerve to smile, which urged me to hit him a few more times.

When he began to turn the car, my lips parted again.

"What are you doing?" I questioned. He flipped the light to dimmers, making the inside panel light cast an eerie glow against his face.

"I can't leave them there to come after us again. I think they were camped out near your apartment building." He parked about four car lengths from the flipped SUV.

I knew we were taking a risk going to my apartment, but I was hoping that DG6 had given up the chase by now. These people were persistent. Were Laura and I ever going to be able to go home?

The sound of metal connecting with metal led my eyes to Luke screwing a silencer on the barrel of his gun. "Stay low, lock the doors when I get out, and shoot anyone you don't recognize."

Those were the words he had chosen to leave me with before he exited the car and slammed the door shut behind him. The rest of my questions died on my tongue as I peered after him, gun in hand as it sat like a heavy weight across my lap.

I engaged the lock using the switch on my door panel. The moon's glow cast enough light for me to spot Luke running toward the SUV that flipped at least twice and landed upright. Its bent and broken body sat crumpled on its warped tires, part of the hood peeled back to the windshield. Thick white smoke billowed from the exposed engine that continued to hum.

The dimness was playing with my vision because it looked like Luke had ripped the passenger's side door off the vehicle. The muzzle flash of his weapon gave me a glimpse of the passenger's terror-filled face before the dark spray of his head contents dotted the headrest behind him. Another muzzle flash revealed the driver slumping as his shadowy body convulsed against the steering wheel.

Luke reached into the car and took something from the dead men. What was he doing? Was he taking their wallets to find out who they were? Was this my life now? I'd been transported into an action film without a script. I was surrounded by death and danger all my life growing up in Crestwood, but this was on a whole other level.

The light on Luke's phone revealed him lifting it to his ear. While talking on the phone, he strolled back to our car leisurely like he hadn't just played Russian roulette with two tons of fast-moving metal and killed two men. I popped the door locks for him to get back in, angling my head and turning so I could observe his every move. He cracked the door and peeked inside.

"I'll get this taken care of as fast as I can," he calmly told me before he continued his conversation on the phone.

"Yes. I led them to a back road, so the vehicle shouldn't be spotted. I'll take care of the bodies."

What the hell did I just hear? My ears perked as I fought for understanding. This was the second time *taking care of bodies* was mentioned. The first time was with the men at the airport and Dax wasn't too worried about leaving Luke there alone.

He continued giving someone a set of what I believed were grid coordinates. What the hell did it all mean?

The buttery leather crinkled under me as I twisted in the seat to catch a view of him walking to the back of our car. The phone went black before he shoved it into his pocket and popped the trunk. The car rocked as he rummaged through the trunk. With something tucked under his beefy arm, he headed back to the wrecked SUV.

For a while now Luke was rummaging through the damaged SUV. I decided to go and check on him. As soon as I edged past the back of our car, he turned to face me. At his distance, he had the hearing of a vampire.

"Beverly?"

I loved the way he said my name. But he made it sound like a question this time.

"I don't want you anywhere near this mess. I made it. I'll take care of it," he stated like he was collecting piles of trash. Based on the way the body was wrapped in plastic wrap, he truly intended to take out the trash. It took effort, but I pulled my gaze from the dead man who was shrink-wrapped like a mummy.

"Are you sure I can't help? It's my fault you have to do this. It's my fault we were being chased." I was offering my help but prayed he didn't want it. I wanted nothing to do with dead, bleeding bodies.

"Beverly, none of this is your fault. You didn't do anything. There was a monster out there sending groups of men after you. Although he's dead, his orders are still being followed. I've got this," he stated.

We stood staring at each other, the night breeze kissing my cheeks. I took another quick glance at the bloody, shrink-wrapped body before I headed back to the car to wait.

Chapter Forty-one

Luke

Beverly had grown unusually quiet. I prayed I hadn't freaked her out with the two bodies I placed in the trunk. I placed a call and asked Gavin to call in a tow we could trust in this area to pick up the SUV and destroy it. However, after D and Dax shared the way Laura and Beverly handled these situations, I was positive she would be okay.

Of all people, I was not the go-to guy for pep talks or therapy. However, for Beverly, I wanted to try.

"I apologize if my actions frightened you. Are you okay?"

"I'm fine. I ... I just want to get back to work and be normal again. Living a lifestyle on the run is stressful. Scary. I wish these people would just leave us alone," she stated, losing her voice in her emotions.

I sat my hand atop hers, noticing the slight tremble in her body. "You'll be fine. I won't leave you until I know you're safe. You will get your life back. I promise."

She nodded, biting into her bottom lip.

"Thank you, Luke. I hope you know that we don't take your help for granted."

I squeezed her hand. "I know."

Turns out, the hardest part of our talk was letting go of her hand. It was so soft, warm, and alive against mine. I'd dealt with so much death throughout my life that a live human touch was foreign.

Beverly's touch intoxicated me. It was genuine and caused sparks of warmth and excitement to course through me, fast-moving currents that rose up and made me high. Her touch was turning into something I craved. Wanted. Needed.

Dax's AMG G6 Mercedes wasn't out front, but it didn't mean he wasn't there. The BMW I was driving had sustained serious damage, and although I offered to pay for the repairs, I already knew he would shrug it off. He was the only man I knew who changed cars as often as he changed shirts.

My phone pinged. It was a text from Dax telling me to drive around the right side of a huge two-story mansion. As we edged around the side, a large garage sat waiting with one of the six doors open.

I spun the vehicle around the wide, paved driveway and backed into the garage. Dax and Laura stood waiting, their faces fixed with deep scowls of concern. They argued like a married couple on the plane, but I think it was a front. They were playful with each other at Ansel's, cordial even. The way and how often Dax stared after Laura told a story I don't believe either knew how to put into words.

Dax was at Beverly's door, assisting her from the car before I could. I opened the back door, reached in and grabbed her bag. A deep smile creased my face at the sight of Laura wrapped tightly around Beverly. The women were as close as sisters, like how I was with the guys. It was a side of this situation I enjoyed witnessing.

It wasn't until I opened the trunk that Laura let go of Beverly, who was talking low into her ear, likely relaying to her the type of drama she'd encountered.

Beverly remained in place near the door to the inside of the house as Laura and Dax crept to the back of the car, lured closer by their morbid curiosity.

"They look like fucked up mummies," Laura's words bounced off the trunk. She leaned in, bending to within a foot of the dead men for a better view.

She cast inquisitive eyes in my direction. "So, Richie Rich had me helping him to set up that spa like we were putting a condom on it. He says you're about to perform magic."

Richie Rich?

My gaze traveled to Dax's. If he revealed to her what I did to people, I was even more convinced there was something going on between them. Her supposedly being gay was apparently a nonfactor.

I needed to get the task of taking care of the bodies out of the way, but there was something more important that called louder. Beverly. I left the two body-gawkers where they stood and approached her. I switched her bag to my right hand and placed my left on her lower back to usher her forward before opening the door.

"Dax?" I called back to capture his attention.

"This way," Dax said while taking the lead ahead of us to show us inside. We followed as Laura lagged behind us. When we entered the house, the foyer led into a large kitchen that resembled something off of the Food Network. I took in the stainless steel, black granite countertops, and gleaming smoke-gray marble floors. The large and darkened recessed area undoubtedly led into a formal dining room.

Next came the side view of the living room. Sparkling gold marble floors gleamed under our feet and introduced a royal-palace style theme. Cream, white, and gold furnishing accented by fine leather and crystal fixtures and a massive chandelier dangling from the ceiling.

The lamps standing between the sofa and adjourning love seats were two life-size statues of goddesses holding up large glass bowls that housed the lights. The furnishings gleamed with intricately placed gold finishes. A wide set of skylights sat over a painting from a long dead and famous artist as three wide windows filled the adjacent wall. The luxurious setup was breathtaking, although expected of anything in which Dax was associated.

"There are no attendants because it's not set to open for another month. We are the first guests. A bed and breakfast," he informed me, answering a few of my questions. "I called in a favor for them to clear up a few rooms and stock the kitchen."

I nodded at him, but my focus was on Beverly. I liked it better when she was making me talk. This more subdued version made me afraid that I may have erased the connection I hoped would grow stronger between us.

When Dax sprang the door to the upstairs bedroom open, I noticed it wasn't a room at all. It was a suite with a sitting area, a kitchenette, and a raised area for the bedroom. Mine and Beverly's bags were sitting by the door.

"Here's your suite, guys," Dax announced as he winked a sneaky eye at me. Beverly hadn't replied to Dax suggesting we be roommates. The smile on her face as she took in the suite was all I needed to see.

"I'll meet you downstairs," Dax informed, exiting the room first. Laura and I lingered. She stared at me before she turned her gaze to Beverly. "I'll check on you in a little bit."

"Okay," Beverly replied while nodding toward her retreating friend.

"Are you okay?" I took a few steps closer.

"I'm fine. This place is off the beaten path, and you're here, so I feel safe." Her words filled me with that tingling warmth that came only from her.

My fingers skimmed her arm to squash my need for her that I had so quickly developed.

"If you need anything, you can yell down or text me. I'll sleep downstairs on the couch. Relax, and I'll check back later." I turned away from her before whatever stirred every time I was near her gripped me and drew me closer. The last thing I wanted was her changing her mind about not being afraid of me.

Chapter Forty-two

Beverly

A long hot bubble bath was all I needed. Now, propped against the thick, fluffy pillows, I attempted to relax with a soppy romance book, but my mind latched onto other ideas. I paid attention enough to the men to have an idea of what Luke was about to do to those bodies.

I clutched at my chest when Laura busted open the door and scampered into the room, appearing to be hopped up on drugs. The front edges of her hair poked up and her high ponytail was a bird's nest of curls. Her eyes were wide, as her body buzzed with what I believed was excitement.

"Beverly, Beverly," she repeated in a breathless whisper like one of those gossiping bitties who'd eavesdropped juicy news.

"What girl? What's wrong? Is everything okay? Are the guys okay?" She made my jittery nerves go from zero to a hundred in a second flat.

"Bev, it's been confirmed. If we didn't believe it before, we need to believe it now. They are professional fucking killers! All of them!" She shot her words out in a mixture of excitement and what I assumed was astonishment. My face fell into a deep wrinkle while staring at her. "I'm convinced that those damn men will be okay, no matter what they face," she added.

A deep sigh followed. Her expression had lost its excitement, and a hint of worry climbed onto her face. "What I need to talk to you about is that big one."

She was scaring me now.

"Is he okay? Is Luke okay?" I questioned, losing my breath as my heart swam into my throat. It took me a while after the car chase to settle my nerves, only to have Laura rev them up again.

"I just watched that big motherfucker cut up two bodies like a chef cutting up chickens. Do you know his friends call him, The Magician? And now I know why. He literally made two bodies disappear."

I sat up higher, not missing the excitement in her tone. My eyes followed her hands when she lifted and waved them to express her words.

"I mean, he knew exactly where to place that blade, right between the bones where the sockets turned and rotated. When he lifted and turned that leg, the damn blade slid between those bone joints like butter—"

"Please," I begged, cutting her off. "I don't need, nor do I care to know the details."

"Yes, you do need to know this shit because I don't want to wake up one day and find out that you're gone. Poof!" She mimicked a magician waving his magic wand over me. "Watching him cut those bodies up was some freakish shit. And, he also knows how to mix a blend of chemicals that melted those bodies down to nothing but liquid." She paused and shook her head with closed eyes for dramatic effect. "Do you hear the words coming outta my mouth, Bev?"

She gripped my arm and gave it a shake to get my attention. "That man turned those people into nothing but a green substance you can pour down the fucking drain. Dax let it out that Luke was who taught Megan's husband how to do it. Now, Dax is down there taking lessons."

I shook my head at her and fought a smile. Laura didn't want me alone with Luke, but she was excited about what she witnessed him do, so shutting her up wasn't going to be easy.

"Dax put you together with him in this room. I think he was attempting to play matchmaker, but if Andre the Giant comes up in here, don't you let him stay with you," she continued, ordering me around like she'd birthed me. "This place has five other rooms. He can pull the plastic off one of those beds," she pointed over her shoulder in no particular direction.

"His name's Luke, and what are you now? My mother? He already said he was sleeping downstairs on the couch, but I'm not turning him away if he comes up here. He scared the hell out of me doing it, but he saved my life again."

Wait a minute. Where were she and Dax sleeping? Before I could spit the question out, she was right back at it.

"Bev, you better shake off that damn glimmer he's put in your eyes. You get out of line with him, and he can cut your ass up and make you disappear. Not to mention he's about ten-foot-five and appears to have superhuman strength. Did you see his feet? He can probably make Mr. Ed jealous. Dick's probably the size of an elephant's trunk. You don't have all that extra cushion you used to have when you were in your teens. He looks like he could do major damage," she warned, causing me to choke on the laugh I failed to suppress.

"You hear that?" she questioned, her eyes peering up as her head jerked up at a sound I didn't hear.

"What?" My face squinted in curiosity.

"It's your fucking uterus trying to convince me to talk some sense into you," she joked, biting back a smile.

I knew her well enough to know she was far from done. I loved this woman. I truly did, but she was about as crazy as crazy could be. My stomach quaked as I stifled a laugh.

I loved Luke's size. There weren't many men who were interested in me who made me feel small and pretty at the same time.

"Why don't you come clean about you and Dax the Assassin?" I asked her, stopping my runaway ideas and finding a subject that would put an end to her rant about Luke. "I've caught bits and pieces about Dax's activities. He's like one of the highest paid assassins in the country and probably in the world for all we know. So, maybe you should be worried about who's going to make who disappear," I warned, making her go quiet for the first time.

However, it wasn't fear that laced her thinking gaze, aimed at the bedside table all of a sudden. She liked that Dax was considered one of the most dangerous men in the country. It intrigued her, and I wouldn't be surprised if she'd put in a request for him to teach her a thing or two.

"I'm just saying," she finally replied, unwilling to talk about what I suspected was happening between her and Dax. As a matter of fact, she'd grown almost uncomfortably quiet and started chewing on her bottom lip. That lip chewing was a dead giveaway. Laura was keeping secrets.

"I knew it!" I yelled, causing her to jerk her head up at me. "I knew that something was going on between the two of you!" I shouted in a controlled whisper, pointing an accusing finger at her. "You've never kept anything from me before, so I refused to believe what was so clearly in front of me."

"It's nothing—the excitement of this mission and what's going on with this DG6 mess. After this is over, he'll be back to assassinating people, and I'll be back at the center keeping the kids from getting locked up or pregnant."

I smiled. "I miss being at the center too. Miss the kids, even though they drive me nuts sometimes."

A fast hug came next. "Love you, Bev," she whispered into my neck.

"I love you too," I returned. "I'm also glad that you're no longer a virgin," I blurted. I wasn't going to let her off easy.

My words froze her in place with her nose buried in my neck. When she moved, a coy smile was all that followed my statement. It was also confirmation that my gay best friend was now bi-sexual. The revelation floored me, something that would have to gradually settle into me.

"First, I was not a virgin. I've had more sex than the law should allow."

I pursued my lips. "With women. Who didn't have dicks?"

She didn't reply, only cast a far off stare at the wall above my head. Laura liked Dax more than she was letting on, but I didn't call her on it. My brain attempted to feed me the idea of delusions of their relationship being a spur-of-the-moment fling, but I didn't believe so. I'd been around her for half my life. For Laura to take things to a sexual level with a man, things were serious, deadly serious.

Instead of holding the therapy session she would deny she needed, I decided to forgo it until she was ready to talk about it. It pleased me she could find a semblance of happiness outside the open legs of another woman.

This was also the longest I could recall her being around someone she was romantically involved with although her choice to flee wasn't currently an option. The poor women she caught and turned out usually lasted a week, two tops, before she was ready to trade them in for the next victim.

A smile crept across my face as she tossed me a quiet wave and ambled out of the door. She was the toughest woman I knew. If she cared for you, she would be the first one riding a flame to fight for you. Dax and I needed to have another talk. World's best assassin or not, if he hurt my friend, I would kill him.

***

The low squeak of the door sounded and drew me from a light sleep. My smile came easy at the sight of Luke. His tall frame blocked the light shining in from the hallway. The lamp gave enough brightness to showcase his handsome face and the shimmering blue in his eyes.

I sat up, needing to get closer to him. I didn't care what Laura said about him, I wanted Luke, and I was just realizing how much I was beginning to care for him.

My hand rose, reaching for him, drawing him closer and wiping away a bit of the tension he stepped into the room with. He took my hand and sat on the edge of the bed. The quiet intensity in his gaze caused a chill to ripple up my spine before it settled in the pit of my stomach.

"I needed to check on you and make sure you were okay," he said. My smile and nod gave him the confirmation he sought. After way too short a moment, he stood, letting my hand go, his warmth slipping away.

"Good night, Luke."

"Good night, Beverly."

My gaze traced the lines of his muscular back working against his shirt. Why couldn't I open my damn lips and tell him not to leave? Luke was being a gentleman because it's what he assumed I wanted. I appreciated this aspect of him, but I wouldn't have minded one bit if he crossed the line.

Chapter Forty-three

Beverly

An hour of tossing and turning was enough. I was craving something sexy. All I needed to do was be brave enough to walk out the door and go and get it. I threw on the fluffy robe from the bathroom and headed out.

Be brave. I kept repeating to myself as I took unsure steps that edged me closer to Luke. He was no doubt the genie who had the magical powers to make me set the vow I made concerning men and relationships on fire. I was setting myself up for a heartbreak, but I couldn't resist the pull Luke had on me.

When I entered the living room, he was sitting with his back resting against the large arm of the couch. The television lit part of the room, but his face was aimed at the skylight.

While sitting up, his feet reached the opposite end of the couch. Therefore, when he laid down his feet would hang over the edge.

His head snapped in my direction, and a huge smile bent his lips at the sight of me. When I eased closer to the couch, he turned his feet over the side to allow me a place to sit. A sheet was spread over the sofa, and the blanket he would use for a cover was slung across the back.

"I couldn't..."

"You..." we spoke at the same time.

"You first," he said before pointing to the remote and lowering the volume on the television. The lights were all out so the television and moonlight gleaming in from the beautiful slanted skylight windows provided a dim glow. It was enough light for me to see all I needed to see.

The robe slipped off my leg when I adjusted myself to sit closer, and I didn't close it. The sight of him excited me, sparking an array of emotions I was losing control over.

"Luke, please tell me I'm not the only one who's feeling chemistry here?" I questioned and like on the plane, my breath caught and I refused to release it until he answered.

His eyes raked leisurely down my body, so filled with lust, I swore, my panties were melting clean off and leaking to the floor.

"You're not the only one feeling chemistry. I didn't want to cross the line with you," he admitted.

My smile spread wide as his words warmed my insides.

"Cross it," I urged in a breathless whisper. "Whatever line you're avoiding, I want you to erase it, destroy it, make it go away."

His low chuckle sounded at my words, but he didn't make a move to get any closer. There remained a depth of uncertainty with him that I didn't understand.

I was skeptical about asking, but I was doing my curiosity a disservice if I didn't.

"Can I ask you something, Luke?"

"Sure," his eyes sparkled when they met mine.

"I've never dated a white man before because there are those who have managed to make me feel like I was a creature they feared touching. Have you ever dated a black woman before?"

"No," he answered, while allowing his fingers to skim my forearm. His caress was making more of my questions and concerns disappear. I wholeheartedly believed we accepted each other at first sight.

His fingers were steadily sliding up my arm, causing goosebumps to rise.

"I didn't have any childhood friends or family growing up. I didn't even have an imaginary friend. My friends were blind, deaf, and mute, the dead." His statement reminded me that he grew up in a funeral home.

"When I talked to them, silence answered back. My existence was lonely and solitary. Without guidance or influence, I learned early to appreciate good people, no matter the color, as long as they were among the living."

I rolled my arm around his and brushed my hand over the top, mingling his seashell white with my dark brown. His broad smile surfaced at my action, the sight sending a rejuvenating tingle through me.

"Whether it was manufactured by society or self-imposed, anyone who fails to see the many ways that you are beautiful is blind," he said, destroying my questions altogether.

"Thank you," was my basic reply, but his beautiful words had my heart ready to hop out of my chest and skip across the floor.

"You asked about chemistry. I felt it instantly. From the first moment our eyes met it was like a warm hand reaching out. We hadn't said a word to each other, but it was like we were speaking all the same," he admitted, taking our encounter to a depth I liked but never expected. It let me know I wasn't imagining our connection when I was sitting at Ansel's table.

He leaned closer, observing me, requesting permission to kiss me with his pleading eyes. When our lips brushed across each other's, my eyes slid close, and my body relaxed. My mouth melted into the soothing flow of his, the sensual caress spreading a blanketing warmth over my body. His kiss was gentle, smooth, and filled with an emotion-infused pleasure I never experienced.

My heart tapped a maddening beat in my chest as the pulse points in my neck and lady parts blazed with heat, the ambers combusting into a slow burn.

A moan escaped and vibrated against his mouth. The sensual glide of his tongue slipped along the contours of my lips, enticing me to open for him. He slipped his tongue into my mouth with an easy unexpected slide.

How could he be so big, tough, and hard and be so ingeniously sexy and gentle, breathing pleasure into me through a simple kiss? I gripped the edge of his T-shirt angling for our bodies to connect, needing more.

He eased back because we needed to breathe, but I was intoxicated off him, buzzed in a new way. He gave me a taste, but I wanted the whole meal. I wanted *all* of him, all six-foot-eight well-built inches.

I stood on legs weakened from our kiss. When I placed myself on his lap, sitting across his strong thighs, hints of shock reflected in his features before it was replaced with lust.

His eyes grew heavy. His strong arms encircled me, melding me into his body as my arms met at the back of his neck, my nails raking through the short hairs at his nape.

"Beverly," he breathed against my lips. Calling out my name in the heat of the moment and making the warmth from his breath coat me like an addictive toxin he sprayed.

"Luke," I whispered back.

His firm hands massaged my back, thighs, and arms. It didn't matter where they were placed as long as his hands were on me.

"I want to be with you," I managed between our kisses.

My words stalled him, causing him to leave our kiss and seek my eyes.

"Are you sure?" he was being the gentleman I didn't need him to be. Judging by the thick hardness pressing into the backs of my thighs, he was as ready as I was, if not more.

After I stood, he picked up his gun from a nook on the couch and his wallet from the end table. He tucked the gun down the back of his shorts before he reached for my hand and allowed me to lead him to my suite. We remained quiet on our journey as we drew nearer to what would either ruin us or bring us closer together.

My damp palm twisted the knob before I sprang the door open and led him to the huge bed. He placed his wallet and the gun on the nightstand before he turned and stared at me, eyes wide and observing my every move.

An odd silence fell between us. Was he nervous or excited? I made the first move, leading his hands to the belt of my robe.

He pulled it apart with ease before he allowed his fingers to slip behind the material and ease it open and away from me.

My teen years had done a number on me. Within any group, I was always the fat one, the cute-faced fluffy one. Although I picked up inches in height and a lot of what I called baby-fat had melted away, the images of that chubby teen face and body were stapled to my psyche and sometimes reflected back at me in the mirror.

When lusty male eyes examined me, it always brought up that girl in me who hated her body and cursed her dark skin. Back then, I received numerous not-so-subtle lines from men reminding me that I might have been dark and fat, but I was a good lay. It was meant as a compliment, but the cutting words had sliced deeper than even I knew.

Being teased for being dark and fat for years left me with a self-conscious attitude. Although I made efforts to work on myself, using the gym at the center or playing sports with the kids, I continued to struggle with my body image.

However, Luke looked at me like I was the most beautiful thing he ever saw. He caressed me like my skin was a precious keepsake. His genuine interest shined through without a single spoken word.

He stared at me the way Aaron stared at Megan and bestowed looks similar to the ones Ansel was sneaking in Regina's direction. With Luke, my most haunting insecurities were going up in flames as I sought to embrace the woman I was becoming.

He eased the robe from my shoulders, his warm fingers seizing every opportunity to brush the parts of my skin he exposed. The material slipped over my braless chest, my hard nipples poking at my thin pink top, revealing more of my lust. My matching pink shorts hugged my hips and barely covered my ass.

When his hand journeyed and slipped over the globes of my thick ass, my pussy flooded, and I caught fire. My breaths came faster, needing him to speed things up, but I was determined to stay calm.

"It's been a long time for me, Luke," I whispered harshly.

"Me too," he confessed.

"Good." Relief swept through me at his admission.

"Good?" he questioned, his face wrinkling with curiosity.

"Yes, it means we're not going to last long on the first go, so we should make plans for a second." How presumptuous of me to assume a second time when we hadn't gotten the first underway. But, I felt it in my soul that we would be good together.

He released a low chuckle. My anxious hands glided down the front of him until I took a hold of the bulge that was tickling the backs of my thighs earlier. He hissed in a quick spurt of air but did nothing to stop me.

My mouth dropped open once I discovered that one hand wasn't going to be enough. I lowered myself to my knees, as eager to see it as I was to get it into my mouth. With a firm grip of both sides, I tugged his shorts and underwear down. His dick sprang free and nearly took my head off.

"Jesus!" I whispered. "Instant hysterectomy," I muttered under my breath, my gaze glued on a gigantic white jungle snake. His size-fifteen foot was telling the truth, the whole truth, and nothing but the truth. I'd never seen one that massive, let alone had it roaming around inside me.

"We don't have to if you don't want to," he said, seriously while considering my reaction. I'd been without sex so long, that looking at him had me ready to come. I maintained a firm hold, moving my hands up and down, making his teeth sink into his bottom lip.

"Do you really think I want to stop? No way," I responded, glancing up at him. My gaze fell back to the magnificent wonder of the world cupped in my palms. He had enough to break me in two if he tried, but I couldn't be luckier if I planned it. After the drought I was in, one night with him would create an ocean across my desert.

This was the first time I was hypnotized by a man's dick, my mouth inching closer like I was going in for a long-awaited kiss. I was ready to say "hello" and "pleased to meet you" with my tongue. In my eagerness, I hadn't even allowed him a chance to get out of his shirt.

When I eased the tip into my mouth and widened my tongue to lap at the underside, a harsh moan left his lips and his body tensed. Bulging thigh muscles sprang up, and his ivory skin pulled taut, giving me a show while I performed.

His hands remained at his sides, balled into tight fists. I eased him from my mouth and glanced up after I placed a sweet kiss to the tip that caused him to jump.

"Luke, touch me. I want your hands all over me." Any decency I possessed was being devoured by lust and my long overdue need to chase satisfaction.

His fingers uncurled at my words. A firm hand gripped the area between my neck and shoulder, and the other started at the front of my hair and tangled its way into a tight grip.

If I had anything to say about it, I was about to sweat my fresh perm out in one night. The more of him I eased into my mouth, the tighter his grip on my hair became. His member tickled my tonsils, and I wasn't even at the half-way point. My slick hand movements massaged the rest of him, unwilling to leave anything untouched.

I was a scientist studying my subject with vigor and eager intensity. I gave my throat a good workout, tongued his balls, palmed, licked, and sucked them to my satisfaction. My lips kissed and caressed the velvety skin of his shaft before I tongue-kissed the head that leaked his sweet juices.

His dick was so heavy my mouth, throat, and hands were getting the ultimate workout, but the strong force of lust and the tingling sparks of desire kept me hungry. Like I expected, it didn't take long before his body started to shiver, and his harsh moans grew more intense.

"Ah. Shit. Beverly!" he yelled as his body started to tremble. I waited for the flow of his warm cum, anticipating how delicious it would be when it coated my tongue. However, right before I got my taste, he attempted to jerk away. I dug my fingers into his muscular thighs and kept him in place.

I believe I moaned louder than him when the first sweet taste flowed into my mouth and enticed me to suck harder and lap up every drop. When I finally released him, he fell back onto the bed, making it creak under his impacting weight. With his eyes clamped tight, he fought to take in oxygen as his chest heaved hard and fast to keep time with his ragged breathing.

A knowing smile made his lips twitch. I stood before sitting next to him, rubbing his back. My skills were rusty, but it pleased me to see that he enjoyed my work. His head was bowed, and his shaking hands were up to his forehead like he was crying. I edged closer, eager for any contact as my hands stroked his solid hot body.

Chapter Forty-four

Beverly

"Are you okay?" I knew better than anyone what a good orgasm could do to you after you abstained for a while.

He lifted his head, and the bright smile on his face eased my building tension.

"Yes. I'm fine. I was a little light-headed for a few seconds. That was incredible," he managed to get out over his quick breaths.

He was clueless as to how sexy he was with satisfaction riding his body and written on his face. His hand eased up my thigh and had me dripping in seconds. At this point, I couldn't have cared less about what was next. I was hot and bothered enough to try almost anything.

He stood. Unfortunately, he found and slipped his shorts back up, covering what I wanted to see. When he tugged my top, attempting to lift and separate it from my body, I helped, shaking my arms to get out of it. I didn't know I was distracting him until his gaze landed on my tits and remained aimed at my chest.

A smile tugged at my lips, realizing he was able to resist my double D's while they were covered, but now that they were naked and flashing him, he stalled. His tongue slid across his lips before he started to move again, pulling my top the rest of the way down my arm, his gaze still on my chest.

I decided to help him by shoving my shorts over my thighs, leaving me in nothing but my panties. His gaze fell from my chest and scanned down my body, chasing my shorts as I wiggled them down my legs until they pooled at my feet.

I fought to control my eagerness, especially when I had intimate knowledge of what Luke had waiting for me. He was moving too damn slow, so I reached and started lifting his shirt. He caught on to my eagerness and didn't waste a moment dragging the shirt the rest of the way over his head.

His thick bicep got caught in one of the sleeve holes, and I gladly helped, stroking and squeezing bulging muscles, multitasking. The picture of the muscular top half of his body was a feast for my eyes. The ink was icing on the cake, giving me a reason to stop and admire, even as my body begged for more attention.

I previously admired the art on his arms, but without a shirt, I could fully see the canvas of art his chest, back and arms were. The sight sky-rocketed my lust and I was forced to take deep breaths to keep calm.

I touched and admired, taking it all in while beating back my lust. My eyes traced over skulls and crows, angels and demons, ancient symbols, and what I assumed was his military tattoo on his upper arm area. It would take me weeks to go over all the symbolism and art he possessed, but it was a task I would eagerly undergo.

It wasn't until he gripped my shoulders that I peeled my lusty heavy gaze from his body and allowed him to turn me to the bed. Distracted, I fell back rather than sat, making the mattress release a protesting squeak.

He eased me back into the center before climbing in after me. Stopping at my knees, he took his time admiring, and I enjoyed being the object those beautiful eyes devoured.

A few more seconds, and I couldn't resist any longer as I lifted off my elbows and went in for a tasty kiss he gave back in abundance. We moaned into each other's mouths, and our noises elevated our lust to a burning level.

Once we quenched our initial thirst, he caressed and massaged my tits, making love to them. The way his hot, pink tongue chased my dark berries and drew circles around them, I panted and was only able to take in small spurts of air.

The visual heightened my arousal as the sensation he fed me made my sex heavy with overflowing need. When he drew one puckered tip in and sucked hard, an elongated, "Oh!" rushed out before my eyes snapped closed and rolled in my head.

The weight of his taut warm body between my thighs, his unexpected soft stroke and his hot wet tongue sucking and plucking my nipples had me fighting back an orgasm already. When I was able to open my eyes, it was the sight of us that boosted my lust past the boiling point.

His warm milky skin teased my chocolate, melting us into a swirl of creamy perfection that invigorated each of my senses and heightened my arousal.

He eased back, sensing my lurking release and admired my body once more. I was rising too, following him up, until he placed his wide palm on my shoulder and urged me to lie back.

When he slipped his finger between the waistband of my panties and began slipping them off, the sensation of them gliding over my thighs and down my legs was enough to make me whimper. My tongue swept my bottom lip as my heavy lids shuttered before my head dipped to the side.

I jerked up when his hand gripped my knees and parted my legs before slipping down the inside of my thighs. His scorching gaze roamed as his hands moved back up and caused me to leak shamelessly, my body revealing my desperation.

The contrast of his hand sliding down my legs brought forth images of vanilla ice cream melting over the top of molten chocolate cake. I knew the sharp contrast in our complexions would play a seductive role. I just hadn't expected the overwhelming intensity it brought to our mingling caresses. I tore my gaze from the sight of us and allowed my heavy head to fall back onto the fluffy white comforter.

My legs were eased up until my calves kissed the back of his sturdy shoulders. His body was warm against mine like he had a fever, sending flaming heat into me. My lips kept spreading farther apart as he eased his face closer to the sweltering heat between my thighs. A gasp left me, my eyes snapped closed, and I damn near passed out when his mouth touched my pussy.

"Aww!" I yelled out against the sudden flow of pleasure that began to fill me to the brim. The exceptional movement of his lips and tongue combated my erratic movements. It was so much all at once and so shockingly good, I didn't know how to take it. Shivering one second, yelling out another, and fisting the sheets the next.

Luke had my pussy soaked, and I feared he may need a towel to dry off once he was done. However, he lapped up my juices like he was sucking on a snow cone melting under the sun. When my legs started to quiver uncontrollably, and my chest heaved, desperate for oxygen, I knew I was about to explode at any moment.

In mere minutes, he had my pussy humming a thank-you-Jesus tune as my mouth shouted curse words I didn't normally use. Whoever said the pen was mightier than the sword lied because at that moment I was certain that his tongue held that title.

"Luke!" I yelled at the top of my lungs, as the explosion of my orgasm possessed me. My legs snapped shut around his head, squeezing like a vice as his tongue remained buried inside me. I didn't care if the state of Texas heard me, screaming was the only way I knew to deal with the pleasure riding my body straight to heavenly bliss.

Luke gripped my thighs, his strong hands keeping me in place as I bucked and screamed my head off. My nails dug deep and hard into his shoulder and arm, leaving no doubt that there would be marks.

A long exhaling sigh left me as he eased up, lavishing me with feather-light tongue strokes while I came down the mountaintop he set me upon. I was too weak to lift my head, so I expressed my appreciation through labored breaths.

"That was out of this world," I panted as my chest continued to move up and down. "Mmm," bubbled past my throat and remained trapped in my mouth.

He'd licked and sucked until every ounce of my control vanished. Spent, he lowered my limp legs gently to the bed. I attempted to sit up but failed, so he assisted by gripping my arms and tugging. He remained on his knees before me, studying me like I was a secret he was discovering.

"What?" I asked, curious about his ideas at this moment.

"You're a beautiful woman, Beverly." The sincerity in his melodic tone and the glint of appreciation that sparked in his smiling gaze presented his truth. With Luke, I was able to accept I had graduated from a woman who was wanted and desired for more than a few well-placed body parts. Luke wanted all of me.

Chapter Forty-five

Beverly

My hand glided over his chin, enjoying the prickles of hair that spiked under my palm. Unable to help myself, another kiss followed. There was something on the tip of my tongue that I was about to say, but I couldn't keep my hands or my lips off the man.

"Stand up," I whispered against his lips before my tongue traced the edges. He lingered there, accepting my kisses before he backed off the bed and stood. I needed to relieve him of his last stitch of clothes.

With me sitting and him standing, a mountain had sprung up before me, but it was a mountain I would gladly climb.

I stood before him, my neck craned to hold his gaze as my hands dropped down to his shorts, knowing first-hand what was down there, waiting, lurking, and brushing against my stomach. My thumbs slipped between his warm skin and the nylon shorts and dragged them down.

When he popped out hard, ready, long and strong, I gawked for a second time, swallowing my reaction before I continued to slide his shorts down his muscular legs. His skin was soft and hot, but his strong muscles, working beneath the softness, gave him a lure I couldn't get enough of. He was manly but harbored a soft and calming allure. Once I got the shorts as far as his feet, he kicked them away.

His dick slapped the burning flesh of my stomach and licked my skin when I closed the space between us. He fit his hand around my ass and lifted me with ease, causing a moan of surprise to escape. The unforeseen movements didn't stop my legs from wrapping around his waist. His hardness pressed deep into my stomach, making its presence difficult to ignore.

He moved us closer to the bed before climbing in with me still wrapped around him. I never had a man handle me this way. None were ever able to or just didn't know how. This was one of those sexual positions I was jealous of because I assumed I would never get to experience it. Luke made it feel natural, right.

The mattress groaned under our weight as I was lowered, shifting to my knees in front of him. My hand automatically went to his dick, massaging and making him suck in quick breaths. I glanced down at my hand moving over it, fascinated by the size and weight.

"We don't have to do it if you think it's too much," he suggested with a deep crease of concern etching his face. He hadn't expressed the statement as an arrogant crack about his size. His concern about hurting me was genuine.

My hands never stopped gliding up and down his length. "I want all of you, Luke, every inch. I don't care how long it takes or how many times we have to do it. However, I suggest you get me slippery-wet before we try."

My words put another one of those big shiny smiles on his face.

"One more thing," he added. "And I pray you don't think less of me for asking, but if it doesn't feel good or if I'm not doing it right, I'd rather you tell me, so I can make it right."

Now, I was the one with a Kool-Aid Man smile. "Luke, that statement alone has increased my respect for you. I have no problem telling you whatever you need to know."

With those words aired, he didn't have to tell me to lie back. Hell, I didn't even know what position he wanted. When I saw his tongue skate over his lips, I reacted like a soldier who was given a command.

He retrieved the condom from his wallet on the dresser. My eyes widened at the sight of it gliding over his length and noticing that although it fit tight around his girth, it wasn't long enough.

Dayum! My drought was about to be washed over by a tidal wave.

He moved with the quickness I didn't think a man his size should possess. His lips reconnected with my lower ones, giving another sample of his intoxicating tongue. He worked me into a breathless frenzy. My hips quivered, my stomach muscles drew tight, and my pussy was flowing like a faucet by the time he came up for air.

He hovered above me, putting his weight on one elbow as he aligned his magnificent piece with my sopping wetness. I jumped when it brushed my wet lips, causing him to stall his movements.

"I'm okay. I'm just excited. Don't stop," I urged as my breaths escaped and merged with his quick ones.

He pushed and I cringed, expecting pain, but he was gentle and careful with his movements, not forcing it. He eased into me teasingly and slowly, enticing me to want more, knowing that he had more to give.

His languid movements were deliberate, well-timed thrusts that had me whispering hot words in his ear and my nails digging into his back. "Luke, baby, it's so good," I whispered hotly in his ear.

He maintained his easy pace, opening me to him, coaxing me to allow all of him into me. "You're so big," flew past my lips as a downstroke took my breath and had me biting into his shoulder and sucking the skin I'd bitten.

Just when I believed I couldn't take anymore, my pussy muscles spasmed and released enough to allow him another inch.

If my clawing nails and biting were hurting him, he didn't care because his loud hisses and sighs of pleasure mingled with mine. Once I started to accept his size, my feet slipped over the backs of his thighs when he slid in and inched back down his muscle tight skin when he eased out.

When he started to rotate his hips, I believed I was dying a glorious death. "Lucas," I breathed out as, "So good," continued to hiccup past my lust-clogged throat, like a broken rap song. I'd had okay sex and was lucky enough to have good sex a few times. But this? The sexing Luke was putting on me had me sprung, and we weren't even done yet.

He took his time with me, making sure he was doing whatever turned me on the most and he wasn't missing a beat.

"You're so beautiful," he whispered hot in my ear. "A sexy Goddess that feels like heaven." His words were as hypnotic as his sensual possession of every part of me. His tongue found the thumping pulse in my neck and caressed it with tender flicks. The thrill of his mouth on me along with his enticing thrust sent my hormones into overdrive.

"Shit," I retracted my nails from his back and allowed my hands to drop lower over his tight ass. He thrust in deep, allowing the ridges of his dick to massage my slick walls before he eased out and massaged my wet fire in the opposite direction.

Luke's sex wasn't something I endured, waiting until the right thrust hit me in the right spot. With him, I was in love with every stroke, every twist and turn, and didn't hesitate to vocalize as much. Yelling with colorful words about his exceptional size, repeating to him how deep he was when I knew he felt it, telling him how much I loved his dick being inside me when he clearly noticed my rolled back eyes, gasping breaths, and cries of ecstasy.

"Beverly. Beverly," he whispered repeatedly. His tightened facial expression revealed his difficulty with speech as his warm breath caressed my face. I loved the way he said my name, but him saying it while he was buried deep inside me caused my muscles to quiver around him as my juices bathed his thick penetrating member.

It was hard to believe he was afraid that I wouldn't like it. He was lavishing my inner walls with so much pleasure I didn't realize I was crying until the wet droplets rolled over my cheeks. *What the hell?* I was unable to hold back as the telling emotions sprung up from nowhere.

I was the one who rolled my eyes when women would say the sex was so good it made them cry. Getting to experience firsthand what they bragged about, was an unexpected revelation.

I was helpless to hide the tears that just kept seeping out like I was a big baby. My moans refused to be silenced, despite the flowing tears. My mouth refused to stay shut despite overwhelming emotions. Our meshed bodies, deep connection, and emotional penetration were too much to keep contained.

Thankfully, by the time Luke lifted his face from my neck, I found a new tone, yelling for him not to stop. The orgasm hit, took control, and made me its bitch. My out-of-control muscle spasms and shivering body must have coaxed his orgasm. The distant sound of him calling my name peeked into my consciousness as I coasted on bliss.

Our cries of pleasure eventually ceased and gave way to our harsh breaths filling the room. His weight on me was heavy, but just right and was what I believed kept me from floating away. I didn't notice how tightly I was squeezing him against me until I unhooked my arms from around his neck and back.

Free to move, he lifted, easing out of me and making me want to rise to chase his movement. The fullness of him was immediately missed, leaving a lusty need I craved. Once he was free of my body, he laid beside me, his gaze scanning me.

"Are you okay? Did I hurt you?" his concern spilled out between quick breaths.

I forced my neck to turn my heavy head in his direction. "I'm more than okay," I managed as my lips rose and a deep smile filled my face.

The bed shifted, but my relaxed state kept me in place. Once I gained enough strength to lift my head, my gaze caught Luke's ripped back and perfect ass as he entered the bathroom to get rid of the condom. I enjoyed the way his muscles moved under his glowing ivory skin. The man was built like a Marvel hero, and he had no idea he had my nose wide open.

When he returned, I managed to lift onto my elbows. I took in his handsome face for only a brief moment before my gaze quickly dropped to the area that took me on the ride of my life. He was the best I'd ever had, and the admission was making a silly smile slide across my face.

He climbed in making the bed dip. I only vaguely acknowledged him speaking because I was unable to stop gawking at his dick. It had softened but remained plump enough for me to conjure dirty sex images. With a pink tint darker than the rest of his body, it laid against his thigh, winking at me and whispering my name. *Beverly.*

"Beverly," Luke called, caressing my arm to get my attention.

"Yes," I mumbled as my teeth sank into my bottom lip and my eyes reclaimed the magnificent piece that had filled me splendidly, stretched my walls to the brink of their resistance, and made me lose all control.

After all this time, I finally understood something. This was how men were when I talked to them and they talked back to my tits. Luke's fingers slid under my chin and lifted my face to meet his teasing smile.

"I think you need to go and ask Dax for another condom," I shamelessly suggested.

The sound of our shared laughter filled the space around us as sheer joy enveloped me. I wasn't like this with anyone.

"So, you liked being with me," his brows lifted expectantly. He was clueless as to how good he was in bed.

"Yes. I want more, a lot more," I admitted, not caring that I sounded like a slut.

Nothing more was said. He hopped out of bed, threw on his shorts and shirt and headed for the door. I didn't know Dax's dick business, had no clue if his condoms would even fit Luke, but we were going to work something out.

***

Luke

A few minutes later, I returned. The look on my face caused Beverly's expression to change from expectant to confusion. Based on her fixed hair and the large towel she'd haphazardly tossed on the bedside table, she'd used the bathroom, freshened up, and prepared for more.

"What's wrong? He doesn't have any? Not the right size?" she questioned, naked and waiting, body sparkling like a beautiful chocolate diamond.

"I don't know. I didn't get a chance to ask. He … they…." I started, but paused as my head tilted to the side. "From the sounds of it, they were actively engaged," I finally finished.

Beverly's smile let me know she already knew what I pondered a time or two based on the way Laura and Dax acted around each other.

"Isn't she a lesbian?" I questioned, shaking off my confusion.

"Not anymore. She's officially bisexual," Beverly shared , smiling from ear to ear.

"Sorry about the condoms. I'm not the guy that gets lucky."

"It's okay. Come here," she called, reaching for my hand. I flipped out the lamp before climbing in. The moonlight spilled in from the open drapes in the large window, allowing me to soak in more of her glowing, radiant skin.

We cuddled, wrapped around each other as she turned her body and adjusted my head to rest on her chest. No one had ever held me this way. No one in the world could have convinced me there was any place better than the warm, soft pillows of her chest as her heart drummed against my cheek.

After a while, her leg glided up the side of mine before she eased it back down. We were positioned so that half my weight was on her body. There was no doubt she wanted me where I was, the way one of her hands was gripping my side as the nails of her other raked their way through my scalp. A deep sigh eased out, and I relaxed, easing into her welcoming warmth.

Again, her leg slipped up mine, the inside of her warm thigh crawling up the outside of mine. She was so warm down there it was getting me hot all over again, causing my breaths to race my quickened heartbeat. I wasn't an expert on reading women, but I was certain that she wanted me, condom or not.

"Beverly," I whispered into the quiet silence.

"Yes, baby," she answered, causing a whole different set of emotions to flip on inside me. Hearing her call me *baby* was a verbally seductive tool she possessed that could get her anything she wanted from me. No one had ever used that term of endearment with me, and when she'd expressed it while we were having sex, I'd almost come on the spot.

"Are you okay?" I asked although I had an idea what was wrong.

She shoved her pelvis into my hip, solidifying my suspicions. For the first time in my life, I loved what was wrong.

"I can't sleep," she whispered, sounding frustrated.

She sat up and flipped the lamp on, on her side of the bed. She pointed at the outside of her arm and waited until my gaze landed on the area.

"I've had this birth control device in for almost a year, and I've never tested the 99.9% effectiveness of it." She paused and let her words sink in I suppose.

When I connected the dots, my smile widened. I placed a soft kiss to the top of the area she pointed out on her arm.

"I'm clean," I volunteered. "About as clean as a man could get and would never risk your health if I wasn't sure."

"Me too. I want you again so badly," she confessed, her eyes so heavy with lust she looked high.

My need for her ripped through me, heating my blood, before sending a tremendous amount straight to my groin. I drew her in, allowing my lips to crash into hers as our bodies collided like pulled apart magnets set free. We devoured each other, exploring, pleasing, and sharing a connection I didn't think could be broken.

Green and blue met with each glance, brown and ivory mingled, flirtingly with every caress. Those were the primary colors reflected in the kaleidoscope of us and projected our physical magic. My eyes, my lips, and my fingers feasted on her skin, a deep, flawless brown of sweet perfection lightly dusted with sparkling flecks of gold under the lamplight.

When I entered her body a second time, skin-to-skin, hardness to wet, tight, heat, I died, and each stroke re-birthed me into a new man. This time was different, more emotional. It wasn't plagued by our eagerness to chase satisfaction. We were rewarded with a more intense pleasure that soothed our bodies, easing us into every move, coaxing us to enjoy every kiss, caress, and thrust.

My throat tightened, and I choked on a jumble of emotional words that threatened to spill free when our eyes connected and held. My brain stalled, never having experienced a set of emotions that connected me so fantastically deep with another person.

This connection we shared was addictive, intense, satisfying, and although my mind rallied against it, I chose to believe Beverly shared my feelings. I trained myself not to overindulge in anything too good, but with Beverly, I would gladly overdose on her, consequences be damned.

Chapter Forty-six

Beverly

Dax placed the phone on speaker so we could hear Ansel speaking.

"Just like the group you encountered when you got back to Texas, another group showed up here with the intent of capturing Regina. The one I tortured claimed he didn't know who DG6 or the Dominquez family was. This could possibly be a group left over and following old orders but be careful, in case we've missed something or someone," Ansel warned, spiking my stress.

Hearing this latest news was disheartening. It meant we weren't out of the woods where DG6 was concerned. How deep did this order to capture us run? Was it over? Were we ever going to return to a normal life? Were we going to have to leave Texas or be stuck glancing over our shoulders the rest of our lives?

"Fuck," Laura uttered under her breath at Ansel's news. Her response gave me pause.

One measly fuck was all that Laura had to offer in response to the news Ansel delivered. I believed she was the Laura I knew, but she certainly wasn't acting like her. She was too quiet.

"Are you okay?" I asked, concerned and already blaming Dax for what might be wrong.

"Yes. You think this DG6 mess is ever going to be over?" The perplexed expression on her face was hard to discern.

"I hope so. You heard Ansel. The guys in Cali after Regina may have been left over from before they killed their targets. Regina believed that we were the women who's ashes Sorio was interested in when she and Aaron were on that farm. She said he was bragging about two women he was planning on catching. We don't know how many teams of men he deployed to look for us. After Regina went missing, he probably sent more."

"And people think I'm crazy," Laura said. "That sick son-of-a-bitch wanted to kidnap us to burn us, probably alive, for our ashes that his sick ass would probably masturbate on."

"Okay. Okay. Laura, I don't want to think about what that crazy man wanted with us. Aaron killed him. Now, we have to pray that the guys have taken care of whoever remains in his wake."

I pinned Laura with a firm gaze, and she returned with a muted expression, playing poker face with me. "So, you and Dax, huh?"

She threw up her hands. "Please don't ask me about that man. I don't want to talk about him."

"So, like I was saying. You and Dax. How? How the hell did he convince you into a relationship?"

"No! No! No!" Head shaking, scrunched face, and nostrils flaring, she was ready to rip me apart. The guys glanced back at her outburst, and I fanned them away with a playful smile.

"First, it's not a relationship. We're *fucking*. And that's bad enough. When this mission is over, we'll go our separate ways. Finished. Complete. Done."

I didn't think for a minute she believed what she was saying.

"Well, I'm being honest with myself. I like Luke. I like him a lot. I know I just met him. I understand that under stressful situations, things happen that normally may not, but I don't think I can be finished and done with him after this is all over. It has taken me all these years to find someone who can glance past my tits and ass to find me."

A deep sigh left her as she gave me her mothering eyes. "Bev, I'm telling you now. These men are used to having women at their disposal. Once this mission is over, they will be in the wind, no matter what they're whispering in our ears now. Didn't I warn you to stay away from Mr. Big? I'm surprised your ass can walk with all that damn screaming and cursing and knocking and bumping I heard."

My hand flew up to cover my mouth, horrified even as I failed to keep a smirk off my face.

"You heard us? I'm so embarrassed." My hands rose to cover my hot face.

"You should be embarrassed." She playfully shoved my shoulder. "The shit I heard had me blushing, and I'm not the blushing type."

Her smiling gaze let me know she was teasing.

"Luke, you're so big, you're stretching me to my limits, don't stop, right their baby, take it out so I can feel you sliding back in," she goaded, repeating statements I couldn't deny shouting last night, especially by the third round.

My face was hot with embarrassment, but I managed to gather a few words.

"I've been in a drought for nearly a year, Laura. Do you blame me?"

"No," she replied, surprising the hell out of me. I glared at her, unwilling to even blink.

"I can see that he makes you happy," she admitted with a smile teasing her lips. "It also seems he's head over heels, so be careful. You don't want to create yourself a stalker. I say we have fun while it lasts, build a few good memories and move the hell on when this is over."

I nodded, but I didn't think Luke was the only one head over heels. I was coo-coo for Coco Puffs and wanted to be under and around the man every chance I got.

Luke had fucked the bejesus out of me, and he didn't do it with ass slapping pelvic-breaking pounding either. He was so well endowed I don't think it would have been good that way. We went at it three times before our bodies gave out. He was the best medicine in the world.

My mind hadn't eased up on calling up images of us, highlighting every moment and playing it on repeat. I squeezed my thighs together and crossed my legs at the ankles to keep my pussy from quivering. I couldn't let this man know I was hooked.

***

The men left to do a reconnaissance mission for a few days, but it felt like a year. Like a hawk, my wide gaze was glued to the door, even when they informed me of their return time. Luke was texting me the whole time.

When the sound of a car engine found my ears, I was up and on my feet, heading for the front door. Laura produced a gun as she peeked out of the window. I shuffled from foot to foot as Laura shook her head at the way I was acting.

"It's a damn shame," she said under her breath, flashing me a side eye that turned into a deep eye roll.

When I realized they were coming in through the garage entrance, I made my way toward the kitchen.

I did a run, skip, and hop getting to Luke when he emerged and opened his arms at the sight of me. He gripped me in a tight hold, his fresh scent, and warmth wrapped around me along with his strong arms. His breath whispered into my ear. "You missed me?"

"Yes. I missed you so bad. I was so worried about you," I whispered back to him.

375 · TWISTED REVELATIONS

I squeezed, tightening my arms around his neck, loving the way he made me pulse with life. When I was around Luke, I forgot about the bad. I forgot about the storm swirling around us and embraced the heady sensations he made me feel.

The repeated clearing of Laura's throat urged me to loosen my grip on Luke. Dax wasn't anywhere in the area anymore, but Laura presented Luke and me her stink-face like our affection made her sick.

"Are you two done yet? Two days apart and you're acting like you're an old married couple or something," Laura spat.

Having Luke back filled me with such delight, it didn't allow me the room to be irritated so I tossed a smile at Laura for her smart comments. Luke did the same. She was a grumpy cat if there ever was one.

It wasn't our fault she and Dax were pretending they were less than what I believed they were to each other. And I knew she wasn't talking about somebody acting married. She and Dax acted like those couples who were sour and boring in public and tore each other apart in the bedroom.

"You mind telling us if we are free from these DG6 assholes or what?" Laura glanced up at Luke while holding her hand above her forehead like she was blocking out the sun. "Your grumpy buddy didn't say shit before he took off. What's his damn problem anyway?" she continued, not realizing her irritation at Dax was being aimed at us.

"The coast was clear as far as we could see," Luke replied. "We even put in a special request for D to use his tech expertise to spy on people and any areas we presumed to be suspect."

With that, Laura walked off, no doubt going to give Dax a piece of her mind before they found their way into bed together.

Chapter Forty-seven

Beverly

Without a word, I gripped Luke's hand and led him up the stairs.

"I hope you're not too tired because we have a few extracurricular activities to participate in," I announced, glancing back at him.

"Nope, I'm never too tired for that," was his reply.

Once we crossed into the bedroom, I reached around Luke's side and locked us in. The little kitchenette in our room was stocked with water and a few snacks. I planned to take full advantage of the time me and Luke had left. I could worry later about my stolen heart that he would no doubt take back to Georgia with him.

For now, I was about to show Luke that my tits weren't just for show. We stripped naked on the short walk to the bed, leaving a trail of forgotten clothes. The anticipation of what was coming had my blood blazing through my veins and my pulse drumming in my ears.

At the foot of the bed, I placed my hand against Luke's strong chest and nudged him back. He fell atop the mattress with a hard *swish*. Once I managed to lift my eyes from his dick, I was gifted with the boyish smile that lit his face.

He eased back with my guidance until he was positioned with his legs spilling over the side of the bed. Leaning back on his elbows, his enchanting gaze tracked my every move.

I stood in place, allowing myself time to admire his ripped body, the intricate designs of his tattoos, and the mesmerizing sight of his gorgeous dick. The man was unbelievably sexy and had the ability to make me high off his presence alone. Unable to hide my broad smile, I shook my head to ward off the spell he had the ability to cast over me.

I bent forward, placing soft lip-smacking kisses and lazy licks against his chest, rippling abs, and lower against his bulging thighs. His muscles twitched as his teeth pinched his bottom lip. I positioned myself on my knees between his splayed legs with his mouth-watering dick standing in front of me. *Lord have Mercy.*

When I adjusted my breast to cup his stiff shaft, his blue eyes darkened with a mixture of lust and wonder. Although most of his dick was sandwiched between my tits, a good portion stood stiff and exposed. The visual of my dark ample tits surrounding his thick pink dick had my lady parts clenching with anticipation and dripping with wanton desire.

With my hands cupping the outside, I wrapped my tits snug around his shaft as I swayed left and right. My waving motion caused the exposed portion of his dick to swing left and right like a slow moving pendulum.

Once I had his dick swinging the way I wanted, I dropped my head and extended my tongue, allowing it to swipe across the leaking swollen head with each pass. My actions had Luke going nuts, as he hissed in air one moment and heaved it out the next. His thigh muscles were drawn so tight, they appeared ready to pop.

"Shit!" he blurted on an exhale as I squeezed my tits tighter around his dick, sliding them up and down his shaft while keeping the head swiping across my tongue.

His sighs chased an exhausted moan as his easy thrust joined my movements. He closed his eyes when the sensations started to consume him, but he caught himself and snapped his eyes open to resume watching.

I believe the visual kept his lust soaring just as it did mine. When I added speed to the process, his chest bobbed faster. His breaths grew sharper as he gripped the covers tight in his fist. His abs and pecs flexed as his biceps and triceps bulged.

When the vein in the center of his forehead protruded, revealing that I had him on the verge of relinquishing his sanity. His ivory skin was tinted with a pinkish glow. I'd given out lazy head and sex before, unmotivated by my sexual partner. Not with Luke. He made me want to give it my all because I knew he would give it back as good as I gave it.

"Beverly!" He yelled breathlessly, gripping the comforter so hard it made a ripping sound. "God. Bev," His voice faded. Eyes clamped tight, he twisted his head left to right, failing to ward off the inevitable. His arms shook under his weight as he fought to stay on his elbows. I kept my pace, jacking him off with my tits as my tongue made sweet love to his swollen velvety head.

The flow of his hot juices shot to the tip, making him grow so impossibly hard, it was like massaging a pipe. I kept my tits bouncing around his big shaft as I took the head into my mouth. "That's it baby, I've been waiting for another taste of you." My words caused his eyes to go darker.

"*Shit!*" He cried out between gulping air before a surge of trembles started in his legs and marched up his body. Licking and sucking, squeezing and massaging, his dick swelled in my mouth before an explosion of his sweet juices rained over my tongue.

"Bev...er...ly!" He yelled, stretching each syllable of my name as the mattress squeaked under his jerking movements. Hearing and seeing such a big strong man lose his shit, knowing I was the reason for it, had my confidence floating on cloud nine.

He came so hard, his sweet nectar swept over my tongue, some shot down my throat, and drizzled down the side of his shaft. My gaze followed the drizzle that escaped. "Let me get that," I stated, my heated gaze finding his dreamy one. My tongue trailed up the thick column of his dick catching every drop as I eyed him.

"Holy shit!" Flew out of his mouth before another hot shot squirted from him, his body trembling uncontrolled, his toes curling into the carpet.

I remained in place staring at the marvel he was, my eyes feasting on him until he came down. He eased up, still a bit shaken, but the lusty glint in his eyes revealed another story. His usual light crystal eyes were shaded a deeper shimmering blue. He eased me up by my shoulders and proceeded to walk me back and away from the bed.

His gaze remained on mine and revealed a stalking quality that suggested he was about to shake up the world as I knew it. A low *humph* sounded when my back collided with the wall.

Luke moved forward until the front of his body pressed into mine, pinning me in place. His dick nudged my stomach, alerting me to its presence, already hard and ready for another round. When he reached down, gripped me by the thighs, and lifted. I gasped at the speed and sheer power he possessed. My lips hung open in shock, but it didn't stop my legs from wrapping around his waist or my arms from going around his neck.

"I wouldn't want you getting bored with me. Do you mind this position?" The smirk on his face said he didn't need an answer. Him putting me in this specific position in the first place made me wonder if he paid attention to my pleased reaction the last time he held me this way.

His big hands cupped the globes of my generous ass and squeezed, causing me to gush shamelessly. His

creamy skin covering my dark chocolate, the lust sparkling in his gaze, and my legs splayed around his powerful
body all teamed together and had me flowing like an open
fire hydrant. Luke was quiet, but he had some freak in him
that I was claiming credit for bringing out.

"I don't mind this position at all," I finally answered,
unable to keep the excitement out of my voice. The tingle
in me had turned into a buzz of anticipation so strong I
started to tremble with need. "Fuck me now, Luke.
Please," I begged.

He backed away enough to reach between us, his fingers skimming my clit before circling my wet pussy lips.
"So wet," he whispered before he eased back, aligned us,
and slid into me as far as he could go. The action knocked
curse words off my tongue and caused me to shiver like
an addict getting the first hit of the good stuff they were
craving.

He worked his dick in, opening me so deliciously I
wanted it all. Only when he was seated balls to the wall,
did he pick up the pace and fuck me harder. With each
powerful thrust, I lost my vocabulary, screaming bits and
pieces of words that weren't English.

My breasts bounced in time with each thrust. My fingers dug into a tribal tattoo that ran up and over his
shoulder, my other hand gripping the back of his neck as
he pumped in and out of me. Each time his lips dropped
to my ear, he told me I was beautiful. The verbal praise
added to my lust and amped up my already heightened desires.

He took complete possession of me, making me relinquish control once he was inside me. The wall smacked
me from the back as his powerful body beat against mine
from the front. His strong thighs slammed into the inside
of mine, opening me wider before his length impaled and
gifted me with addicting shots of pleasure.

The knocks grew louder and harder with each upward thrust. I was certain the wall would have to be repaired before the owners opened for business.

My pussy quivered as my muscles contracted with the need to adjust to the massive amount of dick being shoved into me. "Luke. Fuck. Oh God!" I yelled, breathless and dick-drunk. His warm breath and soft lips played at the pulse in my neck while his dick licked my hot spots, lighting them with sparks that set fire to my soul.

"Bev...er...ly!" This time, when he broke up the syllables of my name, each was punctuated with a hard upward thrust that had me crying out in throat-scratching ecstasy. My thighs tightened around his waist allowing me to cross my ankles above his tight ass.

The firm muscles in his back danced under my clawing fingers as he drove pure pleasure into me. "So good. Luke. Fuck," was all I could get out before I exploded. The orgasm unhinged me. I forgot my lungs needed air. I forgot I needed my brain to think. I forgot my own name, didn't know if it was one syllable or two.

After my mind limped back and reconnected with my brain, Luke came, screaming my name. The flow of his hot semen coating my insides snatched my already sputtering mind and delighted my body so deliciously it induced another orgasm.

This was the first time I experienced the joy of multiples. The power of the pounding impact shook my core before it shot through me and broke me down into a weeping mess of heaves and cries.

There was no need in denying that I was ruined, addicted, and royally fucked from ever enjoying sex with any other man.

Chapter Forty-eight

Laura

When I marched into the room, the sound of the shower let me know Dax was cleaning up. Something was wrong because he'd hardly said hello after he and Luke returned from their recon mission.

Was he upset I hadn't skipped and hopped into his arms like Beverly had done to Luke? He knew me well enough to know that would never be me. I had a hard enough time trying to figure out why we had chemistry in the first place.

Lately, we could hardly agree on any subject, so whatever was bothering him was something else we weren't going to agree on. Our arguments were different than they were in the beginning. Now, we argued, said what we needed to say, then we went quiet on each other for long periods of time. I much preferred us constantly biting each other's heads off.

He entered the room with his shorts hanging low on his waist and no shirt as droplets of water drizzled down his solid, lean body. The scar where his brother had removed the bullet was visible, and at times it still pained him. He never complained, and I understood that he didn't want to be babied about it.

I believe he walked out of the bathroom half naked on purpose—his attempt at seducing me. I wasn't going to let him know it was working, so I took the seat in the desk chair with my back to the desk and folded my arms across my chest.

"Care to tell me what's wrong with you?" I cocked my gaze until my damn eyes defied my brain and ran down the expanse of his body.

He didn't answer me. Instead, he stalked across the room and stood in front of me. His warm energy and fresh scent wrapped around me, comforting me. Not answering my question, he dropped to his knees before me, his chest bumping my knees apart as he drew closer.

With him positioned between my legs, staring up at me, every bit of the anger I built up disappeared as my heartbeat quickened. He reached out and brushed his fingers along my cheek, his steel gray eyes peering into me. My first instinct was to pull away, but I didn't. I couldn't.

"My problem is nothing you should be concerned about. I'll deal with it," he murmured. There was a strange note in his tone that I pondered and attempted to decipher until I gave up the quest.

He reached around my waist and tugged me into his body, drowning me in his masculine strength. A jagged restlessness filled me. I wanted to touch him and fall into the urgency of the heady desires he incited. How was I supposed to return to being normal if he kept making me want him?

My hands worked their way up his arms before I raked my fingertips through his silky hair, enticing him to close his eyes, and relaxing his tensed body. With his face in my palms, I just stared, struggling to make sense of this, of us.

Why him? Why couldn't I fight this? Why did I so easily give in when we were this close? He stared up at me, eyes pleading. I drew him closer until our faces were inches apart, hesitant, scared, and unsure. He closed the last inch of space, allowing his lips to hover right below mine. "Please, Laura," he whispered against my lips, and I lost the last of my control.

Soft, smooth strokes of our dancing lips started the kiss. He delved deeper, intensifying the pressure, making me feel it so deep, I didn't know if I was feeling my heartbeat or his, hearing his pulse thump or mine, tasting his truth or the truth I was determined to deny myself.

His tongue brushed my lips and urged me to open for him. The kiss evoked a tingling depth, and I allowed myself to connect with his flowing emotions and embrace my own.

Dax was the only person I allowed myself to connect with on this level, and I didn't know how to process it from one moment to the next. I always had the ability to hold firmly to my terse and snarling will because it kept me strong. Would I be forever changed by this connection? Would I lose the tough edge I needed to keep me safe from all the harm out there in the world?

He led me to the bed, sitting me on the edge. I was switched to autopilot, and I didn't protest anything he did, even when he went slow and hit me with what I was beginning to understand was intimacy. I took it all: the emotion, the tender caresses, and the easy and affectionate moments, until I was presented to him nude and lying across the bed.

He stood in place, staring, making me squirm under his gaze and feel like a superstar all at the same time. He shoved his shorts down, and my gaze raked over him slowly. He was a sexy man, a truth I still had difficulty accepting.

A sigh huffed from deep within my lungs before I backed further onto the bed, eager to receive the addictive high he had the ability to give me. He climbed in and fit his body against mine. His fastest movements came when he tore open the condom and pinned my gaze while slipping it down his length.

His warm hardness spread my wet heat apart when he started to slide into me with a lingering ease. The only person I allowed inside my body, I believed he coveted that truth like a priceless possession. Life was proving I didn't know it all, that I couldn't find all my answers in the streets, and that embracing a tough attitude wasn't always necessary.

No matter how urgent our start, he always eased into me first. Once he was able to go as deep as my body would allow, our releasing sighs met and kissed in midair. He moved with meticulous strokes, making love to me instead of the fast and hard fucking I sought. I believe I wanted it to be harsh and painful as some type of punishment to myself for wanting him.

Painfully slow, affectionate, intimate. I didn't fight the emotions stirring between us although they terrified me.

I was grateful when the pleasure started to combat the arsenal of emotional weapons he'd unleashed on me. Our moans and harsh breathing joined the overwhelming currents that took my nerves by storm. With every thrust he flooded me with pleasure that caused my eyeballs to roll and sent my hips chasing his movements.

"Don't let this be it, Laura. We're good together." His hot whispers floated into my ear.

I believe he'd just revealed his problem. He wanted *us*, and I was firmly against it. He was convinced we could be a functioning couple. Whenever he attempted to convince me of it, I would laugh in his face, and it led to an argument.

"Do you feel that?" He slid into me with a strong downstroke.

"Yes," slid past my lips as I reacted with light shutters. My nails clawed into his upper and lower back as I trembled from the explosion of pleasure he drove into me.

"Only you and I can create this kind of magic. Only you can make me feel this good, this high, this special," he whispered, causing that pinging in my heart to spread a delighted ache through the rest of me. He was turning me against my own body, against my own mind and although I didn't like it, I accepted it.

Instead of responding to his comments I placed my hand behind his neck and tugged until his lips were on mine. He backed off, staring at me with a perplexed expression. It wasn't like me to initiate a kiss, but he resumed it, caressing my lips with his until desire urged him to seek out my tongue.

His deliberate movements sent our bodies into a sensual dance. We clung and took from one another until our worlds collided and became one sensational universe.

Dax was making love to me, and I embraced every moment of it. We breathed each other in until the haze of our bliss started to dissolve us into a relaxed state. I embraced the pressure of him buried deep inside as we remained clinging to each other, neither of us willing to let go of the other.

This was the fifth time this wasn't supposed to happen between us. The fifth time I insisted we couldn't do this anymore.

I was the first to let go, but it wasn't because I wanted to. I let go because he refused to stop pulling me in, mentally and physically. We lay next to each other, neither of us speaking a word. However, the silence that hung around us was alive with what had been left unsaid.

Chapter Forty-nine

Beverly

The days that followed consisted of sex, sex, and more sex. Luke and I were so strung out on each other, enough was never enough. We'd skipped several meals to have each other. Dax had one of his family's cooks come into the bed and breakfast and make us a gourmet meal we didn't eat until the following day for breakfast.

Other than inviting us to dinner, and although we were under the same roof, Dax and Laura made themselves scarce as well.

"Luke," my call whispered across the dark room. He stood in front of the window staring out at a moonless sky. A few stars fought the darkness and broke free but weren't strong enough to break up the thick dark clouds.

"Yes," he answered, his gaze wandering aimlessly at nothing. His ivory skin glowed in the darkness, providing my eyes a lighted pathway to him.

"Will you tell me what happened to you?" I asked. "One day," I added, in an attempt to stamp back my eager desire to know more about him. In spending time with him, I suspected the demons from his past were hunting him.

He slept like he was being tortured in his sleep. I wasn't a therapist, but something terrible happened to him and he either hadn't let go of it or couldn't let go. I didn't know if it was something that happened before or after the military.

390 · KETA KENDRIC

He presented a calm, well put-together man for everyone to see, but I knew far too well what post-traumatic stress could do to a person. He was shouldering something heavy, and I prayed he trusted me enough to let me into that part of his life.

We were all haunted by our past, but Luke's demons were more pronounced, more insistent on plaguing him with reminders that caused his mind to drift. He was always happy to return to me, or at least I hoped so, because I was happy to receive his affection and care he was capable of dishing out in abundance.

He stepped away from the window, letting the heavy drapes fall back into place. I didn't go to him right away when he climbed back into his side of the bed. The last thing some people wanted when they talked about difficult subjects was to be touched.

When he opened his arms, I went, draping my arms around his waist. The tension in his body spoke volumes, and for a while, we sat in the darkness allowing the sound of our breathing to fill in the quiet space.

"My mother died when I was too young to know her," he started. "My father said I was three when she passed away. Sometimes he claimed I was four and sometimes five. I honestly don't think he knew. All he'd tell me was that she died of natural causes. There were no pictures, no reminders, no letters, clothes, nothing left of her to even let me know who she was or that she'd even existed."

He paused, and I could hear him thinking.

"My father, Luther, was his name. He was an uncaring man. There were no hugs or pep talks or helping with schoolwork, just his taunts and constant reminders that I was stupid, worthless, and that I took after my dumb ass mother. After a while, I started to believe that maybe I was stupid, even though I did well in school. I was always on the honor roll, I supposed attempting to prove to myself that I wasn't dumb. I don't even think my father knew or even cared about how well I did in school. If it weren't for child services, I doubt he would have even cared if I went to school."

I was already fighting to keep from shaking my head. There was a whole sermon in my head about deadbeat, uncaring ass parents that would do nothing but ramp up my anger. I beat back my urge to say something to allow him to tell his story uninterrupted.

"All my father cared about was the number of bodies that came into the business. He never wanted me. He dealt with me because I inherited the title of son. I didn't know enough to understand at the time, but death was a lucrative business, yet my father barely kept the lights on or food in the refrigerator. He did the bare minimum where it concerned the household. As far back as I can recall he drilled it in my head that I needed to do my part to earn my place. He got me familiar with seeing dead bodies early on."

My head remained against his shoulder, while his words poured into me.

"At first, my job was to clean up after my father embalmed the bodies. I'd take out the trash, cut the lawn, cook, and clean the house. By the time I was twelve, I knew how to embalm and cremate bodies. I was skinny, tall, gangly looking, the ideal look of an undertaker. School wasn't a pleasant place. Home was twice as bad, so I learned to appreciate the better of two evils. It wasn't until I was about fourteen that I discovered my father's gambling problems, which were so bad he'd gone into debt with the nasty people he called his friends."

When I first got Luke talking on the plane, it was evident that his father was a huge part of what troubled him. Now, he was painting me a vivid picture of what haunted him.

"There was one night those friends showed up, prepared to collect money my father didn't have. They took the payment out of his flesh. Even though my father never showed me an ounce of care, I grabbed the bat I kept in my room and attempted to defend him. With three guns in my face, my father bloody at my feet, I was as helpless and useless as he always insisted I was. The men taunted me, making sure I knew I was as worthless as my father. His debt was over a hundred thousand dollars, and they gave him a week to pay. He offered up the deeds to the funeral home, which they took along with me."

A deep gasp escaped me, making him pause. I molded myself to him, pulling him closer, knowing that things would get so much worse. My action caused a weak smile to trace his lips.

"My father had a week to produce the money, or they promised they'd kill me. They tied a rag around my eyes and took me to one of their houses. There, I was tossed into a dirt hole, dug in the backyard and shut in like an animal. The suffocating scent of decay revealed I hadn't been the only person thrown down there. Others hadn't made it out of that hole alive."

To keep from reacting, I shoved my grief down my throat after I slammed my eyes shut. I had to maintain control so he would keep talking.

"Cold and as silent as night was dark, all I had was the loud call of my mind to keep me company. Being in all that darkness and silence caused the voices in my head to sound like screaming trains. My captors would crack the metal door that led into the hole and toss down stale bread and an occasional bottle of water. I made myself believe it was water, but the scent revealed the truth. I wasn't always drinking water."

"Luke, baby, I'm so sorry," slipped out of my mouth automatically. I was unable to keep quiet any longer. A knot of grief was wedged in my throat as tears stung my eyes. My gut clenched and I fought to keep from trembling at his horrifically tragic reveal.

He stared down at me. "It's okay. I'm here with you, aren't I?"

His words enticed a sad smile before he continued.

"Those men were worse savages than my father. A few weeks came and went, and I was never released from that hole. My father came up with enough of the money for them not to kill me right away. However, I eventually found out that my father, being who he was, had won enough to pay them in full, but couldn't bear to part with it all to get me released. My captors informed me that he lost the rest of the winnings at the craps table. After what I assumed was a few more weeks, I accepted that my father's gambling habit was all he cared about."

I stirred, attempting to get a glimpse of his eyes. I brushed my lips across his cheek and kept it there until the tension that had risen in him lessened.

"To cling to a little piece of my sanity, I started digging to keep myself busy, hoping I'd tunnel my way out of the hole. The longer I was down there, the more my human behaviors started to vanish. My mind started to turn against me as I fought the rats for the scraps they'd toss down. They told me they were not going to open that door again until my father paid them. They said I'd find out once and for all if my father cared about me. Staying true to their word, they stopped coming, and all I had was silence, digging, and my warring mind. Voices and images I knew weren't there showed up."

My tears started to slip along with my composure to be strong for him. A long ragged breath escaped as I attempted to hold in my weeping sadness. Luke had to get it all out and tell me the full story, even though I knew it would continue ripping me to shreds.

"Whenever I'd fall asleep, the rats would attempt to make me their food. After a while, with my captors not giving me food anymore, the hunger ate at me so badly I started to eat what was eating at me. I'd suck up the moisture that soaked through the ground for water."

At this point, I was unable to stop shaking, and my damn throat was so tight I gasped for air. I knew Luke had experienced something traumatic, but this was worse than anything I could have imagined. He squeezed me when I should have been the one consoling him.

"I think by then I'd gone feral, wild. My father never paid off the debt, and they never opened that door again, not that I knew of. The tunnel I started digging paid off as I broke through to the surface. Time wasn't something I could discern, so I can't say for certain how long it took me to dig myself out. The surface was only about three feet up, but I'd been digging at an angle with no real strength. Once I shoved myself through the hole, the first sign of anything familiar was the glow of the moon. I was in the dark for so long that even the night hurt my eyes. I stumbled and fell through the wooded area behind the house until I happened upon a creek. I drank from the creek until I drank myself sick, threw up, and drank more. The dirty creek water was the best thing I'd ingested in so long that it was hard to stop."

I wiped at the wetness clouding my eyes, attempting to control my constricting throat, swallowing the audible cries I wanted to release. I had to stay strong for Luke while he was releasing this heavy burden he carried. I would fall apart after he finished.

"I was so out of touch with reality, and had gone so wild, I'd catch fish and small animals and rip into them, consuming them raw. I'd hide myself away during the daylight hours, fearing the sun on my skin. I stayed in those woods for weeks until the local sheriff stumbled upon me sleeping next to the massive hollowed out oak tree I used as my new home. No matter what was going through my head, at night, I always searched for the moon. It was the first thing I saw when I climbed out of that hole.

It was the most beautiful thing I had to look at. It kept me company, helped me sleep when I struggled."

That explained his pale ivory skin. He'd learned to embrace the darkness, the one thing that had helped to trap him.

"The sheriff ended up having to sedate me to get me to a hospital. The hospital staff got me cleaned up, and I found myself strapped to a bed in the mental ward. It took me months and a lot of coaxing from the nurses and the sheriff who never stopped checking on me to convince me to start talking again. My mind started to make its way back, to make sense of the world, and flashes and signs of understanding proved that I was still human. I found out that I'd been down there in that hole for over two months, so malnourished that even the doctors were amazed that I was still alive."

Unable to hold back, I started to rain kisses all over his face, grateful he'd found his way back to reality and safety. My actions caused him to chuckle. I was thankful he could laugh, considering what he went through. Once I settled down, he continued.

"The one thing I didn't reveal to the sheriff or the doctors right away was who my father was. I pretended I didn't know. All I knew was that I was better off in the system. It took me a while to figure out that being in that hole had changed me into someone who wasn't afraid of the darkness, danger, or even being hurt. I went from the hospital into a group home, with help from the sheriff I revealed to him my father was the reason I'd been out there in those woods. They placed me in a home with about twenty other boys, most of them troubled by one thing or another. While most of the boys got into fights, I was quiet and detached. If I wasn't reading, I was in the gym figuring out how to become bigger."

My smile spread wide because he'd done a magnificent job and was *so* deliciously big.

"The sheriff continued to check on me from time to time. After I expressed to him that I wanted to go into the military, he helped me obtain my GED. He was the one who talked to me about becoming emancipated and what it would mean. A week after my seventeenth birthday, I was in the military."

My smile didn't drop. This was the part of the story I could handle.

"Before I was shipped off for training, I took the two-hour bus ride to visit my father. I found him drunk and scratching off lottery tickets. He believed he was seeing a ghost when I appeared in front of him. He had the nerve to apologize for letting his *'friends'* take me. I wanted to kill him but knew he'd suffer much worse living in the hell he created for himself. I left my father that night and never looked back."

"Thank you for sharing that part of your life with me." I was grateful that I had a deeper understanding of him, but saddened by what he'd been through.

A deep, hard kiss followed, hopefully, easing him of the horrific past unleashed on him.

"Will you tell me about your past?" His rebuttal made the heat building in me dissolve.

Now I was in the hot seat.

Chapter Fifty

Beverly

Adjusting our positions, I placed two pillows behind my back to cushion me from the large leather headboard anchored to the wall. Luke's face pinched with concern when I reached for him. I seated him between my legs and made sure his head rested against my chest. He was so tall his feet hung off the edge of the huge bed, but the smile on his face let me know he didn't care.

"I take it this is going to be a hell of a story since you placed me in the most comfortable position there is," he said, nudging his face into the cushions of my chest until his teeth raked across one of my nipples.

"If you keep doing that, we'll have to save this story for another day," I whispered, running my hands across his chiseled back and muscular arms. I've never shared myself with anyone in this manner, never expected to experience such an amazing connection.

"I put you in this position," I said, kissing his forehead, "so that I can hold you down if you get the urge to get up and run from me," I finished, only half joking.

He glanced up at me. "You can tell me anything. I'm not going anywhere."

His words were music to my ears because I believed him. I nodded as I gathered the strength I needed to start. The lump in my throat went down roughly, but Luke's reassuring arms tightened around me and filled me with strength.

"I'm telling you this because I trust you like I trust Megan and Laura. I know that I don't have to say this, but—"

"Whatever you say, it will always be between the two of us unless you tell me otherwise," he reassured.

On a deep sigh, I started. "My father, Calvin Hudson, was everything to me. He didn't treat me like I saw some of my friend's parents treat them. Although we were poor, he did his best to give me everything I needed and many of the things I wanted. Like you, I never knew my mother. The rumors around the hood eventually told the story my father never could tell. Addicted to heroin, selling her body, you name it. She walked out on my father and me when I was seven months old. My father never talked about her and every time I asked, he'd get so sad that I stopped asking. He kept a few pictures of her hidden, but I snooped enough to find them."

My arms squeezed around Luke, siphoning more energy from him. He lifted his head and placed his lips against mine, making me smile before he settled his head back on my chest.

"My father worked at the Meat Market, less than a half mile from our small house. There wasn't an official name for the market that I was aware of. Everyone called it the Meat Market. I often left school and sat in the back while my dad worked. His boss made him a manager, so he'd open and close and handle the money. Most evenings, the place was quiet, and it gave my father time to teach me about knives and basic combat skills since he'd spent time in the military. I learned where to stab a man if he attacked me and the best places to hide knives and blades."

A quick pause allowed me to gather myself.

"One night I was sitting behind the counter less than an arm's reach from my father, doing my homework when an armed man came into the market demanding money. I sat on the footstool my father used to reach for the meat deep inside the display. I was sitting low enough that the man didn't see me behind the counter. My father attempted to talk the man out of robbing him, but the man continued to yell, demanding money. I reached out and took my father's hand. I don't know what I was thinking, but I was about to stand, intending to get closer to him. He kept shaking his head and squeezing my hand. I guess to keep me out of sight. I think the robber took the gestures as a sign my father was telling him no, that he wasn't going to give him the money he was demanding."

Luke's grip tightened around me to ease my coiled tension. I fought to control my fast-blinking eyes that had started to burn with the sting of tears.

"The agitated man stopped yelling, and the sound of the gun blast came instantly. Our hands stayed connected, even after my father tumbled to the floor next to me. At the sight of my fallen father, I clamped my free hand over my mouth to stifle my screams. Loud hammering sounded above us. It was the robber hammering his gun against the cash register. It dinged open, and his arm reached out above me to grab the money. While I was staring up at the register, my father's hand stopped moving, and every drop of my blood froze. I'd seen dead bodies before in our rough neighborhood, but seeing my father, with his head shot open, and me kneeling in a pool of his blood had reached in deep and ripped me apart."

Luke remained silent, his tight hold not wavering one bit. My throat bobbed as I struggled to swallow the knot of sorrow that threatened to choke me.

"I don't know why I did it. I don't know what caused me to do it, but I stood at the sound of the man's thumping feet as he ran from the market. The dull mirrors over the door gave me a snapshot of the man's face. After eyeing him, I snapped free of the trance I was in, ran to the back, and called 9-1-1. The police or anyone else meant to help us were wary of coming into our neighborhood, so I ended up waiting for two hours, crying and yelling for help, but it never came. I eventually ran next door to the pawnshop for help. My father wasn't picked up until four hours after he'd been shot. I was taken into child services custody and put into the system. Three weeks later, Ms. Violent Washington came and picked me up. She convinced the social worker that she was my aunt. She'd grown up with my father, and whenever my father needed to leave me with someone, he only trusted me to stay with her. So, to me, she was my aunt."

Luke's warm breath teased my chest. His breathing sped up and was the only sound until I continued.

"I couldn't eat or sleep for months. I probably needed therapy but ended up with something better—*Laura*. I met her during the brief time I was in the system. She and I became fast friends. The whole hood knew about my father getting gunned down, but none knew I'd witnessed the entire scene. After a while, I revealed to Laura what I saw and even as a preteen, Laura was a force. Why did I tell her I spotted the man who killed my father? Why at twelve-years-old did she believe we were grown enough to pursue our plans for revenge? It wasn't until I started seeing the man who killed my father around our neighborhood that I started considering Laura's crazy idea. I became obsessed with it, spying on him, following him to where he lived. When I overheard him bragging to his friends about the man he shot, it was the straw that broke the camel's back."

Luke's firm grip on me remained as he brushed his lips against my chest.

"It took over a year to build up to it, but I went from being an innocent girl to one who harbored vengeful intentions. Laura offered to help me if I helped her with a problem she was having. For a long while, we made our plans until we met Megan. We assumed *we* had problems.

The shit that girl was experiencing caused us to sit our problems aside as we attempted to help her cope."

I glanced down at Luke, "You're not ready to run yet?"

"Never," he whispered.

"Good. Let me use the restroom, and I'll tell you the rest when I return."

Chapter Fifty-one

Beverly

Reluctance crept into my bones, but I returned to the bed and resumed our position, preparing to reveal to Luke the rest of my horrific past.

I relaxed the instant his caring warmth and solid body wrapped around me. The press of his weight against me gave strength to our connection. He was the best thing to happen to me in a long time. I leaned my head down, brushing my nose against his before giving him a lingering peck on the lips.

I left the lamp on, unwilling to part from him for the few seconds it would take to turn it off. After another stolen kiss, I prepared to tell him secrets I only shared with two others. Was I making a mistake? Was I being too quick in trusting Luke? Was I being naïve? I didn't believe I was and prayed my instincts were right.

He stroked my cheek with a tender touch, stirring my gaze to his. "I'd never betray your trust, Beverly. Never," he stated with an assuring tone that eased the reluctance that crept back into my mind.

"Once Laura and I became close with Megan and found out what was being done to her, we became more determined to start executing the things we were planning. It wasn't just young girls saying the things we wish we could do. We started planning and laying out details. Laura came up with the idea of taking care of the easiest problem first. It would also be the test we needed to prove we could go through with our other plans."

I can't believe I'm telling him this.

"We snuck into Laura's old apartment one night. It was two in the morning, a time Laura was sure the man who was introduced as her *Uncle* Dennis would be too drunk to stop us. He remained in their old apartment after her mother died. Laura was sure he was the one who gave her mother the hot-shot of drugs that killed her. We had to have been the noisiest killers on the planet bumping into things and knocking stuff off shelves while breaking into the apartment. Thankfully, his loud snoring drowned out our clumsy entrance. My father had given me three custom made switchblades. We each had one. Three thirteen-year-old girls, standing around Laura's uncle with knives aimed at different parts of his body."

Luke's eyebrows hiked up.

"As soon as Laura said, "Fuck it" and raised the knife, I stopped her, suggesting we get him off the sofa because of the blood. She marched into the bathroom and yanked the shower curtain from the last three rusty rods they were barely clinging to. We laid the curtain out on the floor and dragged the sleeping man off the couch. He fell onto the floor, landing on his side and on top of the dirty shower curtain. He stirred, and we held our breath until his snoring started up again."

The flashing of the digital clock caught my eye. It was nearly the same time of night as it was when we snuck into our first murder scene.

"Using what my father taught me, I pointed out the area of his neck Laura should stab and the area in his leg for Megan. At the time, I didn't know I had Laura aiming at his carotid artery and Megan aiming at his femoral artery. All I knew was what my father had taught me. That these were the areas that would incapacitate someone. I was at his side, aiming for the area that would allow me to slide the blade between his ribs and deflate his lung. When Laura raised her knife, so did we. She counted down. Three, two, and at one we all stabbed, no one chickened out."

I paused, waiting for Luke's reaction. When none came, I continued.

"Dennis jumped up, eyes as wide as two plates, scratching at his neck that gushed blood. His breaths shot out in loud rasps as he struggled to breathe. His leg convulsed as a wet stain started to spread like he'd pissed himself. I didn't know if it was shock that kept him standing, or that we'd hit the right spots, but he remained there scratching at his neck, eyes scanning our shocked faces, the bloody knives clutched in our hands. It was sad that we'd all experienced enough death that witnessing the man dying wasn't as frightening as I imagined it would be."

Uncertain about continuing, I glanced down at Luke. "Are you ready to run yet?"

"Never," he replied before his warm lips brushed the tip of my nose.

"I won't go into much detail about how we got rid of *Uncle* Dennis, but let's just say, three knocked-kneed teen girls dragging a bloody body down two flights of stairs wrapped in a shower curtain wasn't done with any finesse. Laura was so frustrated at the final cleft of the stairs, we helped her align his body on the edge before she sat on her boney bottom and kicked him over. Megan and I were so tired that we didn't attempt to stop her. We stood our crazy asses there and watched that man's body tumble down the stairs."

Luke's body shook, calling my attention. I glanced down at him. "Lucas Bradshaw, I know that you are not laughing."

This time his chuckle was audible. "I'm sorry. It's the imagery of you guys kicking around a dead body."

My smile surfaced before I continued, surprised at my ability to share with him so easily.

"I have no idea how we didn't get caught getting that body to the dumpster, but we ended up spending most of the rest of that night cleaning up the trails of blood we left behind. A few weeks later and after the uncle's body had arrived at the landfill, we made plans for the man who killed my father. His name was Greg Bernard. I stalked the man for a year, so I knew everything: where he hung out, his work route, and who he bought his crack from. I never knew hate could grow so strong as the hate I had for that man. He'd taken the one good thing in my life."

Every time my voice would crack, or I'd get to what saddened me the most, Luke's hold on me would tighten, reminding me he was there.

"We snuck into his house. Back then it was easy to get into people's houses. He thankfully lived alone in a run-down shotgun house, about a mile from where I lived with Ms. Violet. We went in through a window he left cracked at the back of his house. With no screen on the window, we used the items on the back porch to lift the window, prop it open, and climb inside. Knowing his schedule, I knew he'd be home at or around twelve-thirty. We sat around in his dark living room eating his cans of fruit cocktail, a surefire way to tell that we were turning into three sociopaths."

Again, Luke's body shook as he fought to keep from laughing at the words I'd chosen. He could laugh all he wanted, we were all sociopaths, functioning ones, able to flip our consciences on and off at the drop of a dime.

"Like clockwork, the man arrived home as predicted. After having come from his usual stop at the bar he was shitfaced drunk. He came into the house and slammed the door, talking and cursing. He kicked off his shoes and took his usual spot on the couch. The one we'd just been sitting on before he got home. It didn't occur to us until afterward that he might feel the warmth we left behind. Not to mention, my greedy behind left my empty fruit can on the end table.

"Laura and Megan were behind the sofa, and I was stuffed into the living room closet, breathing in his smelly clothes and shoes. Thankfully, it didn't take long for us to start hearing his loud snores. We stood over him, much like we'd stood over *Uncle* Dennis, except this time we didn't stab him. This time, we put my plan into effect and tied him up so well, it would take weeks for him to pick out the knots.

"Like the little killers we were becoming, we took the alcohol in the house and started pouring it all over him. Megan suggested we use rags to tie him with so the fire would burn them and make it seem like the fire was accidental. During our alcohol bath, he woke up. He did his best to get at us, cursing, and yanking at those ropes and rags with such rage, I knew he'd kill us if he got loose."

A quick glance down at Luke showed his eyes aimed at me expectantly. Was he enjoying listening to my pathway to insanity?

"Once he was soaked, we surrounded him, waiting until he stopped cursing. His mouth dropped open when I revealed who I was, and that I was there the night he shot my father for the fifty-seven dollars he took from the register. He observed how we tied him up and how soaked in alcohol he was and started shaking his head at the realization. Laura poured a trail of alcohol to the kitchen doorway, and I struck the match while he screamed, begged, and pleaded. We didn't run or hide from the sight of him screaming and yelling with flames blazing around him, so big and bright we had no choice but to get out of the house.

"We ran through three backyards and were chased by a dog before we took a dirt alley to the street. We circled back to the front of the house where a crowd had formed, but no one attempted to go in and save him. By the time the fire truck arrived most of the house had gone up in flames and his screams had finally stopped. Are you still with me? Still think I'm good-girl-Beverly after that?" I questioned, glancing at Luke.

"Of course I do," he replied before rising. He switched positions, laying against the pillows before tucking me into his strong chest. I turned into him, placing my ear to his heart, relaxing into the lively rhythm.

He kissed the top of my head. "Are you ready to tell me the rest?"

My eyes snapped wide open, first glancing left and turning to the right as I came up with something to say. He placed his lips to my ear. "I might be five months younger than you, but I wasn't born yesterday. You don't have to tell me, but I know there's more."

"Wait, you're younger than me? How do you know my age?" The revelation put me in a faster tailspin. I attempted to think of anything to skirt the main subject.

"I'll be twenty-five in a few months. You turned twenty-five in February. We have access to someone called D. Michaels, so there's not much I can't eventually find out."

"Oh," was all I said as I settled my head back against his chest. What else did he know?

He leaned closer, glancing into my face. "In case you're wondering, I don't know the rest of your story. None of us do, and you don't have to tell me anything you don't want to."

After a long pause, I decided I was comfortable enough with him to start the last leg of a story I swore I'd take to the grave.

"Like with Laura's uncle and my father's killer, we found ourselves waiting on the inside of another house. This time, we didn't sneak in. This time we were let in through the front door like we lived there. It was one in the morning, so everyone was asleep. Laura used a wedge of wood at the brother's door to keep him inside. The wife had taken her nightly dose of sleeping pills, so we didn't bother with her. Laura and I hid under Megan's bed and waited. The poor girl knew her rape schedule. Carlos Dominquez came snaking into the room and slithered into her bed, just like she said he would. Since the room was dark, we eased out from under the bed in silence. When Megan yelled out, "Now!" we stood, knives at the ready."

Luke had gone stalk still, staring straight ahead.

"The first stab came from Megan. She jammed the knife in his neck. When she opened up his neck, he attempted to choke her, but Laura and I started stabbing him. He came after us, leaking and spraying blood all over the place, cursing, yelling, and threatening bloody murder. I was scared as hell when he trapped me in the corner between a bedside table and the closet, but Megan and Laura were stabbing at his back. He was like the Incredible Hulk.

"He turned from me, and I sent the knife across his Achilles, sawing across the area my father had taught me was a weak spot. He screamed like a wounded wolf before he backhanded the hell out of me. He stood but stumbled to one knee while reaching for Megan and Laura. Blood loss made him weak. He hobbled forward but ended up falling sideways. We pounced on him, counting each stab out loud until we got to the number of times he raped Megan."

Luke released a deep sigh. He squeezed me to him. The things I was revealing to him now about who we killed had his full attention. We killed an original member of the Dominquez Cartel. Me still being alive to tell Luke the story was a miracle and just blind immature luck.

"Once we were certain Carlos was gone, we took the wedge from under the foster brother David's door. Instead of taking the chance of him waking up to kick our butts like the dad, we took our time tying him to the bed. We all climbed in with him and just started stabbing and counting. I honestly can't recall my state of mind. All I knew and could think about, was what they were doing to Megan, and how Carlos had strolled into her bedroom to take what he wanted. We stabbed David the number of times he raped her, untied him, and went for the mother.

"Megan had come up with the plan to get tossed in prison or the nuthouse because of all we had heard about the family. We were too young to understand the kind of fire we were starting, but Megan took all the blame. She wouldn't even go through with the plan unless we let her. It was hard to keep Laura quiet, back then and through the years. Megan mistakenly let her know where she was one time, and there she went, dragging me behind her. Thankfully, by the time we arrived Megan was gone."

Easing up, I glanced back at Luke who was paler than usual.

"Beverly." The stress in his gaze and the inflection in the way he called my name, immediately filled me with worry.

"Yes."

"Do you think that there was any way DG6 could have found out all three of you were in that house?"

Crickets! The chirps vibrated inside my brain. I fell back onto Luke's chest, shaking my head. For a split second, I thought maybe. But, there was no way anyone could have known it was us.

"No. The only way they knew about Megan was because she lived there, and she turned herself in knowing it was the only way to stay safe from the family. Also, it was over ten years ago, and Megan has been hiding from that family since she was released from that institution. What reason would they have to think something different now?"

Luke drew me back in before folding his strong arms around me. "Such Twisted Revelations. So many secrets," he whispered in a low tone. A deep sigh left him before he kissed my neck.

Chapter Fifty-two

Laura

Suffocating silence filled the interior of the SUV on the drive back to Houston. I aimed my gaze at the roving landscape outside the window, staring, but not seeing anything. The reach of Dax's gaze may as well have been tapping me on the shoulder. I resisted the urge to swivel my neck to glance in his direction.

My brain kept making attempts to rethink what I already decided not to do. I was not going to start a relationship with him. Our last spat was on that very subject before leaving the bed-and-breakfast. Luke and Bev were unaware that their lives were in jeopardy because the tension between Dax and me was enough to cause a chemical explosion.

Every time I became consumed with him, I reminded myself of the kids at the center. They needed me. I needed to lead them from the traps I was drawn into as a kid, and I missed them like crazy.

Would I miss Dax as much if we parted ways? Hades had to have been missing his flames for me to dwell on the kinds of thoughts I was having about Dax. He was wealthy, educated, well-dressed, proper in public, privileged, and most importantly, *a man!*

He was my polar opposite in every way I knew. However, for some unfathomable reason, we fit. The strangest most confusing shit I ever encountered. A part of me enjoyed the sparks he brought to existence within me. A part wanted this to end so I could return to my life. The loudest part was screaming that I was changing and needed to at least consider the changes.

Dax was under my skin, so far under it saddened me to think he would no longer be in my life. *What am I now, a fucking Hallmark Card?*

The kids, I reminded myself. Other than Megan and Beverly, no one was more important than the kids.

Damn Dax! Fuck him, actually. He'd managed to climb his way onto my short list of people I cared about, and I didn't know how to get him off it.

My nagging mind spluttered when my gaze landed on Dax's which was aimed at me the entire time. His devilish mind tricks sent my emotions reeling all over the place. One moment, I wanted to hate him, the next, I was thankful he taught me a few life lessons no one else I knew was qualified to teach me.

Somewhere along the line, Dax taught me to accept that I wasn't going to disappear into a cloud of smoke if I allowed a man to connect with me. In a short span of time, he proved that accepting help from a man didn't make me weak. He constantly reminded me that I didn't always have to be defensive because the world wasn't against me. I learned not to be too quick to judge because the surface of a person only gave you a tiny glimpse of who they really were.

Dax wanted to continue our month-long fling, something I figured would've burned out after our first time together. However, the flames had grown out of control and refused to be extinguished.

Logically, he did what I'd done to many women. I don't believe Dax's objective was to turn me. He was upfront about his attraction from the beginning. I, on the other hand, hid my feelings until he forced them out of me with his demanding patience and determined spirit.

Beverly was in the same situation with Luke as I was with Dax. Although, based on the way they were smiling at each other, I'd say they were deciding to keep their relationship going.

I freaked the fuck out when I saw that they had selfies of them together as backgrounds on each other's phones. They accepted their connection with open arms, snuggles, and kisses. She was up there right now playing a game on *his* phone, while most men protected their shit like it contained the launch codes for nuclear weapons.

The buzzing of Dax's phone lured my attention.

"What? Hold on," he stated, his tone firm. His face was pinched with concern as he placed the phone on speaker and sat it face-up in his palm to allow the rest of us to hear Aaron's voice.

"Aaron, would you please repeat, so the rest of the group can hear?"

"Regina's been taken. Ansel, Scott, and Marcus were in a shoot-out with who we suspect are DG6 members. D is meeting us at Ansel's to see if we can get a lead to track Regina down."

We stared at each other as Luke's gaze met ours in the rearview mirror.

Aaron's voice returned. "Where are you guys?"

"We're headed back to Houston," Dax informed him, but the concern in his gaze met the stress that started to fill mine.

"Okay. Stay alert. The bastards are clever at hiding," Aaron warned before hanging up.

Silence fell over us with suffocating intensity.

"So, guys," I called. "Regina is one of us now, and those assholes have her. Should we be on our way back to Cali to raise hell or do you think that hell is already someplace here in Texas waiting on us?"

My question was answered by the alarming growl of an engine being revved and the grated bumper of a large, heavy-duty, black-and-window tinted truck on our ass.

The hard crush of metal pounding metal sounded before our bodies surged forward. The bullying impact caused Luke to fight the wheel to keep us on the highway. My heart fought to stay seated in my chest as our harsh breathing sounded over the vehicle's accelerated speed.

My eyes widened as an SUV sped past us and swerved dangerously to the left to cut in front of us, inches from clipping the front bumper. Luke swerved to avoid the truck behind us as it attempted to bump the rear passenger fender. I didn't notice we were being boxed in until a third vehicle morphed out of nowhere.

The truck behind us was so close it may as well have been connected. As soon as the vehicle in front of us was aligned, it braked to force us slower. Dax, Luke, and I raised our weapons, aimed, and prepared to let bullets loose.

With a vehicle to the passenger's side and a thick jersey barrier to the driver's side, we had no place to go. If Luke was half as crazy a driver as Beverly told me, he was not staying boxed in.

"Hold on!" Luke shouted right before he rammed the back end of the vehicle in front of us. The tail end of the vehicle lifted, flashing us a peek of its underbelly as the tires screamed when they reconnected with the road.

The vehicle on our passenger side attempted to force us into the roadway barrier, but Luke slammed on the brakes and caused them to swerve into nothing when they made another aggressive move. The move also sent the vehicle behind us into our bumper. The pounding impact was delivered with maximum force to our bodies, causing a harsh jerk to snatch me so hard, it uprooted my soul for a second. If we lived, we'd feel the force of the lick in our sore muscles tomorrow.

As soon as Luke created an opening, and gunned the SUV, the truck behind us made other plans. It recovered with a wild swerve and straightened in time to tap our passenger side bumper. At our speed, the driver executed a well-timed PIT maneuver that sent us into a deadly spin.

The swirling vehicle sent my shoulder crashing into the window. Dax and Bev were smart enough to grip the bar in the ceiling to keep them secure. By the time our internal organs caught up with our whipped-about bodies, we were turned in the opposite direction before we crashed into a guardrail on the opposite side of the road.

Luke and I were trapped and unable to open our doors due to the car being pinned by the guardrail. The vehicles that stopped at our rear filled our view, people ducking in their seats gawking, some with their phones visible, recording the scene. Engine exhaust, burnt tire rubber, and dust mingled before the scent swept up my nose.

Before Luke could speed us to freedom, our vehicle was bumped in the front and back and pinned in place. The third vehicle sat at our exposed side, its men already dismounted with guns aimed at us.

They caged us, trapping us in the worst situation yet. When I glanced up, two more vehicles approached. The men dismounted, their combat boots beating loud against the ground. Five vehicles in total had us surrounded with guns aimed at us from every direction.

The crew boxing us in blocked the intersection. Motorists were alert enough to stop their vehicles at a safe distance at the sight of guns. The way the men were dressed, they looked like the authorities in the process of apprehending suspects—*us*.

Motorists on the other side of the barrier sped past, many unaware, as others slowed and gawked.

This scene was reminiscent of one of those police takedowns on *America's Most Wanted*. DG6 didn't intend to take any chances on not catching us this time. They deployed a small army. I knew when I was beaten and didn't bother lifting my weapon, especially when Luke and Dax came to the same conclusion.

When the men in all-black tactical gear stepped closer to our vehicle, resembling armed mercenaries, my heart sank. I survived being kidnapped and cuffed, dangling from the side of a building, turning bisexual, and now, I was about to face DG6's goon squad.

If we didn't come up with a plan and soon, we were all going to die. I gripped the handle of my pistol with the intention of lifting it, but Dax's strong hand rested on my forearm while his lethal stare remained on the approaching men.

My gaze met Beverly's, her expression helpless.

The dark figures gestured for us to roll down our windows. With their weapons aimed at each passenger window, the windshield, and rear glass, we complied.

We tossed our weapons at their command and waited for instructions. These people had to know we weren't going to give up any information if it was what they were after. We'd been tagging each other back and forth in this battle for months. Weren't they tired of all the chasing and dodging and their men dying? If they weren't going to put a bullet in our heads now, what the hell did they want?

Through the front windshield, I noticed the man without a gun growing closer as he made his approach. When two of the men standing guard stepped apart and allowed him a path forward, I knew he was the man in charge. He was also someone I met before. Someone in which I'd been actively engaged. He was someone I aimed and shot at before too.

"No fucking way," I mumbled under my breath.

The man in charge was my height, which was kid-size for a man. Even at a quick glance, I recognized his little-man syndrome. He compensated for his size by abusing whatever power he believed he possessed.

He stood in front of the hood, his head barely breaking the surface as he eyed us. His gaze breezed past Beverly before it found me in the back seat.

"Laura?" Dax called, his questioning gaze pinned on me. They knew Megan kept secrets, but Beverly and I had a few of our own.

"Laura?" Dax called again when the small man stood glaring at me. The knowing hate he revealed dripped like acid from his contorted expression and stiff posture. I tore my gaze from the man and started talking since Luke and Dax's gazes were burning a hole through me too.

"Megan always called us, at least every week. The last time Megan talked to us was after Aaron came here, pretending to be a detective searching for her. After three weeks of her not calling and not answering her phone, Bev and I went to the last place we knew she was," I stated, not meeting anyone's unwavering gaze.

Luke side-eyed Beverly, who was chewing a hole in her bottom lip before he turned in the seat and joined Dax in a stare off directed at me.

"We got as far as Copper County, Florida before the trail got cold. Those damn rednecks weren't going to tell us shit, but we weren't giving up until we found out what happened to Megan. One question too many landed us face to face with a group of gun-carrying Mexicans. They attempted to bully us for information when they found out who we were searching for. One wrong move led to a gun being drawn and the next thing I knew, Bev was driving like a flying serpent from hell were chasing us, and I was shooting. The little weasel standing there eyeballing me was leading the group, possibly this same group of men surrounding us right now. I'm pretty sure I shot one of them, possibly two, so he has a score to settle."

I kept my gaze aimed at the back of Luke's headrest. After the revelation I just dropped, I feared Luke and Dax over the shrimp who was approaching Dax's window.

My eyes did a double roll in my head at the sight of the arrogant smile on his face when he did another once over on both Beverly and me. He took an authoritative stance, folding his arms across his chest as his men opened the passenger side doors, pulling Beverly and Dax out first.

"Nice to see you again, ladies," he greeted, his accent thick. If we survived this, Luke and Dax would kill us. Not only did we have an idea of who was chasing us, we may have started the chase by snooping around in the wrong neck of the woods. In mine and Beverly's defense, how could we have known the bunch of crazy Mexicans we started shit with in Florida was from Texas, let alone be members of DG6?

Once Luke and I were yanked out, we were shoved against the side of the vehicle. Our legs were kicked forcefully apart when they searched for hidden weapons. A double set of zip ties gripped our wrist.

There were two men on each of us like we were mass murderers. The little man in charge kept staring at Beverly and me, telling us with his smirk and deadly gaze what he planned to do to us.

The searching men snatched Dax and Luke's back-up weapons. It was surprising how calm we all were, knowing we were being led to our deaths.

It wasn't until Luke's knees buckled and Beverly's face filled with horror that I understood they'd drugged him. The man stood over him, needle at the ready to hit him with another dose if necessary. Luke's chest continued to rise and fall, so they hadn't killed him. The men struggled to drag Luke's bulky body into one of the waiting and running vehicles.

Dax didn't glance down at the needle aimed at his arm. Instead, his deadly gaze was on the one who injected him. Through all the images racing through my head, one stuck out above all the rest. It was a statement I heard

Ansel tell Aaron concerning DG6 when we were in California.

"Either they die, or we die."

Chapter Fifty-three

Beverly

They drugged the guys away putting them in separate vehicles. Relief swept through me when I concluded that
they weren't going to drug Laura and me. Instead, they led
us to the same vehicle.

Surprisingly, Laura was on her best behavior, but I
knew from experience it wasn't going to last long. If it
was just her, she'd have found a way to escape, forced
them to kill her, or acted badly enough that they would
consider allowing her to be someone else's problem.

My heart sank at the disappointment Luke expressed
when mine and Laura's secret was revealed. We'd unknowingly started a fight with DG6 and after putting it
together that they were who was after us, we still kept it
from Luke and Dax.

I spilled a few secrets to Luke, but I was afraid if I
revealed we might have had a clue as to who was after us,
they would refuse to help us. I felt lower than a snake's
belly for my deception. If we lived long enough to see
each other again, I prayed Luke would find it in his heart
to forgive me.

The zip-ties bit into my wrists when I was forced to
climb into the SUV and shoved into place. I struggled to
straighten myself as Laura was shoved into the seat behind
mine. The front and passenger seats were occupied by the
little man in charge and his driver.

My babysitter, a lean man with dark tanned skin and a scraggly beard, climbed into the middle seat with me. Laura was kept company by a chubby guy with a baby face who reminded me of El Chapo.

The only one I recognized from Florida was the short one who continued to shoot daggers at Laura and me. *Short, big-eared bastard.* If I had that much grease holding my hair down, I'd be angry too. And what the hell was he channeling with a full black Dickie outfit, the 1990s?

We weren't drugged, but they weren't taking any chances by putting us together in the same seat. The view through the window was dim, but it didn't stop me from attempting to figure out where they were taking us. I spotted the lead vehicle, then the one with Luke was next, and the truck they stuffed Dax into followed it. We were fourth in the line, followed by the trail vehicle.

Our damaged SUV sat discarded against the guardrail as traffic began to crawl behind us. The cops not showing up proved how much pull this cartel had in Texas. We crept along the interstate until our five-vehicle convoy separated, taking different routes to the same destination I supposed or more like hoped. Us, together would increase our chances of escape.

It took minutes for them to extract us from our vehicle, take our weapons, drug the men, and move on. This takeover was planned with precision. How did they know where we'd be? Had they been staking out certain locations, waiting to pounce? Did they have a man like D on their team?

We traveled halfway to San Antonio before we stopped to refuel. We wound our way through a country town I missed the name of before we took the interstate back in the direction in which we came. I bet we were headed back to the Houston area. I believe they took us on a trip to lose any tails or spies they believed we might have had trailing us.

I glanced back and found Laura asleep, her tied hands behind her. Her head was thrown back against the seat, her mouth agape. How could she possibly sleep when we didn't know how long we had left to live? The girl had nerves of steel. She and Megan were alike in that respect. I, on the other hand, was the one who only fought when provoked. I was more likely to cry or attempt to plead my way out of a dire situation.

With the men being knocked out on whatever drugs they were given; Laura and I were prey to these men. I counted twelve, and there were likely more waiting to torture us when we reached our destination.

"Don't touch me, you fucking pervert!" came Laura's rowdy voice that drew my bobbing head to a stiff start. The El Chapo look-alike had woken her beast.

"Calm down," he cooed in her direction. "I'm just admiring the assets."

"I don't know how you escaped the zoo, but if you touch me again, you will be begging them to let your ass back in that motherfucker," she snapped, her murderous gaze aimed at the man like a weapon.

"You turn around," my babysitter barked in my direction. "Mind your own damn business. You'll get some of that action later," he promised. His gaze scanned my body as his nasty tongue slid across his lips. I ignored him because I was worried about Laura.

"You are a mouthy little bitch," the man stated. "I'm going to show you what I like to do to rude bitches," he continued, slinging his words in Laura's direction after making a kissing sound. He reached and gripped a part of her body out of my view.

My head shook at his actions, knowing he was playing with fire back there. A few moments later, all hell broke loose in the back seat. Fire and brimstone, black-eyed demons, vampire bats, it was all back there swarming.

Curse words erupted, followed by the thumping sound of Laura's feet connecting with the side of the man's face and shoulder. The driver swerved in an attempt to figure out what the hell was happening as the man in charge barked orders at the fight.

At my angle, I saw a portion of Laura's body, so I repositioned myself against the seat in front of me to avoid getting struck. Her legs and feet worked like an out-of-control bicyclist. My babysitter decided to move as well, pointing his shoulder at the fight.

Everyone except me was yelling at this point as the vehicle began to decelerate. El Chapo hadn't gotten Laura under control and was taking a beating for setting his sights on the wrong woman.

"I'm going to kill this bitch!"

"You shouldn't have provoked her. Now, get her under control before I make you walk back!" The man in charge shouted.

"I'm going to stomp your fucking face in," Laura yelled, her legs standing strong against the protesting man's flailing arms. Silently, I cheered for every lick she landed on him as I fought to keep a smile off my face.

I hadn't noticed the vehicle was stopped until my door flew open and the seat was lifted and thrown into my shoulder. It was the driver pulling Laura out, as the man in charge stood outside barking orders.

"If Sorio didn't want you two, I wouldn't worry about this bullshit. I'm tempted to call him and let him know we were forced to kill that fucking she-devil."

My brain processed what the man said. He was talking like he was recently in contact with Sorio? Aaron already killed Sorio, so he must be operating off of old intel.

"You!" the man in charge yelled across me, calling the attention of my babysitter.

"Switch. Get in the back with the wild one," he commanded.

The men assumed they were resolving the problem by switching out our babysitters, but I knew Laura, and she wasn't done by a long shot.

After things were settled, Mr. Busted Face kept glaring over the seat and staring daggers at Laura, who returned them back to him with the full force of her wicked gaze. Figuring I was as crazy as Laura, he avoided glancing in my direction.

"I'm Luis Dominquez, ladies," came the voice of the man in charge from the front seat. "You could have saved yourselves a lot of trouble by telling us where your friend Megan is hiding out. We tried to be civil with you in Florida, posed the same question in the same manner as I am now. This time, I suggest you answer it," he warned.

His pause left the cab of the SUV filled with charged silence.

"We know that her boyfriend escaped with Regina and fled to California. We know that Regina has been recaptured. However, your slippery little friend Megan is nowhere to be found. Regina is about to suffer for turning against us," his slick tone rang out. The prick liked the sound of his own voice. "So, where is Megan? Is she someplace here in Texas or back in Florida with those rednecks?"

"Isn't Sorio dead? That sack of shit should be in Hell," Laura called across the seat.

"Sorio is very much alive. I don't know what you think you know, but he has plans for you two. It's the only reason you're not dead already. Sorio likes to play deadly games with his prey before he kills them. I'll remind you once more. Save yourself the trouble and tell us where your friend is," he stated as he glanced into the rearview mirror.

"She's up your ass, motherfucker!" Laura taunted.

"You need a fucking muzzle!" He fired his strained words across the seat at Laura. "Don't worry. You'll be quiet soon enough," he promised.

Laura leaned up to make sure he understood her words. "Until then, you can kiss the crack of my ass with your tongue out."

He didn't reply, but the driver released a laugh. "She's a feisty one," the driver pointed out. El Chapo, next to me, grunted. His bottom lip had doubled in size, and the top corner of his left eye had a large knot above it. Scratches and bruises colored his face and neck as he sat, steaming, ready to kill my best friend.

Laura was crazy. I knew it and now so did they, but if he attempted to lay a hand on her again, they would have two crazy bitches on their hands.

At least an hour later, the night swallowed up the last of the sunshine. Instead of heading back to Houston, we took a series of dirt roads that led us to wide open country. When a scattering of buildings started to come into focus, standing against the darkness, the sight had a chill racing up my spine.

The large white plastic numbers, 1236, were nailed to a dying oak tree outside the fence left open for us to enter. Halo Heights was the name painted on an arch that led into an old ranch. My forehead pinched tighter when the number and name on the archway came together in my head. D believed it was an address, but the numbers were a numerical representation for this place, and Halo Heights was what I assumed was the name of it.

Was this the farm where they'd kept Regina? Was it the one that she and Aaron had escaped? It was in the middle of nowhere. My neck swiveled back and forth taking in everything.

"You are now at the farm, ladies," Luis announced. His words struck with the force of a heavy hand across my cheek. They planned to torture us and burn us alive. Our worst nightmares were about to be lived.

Would we escape in time? Where were the men? Were they bringing them here too? There were only two vehicles in our convoy, and I prayed the others carrying the men would arrive soon.

Chapter Fifty-four

Luke

My brows pinched tight, pulling against the thundering ache in my head. An easy swaying effect urged me to open my eyes. Light pouring in from above blurred my vision and made it difficult to make out what surrounded me.

Crumbling cement walls, ash gray, at least a standard size room. A brown mini refrigerator sat in the corner next to a triple stack of black crates that created a makeshift bookshelf, stuffed with books. More books sat stacked at least four-feet high along the wall. There was a dark recessed area that led into another space.

Someone had once called this place home, but the thick coat of dust that settled across the room revealed they'd abandoned it. The squeaky whine drew my head up, painting a picture that sent my gaze tracing the room and down my shirtless, battered body.

Tied to the ceiling, my wrists were stretched taut, the thick rope digging into my skin, choking my circulation. Dax hung beside me, bloody, beaten, and knocked out. The sequence of events that led us to this moment crept back into my memory.

Our capture on the highway. The drugs we were injected with. We were tied up and beaten for the whereabouts of Megan, Aaron, and the rest of the crew who attacked this farm over six months ago. These people wanted good, old-fashioned revenge.

"Shit," I muttered through my busted lip. They threatened to kill Beverly and Laura, who'd unknowingly thrown themselves into the middle of a war while searching for Megan. Their secret was what landed us at this infamous farm. I wanted to strangle them for their deception, but it didn't mean I wasn't going to fight for them. If I could help it, I wasn't going to let anyone hurt them.

My gaze bounced around the tight space. We had to find a way to free ourselves and get out of here.

"Dax," I called, angling my head in his direction. "Dax," I called louder.

Since my feet were left dangling, I grunted as I lifted and wobbled, attempting to kick Dax. When that didn't work, I fishtailed my body to get it to start swinging. My wrists were about ready to rip apart from my arms, but I ignored the painful pull and focused on getting the momentum going.

Once I was swinging like a heavy pendulum, a sharp twist on the swing back was enough for my leg to collide with Dax's body. He stirred and released a weak groan. "Dax, we have to find a way to free ourselves before they come back."

The sound of his groan was his response.

Every hair on my body stood at the sound of an urgent scream.

"Luke!"

The sound lingered, filling me with the frantic need to rip myself free by any means necessary.

"Luke!"

Beverly's desperate tone highlighted her urgent need. Her sharp voice let me know she wasn't far away. Our captors wanted us to hear the women being tortured. Dax was fully awake now, his searching gaze finding mine.

"They left my shoes on," he pointed out. Despite the tension riding me, Dax's observation provided some relief. We were shirtless, but they'd left us in our pants and shoes. Me wearing shoes meant nothing, but Dax having them on meant everything.

"Start swinging," I urged. "We need to find a way to make our bodies collide." Another set of screams sounded. Neither of us commented on the sounds, but we swung our bodies back and forth like we were in training for a jungle tree-hopping race.

We managed to get our bodies to collide three times before Dax's legs connected enough to latch on to mine. With careful movements, he climbed up my body. When his feet reached my thigh, I bent and lifted my knees, giving him a boost.

It was grueling on Dax's part. The straining and grunting could attract attention, but it couldn't be helped. I lifted my knees as high as I could, assisting Dax's climb. His goal was to get to the ropes I was hanging from.

His hard bottomed shoes inched across my chest, kicking and digging into my already bruised skin. When his shoes were at my neck, I angled my head every way imaginable to assist him in getting his feet to rise higher. We battled gravity with no hands and forced our tortured bodies to endure the abuse.

One of Dax's feet was clamped under my neck, the other sat atop my head as he struggled for breaths. His leg shook with the effort he used, attempting to angle it just right.

"Your thumb, Luke, move it straight up," he instructed. My hands were so numb that I couldn't tell if I pressed the nook that would release the knife in his shoe until the spring-loaded blade sounded.

Now the hard part. Cutting the rope without cutting my wrist or losing our connection. Dax moved leisurely, using the leverage of our connection to move the blade across the rope.

As soon as the rope started to unravel, my body lurched as the strings ripped and we nearly lost our connection. The sight of Dax's blade swinging past my right eye was not a welcomed one. Thankfully, I hadn't lost an eye, and we stayed together.

Chapter Fifty-five

Laura

My attempt at channeling more strength wasn't working. Struggling against my restraints did nothing to help Beverly who was being tied to the table in front of me. The worst part was that it was an autopsy table. If blood or body fluids were released, it would all get washed down the drain near her feet.

My wild-woman screams stirred the rancid stench of death in the room when I concluded that they were about to torture Beverly to make me talk. These crazy bastards wanted Megan and the whole crew who'd attacked the farm when they attempted to rescue Aaron.

Tied and hanging in front of a wall of body freezers, my feet dangled a few feet off the floor as a rope bit into my wrists.

"Let her go, motherfucker! Take me, assholes! When I get loose, I'm going to kill all of you!" I yelled and taunted them to pull their attention away from Beverly.

Beverly struggled, giving their asses a hard time, but she didn't have enough strength to fight off three men. One of them was Luis, who wore his arrogant smile like a badge of honor.

They were a determined bunch that didn't pay me a bit of attention until they had Beverly strapped to the table, her limbs and her mid-section wrapped in thick black binds that resembled seat belts.

The one at Beverly's head picked up a large white rag from the top of a smaller metal table. When Luis, at her right side, lifted the hose attached to the autopsy table, my frantic mind struggled for a way to get them away from her. Were these evil, heartless bastards about to do what I believed they were?

The idea set me off, and I screamed and cursed harder while struggling against the tight restraints keeping me pinned to the wall like a useless portrait.

"Let her go, you fucking idiots. If you had any good sense, you'd already know that we don't know shit. Take me. Leave her alone. I'm the mean angry bitch!" I shouted at the top of my lungs.

"Don't worry, mean, angry bitch, you're going to get a turn too. And let's see how big and bad you are when we have you on this table," the one at Beverly's feet spat at me, facing my direction.

"I'll prove how big and bad I am. All you have to do is untie me, you fucking coward, picking on innocent women."

The statement drew laughs from the bunch. Okay, so maybe we weren't all that innocent, but we were women, and these assholes were treating us like we were running buddies with a known terrorist group.

The man at her head wet the cloth, the loud drips of water spilling to the floor. When he reached to place it over Beverly's face, my yells turned into the voice of the demon who possessed me. They were prepared to waterboard my best friend, and there wasn't shit I could do about it but scream and watch.

This was the kind of torture that left you with nightmares and night sweats, the same kind Dax suffered. It was the sort of shit that changed a person, turned you into the evil counterpart that lived within. I believed I'd already given in to my evil counterpart, but Beverly hadn't.

They were about to strip away all the goodness that remained inside of her.

The man drew the wet rag tight on each side of her head, and Luis stared at me while he took up the hose and aimed it toward Beverly's face. At the sight of their actions, I lost it, yanking my wrist against the restraints so hard that my skin was being ripped apart. Where were Luke and Dax? They were former Special Forces. Weren't they taught to escape impossible situations?

Luis turned the water to the steady flow he desired and aimed it at Beverly's mouth and nose. Instantly, she started choking and gagging as her body fought the restraints. Each breath she took turned into gurgling and muffled gasps as her chest heaved. Her body convulsed at the sensation of drowning, choking on her own oxygen and incoming water. She was living inside a nightmare and I couldn't do a thing to free her from it.

Beverly choked for a lifetime before they removed the cloth and presented their questions. Stinging hot tears blurred my vision.

"Lacey Daniels. Where is she? Aaron Knox. Where is he? Derrick Michaels, Galvin Richardson, Marcus Rodgers, Scotland Ross, Wade, Jake, and Jackson Knox," Luis continued down the list, his pointed gaze locked on me for an answer.

He knew the names of Aaron and Ansel's crews as well as the August Knights. The only one they currently had from the group who attacked this farm six months ago was Dax. They weren't going to end their quest until they found everyone.

"*Luke!*" Beverly yelled as loud as she could between coughs and gags. These evil bastard made us listen to their first torture session, which was the constant pounding of flesh as they asked Luke and Dax the same questions they were currently asking me. They wanted us to hear the men getting beaten. Now, they wanted the men to hear us getting tortured.

"*Luke*!" Beverly yelled, coughing and gagging once more before the rag was tossed over her face and they recommenced with waterboarding her.

Another round, Luis pulled the water away, and the rag was removed while he went back to asking questions.

"You tell us where these people are, and we will stop," Luis, standing at her right side, barked at me. He aimed the running water at her side, allowing it to run into the table to be washed down the drain.

Beverly was busy coughing up her lungs as I fought to think of a way to get them to stop. If I didn't tell them what they wanted to hear, they were going to torture Beverly until they killed her. Like the smelly assholes they were, they didn't give her time to regain her breathing before they had the cloth back over her face and were aiming the water again.

Tears ran down my face as I begged for them to stop. "You're killing her. Take me! Please! Stop!" I yelled through my cries. Just when I was about to have a nervous breakdown, the double metal doors were blown open with a resounding *boom* that felt like it rocked the room. Luke's shirtless battered body filled up the frame.

The instant Luke noticed what they were doing to Beverly, he went from Hulk to big bad-ass beast straight out of nightmares. The asshole standing at Beverly's feet lost a portion of his head as blood and brain matter misted into the air. His body lunged forward and landed over Beverly's feet for a few seconds before it did a slow-motion glide and tumbled to the floor.

It was difficult to accept, but hard not to acknowledge. If there was ever someone who loved another human, I was certain Luke loved Beverly despite our situation or how they met.

The sound of gunfire in the background let me know the Silent Assassin had gotten loose and he was saying goodnight to more DG6 members.

The remaining assholes knew better than to test the big man with the gun. Luis dropped the hose, raised his hands, and looked ready to faint. The one at Beverly's head released the rag.

"Take the rag off her face, shit for brains!" I yelled, but the man was too afraid of Luke to move.

Dax flung the doors open and stood next to Luke, shirtless and battered, but strong, sure, and deadly. I was never more thrilled to see a man until that moment.

His gaze landed on me before he charged and struck the asshole standing at Beverly's head. The hard lick with the butt of his gun had the man stumbling back as he fell against the wall.

Luke marched up to the table and yanked the cloth from Beverly's face. He and Dax didn't give one damn about strolling past DG6 members. It was the coldest brushoff I'd ever seen. They were like animals who knew the cowardly prey behind them wouldn't have the balls to attack.

Luis stumbled away from Luke and tripped over the man Dax had knocked in the head. His back struck the wall as he struggled for balance and to keep his hands raised. Dax stood in front of me. Our eyes met for a split second before he observed the rope holding me in place.

Luke fixed his gaze on Luis standing across the table as he made quick work removing the restraints anchoring Beverly to the table. She continued to cough and struggled to breathe as he soothed her into taking steady breaths.

Dax lifted and sat his knee against the wall below me before he assisted me into a kneeling position atop his muscular thigh. He cut me loose with his free hand while he used the other to support my body.

My gaze found the men who had tortured Beverly. They were as sorry as they were dumb. As soon as I was free, Dax lowered me to the floor with careful ease. I shook and rubbed my hands and arms, fighting to regain my circulation.

When my fingers started to tingle with life, I snatched the spare weapon from Dax's ankle and put a bullet in the asshole who held that rag over Beverly's face. His brains and blood didn't spray out like most headshots. Instead, his eyes went wide as the hole in the center of his head oozed a trail of slow-moving blood.

His surprised expression was followed up by his body going stiff before collapsing to the floor, revealing the hole that split the back of his head open. With his body face down on the floor, I glimpsed his brain matter and blood bubbling up from the crack like a swarm of roaches scurrying from an infested hole.

I stood over the dying man, cursing him as his body twitched. "You fucking asshole!" I kicked his expiring body. "That's for punching me in the face!" I kicked him again. "That's for torturing my friend. Torture somebody now, you dick!"

The man was dead. I knew it. His body was all muscle movements and spasms, but I didn't care as I continued to kick him, expelling my rage the only way I knew how.

"Laura, I wanted to question him," Dax stated, not sounding the least bit sorry that I'd shot the man dead. Dax proceeded to talk to me, but I didn't acknowledge his words.

"Dax, will you get her before she finds a way to bring him back to life and kill him all over again?" Luke suggested. Beverly was wrapped tight in his arms, but his perplexed gaze was aimed at me killing a man who was already dead.

Next thing I knew, strong arms wrapped around my waist and lifted me off my feet. I was dragged away from the dead man, cursing and not ready to let go of my anger. Once I calmed enough to focus, I was placed back on my feet. My attention went immediately to Beverly.

Luke had her standing against him, one of his muscled arms holding her weak body up. Tears streamed down her cheeks, and every other second, she would release a deep hacking cough.

Luis was the last man standing. His hands remained raised. If he knew what was coming to him, he'd make one of us kill him.

Chapter Fifty-six

Beverly

Luke pushed the double metal doors open and assisted me out of the room, leaving Dax and Laura inside. They picked up the reins of the torturers while Luke's concern was taking care of me.

Normally, I'd be the voice of reason. The old me would have attempted to talk Dax and Laura out of doing to Luis what he'd done to me, but my compassion refused to answer my call at this moment.

It was heaven on earth to get a steady flow of oxygen into my lungs. I'd never experienced anything so horrific in my life, fighting to breathe, chasing after air, when there was nothing there but water. I fought for my life, knowing I didn't have any hope of saving myself.

Breathing water, choking, and suffocating as your lungs and nasal passages are being burned from the inside out was the best I could describe the sensation.

I assumed I was tough because I grew up in an area where death sat and waited for you with open arms. By twelve-years-old, I'd witnessed more dead bodies on the streets of my neighborhood than some doctors saw during their whole careers. I was convinced, I was no stranger to the chill of death as it lurked and crept up on the unsuspecting.

Today was different. Today, I came face to face with the faceless demon. The hands of death had gripped me, dragged me, and snatched at my soul. Death was right

444 · KETA KENDRIC

there on that table with me, waiting until I gave up the fight, until my lungs burned into flames, and my heart exploded in my chest.

Luke rescued me in the nick of time. Anymore and I believed they would have succeeded in killing me by inducing a heart attack, stroke, or suffocation. One of those three was seconds from taking me out.

I was waterboarded, a form of torture I only witnessed in films. But, unlike the movies, no one could fully comprehend the experience unless they went through it.

This incident proved that DG6 would stop at nothing to get what they wanted. When Regina told us about the farm, I was wrong to assume I understood what she went through. Now, I had a visual and a physical understanding of the hell she lived for those three years.

Luis's screams followed Luke and me as we exited the cellar. Dax and Laura torturing him gave me a sick sense of pleasure I didn't deny myself. He was the one to suggest my punishment to the others. He stood proudly aiming the hose at my face, enjoying my pleading desperation.

After a hair-raising half hour, Dax and Laura emerged from the cellar like they'd just had explosive sex rather than torturing someone to death. Smoke from what I assumed was the incinerator billowed into the darkness. I was beginning to understand why Laura had allowed Dax into her world over any of the hundreds of other men who had failed to get her attention.

She and Dax were cut from the same cloth. Dax was a quiet storm who released his anger through death and torture. Laura was a roaring thunderstorm, but like Dax, she had anger issues, and now death and torture were a way I believed she released it.

Since we managed to kill the crew who snatched us from the interstate and dragged us to this farm, Dax and Luke discussed plans for *clean-up* as Luke called it.

"I've already made the call," Luke announced, talking to Dax. "They will be here in a few hours. This is a big cleaning job, so I'd like to wait until they arrive before we take off."

We waited. Luke and I sat in the back of one of the SUV's that he mentioned would be destroyed along with everything else on the farm once the cleaning crew arrived. My grip on Luke was so tight my hands and arms ached.

Luke's steady heartbeat against my cheek gave me the strength I needed to forced my brain to stop repeating the nightmare I'd just survived.

Dax and Laura talked in hushed tones in the front seat. Their voices sounded, but my brain didn't process what they were saying. I was in and out of focus, dozing only to be awakened by the ghosts of my own screams.

When the lights from an approaching vehicle came into view, the sound of guns being cocked registered. Luke, Dax, and Laura were ready to strike at any opposing forces. However, their warrior spirits weren't necessary. The phone Luke borrowed from the dead guys went off, and the cleaning crew identified themselves.

There were no introductions as Luke and Dax exited the vehicle to greet the crew of six. The darkness revealed shadows as their muffled voices found a way into the cab of the SUV.

"These men are connected into all kinds of shit. Can you believe this? A clean-up crew?" Laura questioned as she stretched her neck for a better view. She cracked her window to eavesdrop, but the men were too far away for us to make out their words.

I didn't want to know what they were saying. I didn't want to know what they would do. All I wanted was to part ways from anything criminal and get back to my normal life as a director of a local youth center.

We waited as the shadows unloaded their equipment and vanished into the darkness. Dax and Luke came back to the vehicle and informed us that we were taking one of the trucks from the cleaning crew and that our suite was ready and waiting.

***

Luke got me cleaned up and settled as my head rested on his sturdy shoulder. He talked me into eating a small portion of my chicken Caesar salad. He also attempted to sweet-talk me into seeing a doctor he and Dax would call from a connection they had, but I strongly refused, and he dropped the subject.

Luke was the kind of man dreams were made of. Not once had he mentioned that I lied by omission about our encounter in Florida with Luis and crew. He was the kind of man you clung to for dear life.

My torture session kept a chokehold on my concentration as I continued to lurch with the urge to cough up one of my burning lungs. However, a more urgent topic fought for the number one spot. My relationship with Luke was coming to an end, and I didn't want it to. Neither of us had discussed what we were to each other. Were we in a relationship? It certainly felt that way.

I wasn't ready for bed, so we settled into the large common area of the living room. Dax got us the royal suite at The Regent. I knew from magazine browsing that any top-level suite in the place ran at least twelve grand a night. It contained two downstairs bedrooms and an upstairs bedroom. I believe it was owned by his family, like we were finding most things were.

Luke and I took one of the downstairs bedrooms, and Dax and Laura took the one upstairs. Dax had grown on Laura, and it would be interesting to see how she would react to their time coming to an end.

Dax came down the stairs in sweats and a T-shirt with Laura on his trail, his phone against his ear. His pinched brow had me sitting up in concern. He sat on the large couch beside us, and Laura squeezed her small body in next to him.

"Aaron, I'm putting you on speaker. Repeat the updates for the group," he stated before placing his phone on the fancy glass coffee table and hitting the speaker button.

"It was that fucker, Sorio, who was after Regina. He had a twin, and that's who I killed at Ansel's house. Sorio sneaked into the city and lured Regina away from Ansel's apartment. His men snatched her during JG's attempt to get her to a safe house. JG sustained a serious gunshot wound, but he's going to live. Thankfully, Ansel had a tracker on Regina, so we found her in one of DG6's local dope houses. Ansel is in the garage playing with Sorio right now. This time, he is not going to escape death," Aaron said, and I could hear the certainty in his voice across the phone line. The way he said Ansel was playing with Sorio didn't need a translation.

Sorio was the one who kept sending his soldiers— keeping up a war we assumed had ended. It also explained why Luis was insistent Sorio wasn't dead. Our run-in with Luis in Florida had dropped us into the middle of the ongoing chaos.

After Aaron's call, we chatted and dispersed to our rooms. With Luis dead and the news of Sorio's impending death, we should have been free from DG6 hunting us. However, Luke and Dax had plans to do another recon mission before they took us home.

Dax also put in a call to Kadeem, who was willing to watch over us for as long as it took. Laura still didn't know how to take Kadeem and Dax's uncharacteristic friendship, but she didn't comment on the matter.

I was selfish with my time with Luke. We had a handful of days left, so I would do my best to make them count.

Chapter Fifty-seven

Dax

I paced, my gaze fixed on her, blazing with heat as she sat with her arms folded across her chest. Her face was set in determination, letting me know my words would hit a stone wall. I decided to speak anyway.

"Just because you're afraid...." Her hand snapped up and cut my words off.

"Who's afraid? Not me. It doesn't make any sense for us to keep this train wreck we had going on so that it can keep scratching up the tracks. It was fun, different, damn sure interesting, but I need to get back to my life and so do you."

She'd already put our relationship in the past tense. She was calling it nothing, but I was calling it what it was, an unshakable connection.

"Laura, I live three hours from here, in Dallas. I own a place here in Houston I'd move into. All you have to do is say the word."

She didn't answer. She just sat staring at me.

"Laura, I can get any woman I want, anytime. What I can't get is the fire you set off in me. I can't get anyone who's not afraid to stand up to me and force me to view the world through different eyes. Someone who's not afraid to kick my ego around a bit, so that I remember that I'm human."

Confusion, interest, and maybe understanding were expressed on her face. I may have been getting through to her.

"No, Dax. I'm sticking to my decision," she stated as her arms went back across her chest.

"You're being hardheaded and selfish. Unwilling to stand outside your comfort zone because this is tough, hard, and requires feelings." After a head shake I released a deep sigh. She had me so damn frustrated I couldn't see straight. "Why the hell am I even wasting my time on an egotistical lesbian, who'd rather be the man than to allow one to give a damn about her?"

"Finally, you get the fucking point!" She yelled as she stood and stalked toward the door. I moved across the room like a vampire chasing new blood, stopping her before she walked out of the door. I intended to get her riled up, but I feared I was screwing shit up worse.

"Laura, please. You know I didn't mean any of that. I'm not ready to let you go."

She spun to face me, her back to the door. "So, exactly how long will it take before you're ready? Two more weeks? In another month? I have no desire to be your Ms. Right Now. I have no intention of sitting around waiting for you decide to move on, which is why I have no problem making the decision for you. I've appreciated the kind of attention and support you've given me, but there is no need for you to keep wasting your time or mine. Now, move your hand so I can walk out of this door."

I lowered my face closer to her neck, the action causing me to instantly flood with relief. The light mist of cotton candy, her pleasing scent, drifted up my nose. The welcoming warmth she emitted wrapped around me and wouldn't let go.

A low sigh of contentment escaped before I lowered my head and allowed my mouth to hover just below her ear. "What you do to me Laura. You have no idea." Just being close to her filled me with everything I never had: hope, care, understanding, lust, desire, and love."

She gave me everything without even trying. I had to find a way to make her see reason.

"We aren't just a fly-by-night fling, and you know it."

Her brows hitched at my words, but she remained silent. I fixed my eyes on hers. "I've never wanted any woman the way I want you. You've become the voice of my soul. You're in my head, ruling my thoughts. Traces of you are moving through the blood that flows through my veins. The idea of losing you scares me more than anything. Does that sound like a man willing to give up the most meaningful thing he's ever had in his life?"

I prayed she didn't think I was running lines on her because I meant every word. It hadn't occurred to me until I expressed it that I wanted Laura full-time and for good.

My words stilled her as she processed them. Her eyes softened for a split second and I smiled, assuming she would embrace the possibility of us. However, her expression stiffened, and my heart sank. The idea that she'd never go for it hit me before her words did.

"Remove your hand from this door right now," her threatening glare backed up her words.

I recognized that commanding tone she took, so I removed my hand from the doorknob and lifted my arms from either side of her.

She snatched the door open and stalked out. A deep sigh escaped before I shook my head. *Too much.* I messed up and forced too much on her, too soon. I may have blown up my chance of talking her into continuing a relationship with me. However, she could say what she wanted, but she sensed our connection as much as I did.

She made me care about her. She made me respect her. She allowed me to find the beauty within her, and the passion and drive that drove her to act, do, and care for those who didn't have anyone else.

I may have lost this battle with Laura, but I didn't intend to lose the war. A wicked smile formed across my lips. I believe I staked my claim the first night we slept together. Laura was mine, and I was hers, and she was clueless as to how far I was willing to go to prove it to her

.

Chapter Fifty-eight

Beverly

My tits bounced when I fell onto the mattress, my body and mind eased once again by the intoxicating high Luke had the ability to give me. We lay comfortably in our nakedness, just breathing, and enjoying the aftermath of what was my addiction.

However, after a moment, I began to cool, and my runaway ideas started to kick my ass. No matter how much I hid it, my disappointment at the prospect of losing Luke would surface and steal my joy.

Tonight was our last night together before he was set to take me home and move on with his life. We'd made love and sexed each other into several sex-induced comas over the past few days, and I enjoyed every minute of it.

I eased up before placing my head on his chest. I memorized the rhythm of his heartbeat vibrating strongly against my cheek so I'd never forget. He encircled me in his warm embrace, something now as familiar to me as breathing.

He eased up, gripping and taking me along with him as he propped his back against the plush leather of the shaky headboard. We'd managed to unhinge a headboard I assumed was bolted to the wall, causing it to knock and shift whenever we moved.

"Can I talk to you about something, Beverly?"

I didn't like the apprehension in his tone and believed I knew what subject he was about to broach. He was so kind and considerate I knew that he would do his best to make our transition easy. My hesitation prompted him to call my name again.

"Beverly," he whispered before placing a sweet kiss on my cheek.

"Yes," I finally answered. "We can talk about whatever you want," I stated, forcing a smile onto my face.

"I know that we just met. I know that going too fast in a relationship can be a disaster. I know that we may have acted on impulse and adrenaline because of the dangerous situations we have been in."

His long pause led me to search his face for a hint of what was on his mind.

"I care for you, Beverly. A lot. I don't want tomorrow to be our end, but I'll understand if you prefer that it will be."

"No," was squeezed out. I was so nervous, my heavy breathing continued to rush out. "I don't want it to be our end either." I breathed a deep sigh of relief.

"Phew!" he blew out and pretended to wipe sweat from his brow. His reaction caused me to giggle, my smile about as wide as the Grand Canyon.

I shifted, fitting my naked body into his, as I allowed his warmth to wrap around me. His lips raked my jaw when I shoved my face into the nook of his neck, inhaling him, loving him, and overjoyed that this wasn't our last night together.

"You mean everything to me." His words brushed against my neck before I lifted my head and met his gaze.

"And so do you, to me. I couldn't have dreamed up a better man than you," I complimented, loving the big smile I was putting on his face.

"I don't have a plan about how we are going to work things out. Even if I have to telework or set up a remote office here in Texas, we'll make it work," he assured. The certainty in his tone wasn't lost on me. His willingness to make it work for us; meant everything. How in the world had I gotten so lucky? The sentiment behind his revelations had tears stinging the backs of my eyes.

I nuzzled tighter, squeezing him with a massive hug. "I love you so much," tumbled out of my mouth, muffled but assuredly released. My breath hitched at my slip.

He froze. So did I. Had he heard me? My face remained planted in his neck. I was too afraid to face him and the bridge I slipped and crossed.

He wanted to keep seeing me, but I knew better than anyone that it didn't mean he was ready for the kind of relationship I just alluded to wanting. I silently cursed myself as my heart hammered against my ribcage, cracking a few I believe.

Fear at my unintentional slip kept me immobilized and unable to breathe. Was he going to change his mind about us? Did he want the kind of relationship I coveted? Did he feel the same way?

When I refused to move, he inched his shoulder away from my face. I sensed his eyes on me as I attempted to stay hidden.

"Beverly, look at me please."

I couldn't tell anything by his delicate tone, but I forced myself to stop being a wimp and face him. My heart was on pause as a zillion thoughts coursed through me.

"Did you just say you love me?" His face was pinched and I couldn't tell what was playing out in his expression. I couldn't answer him, so I nodded, not trusting my voice. The calming smile that teased his lips before spreading across his face was enough to make my heart sputter in an attempt to start again.

He placed his thumb under my chin and lifted so he had full access to my face.

"Beverly. I love you, too. More than you could ever know. More than I can express." His intense stare drove

456 · KETA KENDRIC

more meaning into the words, making them sink in and light up my entire body.

My speechlessness remained until his warm lips fell over mine and awakened me. Unbridled passion overpowered the kiss, solidifying the words we'd expressed to each other.

Truth was, I believed I loved Luke from the first time I saw him. It was something I sensed, over something I knew right away. Being around him had proved instincts and forces beyond our control had a hand in bringing us together.

I believed I was set on a path to meet the person I was meant to love. It was a rocky path but being around Luke was all the confirmation I needed to accept that I, a girl who never believed I'd find it, was meant to be loved.

The sparks that brought me to Luke and compelled me to acknowledge him had never died. The chemistry had always been there between us, and I knew now with all certainty that it had always been love.

Epilogue

Dax

I gave it a valiant effort, but I couldn't stay away. Laura was a part of me I wasn't ready to let go of and I didn't know if I would ever have the strength to cut the connection tying us together.

"I love how hard and long it is." Her sultry tone purred into my ear, awakening my senses.

"Put your left hand right here," I coached; delighted that she was listening. "Place your fingers here. You're going to use your pointer finger to tickle the tip, right here," I continued giving her instructions.

"Like this?," she questioned, sliding into this better than I assumed she might.

"Yes, just like that," I squeezed out. She was making my lust rise. My breaths lodged in my chest, building until I released a long exhale.

"Since I have you in the one position I know you'll listen, let's talk about us."

"Let's not. Do you really want to talk about something that doesn't exist at a time like this? There is no us," she insisted.

"Laura, if there wasn't an us, you wouldn't be lying here next to me, my dick wouldn't be this hard, and this long hard masterpiece wouldn't be in the palm of your hands," I pointed out, making her giggle.

"You have a point, but I don't want to talk about it," she reiterated, sliding her palm along the hard base. Every vibrant spark she emitted stroked my sense of longing and caused my pulse to quicken.

"I believe you're my poison *and* my antidote," I blurted my thoughts.

"What the hell is that supposed to mean?" she questioned, her attitude jumping from the shadows, ready to pounce.

"It means you have the ability to weaken me to the point of making me nonfunctional before you let your guard down and restore me. You make me feel better, powerful even. You have the ability to inject me with a fatal dose of your special poison before you administer the cure."

She lifted a brow.

"If I didn't inject you with my poison, you'd be bored, and I'd be your afterthought. Women gravitate to me because I pique their curiosity. Men don't know how to deal with me. Some shoot their shots and fail, and others choose to dislike me. Not you. You can take it. You like me the way I am, poison and all."

Her cute brows arched higher. "However, what you clearly know and haven't accepted yet, is that I'd gladly leave you hanging on to your last dying breath just to see if I could bring you back."

At those words, I chuckled. She had me in every way imaginable. If I could get her to believe it, we'd become an unbreakable force. I decided to stir the conversation back to my original concern.

"When do you want to talk about us, Laura? When I give you enough time to convince yourself that we don't have something worth fighting for? When I give you enough time to put me in the category with all the other men you hate? I want you. I care about you. I'd do for you what I wouldn't for anyone else. You know me, *all* of me," I professed, forcing her to turn her side eye into a fiercely intense gaze that bore into mine.

My gaze pierced deep into hers, concentrating on the emotions stirring between us.

"Laura, I—"

"Aww!" She yelled, cutting me off.

"Don't you dare say another damn word. This is not the time for you to get weird on me," she whispered-shouted, making me laugh.

"I wasn't going to be weird. I was about to tell you that I believe he's arrived."

***

Laura

Three days was all the time Dax had allowed to pass before I saw him again. Over the past month, he has refused to let go of the strange connection we've developed during all the high-pressure, life-and-death crisis dogging us. He called, texted, and showed up at the center unannounced enough for the kids to start calling him Mr. Dax.

He was reluctant to offer me money directly, knowing my personality well enough to understand I wasn't impressed by a big bank account. However, I wasn't stupid enough to say no when he offered to upgrade my car and the apartment Beverly and I shared.

Instead of concentrating on buying my affections, Dax helped me in ways he knew would land on my heart. He worked with me and poured an insane amount of money into renovations on both centers.

The lonely carpenter who did volunteer work at both locations had company now, and they were adding a new wing to my building that rivaled the size of the original structure.

Dax had officially asked me out on a date, the kind of date he knew I wouldn't turn down. Currently, we were twenty-seven stories up, perched in one of the many secluded nooks on Central Park Tower in New York. I was positioned on my stomach lying beside him on a cement slab, his pelvis pressed against my backside, his warm body flush with mine.

My left hand rested under the hard metal exterior of Dax's sniper rifle propped up on a tripod. My right pointer finger tickled the hard tip of the trigger. He called the rifle, Alberta.

The crazy man had invited me on one of his official hits. A fucking paid assassin. I'm sure he was breaking one of the biggest rules in the hitman handbook.

I lowered my head before glancing through the sight. The white rag Dax tied nearby helped me understand wind-direction and how to properly adjust with respect to the wind. He'd even taught me about breath control.

Through the scope, I glanced at the target, a snuff-film collecting billionaire who managed to keep his misdeeds hidden because his pockets were deep. Dax had taken the contract after witnessing video proof of the man's dirty deeds which were overwhelmingly disturbing. He had raped, beaten, and murdered women and filmed it so he could enjoy the aftermath of his destruction.

Dax would be paid two hundred and fifty thousand dollars for this hit. There were many secrets he hadn't yet revealed to me, but he was in the process of luring me deeper into his world. I was impressed to find he always donated the money from his jobs to charity.

Now that he saw firsthand what went on in hoods like mine, he refocused, concentrating more on what his money could actually do for the people who needed help.

"I have a clear shot," I stated, as adrenaline raced through my body like liquid fire.

"Breathe in, slow and steady," he coached. "When you exhale, execute."

The impact of my next decision filled my brain. Once I allowed my finger to flex against the trigger, I'd be going past a point of no return: in life and with Dax. In his world, this was as good as us getting engaged. Was I ready for what came next with him and within his secret underworld?

I released my breath and squeezed. When the spray of blood splattered the wall behind the target before his body slumped across the table, I knew I'd hit my mark. A warm kiss brushed my cheek, a gesture I called Dax's Kiss of Death.

End of Twisted Revelations

Author's Note

Readers, my sincere thank you for reading Twisted Revelations. Please leave a review or star rating letting me and others know what you thought of the book. If you enjoyed it or any of my other books, please pass them along to friends or anyone you think would enjoy them too.

Other Titles by Keta Kendric

The Twisted Minds Series:

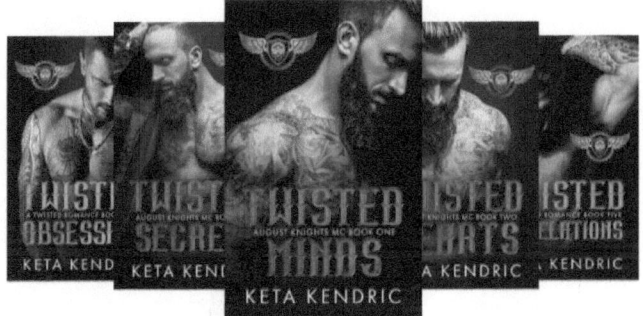

Twisted Minds #1
Twisted Hearts #2
Twisted Secrets #3
Twisted Obsession #4
Twisted Revelation #5
Twisted Deception # 6 (2024)

The Chaos Series:

Stand Alones:

Novellas:

Paranormals:

Kindle Vella:

Love Lied Series
(Seasons 1-3)
Keta Kendric

Audiobooks:

Connect on Social Media

Subscribe to my Newsletter or Paranormal Newsletter for exclusive updates on new releases, sneak peeks, and much more.

You can also follow me on:

Instagram:
https://instagram.com/ketakendric

TikTok:
https://www.tiktok.com/@ketakendric?

Bookbub:
https://www.bookbub.com/authors/keta-kendric

Goodreads:
https://www.goodreads.com/user/show/73387641-keta-kendric

Newsletter:
https://mailchi.mp/c5ed185fd868/httpsmailchimp

Facebook Page:
https://www.facebook.com/AuthorKetaKendric

Facebook Readers' Group:
https://www.facebook.com/groups/380642765697205/

Twitter:
https://twitter.com/AuthorKetaK

Pinterest:
https://www.pinterest.com/authorslist/

www.ingramcontent.com/pod-product-compliance
Lightning Source LLC
Chambersburg PA
CBHW031151050726
47495CB00019B/1428

* 9 7 8 1 9 5 6 6 5 0 1 6 7 *